Mob Sisters

JEANNE REJAUNIER

Copyright © 2012 Jeanne Rejaunier

All rights reserved.

ISBN-13:978-1475165814

ISBN-10:1475165811

DEDICATION

To Vadim

CHAPTER I - DAVID CATES - 2012

Three years ago, my mother Kristin Cates vanished. How did she disappear without a trace, and why there are no clues to her whereabouts? As I told the FBI, which has been trying unsuccessfully to locate my mother, I can't answer these questions.

Does the name Kristin Cates ring a bell? If you follow crime, you know that over past decades, my mother, Kristin Cates, led a notorious, albeit largely low profile life as a member of the La Femmina female mafia. For those few who haven't heard, the La Femminas are the most powerful cartel of lady criminals in the world, in fact, the only criminal cartel composed exclusively of women, and they do it all — gambling, loan sharking, numbers, counterfeiting, narcotics, and you name it. Besides this, LFM women own some of the most profitable legitimate businesses in the world in sports, entertainment, fashion, real estate, casinos, financial services, and much more.

What do I, as Kristin Cates's only child, know about my mother's life and career? Actually, not that much, since Kristin kept her criminal movements well concealed from her son. However, what I can offer to shed light on my controversial mother's life, is, interestingly enough, a novel Kristin left behind when she fled, which touches peripherally on her activities as a member of the La Femminas. Rather than focusing wholly on my mother's own personal story, her work of fiction is a primarily roman à clef revealing how the La Femmina women's mafia came into being, and how its' celebrated crime queenpins grew, prospered and defied the system. So historically, I think you will realize when you read this, that my mother's tell-all is an extremely important work.

I don't know if my mother ever intended to publish this book, whether she wrote it for posterity, to enlighten, or merely as a creative effort, but if I had to guess, I'd say all three could apply. What I do know is that upon completion, the manuscript was tucked away in a drawer and that Kristin never made any effort to have it published, although she certainly could have, given her connections. Now that she is living in the shadows (as we believe), and particularly since e-books are so prevalent today, it was my decision to go ahead and bring this story my mother wrote to the light of day. I believe my decision could prove instructive and informative to many.

And finally, I hope upon reading MOB SISTERS, that you, the readers, will agree with me that my mother's chef d'oeuvre deserves an honored place in our nation's cultural history.

David Cates, New York City, 2012

CHAPTER 2 - KRISTIN CATES - 1990

It was the final time I'd be returning home from one of the dangerous drug runs that had been my stock in trade for the past six years. At last, I'd be moving up in the ranks of organized crime — not that I had complaints about my probation period; one million eight hundred thousand dollars in cash under the table last year, for example, made my activities on behalf of the La Femmina female mafia syndicate — the LFM, as it's called — more than worth the risks. Nevertheless, I was pleased the unusual organization to which I owed allegiance would now be promoting me.

I settled back into the luxurious pleasure of Thailand Airlines' Royal Orchid Service, trying to put worries aside. This Bangkok to New York flight was one of my favorites. The stunning hostesses in bright colored saris always pampered us passengers, offering hot perfumed towels and purple fans, serving jasmine tea, cherry wine, exotic cocktails and spicy Thai food. That part I'd miss. What I wouldn't miss was the constant fear.

I recalled the culture shock of my first Thailand run. It was October, the cool season, and the stifling air was blazing hot. The Thai capital is a city of contrasts. Extremes of wealth and poverty coexist. You can be walking in rat-infested slums, the smell of human excrement pervading, then just around the corner discover a lush tree-lined section of sumptuous villas.

This is a city where one can easily hire a killer for less than a hundred dollars. Everywhere, one sees ragged beggars hawking pathetic skeleton-like children, and for fifty dollars, you can buy a nursing baby. I don't like telling you the usual fate of such infants is that they are slaughtered, their internal organs removed to stuff their bodies with drugs. I thanked God I was never asked to do anything like this because I never could.

The first time I ever hailed a cab on a Bangkok street, a well dressed stranger approached me to advise against getting into a taxi unless I wanted to end up dead in some alley. Later that night in my hotel room, I noticed the door handle to the adjoining room was turning. I put a chair against it and lay awake the entire night, my heart pounding till dawn. No matter how satisfying it might be to take the money and run, the fear never ended.

As an LFM soldier, my main activity was drug courier, and there was always the risk, particularly with large orders, that someone might deliberately leak information to the police. This was part of what I'd had to contend with these past years, and it wasn't over yet.

At the outset, as a struggling single mother in dire straits, I desperately needed what this life could offer. Working with the LFM's was a way to earn lots of money. For the La Femminas were the most powerful cartel of female criminals in the world, in fact, the only criminal cartel composed exclusively of women, and their lucrative interests were spread around the globe. Opportunities for advancement were enticing.

How did I have the good fortune to connect with them? If you are a devotée of obscure cable TV shows, you know Sandra Martinez, exotic, dark-haired psychic and astrologer. A fated 900 number phone call to "Sandra and the Stars" led to an appointment for a private reading. I'd been praying for some way to pay off mounting debts and at the same time escape the 9 to 5 rut. Well, I got everything I asked for and more. Sandra, a capo in the Jasmine Shields mafia family, introduced me to the LFM, and the rest is history.

Think what this would mean to my son David — the best schools, his future assured. My boy, just nine at the outset of my involvement with the LFM, was the reason for it all. My thought always was that women like me must opt to make it through any channel we can, no matter how unorthodox. I make no apologies. Even so, the LFM didn't accept me all at once; I had to prove myself.

That watershed day half a dozen years ago, I opened the door to the Manhattan hotel room where I'd been told to go. Keys were left for me at the desk and a note was placed on the bed. I picked it up and read: "Fill out this form. Be at McDonald's, 8th Avenue and 56th Street, at 3 p.m. But be sure you intend to go through with this and are willing to face any consequences. Check and double check your replies to all questions. The information must be accurate, because if anything proves false, consequences could be serious."

Were they trying to scare me? They were succeeding. My initial thought was that if I could do this job even just once, better yet up to a dozen times, I'd be home free, and then I'd quit. I'd made my share of mistakes and poor choices in life; the goal now was for a source of income. This gig could provide it.

I was shaking. "Form 20" required name, address, phone and passport numbers, age, race, and answers to several questions, such as: Would you go to any part of the world? Can you read maps? Can you read instructions in English? Yes, I wrote, my hand unsteady, U.S. citizen, born in Richmond, Virginia. Have you ever been involved with anything like this before? No, never. What are your qualifications? "Willingness to risk," I wrote. How much money do you want? The max, I wrote, and added "please."

Still trembling, I re-read the final orders. "Leave this folded with your passport. It will be returned to you soon. Good luck." I had the feeling I was dealing with a mysterious league that kept itself well insulated, hidden from view. How right I was.

They contacted me two days later, met and escorted me to three separate locations. At the ultimate destination I found a note reading, "Go to Grand Central Station. Pick up a double-bottomed suitcase. Inside you'll find money." I was to purchase a ticket and leave on a trip. I followed instructions to the letter. As it turned out, this was a trial run. The same procedure happened again; I went where I was told, was directed to be at another and still another place, where I was met and escorted yet elsewhere. I sat and waited. When would it all gel? When would I start making the big money Sandra had said I could?

Finally, a few weeks later, apparently satisfied with my performance thus far, they had me buy a plane ticket to the Far East, where upon arrival I was to purchase another special double bottomed suitcase. I was given an envelope containing twenty thousand dollars in cash, half of my fee in advance. The balance would come on delivery of consignment. Everything was finally falling into place, my problems were being solved, my life was opening up! This marked the beginning of my career of sitting in hotel rooms around the world and waiting, waiting for phones to ring, afraid to go out for days on end for fear of missing a call.

And now the waiting was coming to an end. Thank God I wouldn't have these worries anymore. What a relief; what satisfaction to know that bigger, safer ventures were coming my way, and that from now on, the money promised to be even better. As I gazed out the plane at the New York skyline, I smiled to myself. These fears of mine would soon be over.

"Kristin Cates, you are in violation of United States Code 16443.052, Section II, Article 27 — "

I stared incredulously at the two federal agents who were waiting on the tarmac. The full impact didn't sink in at first. There was an air of unreality about this; it seemed that ten thousand pairs of eyes were boring into me and that everybody at Kennedy Airport knew what was going down, knew it was all over for me. The feds were taking me into custody, making my worst nightmares come true. At once, I could predict the scenario — scare tactics, threats of grand jury indictments and plea bargaining — cooperate with us, Kris, and you can keep out of prison, strike a deal, plead and we'll give you immunity, we'll put you in the Witness Protection Program (God forbid) — all the ensuing scenes played through my mind in advance. They'd want me to tell everything I knew, the truth and the myths, every piece of information I could dredge up about the La Femmina female mafia. While I was not a part of the LFM power structure at that time, I did have information about the organization the authorities wanted to hear. What I knew, covering more than two decades in scope, contained facts about LFM leadership and expansion, their romances and vendettas, and how these remarkable women, over a period then approaching thirty years, managed to parlay rackets and vice operations along with legitimate enterprises into a multi-billion dollar empire. Looking back, I can categorically state that today, the La Femmina women's mafia power is unparalleled, a subject I hope to address in future books.

Of great interest to law enforcement, I knew, would be how the syndicate women brought the global drug trade under their jurisdiction and became the leading voice in the American underworld.

"A mafia of women? A mob not of male hoods called Vito, Sal, Tony and Joe, but of beautiful and charming ladies named Tania, Laura, Jasmine, Victoria, Susan and Sandra?"

The scene was Federal Plaza, FBI New York headquarters. I'd been led through the Bureau's rabbit warren into the offices of FBI Special Agent Tom Madigan, who appeared bemused as he leaned back from the desk in his brown leather swivel chair. On the wall to Madigan's left hung a chart depicting the La Femmina Mafia's alleged leadership coast to coast. The chart was not completely accurate. I thought, is it possible we women have been operating under the FBI's noses all this time and they were only now getting around to finding out? Another proof of our cleverness. But I kept those thoughts to myself.

A second agent, Ronald Haines, a patronizing type who also seemed amused by the idea of the La Femminas, joined in, "Ladies raking in hundreds of millions annually from a cartel founded on gambling, loan sharking, numbers, narcotics, prostitution and labor racketeering! Laundered money recycled into legitimate enterprises — trucking companies, mortuaries, restaurants, dry cleaning establishments, pizza parlors, fashion houses, banks and brokerage houses — "

"An empire worth today an estimated cool two hundred billion dollars," Madigan finished, then looked at me again to ask, "Tell us how it all began, Kristin."

Madigan, Haines and I were at an informal transitional phase, legalities having thank God been settled. When I was brought into the FBI office following my arrest, it had to be determined if I was going to be a cooperating witness, if they were going to bring me down to the court and arraign me, or have me held over in the Metropolitan Correction Center. To make a long story short, I became a cooperating witness.

My actual testimony would come much later, when the U.S. Attorney had the cases ready. At this point, I was at a preliminary stage with the FBI; we were painting the broad strokes. I would tell them what I knew, they would listen and transcribe hours of what I said on tape.

Trying to answer Madigan's question about beginnings, I said, "Sex discrimination and sexual harassment were definite factors impacting women's lives. You could say that some women, conscious of being closed off from the system, were eager to correct the balance by whatever means, no matter how radical. These women joined ranks and formed a 'mafia'. They began small — floating craps games out of their apartments, cigarette smuggling up from the Carolinas, fencing hot stones "

"Who were the founding mothers?" Tom Madigan asked. Madigan was I guess what you would call a fairly decent fellow, as FBI agents go. He was about 45, sandy-haired, with a broad forehead and a receding hairline.

"There were probably two major queenpins to begin with, which later escalated to four," I said. "You've heard of Joseph Lo Bianco?"

Of course they had. Although Lo Bianco was murdered back in the early 70's, law enforcement wouldn't forget this mafia don for a long time to come.

"Lo Bianco, as you probably know, had a beautiful daughter named Laura. The family lived first in Brooklyn, Lo Bianco's main turf, later in Brookville, Long Island. When Joe Lo Bianco's wife, Laura's mother, was dying over a ten year period, all during that time, Joe had a girlfriend, a mistress by the name of Victoria Winters — tall, blonde, goodlooking — "

The two agents nodded, remembering the legendary Lo Bianco, shot with a cigar in his mouth in the garden of a Brooklyn restaurant.

I continued, "Initially, Laura Lo Bianco had no great love for Victoria Winters; in fact, very few people did, since Victoria is actually not a particularly endearing person — however, Laura and Victoria reached a working relationship that was mutually beneficial. As I understand, even though Joe Lo Bianco provided to some extent for his daughter and his mistress, nevertheless, after his death there was internal strife in his organization, a lot of assets were missing, and at this point, Laura and Victoria found themselves in circumstances that compelled them to join forces, although they probably never would have otherwise.

"It seemed natural to continue some of the things the two had absorbed from Joe and strike out on their own. Victoria was full of ideas to make money. As for Laura, when Joe died, she was in deep trouble — being family, she was the one who inherited her father's headaches.

"So here were these two arm's length friendly enemies, rivals when Joe was alive, now in a state of truce. They had a mutual goal, to make up for the money that wouldn't be filtering their way anymore through Joe. And if the truth be told, Joe had held them both down. Lo Bianco was hardly what you'd call a feminist — like they say, the Mafia is not an equal opportunity employer, and both Laura and Victoria were victims in that sense. They reached an agreement to split percentages. Both had a network of friends; they expanded.

"The other two leaders of New York's Four Families, Tania Cutler and Jasmine Shields, were, I think, either school or social friends of Laura's. Anyway, these four soon banded together and formed a loose alliance; in the beginning they joked about being a female mafia; then it became a reality. One thing led to another.

"My association with the La Femminas, my knowledge of their operations began around two decades after they were up and running, but I know the legends and the lore about how it all began."

CHAPTER 3 - VICTORIA

Eyes glinting at the barrel, Harry Sutro cocked a .357 magnum and held it pointed it at Victoria Winters' temple.

"Very fucking funny, Harry." Vic moved out of the line of fire with a disdainful look. "I hope for your sake that piece isn't loaded — or automatic."

"Hell, no. Think I wanna blow my pecker off? Shit, an automatic could jam."

"Listen, put down the firearm and let's talk."

"Sure, hon."

As Victoria's bodyguard, houseman/henchman, jack-of-all-trades and steady bed partner, Harry Sutro also doubled as her unofficial male *consigliere*. Vic relied heavily on his advice, even though being a man, he was ineligible to officially join her female mafia borgata. Dr. Caroline "the Cow" Stoll, Vic's consigliere of record, didn't have much time to counsel, so Harry's role had expanded to encompass areas that the Cow would have handled had she not been so absorbed with her cardiac patients. If the other three LFM capos of New York's "Four Families" knew how intimately involved with Vic's operation Harry was, they would disapprove. But then, there was a lot about Victoria that caused the others to lift an eyebrow — to which Vic said, fuck them.

Victoria's short brittle laugh was a snigger. She wore a soupçon too much lavender eyeshadow rubbed onto the lids of her narrow and darting, deepset cinnamon colored eyes. When she smiled, which was seldom, the effect was cold and fiendish. One corner of her mouth raised to curve slowly under while the other side remained immobile, formulating a twisted and uneven, diabolical grin.

One of the most colorful mafiose, Victoria took to the La Femmina mob the way a basking shark takes to a school of fish. As one of the outfit's most astute businesswomen, she displayed brilliance in her inaugural rackets of fencing, hijacking, pornography and piracy.

She was slender and tall, 5'11 in stocking feet. Though it often seemed she carried a non-removable chip on her shoulder, men found the ice cold sex she projected interesting, and in fairness, her sometimes offputting exterior was a defense. Behind her back, she was called Vic or Tip O'Neill, sobriquets she disliked, preferring the regal Victoria.

Victoria plopped down at the kitchen table and contemplated space. Lighting a cigarette, she began smoking in compulsive gulps, blowing rings out in spurts. She was rough and edgy today.

"This Jasmine Shields is un-friggin' believable," she complained to Harry about her biggest rival, the skipper of one of New York's mafia families. "Trouble is, she's got influence in her corner and it makes a difference. She sure can get a guy by the balls."

"Well, you got me by the balls, baby — you know that."

"You're different, Harry. A guy like you I can fart with. What I'm talking about is getting the kind of guy you can't fart with by the balls."

Harry started cleaning his gun. He was always cleaning things. In fact, he was the cleanest man she knew — he was a born homemaker, constantly vacuuming, dusting, washing dishes, putting garbage out, doing the laundry.

"Harry, you know my goal is to become the biggest powerhouse in heroin in the tri-state area. But it takes cooperation, and thus far I'm not getting any from the other Four Families."

"I keep telling you, what do you need those bitches for? Your crew can out-perform them any day of the week."

"That may be, but we La Femminas are an organization, we rely on each other's support — that's why we mobilized into a mafia in the first place. As you know, Tania Cutler's boyfriend's uncle, Tom Kelly, is head of the longshoremen's union. This SOB could work something out for me to use the docks for bringing the stuff in, but Tania hasn't come through."

"Your own captain, Georgia Jensen, is Mike Giordano's girlfriend, and Mike rules the Jersey seaports. I still say Georgia should be able to swing things for you."

Vic shook her head. "You know how hard Georgia tried." Mike Giordano was a captain in the Genovese family, which already had heroin coming through the ports Mike dominated, and he was not about to get into a conflict of interests with the male mob. "Anyway," Victoria said, "Giordano's such a big male chauvinist he doesn't even want Georgia involved with narcotics."

"If only you could reach out to Anthony Zino."

"Don't I wish."

Zino, a captain in the Lucchese family, controlled the airports. His iron grip on Local 295, the union that supplied manpower for the flight terminals and warehouses, enabled him to put the squeeze on any national firm operating out of any airport in the whole USA. With just one phone call, Anthony Zino could paralyze the entire American transportation system. He was the heaviest guy in unions on the east coast. While a prison sentence had precluded his rise in the official labor movement, he was the man who called the shots from a ringside table. People cooperated with this guy or else. Zino had made mayors and judges, put congressmen in office.

Unfortunately, Jasmine Shields had gotten there first. As her mentor, Zino had been opening doors for Jasmine in finance, the schmatte trade and in food distribution, working out union contracts with truckers, arranging introductions to suburban bankers who'd make compensating balance loans in exchange for rented CD's and money under the table. He sent a lucrative fat rendering deal her way, enabling her group to purchase byproducts from his kosher meat business, which were then used to manufacture detergents that with his assistance would be pushed in the supermarkets under the no-brand label. It was hard to accept Vic was closed out of this action, just getting a small override.

But that was Jasmine for you. You couldn't trust her. For instance, there was the cocaine situation, on which Vic suspected, even though she had no proof, that Jazz and her consigliere Sandra Martinez were jointly screwing her. Their pipeline was flowing unabated, a gold mine. Ok, so Vic was getting a nominal override, but why should she have to settle for that when Jasmine and Sandra had the lion's share? Well, Jasmine Shields might have cornered the cocaine market, but goddamnit, she wasn't going to get the better of Victoria on the heroin. This time, she would control the deal.

Vic said to Harry, "Jasmine's jacked me around for a long time, but it'll all come to a head in Beirut soon — "

End of next month, they were holding a policy summit in the Lebanese capital. Here, Vic was counting on meeting another connection of Jasmine's she wanted to exploit, Maurice Hirsch, one of the most influential men in France, a low profile, quasi-shady billionaire who secretly financed heroin on the side. Jasmine had long promised action from Maurice's corner, but thus far, zip. "I don't know why Shields has been pussy-footing, but just let me get to Hirsch — I'll make it happen. And don't forget, there's Hirsch's partner, Charles Cestari." A Corsican drug dealer, Cestari owned the largest casino in the middle east right in Beirut. She wanted to corner one or both of these guys, get things rolling.

"Listen, Harry, I was thinking about a project for you. Charles Cestari visits New York several times a year. Ask around, get a line on him."

"Sure, hon. I'll get right on it."

"And while you're at it, I'd like a wiretap on Anthony Zino's lines. Not his home in Queens, but the joints he hangs out at, particularly the San Carlos Hotel."

"Piece of cake. Honey, we're not giving up on Zino — who says Jasmine has exclusive rights? We just gotta figure out a way to give the guy something he wants."

Harry always had her best interests at heart. He was one of the wisest decisions she ever made. He was a complete switch from any of the previous men in her life, especially from her late, longtime lover Joe Lo Bianco. Joe was a dapper dresser, whereas Harry had lousy taste in clothes; Joe was exciting, a guy you said yes to, Harry a man who took orders. It took a while to appreciate Harry's true worth, but he exemplified everything a good man should be — affable to have around the house, domesticated, a good homemaker, and always ready when she called for action in the sack. He was also an amateur lockpicker and wireman of no mean ability. Added Sutro credentials were an ability at karate, massage and marksmanship. Perhaps his major talent, however, was his tongue.

And a propos of what she'd said about farting, it was true. There was the old adage that a woman should find somebody she could fart with, and Harry certainly filled the bill. Not only did he give no objection her farts, he even found them attractive.

The first time she brought him up to the penthouse, right after picking him up at one of her massage parlors, she found out in short order what a fanatic he was on cleanliness. It was after midnight, the lighting was dim, but his eyes didn't miss a trick. "This joint's a mess," he said, indicating clutter, dust and disorder. "Honey, under these circumstances, I could never get it up."

"Sorry," Vic shrugged. "Maid service isn't my thing."

"I really wanted to ball you, but like this — no way Jose," Harry said. "You got any supplies around here?"

"I'll see."

"You're kidding," he scoffed when she handed him a bar of Ivory and an old sponge that fell apart to the touch. Consulting his watch, he said, "Look, I'll be back in a while."

She thought it was a brush off -- he was probably impotent anyway -- but lo and behold, forty minutes later, he returned from an all-night supermarket carrying a bag of cleaning equipment. He went to work moving furniture, vacuuming walls and ceilings, scrubbing under rugs, even behind picture frames. In five hours, he waxed the floors, washed the dishes, did all the laundry and changed the sheets. While he was working he told her all about himself, how he'd been toiling as a pallbearer in a mob-owned mortuary, specializing in carrying duplex coffins in which the rub-out victim was placed under the displayed body of record. You needed strong guys to carry these heavy duty doubledeckers. Corpses disappeared without a trace this way. It was foolproof. Victims would be six feet under in a matter of hours, long before they were stiffs even, much less before anybody realized they were even missing.

The sun was rising when he finally put everything in the cabinets and sat down for a well earned cigarette and can of beer.

"You must be exhausted after all that."

"Nah. Just give me a few minutes and you'll see." His porcine eyes turned erotic, or as erotic as Harry's eyes ever got. "As it happens," he said, "I got the fastest tongue in the east," he winked, "and my tongue never gets tired."

As a matter of fact, he did and it didn't.

Later, as they lay in bed, Vic explained how she earned her living. "In a way, you could say what we're doing is revolutionary, inasmuch as we're organized along business lines, like General Motors. It's probably the first time you've heard about a group of women like us before," she said. "Those wise guys wouldn't let us in their mafia, and we wouldn't let them in ours, but let me tell you that in a lot of ways, we're on our way to being even more powerful than the male mob. Any dude who gets involved with me has to understand my lifestyle and fit in with it."

"I hear you," Harry said.

"Women in so-called crime is a long established reality. Females have been dealing dope for a long time — the biggest drug dealers in California are women, most of them ours. Women have traditionally functioned as madams, run brothels and casinos, been couriers and mob fronts," Victoria said.

Harry licked his lips. "Sure, I know women can do all this, as much as the males who've been hogging the action."

"The difference with us LFM's," Victoria said, "is that for the first time in the history of the world we have an organized cartel of women."

"Mazeltov," Harry said. "Who could blame you? Look at how the establishment operates — can these people throw stones? States are into gambling and shylocking; what are most banks and credit card companies but legal loan sharks? You gonna tell me they don't have a racket? Who gave them permission?" Harry loved the idea of her organization, and wanted to know everything about it.

"We take vows of omertà," Vic said, emphasizing the last syllable of the traditional mafia word for silence, "so there's lots you can never know."

Harry said, "Listen, I'm a feminist. Everything a man can do a woman can do, if not better. A female mafia, is that a helluvan idea. Sure wish I could join."

"Being the wrong sex, you can't, but off the record, you can be an unofficial part of my team, my male associate."

"You got a beautiful set up," Harry said. "I mean, what law enforcement officer is gonna go after you? Even if they considered it, all you'd have to do is fuck their brains out to get yourself off the hook."

Harry was a treasure, worth his weight in gold, supportive of her aims in life; it was he who even encouraged her to make useful outside sexual liaisons.

"You mean you wouldn't be jealous?"

"Nah. What's nookie among friends? Can anybody begrudge a little head here and there?"

At first Vic wasn't sure she wanted to play that angle. She'd fought hard for her independence and wanted to keep it that way. She was a strong woman who, goddamnit, didn't have to take crap from any direction. She and Harry had had a number of discussions in this vein, Harry's contention being that she should use her cunt to advantage, while Vic argued it was a point of honor to make it on her own wits.

"You got wits in your pussy too," Harry pointed out. "If you don't use it, you lose an edge that every other female out there, despite what she may profess, is cashing in on. You're cutting off your nose to spite your face."

Given her enviable status in life, she thought she was long past that bag. "Harry, I've been down that road and learned the hard way."

"Listen, if you're smart you can call the shots and still fuck these guys in every sense of the word, and that's how you should look at it. This may be a female mafia, but who's to say getting the right man in your corner isn't still one of the best ideas a lady mobster can come up with? You see how your pal Jasmine operates."

"Still," Vic argued, "look at my accomplishments, look at all I've achieved."

Victoria's troops were the best. She had a fabulous crew of tough, aggressive don't-take-no-crap-from-nobody, ballsy winners. Her girls were producers, whether they were working contraband cigarettes smuggled up from the

Carolinas, precious gems, loans, gambling, hooking or you name it. She had a group of foot soldiers adept at hijacking and a team who ran the car theft end of the business, and owned chop shops in two boroughs and two outlying suburban counties. She had been in the avant guard of the gay revolution with her out-front, no holds barred homosexual bars, and she had some pretty decent porno action going too. In fact, the living room table was loaded with X-rated scripts, and just last month they'd shot a hot Perfumed Persian Garden erotica video in this very apartment, a steamy followup to her smashingly successful Cunt's Guide to the Kama Sutra offering.

Her penthouse suite at the Woodward was incredible -- rent controlled, dirt cheap, with a wrap around terrace that offered a view to kill for on all sides. On a clear day you could see the five boroughs, Jersey, Connecticut, Westchester and Long Island. There were eight rooms. Harry tended the rooftop garden where a hardy crop of marijuana grew alongside the pretty flowers and plants that were his pride and joy.

Vic had done all the decorating herself and was proud of the results. The color scheme was antique gold, baby blue, apricot and white. Velvet, the main fabric, was draped everywhere, carpeted, upholstered and hung. The floor was covered in blue carpet and apricot and robin's egg blue harlequin tiles, and there were gauzy apricot curtains. Chandeliers hung from a filigreed ceiling, and in the long harlequin tile entryway were two surrealistic murals of naked people in languid poses painted by one of her crew members, an artist who'd taken up crime to support her creative habit. In the center of the living room stood an oversized, polished Carrara marble statue of an idealized blond goddess — herself — posed with bow and arrow, knee-high sandals and a clinging Greek-style garment, leaning against a Corinthian column. That statue was so perfect it could have been sculpted by Praxitiles; instead it was the work of another one of her artistically inclined borgata members — Hoboken loan shark Mary Beth "Shybaby" Fudderman. If the art scene weren't such a scam, Shybaby wouldn't have had to have a second career as a shark.

The three other New York area LFM crime chiefs, Jasmine, Tania Lynn Cutler, and Joe's daughter Laura Lo Bianco, though skippers like herself, lacked her brilliant managerial skills, and their soldiers weren't the workers her team was. Vic's was an operation like no other. She was putting in 18 and 20 hour days and it was paying off handsomely. Take the phone room, for instance.

At one end of the penthouse, just off the kitchen, they'd torn out a wall of the former utilities/laundry room which Harry had then painted a delicate shell pink. After that he'd installed fluorescent lighting and put in banks of bootlegged pastel-tinted phones, ten lines in all, all of them illegal. Her phone people sat in plasterboard cubicles manning calls all day long, tending to a burgeoning commodities business. Gang members on the horn bought and sold stripper oil and discarded, dirty left-over petroleum mixed with heating oil for use in schools and hospitals; made-in-Portugal "scotch whiskey;" and gold with forged hallmarks under LME.

Vic had at least two dozen phone room legwomen on her rolls working staggered shifts. They were doing all kinds of deals — contracts on iron oxide pigments, sludge piles in West Virginia, gob piles in Kentucky, coal mines in Tennessee; she had them pushing precious stones; shrimp and other frozen foodstuff from South America; her phone crew had just closed a supermarket deal for Ecuadoran coffee, and using counterfeit collateral, had recently financed the purchase of some tractor assembling plants in the midwest. In addition, they were selling American made cars to Arab countries at inflated black market prices the Arabs were more than willing to pay.

Cement, rice, sugar, paraffin, fruit juice and railroad ties were but a few of the staples her troops were pushing now, and they were making great money from them.

Every day Victoria's time was occupied with a myriad of tasks, hopping between her penthouse home and her other headquarters at two social clubs, one downtown in Little Italy, the other on Vernon Avenue in Long Island City, where her Queens crew hung out. A typical day might find her discussing a hijacking with Millie "Bug Eyes" Newins, for instance, a car theft problem with chop shop owner Darilyn "Four Fingers" Houston, or going over a few shylocking moves with Alexis "The Cat" Knight. Uptown, downtown, east side, west side and all around outlying territories, Harry chauffeured her in a Ford Galaxie, and waited patiently for her to transact business.

Somewhere along the line, he found time to go out shopping for fresh produce, tend to the planning of healthy menus, do the vacuuming and dusting, walk the dog, wash the clothes and dishes, water the plants, and see that fresh flowers were on the tables.

A fabulous gourmet cook, Harry loved nothing more than puttering about the kitchen. Tonight, he had whipped up a tasty pasta al pesto dish, followed by steamed filet of sole véronique, baby carrots julienne, and a lightly tossed salad vinaigrette. Vic's guests were her underbosses and official consigliere.

Following an enthusiastically received dinner, Vic said, "We have business to discuss, ladies. I've asked Harry to sit in, because I value his opinion, and five heads are better than four." No one objected, so Harry joined them in the trophy room for an evening of plotting, planning, and scheming. Her girls had it in them to do big things, and Vic wanted to move some of them presently involved in rackets into something higher class, like narcotics.

Vic's actual consigliere, the physically large, rawboned Caroline "Cow" Stoll, M.D., a graduate of a Spanish-speaking Caribbean medical school, had interned at Metropolitan Hospital, done her residency at Queens County General and now was in private practice as a cardiac surgeon. A high school dropout who never went to college, the Cow seldom even attended med school classes since she spoke no Spanish and thus couldn't understand what was going on in the lectures anyway. It was a miracle she'd learned to perform complicated surgical procedures — heart bypasses, angioplasty, implanting pacemakers and the like — since the school had no cadavers, but somehow the Cow did manage to get a medical degree, now prominently displayed on her office wall, and in fact enjoyed a flourishing East Harlem practice. With a bi-lingual clientele of mostly Puerto Ricans, even her Spanish had been improving these past few years.

A gifted surgeon, Cow had the most phenomenal hands — long, thin, artistic — that looked like they were always performing feats of prestidigitation, even when engaged in mundane activities like writing out a prescription for Quaaludes.

Like many in her profession, Dr. Stoll's greatest asset was her intuitive knowledge. If anyone had the calling, Cow did. It was a reflection on the system that she had to go the route she did. But the Cow was a healer and she cared, in fact was so dedicated she treated inner city patients gratis. Not only that, she was always running off to third world earthquake-prone countries like Guatemala and El Salvador to help poor devastated natives. Stoll was a humanitarian soul, unselfish and altruistic. Well, she had to make a living somehow, didn't she? La Femmina mafia deals were her answer.

In addition to her medical practice and La Femmina responsibilities, the Cow, a gifted musician, sang second soprano in the New York City Physicians and Surgeons Choral Society, where her thrilling mezzo could give both Marilyn Horne and Jessye Norman a run for the money. Now Cow's Amazonian-proportioned body occupied a large armchair, and she had donned her most serious looking horn-rimmed glasses for the meeting.

To Victoria's right was her captain, Georgia "Legs" Jensen. Bosomy, sloe-eyed and blowzy, clad in a micro-mini skirt, Georgia, in blue-tinted shades, sat inhaling contemplatively, blowing fat smoke rings across the room. She seemed far removed from the Union City rackets she ran, including a shylocking concession out of a south Jersey bar whose flashing neon signs advertised topless dancers. Georgia always looked as if she'd spent the better part of the week rolling in the hay. A slack mouth and benign expression added to her fucked-out appearance. Occasionally she would reach down to stroke the fur of Marlene Dietrich, the German shepherd bitch who accompanied her everywhere and passed easily for a seeing eye dog, although she was not. On the fourth finger of her right hand Georgia wore an enormous ruby ring, the gift of her boyfriend, New Jersey labor leader and Cosa Nostra mobster Mike Giordano.

Grey-haired Rose F. Dyson, mob moniker "Rosie the Pelvis," was a good woman, a heavy hitter who owned and operated a thriving funeral parlor, the Shady Grove Mortuary in Valley Stream, Long Island. One of Ro's greatest satisfactions in life lay in dressing a corpse to give it the right appearance for its final scene on earth and sendoff to the Great Beyond. Cosmetics were Ro's specialty. A while back she was doing makeup for a TV studio in Manhattan. When they moved to Hollywood, Rose was invited to come along, but she preferred running her own scene on her own turf. The mortuary was it. With help from female mob money, she now owned the business, and was so good at it she'd been elected to serve as Vice Chairman of the Tri-State Morticians and Casket Association. The versatile Pelvis was not only a premiere funeral director, but also active in the Nassau County Cancer Society as a fundraiser, and an 8 handicap golfer at the North Hempstead Golf Club.

Displayed against purple velvet in the trophy room was Vic's gold plaque award for being elected, some seasons back, "Miss Kosher Hot Dog" at a Miami delicatessen, along with Harry's collection of ancient weapons — jewel-encrusted samurai swords, daggers and such; one of Sutro's hobbies was weapons, including esoteric Asiatic torture instruments, the latter exhibited in another room.

The group plotted for the next couple of hours, covering various aspects of gambling, loan sharking, prostitution, commodities, financial deals, and other weighty matters.

Enterprises were going well; nevertheless, as skilled an organizer as she was, as great a team of heavy duty earners as she was overseeing, Victoria urgently wanted to shake loose from the bottom of the rung rackets to concentrate on clipping coupons and enjoy the ease of money floating in without a lot of effort. Establishing a powerful narcotics set up was the major purpose behind all high level meetings recently. Dope, that would give the bankroll and independence she craved for herself and her team. Now, while she had the drive, energy and motivation, she had to get it all moving. Her vision was limitless. But a number of basics had to be worked out first.

"Why can't Zino be used for the airports?" the Pelvis wanted to know.

"He's paranoid because of government surveillance, so he's trying to stay as clean as possible in that area for the time being. At least this is Jasmine's story."

"What do you want to bet he's letting her cocaine in?" Cow remarked.

"Mike is still resisting our using the Jersey seaports, and I doubt I can change his mind. He's adamant," Georgia said. "But inasmuch as it's going to be difficult to get direct local cooperation, why lock ourselves into the ports of New York and New Jersey? So we take delivery elsewhere and ship east via Amtrak, Federal Express, UPS, the post office, Greyhound — or use mules, or whatever."

"Sure, we devise alternative routes from the south or use small airfields and so forth," Rose agreed.

Vic said, "It's just that keeping close tabs helps, and local cooperation would cut our overhead. Using circuitous routes, transhipping to entrepôts won't be as cost-effective."

"Besides," Cow agreed, "who wants to work these elaborate routes half way around the world and back again, from Europe to Hawaii to San Francisco, then Amtracking to the East coast — think in terms of efficiency. This is a business, you have to run it like a business and watch the bottom line."

"We could bring it in in containers to the ports without clearances," Georgia suggested. "They only do spot checking."

"An idea worth considering," Harry said. "However, one slip up is all it takes. Better safe than sorry?"

"In any case, the upcoming Beirut meeting may well advance us on one front," Vic said, "and I think I may have an idea for a hook into Zino. I believe I may be able to change this guy's mind. Stay tuned."

CHAPTER 4 - TANIA

Texans, it was said, had a brand that set them apart, and luscious Fort Worth rose Tania Lynn Cutler was a prime example. You immediately recognized the Texas in Tania from her determination and zest for adventure, her grand sense of life. Hers was a sensuous face, compressed, vicious, with a small nose, large mouth, and a look of innocent depravity. A gold Phi Beta Kappa key hanging on a delicate chain glinted at her cleavage.

When Tania Cutler's live-in lover and business partner Jack Riley asked, "Can I hit you for a loan for fifty dollars?" Tania immediately reached for her purse, not realizing that in gamblers' lingo fifty dollars meant fifty thousand. When Jack explained, Tania was aghast.

"Fifty thousand?" she repeated.

"Yeah," he said, as if it were chicken shit. He was only short temporarily; it wasn't a problem, because it was all coming in on a week to week basis from their joint gambling concessions.

Fifty thousand dollars was a lot of money to lend, even to a trusted lover, though. So Tania replied, "I'll have to think about it."

Jack had played a key role in the initial stages of the female mafia. Tania and Jack met one fated night at a charity event where Jack's uncle, Thomas Kelly, head of the International Longshoreman's Union, was receiving an award. Tania noticed Jack immediately, making his way to her table, walking slightly crouched over in a relaxed, loose-jointed manner. He was darkly handsome, and seemed not unpleasantly harassed as he took the empty seat next to her and lit a cigarillo. In the course of the evening, Tania confided she was depressed over having lost investment money she'd borrowed from her parents, how she'd expected a big return, but instead lost nearly every cent.

"I hope it wasn't that much," Jack said, sympathetically.

"Five thousand dollars."

"That's all?"

"Five thousand may not be much to you, but to me it's a fortune. The worst part is it wasn't mine, it was my parents', and they really need the money."

Jack's business card identified him as VP Creative Affairs of one of Madison Avenue's biggest ad agencies, but his actual function behind the title, he said, was that of official shop bookmaker. Gambling was actually his full-time occupation, and if you knew what you were doing you could make at least 25% on your money annually, usually a whole lot more.

"Look," he said, "I got a gut feeling. If I'm the winner I think I am tonight, you can pay your parents back, no sweat, and no strings attached." He consulted his watch. "Suppose we split and give the craps tables a whirl."

Their next stop was a tavern in the East 80's. Weekends Jack ran a couple of independent concessions, attracting a Madison Avenue, Wall Street, and show business clientele. In the back they booked horses, he said, and there was a room upstairs where patrons could play craps and Georgia skin. As houseman Jack got a cut from every pot. Without even trying he was clearing a grand a night at each location.

"Here you go," he said, handing Tania a wad of well-worn bills. "No questions asked. All yours."

It was a little over five thousand dollars and it hadn't even taken him a half hour to win it. Tania was flabbergasted.

After they were seated at a table in the front having drinks, she asked, "Tell me more about the gambling business."

They were "outlaw" games, Jack said, protected by the NYPD. "Outlaw means the mob lets you run. If you get too big you could end up paying the LCN a tribute."

"LCN?"

"La Cosa Nostra. Their allies — officially their apprehenders, but more often co-conspirators — are LEO's — law enforcement officers."

"Really! Can anybody do what you do?"

To her questions, he said although organizing and planning were challenging at first, after the word was out and you had customers hooked, the concessions could run themselves, providing you had the right personnel to mind the store.

Thoughtfully, Tania twirled the chain around her neck that held the gold Phi Beta Kappa key decorating her enticing décolletage. She asked, "Suppose my friends and I wanted to operate something like this — could we learn?"

Jack laughed. "Working a crap game's tough. You gotta call it all automatically, worry all the time about the bust-out men — craps is the fastest game in the world. But in time you'd pick it up."

Territories could be tightly divided, Jack said, but there was room for give and take, depending. "Cops will deal, the mob will deal. Why shouldn't they? Half a pie or a slice of it's better than none. You can't even count the number of joint ventures that go on with the Italian organization and the police. What the mob mainly offers is muscle, often through the unions."

"It's that simple?"

"Sure. You learn to trim the edges off of whatever system you're working."

Tania's mind was clicking. She told Jack she had friends who needed money. This sounded perfect for them: they could pitch in with food and manpower. "Do you think you could teach us what we need to know?"

Jack grinned, his Irish eyes twinkling in reply. "Say when."

It wasn't long before Tania and Jack were both bed and business partners. Jack, lured by the idea of expanding his own concessions, was happy to serve in an advisory capacity in a 50/50 joint venture with Tania and her friends.

So together the heads of New York's Four Families embarked on gin, poker and floating craps out of their own and other apartments. The games took off immediately, became fabulously successful and kept escalating in size and number.

Soon there were horse books, baseball pools, punchboards, and slots. A mini-casino Jack helped inaugurate had two craps tables, three for blackjack, two roulette wheels, one baccarat table, a bar and the best food in town, without exception. The gambling operations were works of art, their decor, food and flowers all creative touches Tania loved providing.

The foray into gambling brought revenues that began working in a number of directions. Their take was 10% of the winning pot. As Jack trained more and more personnel, Tania and the others became increasingly independent, able to leave the concessions in underlings' hands, and devote their time to other enterprises.

Since then, Tania's interests had branched out, so that she now had three thriving escort services and two massage parlors operating in Manhattan; there were several paper deals involving "dead" collateral with an Australian partner, and similar off-shore situations with dummy corporations in a number of Caribbean tax havens; she was involved in a large captive reinsurance loan out of Bermuda, and had some intriguing Wall Street operations going as a partner with other LFM interests. But the project that most held her attention now was an enterprise in the planning stages, a stud service for women to be named "Balls." She had been looking to rent space and had three locations seriously under consideration. Once she signed the lease, she'd be ready to plunge into other aspects of the promising venture.

Jack and she had been living together for the past year. They were as unmatched, he said, as an ace and a joker, but it seemed to work — at first. What Tania was looking for in a man was an intellectual, sophisticated connoisseur of the arts, a man who was well-read, world-traveled and into art, classical music, foreign languages and philosophy, preferably a Harvard, Yale or Princeton graduate, although Brown or Williams would also do. Jack Riley, University of Miami bookmaker, while none of the above, had managed to conquer with his charm, and the fact that he held the key to a life that would eventually be all she'd ever longed for. Had she even wished, Tania could not have resisted his sparkling Irish eyes and conspiratorial grin. Jack's warmth and loquaciousness made him one of the most likable individuals she'd ever met, added to which, he was so great in bed — in the beginning, at least — that it blinded her to potential problems other women would have recognized. Perhaps all this could be attributed to the weirdness of her brain.

Twenty-six years ago, purple faced and choking, Tania Lynn Cutler made a traumatic entrance into the world with an umbilical cord wrapped twice around her head, and was nearly asphyxiated in the process. She had traveled through a birth canal so narrow it was impossible to pass beyond her mother's cervical area without the use of forceps that were inserted high and clamped tightly around her tiny infant head. Doctors said certain brain cells were affected in the process, only no one predicted the strange manner in which these cells reacted.

At two, she taught herself to read and write, at seven had mastered French, German and Spanish, self-taught; her Regents exams were the highest in Texas history, she could do complex calculus problems in her head and learn a foreign language in no time; but on the downside, she had trouble handling some of the most basic human situations. For instance, she needed a string around her finger to remind herself to get off at the right subway stop, and on the dance floor she had to count to consciously tell her feet where to move, rendering conversation with a partner all but impossible. Perhaps the most unfortunate lack in brain function, however, was in the area of human relations, particularly with the opposite sex. She was a lousy judge of character, too often misreading motives, trusting others only to discover they were not what she thought.

Quite apart from her unusual mind, Tania had been forced to grapple with another problem of an entirely different nature: money. When people heard Hockaday and Wellesley, they smelled bucks, not realizing Tania had attended these elite schools on full scholarships. Accustomed to being praised for her intellectual achievements, she'd expected doors to open after college, but found an ugly awakening in how tough the New York market was, especially when a woman lacked adequate financial backing. Though it was hard to understand, she had found no decent jobs available in New York City for a Phi Beta Kappa summa cum laude valedictorian Ivy League graduate who spoke nine languages fluently. Money was the root of the problem. Money was power, freedom, security. Once you licked that, all else fell into place.

Tania saw herself against a vast panorama of history, a synthesizer of past ages, reaching out across time to flower in the unique era in which life had placed her. She was destined to express a grand design, be the guidepost of an age, enliven the cultural scene, sponsor theatre and dance companies, collate and promote art and culture, create a philosophy to shape her generation and leave her mark on humanity. She had always dreamed of being a genuine Promethean Athena/Minerva of her time, all things to all men.

In Fort Worth, the place to live was Westover Hills on the first hill, with all the winding streets, tall trees and big houses behind brick walls, where the old money was. Only her family didn't live on the first hill, and they had no money. Her father was a downtown auto mechanic — so unfitting for the person she both innately was and had shaped herself into.

There was such sadness in being a have-not in a world of luxury and beauty. Her junior year at Wellesley was spent in Perugia and Florence in a daze of desire, delirium, euphoria, exhilaration, passion and longing. She wanted to live ever surrounded by great art and beauty, but for so long everything had been beyond her reach. She felt out of synch with the world, killed by its confinement. Here she was, involved in the pettiness of a struggle for survival when she was full of great uplifting ideas and an enormous flame was burning inside her.

Money, money, money — it was her constant obsession, her mania. She must have it — to live the life of beauty to which she aspired, and to serve the highest good. Given her cultural and social ambitions, and considering that there was no way out playing by conventional rules, the truth sank in. Something had to give.

Where did other people's money come from, she asked? Wheeling, dealing, connections, and a lot of it from previous generations, that was the answer. One or two generations at most was enough to whitewash anything a robber baron grandfather conceived. Behold the aristocrats. They were entitled.

Long ago, idealism would have prevented her from taking measures. No more. Scruples receded, becoming a thing of the past. O.C., organized crime, was the way to go. Nietzsche in The Genealogy of Morals reevaluated all values and proved that so-called evil was good, and vice versa. Schopenhauer said the same thing. Man had been asleep for thousands of years and had falsified the real.

Organized crime was merely an underground economy, an extension of the free enterprise system in which rules were more relaxed, an open, unregulated market. Look around and see how the country's fortunes were made — by nefarious means. Examine the impeccable great families — Rockefeller, Kennedy and their ilk — and you'd see proof that as Machiavelli declared centuries ago, the end justifies the means. And as Balzac said, "Behind every fortune there is a crime."

When the opening presented itself, Tania grabbed it. Hungrily. She would no longer be denied. The way out was bending the law and being a new kind of outlaw. Her noble goal must be realized. She would mold philosophy and shape the sensibility of an epoch in no less formidable a manner than the Medicis.

With her inspired agenda, the entire planet could be upgraded. She would bring a needed aesthetic vision to the waiting world. As a magnetic center, a catalyst, her personal sense of right and wrong was allowed to differ from the generally accepted one. Crime became her enabling force.

At this point, her most pressing personal creation-in-the-making, Balls, a stud service for women, occupied the forefront of her consciousness. She had long felt the need for such a service existed. After all, if men had massage parlors and brothels at their disposal, why shouldn't women enjoy such alternatives? When she heard a similar establishment, named "Dongs & Wongs" was up and running in London, she phoned its proprietress, ex-journalist Fiona Stonemartin-Cartwright. They had spoken several times, and soon now Tania would be leaving for London to see Fiona and her operation firsthand.

Sadly, Jack didn't share her creative vision. He was certainly a nice guy, but unfortunately burdened by intellectual limitations. He didn't understand that gambling, bookmaking and numbers were merely steps along the way, not the ultimate be all and end all. It seemed the more she distanced herself from the environment of roulette, craps, horsebooks, punchboards, poker games and Georgia skin, the more Jack enmired himself in them, and worse, the heavier his personal betting became.

In the beginning, Tania hadn't suspected Jack had a gambling problem. Then, buoyed by success, using increased income that was flowing in from his half of the concessions, he started betting heavier with the proceeds, but as initially he was on a winning streak, at first she didn't notice. Then his luck reversed. Jack said these cycles happened, and swore that in short order, he'd be on the plus side again; he knew what he was doing.

Sports, races, poker, gin -- he thrived on them all, everything that was action. His conversation had become increasingly one note: "Let's see, Green Bay vs. the Rams — it's Rams' home turf, but on the other hand — " "This horse has the speed to score, but on a mile and a half course, can he close?" "Think I'll catch the helicopter for the 8th at Monmouth. Wanna tag along?" "Hialeah's the place to be tomorrow. Can't afford to miss this one!"

"Don't worry, baby," he assured, flashing a smile. "I'm a pro, and if I say my luck's gonna change, you can believe my luck's gonna change." Casually, he'd talk about winning and losing huge amounts — five and six figure sums — as if it were nothing. "You win a few, you lose a few," he shrugged. The pattern was clear: he lived from moment to moment, one day flush, the next broke, always waiting for another streak.

Why hadn't she seen it sooner? They hadn't even had much sex lately, because gambling sapped his desire.

Tania, broaching that subject now, said, "Jack, do you realize how long it's been since we've made love?"

He said, "I'm sorry, angel, but if I could just get my debts cleared up, everything would be back to normal, like before. If you could just lend it to me — "

"Thirty thousand dollars is a lot of money."

"But only for a short time — please, honey, say yes."

Maybe it was her brain, and again maybe it was compounded by guilt and pity for Jack and the feeling that he'd helped her, and now he needed her help and she owed him. And she did love him, after all. Could she stand by and allow him to sink into ruin?

Jack kept pleading with her until, sighing, and still not without reservations, Tania finally said yes, yes, she would lend him the fifty thousand dollars.

"All right, you can borrow the money, as long as I get it back in a week or so."

That was her first big mistake.

CHAPTER 5 - JASMINE

All heads turned as Jasmine Shields wound her way to Anthony Zino's table for their pre-arranged appointment at the Mannequin Lounge in the garment district. Men always gaped at Jasmine that way. It was more than her looks — the greenish-hazel almond-shaped eyes, long silky legs and voluptuous body – Jasmine had real presence. Infectious and hypnotic, with an infinite belief in her powers, she was alternately demure and flamboyant. An ineffable quality set her apart.

Mannequin regulars were curious what business she had with the redoubtable Anthony Zino, one of the most notorious public enemies in the United States. This was the first time they'd met, and Jasmine was immediately attracted to Zino's kinky appeal. She liked the way his mouth dropped into a downward, snarling grimace that looked like he didn't know how to smile, until his upper lip slowly curled, revealing shiny wolfen teeth that gave a dangerous cast to his dark, olive complected, angular face. His style fascinated her -- the cool, abrasive voice and the large, powerful hands. His drink was Early Times straight up, she noted.

Without bothering to ask if she smoked, he lit two cigarettes and handed her one. For a second their fingertips touched, sending an electric shock running through their hands. She knew they would connect in important ways.

An hour later, when she prepared to leave, Zino offered, "Let me give you a lift. Sugar, Barbi — " He called two toughs at the bar.

His hand slid under her elbow with a rough grip as he guided her to his waiting car. Riding together in the back seat, the current of sexuality between them was overpowering. Sneaking a glance at his crotch, she was encouraged to see he had an erection. He asked for her number and said he'd like to call her.

The next time they met, they were all over each other at the table. Even so, she was unprepared for the suddenness of what occurred afterward in the car. Without warning, he grabbed her and kissed her till he knocked the breath out of her. He stopped briefly to order his men in the front seat, "Take us around the park, youse guys, and turn up the music — loud."

Then he moved in again. The sharp teeth, lit from the street lamps, gleamed in lust as he tore at the zipper of his fly and his erection burst out, flopping like a hunk of hard rubber. Reaching under her clothes, he guided his hand through the barrier of her panties, and dipped his finger into her vagina. He was moaning, "Oh, baby, you're so wet ..."

He tugged the bikini panties off, then lifted her skirt and took her bare buttocks firmly in both his hands, emitting a sharp cry as he eased her directly down onto his stiff organ. "Give me your cunt," he commanded, his deep gruff voice muffled in her ear.

His grip was like a vise. Straddling him, she relished the exquisite hot sensations inside her body, as ravenously, she moved her torso around at varying angles, and he met her with long, deep slow strokes, and she closed over him, her legs gripping his chest, feeling the mounting excitement of his slippery bulging inside her. "Sweet pussy, sweet, sweet pussy," Zino whispered under his breath. "You got the juiciest pussy ... God, your cunt is tight ... Christ, you're so juicy ..."

Air escaped from his gritted teeth in rapid, fizzing sounds. He sucked in his breath and grimaced, "Shhh!" gesturing toward the bodyguards in the front seat. Their friction accelerated. Breathless, she pressed closer, her vaginal muscles flexing in continuing expansive rhythm. Their pelvises were locked into each other, rubbing, pumping, swiveling, gliding as one unit now. And then as his engorgement reached a peak inside her, amplified sensations overtook them and the sounds of their joint climax became muffled together. In her paroxysms of release, it was as if his whole cock had burst into flames inside her.

"I knew you'd be like that," he whispered in her ear, tucking his dick back in his pants.

He had connections at some savings and loans in Jersey and Queens — there was a bank in Flushing which in particular interested her. She said, "You mentioned you knew some special banks and hungry bankers — I'd like to meet these bankers. I have a business venture I want to jump start in the garment center, manufacturing sportswear and leisure wear."

He was the man for that. The mob owned 2/3 of the garment center and had a monopoly on trucking.

"A manufacturing operation, huh?"

"I'm into apparel and design, it's my thing. I know what can be done on the accounting end of the schmatte trade in factoring and unreported cash — it's an unbelievable opportunity for book cooking. My friends and I are looking for reinvestment opportunities. I know you have friends who own a sizable portion of the garment district — "

"I'll see what I can do," he promised. "Let me work on it."

Anthony Zino could do a lot. Among other things, he controlled New York's needle trade through respectable fronts. Through influence with the unions, you could open a factory without worrying about payscales and rules; you'd get concessions that gave you an edge over your competitors. The manufacturing end of the rag trade was where the money was, and for that you needed leverage with the unions from sewers to pressers to truckers.

They talked about the logistics of trucking deals. In the metropolitan area, cargoes had to be turned over to the mob; it had to be one of their approved trucks that hauled the material to the factory. There were no formal logs on truckers saying what company they worked for. It was always a gentlemen's agreement, nothing written down. He said he'd help her set up a jobbing business, yeah, he'd find contractors, work deals with the locals, swing everything right, no problem. His price would be to put two of his own people on the payroll in no-show jobs.

"You wanna run a factory, you got it," he promised. "You got nothin' to worry about."

Zino's introductions facilitated her starting the manufacturing facility without putting up a penny. Through his collateral rental/suburban bank scheme, it was a snap. What you did was rent, for a one per cent fee, collateral in the form of certificates of deposit from the unions. These were then put in your name or in your company's name, in FDIC insured banks where Zino had connections, the interest to be collected by the unions. In return for kickbacks, banks would give compensating balance loans for three times the value of the CD's. The trick in working this gimmick was finding the willing bankers, and Zino had a whole slew of them chomping at the bit. In New Jersey towns like Passaic, Manville, Bayonne, Trenton, Clifton, Bloomfield, Edison and Perth Amboy, the bankers were lined up, cups out like beggars, just waiting to grab a piece of the action. Ditto Queens.

Zino said this was the way everybody with half a brain operated these days. He said all the big real estate developers, condo and resort builders worked that way. And from here, there would be more deals, more projects. The potential was limitless.

"Suck me, oh, yeah — I love you to suck me," Zino moaned. "Baby, tell me you like my cock — tell me I got the biggest prick — the biggest, the fattest — oh, yeah, yeah — "

His mouth moved to her taut distended nipples, to the flatness of her belly. She spread her legs wide for him as he began licking the inside of her thighs, pressing on, moving his tongue into the pink junction that was the confluence of his arousal and desire. Then he was inside her again, plunging toward her upraised pelvis that jutted to join him in thrusts of pleasure. She could feel the fullness of his lust raging for her, as his cock, blood thirsting and pulsing, beat against the walls of her hot, swollen vagina. They were throbbing together, embedded in each other, cresting, rushing and meeting in quickening tempo. "Mamma, mamma, o-i-e, madonna! Oh, mamma!" he cried out, as she milked him, deeper, more, deeper, more, until finally he groaned one final "Mamma."

CHAPTER 6 - LAURA

Laura Lo Bianco was an exotic beauty, ripe, sensual, with eyes like black grapes fringed with long dark lashes, creamy rich skin, and a tumble of straight dark hair — striking, alluring, a knockout. "Gangster's daughter," people whispered behind Laura's back. Newspapers had described her late father, Joseph Lo Bianco, as "tough, gravel-voiced cigar-chomping underboss, feared man of respect, a sottocapo with eight captains, each in turn commanding a crew of 30 soldiers... Lo Bianco troops are estimated at 250."

Overnight, Laura's world turned upside down. One day her father was alive, the next he lay murdered in a pool of blood in a Flatbush restaurant rubout. Soon afterwards, endless problems started with the Lo Bianco estate and business interests. The security her father had built, rightfully hers, was eroding, her birthright slipping away, as her father's mob cronies pushed their way in to take over enterprises — the bottling plant, the coat factory, trucking and food distribution companies. Once plentiful income trickled to a fraction of its former amount, and even her father's attorneys were screwing her.

Adversity makes strange bedfellows. Victoria Winters, the woman who had monopolized so much of her father's time and kept him from his family, stepped in with an idea, and Laura's solution was born. But for her accomplishments as leader of the Brooklyn and Long Island branch of the La Femmina Mafia, she would have been wiped off the face of the earth. Thank God for the LFM. Since its inception, the organization had reached into all corners for revenue. It took off like a house on fire, as LFM's made their bones, vowed oaths of loyalty, and jointly helped build families of reliable workers. The structure was formalized in a manner similar to the male Cosa Nostra, with separate families of capos, lieutenants, captains and crews of soldiers. They'd even set up a National Commission to settle disputes and arbitrate policy.

As luck would have it, due to federal heat, many male Cosa Nostra members were forced to lie low, leaving a void in organized crime. In their cops and robbers game, law enforcement prided itself on decimating the LCN, but were oblivious to the La Femminas, which gave Laura and her distaff criminal associates an edge.

It was all building. Laura's tentacles reached into various corners of the tri-state area. Her lieutenant Nancy Jo Corcoran ran a posh bordello on Manhattan's upper east side as well as an S & M parlor downtown; underboss Chinatown mafiosa Eleanor Lee Wong was hooked into some heavy Hong Kong and Taiwan money connections; and another underboss, Deborah Cook, ran Laura's Wall Street operations.

Her ventures were doing well indeed, but even so, she was not out of the woods yet financially. The IRS had come after her with a deficiency judgment; legal troubles had accelerated, resulting in liens; she was being hit from all sides, and was in danger of losing her home unless she could cough up a large six figure amount within the next sixty days.

Laura was sure Frank Gantry, the man she had worshiped since early teens and had always fantasized marrying, would know how to help. He would counsel her, steer her toward workable solutions, and in the process, as they bonded, their relationship would take hold.

"Frank is absolutely perfect for me," Laura confided to her lieutenant, Kamzen Raines. "He and I come from the same background. Frank grew up in Brooklyn like I did. Then, several years back, his family moved to the Jersey suburbs, and even though our fathers were close associates, Frank's life went in a different direction than mine."

"How's that?" Kami asked.

"He went to an high profile eastern prep school, whereas my dad insisted on sending me to nearby Catholic schools so he could keep an eye on me. Frank was an art history major at Princeton. He spent his junior year in Florence. It's pretty funny, because the society columns liken him to a renaissance prince -- they have absolutely no idea he's the son of bigtime mobster Vincent Gantria --"

"You mean the Genovese family lieutenant?"

"I do mean. Frank's father runs a formidable low profile borgata that controls Jersey numbers and loan sharking. If the cat ever got out of the bag -- "

"How are you going to play this, Laura? How will you get together with him?"

Laura told Kami how her path and Frank's had seldom crossed over the past few years, but then, miraculously, a few weeks ago, they'd met at a cousin's wedding. "It was instant magic," Laura recalled. "Dancing with him, being in his arms just swept away the years -- and he flirted outrageously with me. You wouldn't believe this man's pure visceral power, his strength and virility -- incredible!"

"Ok, the guy has charisma, but has he called you yet?"

"No, that's the problem."

"Sometimes men need a nudge. Why don't you call him?"

"I intend to."

Laura was determined yet nervous, as she picked up the phone to dial Frank. "I need some advice. May I come see you?" she asked.

"Of course, Laura. Anytime," was the welcome reply.

Frank Gantry's spacious office was located on the 50th floor of the RCA Building, behind a frosted glass pane reading "FTG Enterprises, Real Estate, Import-Export, Art Consultation." The rooms were elegant and tasteful, decorated with art pieces from all over the world — antique lamps and Chinese rugs, urns and totem poles, 18th century snuff bottles and porcelain clocks.

A door opened and Frank emerged. His strong, handsome chiseled face was graced by a touch of tan that bespoke his privileged lifestyle. His suit was cut with the understated elegance that was the trademark of his tailor, Hayward of London. There was something undeniably stellar about him. Of four Gantry/Gantria brothers, Frank was the one with immediate star quality. "Laura," he said, striding toward her, hand extended. "I do apologize for keeping you waiting."

He leaned closer to kiss her with casual affection, told his secretary not to disturb them, ushered her into his office and closed the door. At last, after so much fantasy, they were at the right stage in life for each other.

"It was great seeing you at the wedding. I must say you're looking absolutely radiant — then and now."

"It's been a long time," Laura smiled, her heart racing wildly. Without hesitation, she began the story of the troubles she was having with her father's enterprises, about how she might lose the house and didn't know what to do.

Frank frowned. Didn't she have a lawyer, he asked? She explained her father's lawyers were all crooks, they had tied up her money and were trying to screw her. Frank shifted his weight in the chair, pulled his tie away from his neck and said he could get her a new lawyer. That was not exactly what she'd been hoping to hear.

All too soon, sliding back his shirt cuff, Frank consulted the black face of his diamond studded Piaget and apologized, "I think I mentioned that today was crowded." (She didn't recall his saying that at all). "Unfortunately, much as I'd love to visit with you, I have another meeting in just a few minutes."

"I don't want to keep you," Laura said, rising, trying to hide disappointment. "I'm grateful for your time and help."

"I'll be in touch on the lawyer," he promised.

The current had been so strong between them at the wedding, but now he was impersonal. He had controlled the entire conversation, despite her being the one who did most of the talking.

Then suddenly, as they stood at the door bidding goodbye, he flashed his dazzling smile, their eyes met, held for longer than was necessary, and for a split second Laura thought there was still a chance. "I hope we can get together again soon," she ventured.

"I hope so." Distance again; he was definitely putting up a barrier.

She tried phoning but had trouble getting through. She heard from him again only through his secretary. He had left a message for her — the name of a good attorney.

Frank's reaction was a big disappointment, but she had to move on, and an idea of how to get the increasingly urgently needed money dawned on Laura. She'd seen an article in The New York Times quoting police and FBI sources, claiming numbers lotteries in Harlem alone earned one billion a month in profits, and that the Genovese family, which had a stake in several Harlem banks, had 27 millionaires among its soldiers involved in the banks. Blacks, Jews and Hispanics were operating in tandem with the Genovese family in joint ventures. What was to prevent women from doing the same thing?

Laura's lieutenant Kamzen Raines would be perfect to organize such an inner city venture. Hence, this meet Tuesday morning at 10:30, uptown, on Kami's turf, in a neighborhood that consisted of a colorful group of fast food operations, record stores, beauty parlors, clothing boutiques, African bazaars, and a center for African dance, music and culture.

A product of the Harlem scene, daughter of a LaGuardia Airport skycap father and a mother who worked for Verizon, Kami Raines had begun her career as a shovel and bag woman in an uptown heroin mill, with a burning ambition to emulate her heroine, Madame Stephanie St. Clair, head of Harlem numbers in the 20's. She boasted gold-plated connections in the African-American underworld community. With the changing face of ethnic crime and her own organizational ability, she was proving indispensable in working inner city rackets.

Dressed in tight jeans and a fur-trimmed leather jacket, Kami stood waiting outside a Pentecostal storefront church by the elevated bridge near Park Avenue. Laura walked the few blocks over from the Lexington Avenue subway, the two greeted each other and went around the corner for coffee.

Laura had invited the other capos of New York's Four Families to the meet. Jasmine and Tania showed, but something had come up and Victoria was missing, though of course she'd want to be part of the deal — who wouldn't jump at an opportunity like Laura was proposing?

"Do tell us about this idea that's going to bring us all millions," Tania prompted, after they were seated and had placed orders.

Glancing around, then speaking in a low voice, Laura began, "The Genovese family has a stake in several Harlem banks that have made over two dozen of their soldiers zillionaires."

Pushing a long, relaxed mane of copper-colored hair off her face, Kami, who had already been briefed, took up the ball. "What Laura has in mind is to implement something along these lines for our organization. I told Laura I can run it. All I have to do is rope the right people in, and we'll have a money-making policy game of our own."

"You mean there's room for another numbers operation?" Tania asked, surprised.

"There's always room; and if blacks, Puerto Ricans and Jews can, we women certainly can."

Laura said, "It can't be done alone, but even as a joint venture it's the goose that laid the golden egg. In effect you purchase a franchise and split with the Italian organization. They provide protection and handle the big layoff action. You pay off the cops, of course. Even so you come out way ahead."

Kami explained the way it worked: "The customer picks a number from 1 to 999. He gives this to his runner, lowest man in the hierarchy. The runner hands the money over to the controller — each controller has at least 12 runners reporting to him — the controller disciplines the runners, keeps accounts tabulated, and passes funds along to the big man, the bank."

"That's Kami," Laura said.

Hip, classy Kami Raines knew the program. Put her blindfolded in the middle of 125th Street and Boston Road, she'd tell you exactly what was going down, point to the hustles, dealing and pimping, crib cracking, boosting and blackmail, show you where the bulls were. She could smell a plainclothesman a mile away, spot cruisers and dudes looking to harass junkies and whores and bust crap games. She knew all the successful pimps, numbers runners, controllers and dope dealers in the neighborhood. Her reputation preceded her: as a mill hand managing smack cuttings, she'd been known as one of the most dependable shovel and bag women around. She'd been looking for a career move and got it from Laura and the LFM; what Laura now had in mind could increase Kami's stock in trade thousandfold.

Kami said, "Being the banker takes connections and organizational ability. Each winning number has to be one that people can trust that can't be fixed — say a figure from the newspapers agreed on ahead of time, like the results at Belmont, or the last three digits of the total amount of money waged that day at Monmouth Park."

"What kind of odds are we dealing with, Kami?" Jasmine asked. Jasmine was tall, tan, amber-eyed and stunning.

"One in 999, so the payoff on the dollar is around $700. That leaves you a margin of $300. You split that — runners, controllers, banker, the organization above us, the Italians, and also the cops — they'll most likely take half our profit."

"What are the cost breakdowns?" Tania wanted to know.

"The banker at top collects 11 cents on the dollar. After incidental expenses, he ends up with 10 cents on the dollar. The runners, collectors and controllers take 25 cents of every dollar, net, and 10 cents of every winning hit, making a total of 35 cents on the dollar. You can end up, after expenses, with at least 10 cents on the dollar, which can be an enormous sum, believe me."

"Sounds right up our alley, doesn't it, ladies?" Jasmine said, enthused.

"Believe it, believe it. Our idea is to make the runners a straight business offer," Kami said. "We pay them better than 20 per cent. They'll be taking some risks, so we offer them extra security and inducements."

"I know you have to pay off the cops, but why cut the Italian mob in?" Tania asked. "Do we really need them?"

"Absolutely. First of all, only a big organization can handle the layoff — pay off when the bank gets hit hard, that is. Only the Italian organization has the muscle and money to keep cops and politicians from breaking up the operation, shaking down the clientele and the operators. So they control at that level. We become part of their organization and get the benefit of their clout."

"Can you get us protection from your father's old crew, Laura?" Tania asked.

"That's the last thing I could do," Laura said. "My father's people have been cheating me blind. I can't deal with them. We'll need Jasmine to get Zino and the Lucchese family behind us. With that connection, it should easy for us to buy into a franchise."

Kami turned to Jasmine and said, "Tell Zino to set his mind at ease. I know what I'm doing. Tell him I can get the runners, which is the whole key. He'll understand. Customers don't know about controllers and bankers. Customers only know the runners. So we bring in the runners and the customers follow. It's like the old pyramid deal. Get Zino in our corner. He'll go for it, I guarantee."

"Great idea, Laura," Jasmine said. "Count me in."

"Me too," Tania said. "How long do you figure before we're operating?"

"Not long. As soon as Zino gives the ok, we'll be ready. We should definitely have a going concern by the time we're heading for Beirut."

It was the solution that would solve Laura's legal and financial problems once and for all. Not for nothing was she Joseph Lo Bianco's daughter.

The LFM, this "thing of theirs," was doing so well that in the past month Jasmine had signed on half a dozen more women to handle the action in her borgata. Thanks to Zino's assistance, it didn't take long before she expanded to mass produce Cartier lighters and Rolex watches, Gucci bags and designer garments out of sweat shops located both in Queens and offshore. The counterfeit merchandise, knockoff designer jeans, and accessories supplemented the legitimate manufacturing operations that Zino had facilitated.

Again due to Zino's support, the numbers franchise quickly became a done deal, and was operating bigtime, a real winner. She was on the road to riches, loving every moment of it.

"I'm gonna miss you, doll." Anthony Zino reached across the bed to tousle Jasmine's hair. "Where're you off to this time?"

"South America, as usual, then on to the west coast followed by Lebanon — Beirut."

"Beirut? Lebanon? That country's a ravaged wasteland war zone."

"Only according to media portrayal. Actually, it's not like you think at all. Beirut's a fabulous place to shop, eat, gamble, be entertained, launder money and/or spend money as the case may be, and have an absolute ball. It's very chic, very fashionable, and it's got the best nightlife in the entire Mediterranean -- Europeans go there all the time. It's a totally fun place to visit and hang out."

"No shit? You learn something new every day. Hey, babe, let's have one for the road, 'cause I'm gonna be horny as hell while you're gone. Why're you leaving me high and dry again?"

"You know why. Some white powder that's going to give you a real hard-on when you get your cut, among other things."

"You give me the only kinda hard-on I want. C'mere."

"Will you be a good boy while I'm gone?"

"You bet. Oh, honey, yeah, oh, yeah — suck me, suck my dick. I love you to suck my cock."

Life was on the move. Jasmine had the feeling of freedom and riding the crest of a wave. She was unstoppable.

CHAPTER 7 - THE ST. PATRICK'S DAY MASSACRE

It took a while for Harry to convince her. It hadn't been easy to come around to his point of view.

"I told you before, I'll say it again — you got a gold mine in that pussy of yours, pumpkin," Harry said. They were breakfasting at the kitchen table while Harry was opening the mail with a switchblade. "You oughta be out there using it to advantage."

"I understand only too well what's entailed in being a hooker," Victoria retorted, cutting open the poached eggs on toast Harry had made and letting the juice ooze out onto the plate. "And listen, even Joe Lo B. didn't consider me in that category. It's not my style."

"Don't knock it," Harry said, placing the switchblade down to stir milk into piping hot oatmeal. "But anyway, who's talking about hooking? What I'm saying is you got an edge, you gotta use it. Hasn't it been said that one pubic hair on a woman's body is stronger than the Atlantic cable?"

"Other women don't have my mind," Victoria pointed out.

"No reflection on you, honey," Harry said, "but you gotta learn nobody makes it on their brains alone, not even men. There's no shame admitting everybody needs support from the right auspices. Sex is political. Nobody oughta have anything against using their pussy. That's what God put it there for, to do some good. You got a great cunt — why lose out? You got a complex about not wanting to be considered a bimbo."

"I just believe a woman should get to a point in life where she calls the shots, Harry."

"You're there, baby. Do you realize you're one of the most envied, powerful women in this city or this entire nation, for that matter?"

"Then why should I have to lower myself to cater to some ass hole?"

"Baby, you can play a role and still retain your dignity. Lotsa guys can only accept you in certain roles, as an entre, but after the preliminaries they start seeing other aspects. Only you gotta meet them half way to get things started."

"Christ on the fucking cross, Harry, I've probably been to bed with a thousand different men in my day, and where did any of it get me?"

"Ok, but you're smarter now, so you play the game on a higher level."

"The whole thing is that a penis makes a difference, and that hole we women have louses us up. It's like something's missing and you have to compensate — "

"Men use women. It's the same thing."

"No," Victoria insisted. "It's a man's world."

"Only because you don't understand the male point of view. You'd be surprised if you could get inside a guy's head — or his cock."

"Yeah, I bet I would."

"Honey, there's no shame making sex the modus operandi -- and seldom is it ever that cut and dry, anyway. It's a grey area. You're dealing in guys' egos and things they won't even admit to themselves — "

"Well, I have to say you have a point, Harry, much as I hate to admit it — the right man could be a boost."

"Sure. Look how this Jasmine operates. She's out there putting her cunt to good use. You wanna lose out?"

All right, but it was tough to swallow. She'd really believed she was beyond that phase. How often had she thought of Marilyn Monroe's famous exit line to the 20th Century Fox head honchos when finally released from her indentured slavery 7 year contract: "Ok, boys, that's the last cock I suck." Now if that wasn't the all-time classic example of a female cry of independence! This, Vic thought, was exactly the way things should work out for a woman once she got to a certain stage in life, and the sooner the better. She had fancied herself being there already, and yet more and more it now seemed that she wasn't.

Not that she hadn't voluntarily, even enthusiastically, sucked her share of cocks — still did, for that matter — but the ultimate power was in freedom of choice. All men automatically expected their cocks sucked, whereas not all cocks were suckable; some didn't lend themselves to it; but reluctance to suck a particular cock could cost a woman dearly. Then it was a power struggle, a problem she still hadn't solved, dammit all.

"I see the fine line, Harry. Just as long as I get to call the shots without the guy being the wiser."

"Now you're talking. And Zino should be a priority. He can do a lota good with the drug situation."

"Right you are, Counselor," Victoria said. "The sooner I get to Zino's balls the better."

"He and Jasmine have a non-exclusive relationship, according to the wiretaps. So that gives us more leeway than we originally thought. It's encouraging."

They formed a plan how to get Zino hooked. Now they just had to corner him and start setting it up.

Friday night, the finest judges, politicians and priests in the city gathered at the private Italian club Tiro a Segno at 66 MacDougal Street for the best pasta in town, followed by target practice at the New York Rifle Club downstairs. They struck paydirt with a tip from Harry's wiretap, advising Anthony Zino would be dining there. The plot was ready to hatch; it was all systems go.

Vic and Harry were enjoying *capelli d'angeli*, listening to His Eminence New York's cardinal and others of the Roman Catholic hierarchy in their weekly rendering of maudlin Irish songs when she was called to the phone. Heading back to the table again, lured by the strains of "Mother Machree," Vic's attention was brought to the men's room. An emerging figure, face turned away from her, was lighting a cigarette, the match flame protected by his cupped hands.

The man was impeccably groomed, starched white handkerchief in breast pocket, nails freshly manicured and glossed. He was wearing a shantung suit, and his tie bore the logo of another one of the city's best known Italian clubs. On his right hand was an unusual mark, a rooster tattooed between the crease of his thumb and trigger finger. When he squeezed his fingers, the rooster looked like it was flying. As he skulked away from the men's room, his walk was slow, deliberate. The face was hard and sallow. He had the muscular body of a man much younger than his years. Thick joined eyebrows covered his forehead in a baneful soot black line. He was ultra glamorous, like a character from a Hollywood gangster movie. He was Anthony Zino.

Victoria went right up to the mobster and pitched him. Baring his teeth and grimacing, he agreed to meet her for lunch the following Tuesday at the Black Angus. Holy canoli, the deal was coming alive.

"Too-ra-loo-ra-loo-ra, that's an Irish lullaby." The prelates' strains, the cardinal's tenor predominating, reached a crescendo and died out, as Vic returned to her table, a triumphant smile covering her face.

Skillfully made up, dressed to kill, Victoria twisted her hair back and gazed at her image with approval. Viewing herself looking magnificent in a black matte dress encrusted with brilliants was an antidote to any frustrations she might have recently been feeling. Just give her this crack at Zino — she'd knock his socks off; the guy would be putty in her hands. She'd build an ongoing relationship that would benefit her in a host of areas — she'd sew up the airports, get herself positioned in the supermarkets, work it so she'd replace Jasmine and become Zino's primary side action.

The St. Patrick's Day corned beef caper she had in mind was the perfect entree to Zino's balls, small but stylish, and it made a point. It was an important piece of work. After she'd executed this one to satisfaction, he'd be sure to swing other deals her way. She was due for an upward shift, and this luncheon was the beginning. Donning a short square shouldered capelet with baroque beading, she fastened on a delicate, black veiled, doll-sized dinner hat -- just the right conversation piece — and she was off.

The Angus was jumping at noon, populated today by a disproportionate number of private carters, including the renowned Rocco Portone, garbage king of Staten Island, who was one of Anthony Zino's golfing partners.

Victoria sat waiting for the celebrated mobster to appear. Outside the Angus was one long line of impressive limos, inside, the euphoria of blue sharksin suits, monogrammed shirts and pinky diamonds. Vic was in her element. This was the place where bigwigs in the meat business and supermarket trade, garbage execs and mafiosi met to make payoffs and to scheme, plot and conspire to defraud, rob, murder, and otherwise conceive ill gotten gains. Lunching and enjoying drinks today were controlling factors of the ash can handlers, distillery workers and butchers' unions.

At the table across the way sat bullnecked, bull voiced Morrie Kahn, he of thick hands the size of snow shovels and one glass eye. Kahn sported huge sweat marks under the arms of his shiny silk shantung suit. His specialty was taking contaminated seafood from overseas that had been rejected for American import, cleaning it out in formaldehyde to get rid of the stench, then bribing US food inspectors to give it a stamp.

Even from a distance of 20 feet, you could almost smell bird crap on the hands of Phil Golden, who ran the leading chicken brokerage firm in the city down on lower Fifth Avenue at 14th St. His ravaged face looked like it was made of melted wax, his right earlobe was missing, he had a third grade education and wore a dangling black pearl ornament attached to the protruding zipper of his high-waisted trousers. Golden was immaculate but for the stench of poultry exuding from his pores. It was enough to make a person become a goddamn vegetarian.

She carried a rap sheet in her head on these guys, knew their act, and anyway, she had a photographic memory when it came to essentials.

Present also was the muscle man for the embalmer's union, Frankie Bruno, whose troops were all bums and strongarms helping him operate at the polls. And there was Willie Wolters, the horse meat king, charged with conspiracy to pass seventy-five grand in counterfeit bills, whose conviction was reversed on a technicality by a crooked appeals judge.

Another distinguished guest was Mike Giordano, who ruled an International Longshoreman command post at the Jersey docks, where he was head honcho of Local 564. In addition to being her soldier Georgia Jensen's significant other, Giordano was also a close crony of Anthony Zino's. Giordano wore a huge white star sapphire ring covering half of one finger, and his left thumb was lopped off at the bottom joint. Vic wondered what particular project had brought Mike here today.

Waiting for Zino to arrive, she picked up on the deals going down, bribes being passed under the table, rub-outs being hatched. She watched Bernie Komack, crown prince of Jersey carting -- nothing went on in the state garbage business without Bernie's blessing — she heard him bark to his luncheon companion, "Not to worry, Sy — Abe can always collect, even if he's gotta break the guy's skull open with a pipe."

All this was heady stuff. Victoria felt like the right girl in the right place at the right time. Everyone was staring at her, and why not? She was one helluva great looking woman.

Zino should be here any moment. He didn't have far to go. This was his neighborhood. Opposite the Angus was the Round Table, a few doors down from which, at the San Carlos Hotel, Zino kept an apartment, his home away from his wife and five kids in Bayside, Queens. Every day he maintained his ritual of steam, massage and nap at the Luxor Baths, also in the vicinity.

She belonged in a higher class setting than this, but the Angus was a good base to start from, it was power on a certain level, and it could decidedly be a springboard to better things.

The feather in her cap she sought was Zino's blessing on using the airports to bring in the drugs; but she'd work up to that gradually. The important thing was to establish a relationship, get the bonding process rolling right away. To that end she wanted to hook him into something simple but compelling that would command his immediate respect. Her scheme would involve double crossing Al Steinbrenner, meat business potentate, and she wanted to flatter Zino by asking his approval. Because of his position of elder statesman, she'd ask permission to go for the jugular. Then with what she had in mind for after lunch, better believe it would guarantee her having this guy by the balls.

Zino was winding his way through the tables, saying hello to the contingent of private carters and other nefarious luncheon guests. His lip curled when he greeted her with a firm handshake. He was dressed in an expensive Hickey Freeman suit and looked like he'd just come from the barber --- freshly shaven, trimmed and smelling of spicy aftershave. Good sign; he cared enough to show her that kind of respect. After he was seated and the waiter had taken their order, Zino said, "That's some hat you got on. Can you eat with that thing in your face?"

Vic removed the veil and gazed at him with rapt attention.

"That's better, doll. Now I can see your beautiful kisser."

Progress. Encouraged, Vic launched into a well-rehearsed speech. The real profit in the meat trade, she knew, was in specialty cuts — briskets, corned beef, hamburger and sausage. To have the shops take your product entailed payment of "gratuities," and it was Anthony Zino who arranged all manner of behind-the-scenes payoffs to Local 174 of the butchers' union, among others. From a short-lived affair with Al Steinbrenner, Vic knew the latter had been pumping an extra 8 to 10 cents per pound into all the corned beef he sold the supermarkets in the tri-state area. Steinbrenner had the market cornered. Zino got his cut for arranging things with the mob and for keeping peace in the unions.

But Vic saw a way of fucking Steinbrenner, thus repaying him for his having both dumped her and cheated her on a business deal. At the same time this would enhance Tony Zino's take and upgrade her stock with him.

She said, "Look, Tony, both you and I know that the real profit in the meat trade is in specialty cuts like briskets, corned beef, the stuff ground into hamburger and sausage, et cetera. You know as I do that Al Steinbrenner, the man who has the corned beef and brisket market on the eastern seaboard cornered, has been pumping an extra few pennies per pound into all junk he sells in this area. Now you get your cut from Al for arranging things with the mob and for keeping the unions happy."

Zino stabbed his caesar salad, cut open his sour cream and chives baked potato, mashed it down with a fork, and then, executing a boarding house reach across the table, helped himself to four mounds of butter.

"I see you're a man who's unconcerned with his cholesterol count," Victoria observed, and continued talking shop. "I happen to hate that son of a bitch Steinbrenner and I don't think I'm the only person who voices that sentiment."

She watched Zino's reaction but he betrayed little. "I have a way of screwing Steinbrenner that I know will appeal to you, Tony, at the same time allowing you to increase your take substantially."

Each year Steinbrenner held back from the market all the corned beef he had stored in his coolers down on 14th Street in anticipation of St. Patrick's Day. Then the second week in March, he deliberately jacked up his prices. Since he had a monopoly, that meant carte blanche; everyone was obliged to meet his scalper's prices.

"Just suppose Steinbrenner couldn't deliver for St. Patty's?" Vic said. "Suppose his supply was cut off? Every Irish pub in town, every hotel and restaurant would be willing to pay an extra few cents per pound for the stuff, to say nothing of the supermarkets."

When Vic outlined her plan to Zino, his first reaction was, "You wanna end up in the morgue with a tag on your toe?" But as she explained more fully, seeing dollar signs and feeling no great loyalty to Steinbrenner, he appeared more interested.

"I don't mean to be nosy, but what's Steinbrenner paying you?" she asked.

"That's for me to know and you to find out."

"Look, you owe Steinbrenner nothing. So why be loyal to this fink?"

"Why've you got in for him?"

"That's my business. Just tell me, are you interested in making a buck? Because if I have your backing and blessing, I can move forward. You have nothing to lose and everything to gain."

She could tell he was considering it. Of course he'd go for it. It was money under the table, wasn't it? She'd give him a while to think about it because she had a couple of more ideas worth bouncing off him, including getting another loan shark concession going.

Lowering her voice to a confidential tone, she said, "I need your advice, Tony. Aside from my personal attraction for you and my desire to know you better, I want your help." She leaned closer, aware her tits were practically popping out of her neckline. "Let me be blunt. We both know you're the man to see when you want to give a kickback to the butchers' union."

"They don't call it a kickback, sweetheart. They call it a gratuity," he corrected, carving an obscenely thick steak that was oozing with blood and fatty juice.

"Ok, what I want to determine is how much do we have to offer these supermarket dudes to take our stuff?" Vic said, playing thoughtfully with her watercress.

"At least six, seven hundred a month."

"What about the middlemen?"

"That's included."

"We want to get our goods prominently displayed — private label aspirin, matches, designer meats — "

"Not to worry. They'll do as I say. If I say. What'da ya got to offer them?"

In addition to the aforementioned, Vic had a new product lined up. She began telling him about a fabulous, as yet unknown in the United States, exclusive designer meat from Europe known as Leberkäs, a member of the sausage family. It so happened she had a mouthwatering recipe for Leberkäs, stolen during a one night stand with an Austrian butcher on a trip to Vienna. Butchers were the only people in Austria who knew the secret of how to make Leberkäs. Ingredients were closely guarded, handed down in families for generations. The item was bound to go over big in the American market. Al Steinbrenner had promised to take her Leberkäs and reneged. Worse, he had duplicated her stuff, stolen it out from under her and was planning to launch it under another name. The guy was a schmuck and a crook. And a lousy lay besides.

Vic said, "I have a provisioner out in Neptune, New Jersey, a German guy who made me up some samples. His initial price on the Leberkäs was a bit out of line, but we can alter the recipe, use more fillers — you know, a touch of sawdust and some mouse droppings — "

When Zino made a face, Vic said, "Come on, Tony, why're you turning green? Mouse crap's pure protein, for God's sake. You don't have to eat this shit. The Leberkäs retains its taste, rodent fecal matter notwithstanding — we just bring the cost down. In fact, I have a sample without the mouse droppings in my refrigerator at my home, and I would be delighted to give you a taste, if you care to come up for a drink ..."

"Think maybe I'll pass on that one, sweetheart. I'm a steak and roast beef man myself."

She'd come up with a more provocative invitation before lunch ended. Undaunted, Vic continued. "My kraut guy in Neptune will make the Leberkäs, label and all. He'll also be my provisioner on the corned beef."

"Corned beef? They'd know where it comes from, then."

"No, because this is private label, so to speak generic stuff sold by the guy in Neptune to our shell corporation in the Bahamas, and therefore totally untraceable... the Neptune dude's not on the line, nor are the supermarkets — nobody knows anything — they need product quick, they buy the only game in town."

"Can you rely on this guy to produce quality stuff?"

"Definitely. I've dealt with him in the past."

"So Steinbrenner checks who's the guy, and this dude out in Neptune gets leaned on."

"Why? He's only the provisioner. He's in the clear."

"So they trace the provisioner to you, and you get clipped."

"No way. Like I said, we use a shell corporation, offshore, untraceable."

"What happens to Steinbrenner's corned beef? You just dump it by the wayside?"

"Hell, no, we sell it abroad. I have buyers lined up in South America, Asia and Africa who'll pay a premium — they go ape shit over corned beef in those third world countries — and we don't have to pass inspection. So we make it on both ends."

"This corned beef sounds like a one-shot deal only."

"Right. After this we go onto the next gig. This first one's just to show you who I am and what I'm capable of."

"Why is that important to you?"

"Because I want your respect. I have ulterior motives, and I think this might make a difference in your level of excitement."

He perked up on that one. Gradually, he was getting more interested. He said, "You said something about loansharking?"

"Yeah, concessions in Hudson County."

"From what I hear, you got a woman on your team who's close to Mike Giordano. What'da ya need me for?"

"Coming through your auspices gives me added clout."

He said he'd look into it. And then, just as she knew he would, seeing dollar signs and feeling no great loyalty to Steinbrenner, Zino gave her the nod on the corned beef caper. "But remember," he said, "I keep outta this. If my name ever comes up, I don't know nothing."

"Not a problem," Vic said.

"Because if anything ever comes out, I'm the guy who's gotta deal with the responsible parties in an appropriate manner."

"I'll take that risk. You see, Tony, I want to do this one to prove something... that I can hatch a plot, strategize and execute. Ok, so it's not a zillion dollar deal but it will provide me with satisfaction and increase my standing with you. It makes a statement."

Victoria consulted the diamond studded black onyx dial of the Bucherer Vacheron Constantin yellow gold bracelet watch that Harry, using counterfeit currency, had purchased from a fence, his birthday present to her. They had finished lunch and were lingering over coffee. Everything had gone perfectly. It wouldn't be long before her plans would be reality. Now was the time to lure him back to the Woodward. She'd arranged with Harry to be out for the next several hours. Or if Zino preferred, she'd accompany him to the San Carlos. The plan: they'd shake on it, then fuck on it; the physical act would constitute sign, seal and delivery. He'd switch primary allegiance from Jasmine to her, and all sorts of deals would start opening up.

But something went drastically wrong. Out of the blue, it came upon her, unexpectedly and without warning, something that could only happen to a member of the female mafia — to a male mobster like on the 12th of never. It was her menstrual period — one whole fucking week early.

"Can you believe it?" Vic told Harry in disgust. "No wonder it's called the curse."

"You should've gone for it anyway. You do with me — "

"I keep telling you, Harry, about the difference between a guy you can fart with and one you can't."

"Well," Harry said, "if at first you don't succeed — "

In the annals of organized crime history, it has been noted the famous Sicilian Vespers was a grossly exaggerated event that possibly never even happened, and that the same might also be said of the celebrated St. Valentine's Day Massacre. In that case, possibly the St. Patrick's Day Massacre as staged by Victoria Winters and her La Femmina female mafia crew never happened, either. However, there are those who will swear it did, and all things being equal, the St. Patrick's Day Massacre, like Sicilian Vespers and the Valentine's Day Massacre, is one of those larger than life mythical tales that will be handed down by law enforcement and the media for generations to come. True or not, such events take on a life of their own.

They got right on the corned beef situation. Harry had located a closeout deal, dummies that were ringers for twenty pound packages of corned beef. The discount store owner was happy to unload the lot for peanuts. It was practically free.

Victoria put together a crackerjack team of her best women. Her sexy roadstop decoys distracted Steinbrenner's Teamsters who were hauling the real corned beef, engaging the drivers in erotic motel dalliances, while a half a dozen other La Femminas per truckload set to work hijacking the meat products, replacing them with the dummies. While Sally, Norma, Jessica and Molly were disrobing, unzipping flies and going down on truckers, Vic's four strongarms, Mildred, Ethel, Elaine and Carmen, were unloading the trucks, replacing the real items with the bogus product.

The real corned beef was reloaded into Vic's fleet, driven by her girls — who included a former lady wrestler and a Roller Derby veteran — then driven to Vic's meat lockers in Jamaica, Queens. The theft preliminarily went undetected, since the dummy corned beef was wrapped and resembled the real thing.

Immediately prior to St. Patrick's Day, when tavern-keepers all over town were desperate because Steinbrenner couldn't deliver, Vic's troops manned the phones. Using an offshore Panamanian company as an address, they sold the only game in town. Due to the careful layering of intermediaries, Steinbrenner was unable to discover who was behind the job, but angrily charged his footsoldiers if they valued their lives they sure as hell better find out.

CHAPTER 8 - DONGS, WONGS, AND BALLS

A basket of fruit and a huge vase of flowers from Fiona Stonemartin-Cartwright awaited Tania's arrival at the Dorchester in London. Apologizing for having been unexpectedly called out of town on a family emergency, Fiona planned to return within a few days. Tania, tired from the trip, thought back on the past few days in New York.

Her schedule had been crowded with meetings with her lieutenants concerning massage parlors and escort services; talks with the realtor regarding space for Balls; interviewing decorators with an eye to developing a concept for Balls' interior; sessions at the library doing research on periods, again for Balls' décor; an art auction at Sotheby Parke-Bernet; plus supervising the editing of two pornographic videos she had scripted and produced, one set in the Monet Gardens at Giverny, the other a very tasteful "Beyond the Kama Sutra."

Laura's underboss Deborah Cook had explained to the four families details concerning a new issue the organization's Wall Street arm was pushing. "We tout this as a company with super potential," Deborah explained. "We move blocks of stock through Houston and Toronto. Keep the stock overnight and you can automatically jack up the price.

"A team of young clerks from the big board houses has been romanced and promised a small piece of the action. So we're controlling the box with no problems. We keep the market active through paper transactions in nominee names. The stock moves up to fifty bucks a share, and on every two thousand shares, we clear ninety grand.

"Once you have a stock in position you literally make the price. Some people end up losing their shirts, but the pros know the rules. They can go to Vegas and shoot craps if they want. Instead they're here on the street."

That brought Jack to mind. No, he hadn't repaid the loan yet. Tania twisted her Phi Beta Kappa key nervously. She would have to have a serious talk with Jack. It wasn't only the money; there were other difficulties as well.

Their Central Park West apartment building reeked of past glory and romance. Its Italianate entryway was marked by an extending Beaux-Arts marquee and Della Robbia Revival arch. Jutting out from the grilled door was a carved salamander, a symbol of François Premier, King of France. Jack didn't know it was a salamander or what the salamander stood for, let alone who François Premier was, he was totally oblivious to their building's history or architectural importance; he merely lived there because some gambling crony was moving out and offered the place to them.

That was one of the problems, his not appreciating beauty and culture, not even noticing his surroundings. For instance, when the gambling revenues began pouring in, Tania decided to redecorate. Now an expensive crystal chandelier suspended from the living room ceiling shed warm light on plum seating groups and on new mauve wall coverings. Jack was oblivious to the profusion of plants — cyclamen, yellow calla lilies, begonias, ferns — that graced the rooms in corners and hanging in Mexican terra cotta pots. She had chosen the hanging baskets of broad-leafed calanthea one by one. The furniture, the works of art gracing the walls, the thick expensive carpeting and rich drapes were all lost on Jack. His reaction to her efforts was to shrug his shoulders and say it didn't look much different from before, as he bent over his scorecard and muttered, "Let's see, Miami and Pittsburgh? It's gotta be Miami, and they gotta win by four — "

She'd been fence-sitting, pondering a separation of sorts, not yet ready, still hoping for an outside force to intervene, for something to happen, a miracle.

In the beginning it had seemed close to idyllic, but now she just felt trapped. Their incompatibility had become more glaring. She was a gourmet while Jack eschewed her favorite dishes, saying he was strictly a meat and potatoes man. "Just give me a good hunk of steak, turn it over on the grill and serve it — crawling," he said. He was critical of her cultural interests, blamed her for being a snob and a "professional Texan." He had no interest in museums, fashion, theatre, music, film, books, plays, history or current events. His idea of a birthday present was a denim shirt from Macy's.

Lately, gambling had been absorbing Jack to an even more alarmingly neurotic degree. He would often have two and three games going on televisions and radios at once, all the while manning phones and taking bets. Sometimes he'd stay up an entire night, "studying", analyzing. More and more, his characteristic position was crouched over a pile of tout sheets.

A pattern set in. She went out of town on a deal, resolving upon return to work out a compromise; a romantic reunion held promise of improvement, things worsened again, she went away again, and the cycle repeated again. Something had to change.

The gambling was really getting to her. Like when she asked, "How are you?" his reply was, "The game fell right on the point spread. I broke even, so it was essentially a wasted day. But the thing I'm counting on is a big double. It's gotta happen soon."

"Jack. We have to talk."

"Good idea, honey. Why don't we grab dinner and do just that? I have something important to bring up."

You too? Tania thought.

As they walked over to the restaurant, Jack was scratching his head and muttering in bewilderment, "I can't figure it out, because I'm a very good handicapper, far better than anybody I know. I just can't fathom it."

"Where's my money?" Tania demanded. "You said you were going to pay me back by now."

"You'll get it, it's coming."

"I should've known. I guess I can kiss it goodbye. That's not fair."

"You'll get it already. Listen, my luck's bound to change, it's the law of averages. Gambling's something you gotta keep at. How else are you gonna recoup?"

"By quitting."

Jack shook his head. "It all comes in cycles," he explained. "Everything evens, and then you're hot again! Besides, you can't get bailed being a nickel and dimes bettor."

He had an excuse for everything. It was always somebody else's fault — the coach, the player, it was because of bagging or payola or point shaving, the spread, fixed races, or the jockey dropped the whip or whatever — anything but the truth. "The layoff man in K.C. screwed me, and that's where the whole trouble started," he complained again. Always somebody else, never him.

But hope was always just around the corner. "See, in a bird cage, any two out of three wins, you collect. The odds are good!" His dreams centered on making it with quinellas, perfectas, parlays, exactas, doubles and twin doubles; his life was all finagling, one long round robin.

Jack laid aside his Morning Telegraph to carve a two-pound slab of New York stripper at the neighborhood steakhouse. He said, "Honey, I've been thinking about something important that impacts both our lives. I've been thinking isn't it about time we thought seriously about a making a real commitment?"

"What sort of a commitment?" Tania asked warily, reluctant about the direction she had the feeling Jack was moving things.

Between bites of food, Jack said, "We're in love with each other, we share one another's business interests and we have a lot in common. So how would you feel about marrying me?"

Tania nearly choked on her swordfish. Was he trying to manipulate her? She put down her fork and said, "Jack, not now — with all the problems —"

"That's just it," he said. "There's a sense of commitment lacking with us. If we had a marital commitment, it could do wonders for our relationship."

"What do we have in common, Jack, other than sex, which by the way we haven't had in a dog's age? I mean, look at our tastes in food —"

He waved that objection aside. "Menus offer a wide variety. That's no problem."

"There are other considerations, too. You're always putting me down for my intellectual and cultural interests."

"Honey, I'm just teasing you."

Tania twirled her Phi Beta Kappa key. He said he loved her. Did she love him? In some ways, yes, though not like in the beginning — it was different now, there was more attachment and less illusion, and still this nagging problem that she continued to dream of a person Jack wasn't, a renaissance man, her perfect male counterpart, her all-in-all. Did he exist?

"Aside from everything else," Tania said, "need I remind you again how long it's been since we've had sex?"

"Must be a sure sign we're really in love," Jack grinned.

"It wasn't like that in the beginning."

"Sweetheart," he sighed, "it's just my money problems have put a damper on that department."

"Quit gambling, Jack. It would change everything."

"I did quit. I didn't place a bet in two days, then all I did was make a token wager on a sure thing. The problem right now is interest on debts is eating me alive. That's why I haven't felt in the mood for sex."

"It's been three weeks."

"Yeah, that was just about the time that bookie in Kansas City screwed me. Green Bay vs. the Rams. What a heartbreaker."

"How long can this continue?"

"Honey, everything's been going haywire — eventually it will resolve, only right now if you'd lend me a small amount, I could satisfy this shark in the Bronx who's been hassling me and that would be a load off my mind."

"I already lent you fifty thousand dollars and haven't got that back yet."

"You can afford it. You're making a fortune on the gambling concessions and all the other deals you and your wise gal pals have going."

"You own 50% of our joint concessions, whereas I split the other 50% with three other people. It just doesn't make sense that you need me to bail you."

"I told you — my profits have all been going to the boys uptown and the vig's so high nothing's left over. Owing shylocks and layoff guys is draining, it takes a lot out of a person. If I could just get these guys off my back, I could pay the rest in installments myself. What your loan of even a measly ten or twenty would do now is change the whole picture."

Yes, she could afford it. She'd just made a killing in one of Deborah's stock deals and the numbers franchise was paying a handsome royalty, to say nothing of her take from the gambling and other ventures. It just seemed like throwing good money after bad, but Jack had tears in his eyes and she did feel guilty for not wanting to marry him. He was so pitiful right now, besides which, he'd been kind to her in the beginning when she needed it. Well, maybe just one more infusion of cash would do the trick

Tania hesitated, because she really didn't want to lend the money. She said, "If I knew this would get you out of the woods and you really would turn over a new leaf, Jack, that you'd stay away from the track, avoid poker, gin and football pools — "

"Honey, you have my word!"

"All right," Tania capitulated, "I'll lend you the money. But this is absolutely the last time. As far as marriage goes, it's not what I want at this point in time. I'm sorry, Jack."

The next day when Tania waved the check in front of him, a slow, relieved smile spread across his face. "Thanks, baby," he murmured in gratitude, reaching to take her in his arms. Quickly, they undressed and went to bed. Foreplay continued for a seemingly interminable time with no penetration until Tania could stand it no longer. Nothing could arouse Jack. He was soft as jelly. No use, he couldn't get it up. Tania lay back, frustrated and disappointed.

His hand shaking, Jack lit a cigarillo. He said, "Forgive me, baby. I promise by the time you get back from London all this will be behind us and we'll start a new life together. I love you. Just bear with me."

Waiting for Fiona to return, Tania busied herself at the British Museum, the Tate, and the Ashmolean, Sotheby's and Christie's, doing more research on periods, looking for potential inspiration for Balls' decor. When she phoned London friends to say hello, she found herself invited to a number of intriguing soirées.

Enter international financier Corrado Sofino, suave, sexy, dashing, continental. She first noticed him across a crowded room at a fancy dress party at Christie's where the surroundings had been converted into a 19th century Deauville with a 2 month old tiger prowling among the guests. Corrado appeared to be with a tarty looking statuesque blond, obviously Scandanavian or German. The next time they ran into each other was at a lavish party at Claridge's. Opaline lights filtering down gave a benign cast to his face, but did not serve to make his tall blond date look any less hookerish. What did a man like this see in someone like her, Tania mused.

The following evening she went to a medieval costume party as a unicorn. He appeared once again, wearing a purple sombrero with an orchid in his buttonhole. One wondered what this had to do with the middle ages.

"Do you know Mr. Sofino?"

Ah, Italian. No, Sicilian. Tania turned to face the stranger. The distinction was especially in the eyes — you noticed them — sharp and piercingly blue, ever probing, assessing, relishing, becoming soft and clouded over, then turning slightly amoral, though no less simpatico, just hard to read, again very Sicilian.

As he took her hand, pressed it to his lips and kissed it, his gaze did not wander. Something inside her was moved, shaken up, and she had a very strong suspicion that they would fall deeply, madly in love.

When he heard she was from Texas, he said, "I know all about Texas. I can even sing Texas. I know chuck wagon stew and short ribs and pinto beans, Texas chili --"

Tania laughed, charmed. "How do you know so much, Mr. Sofino?"

"Oh, I know — Dr. Pepper's and Gilley's beer and Pearl's. I like it all. In Texas they cook with lard, and they say the west begins in Ft. Worth."

"My home town!"

"How wonderful. I have great nostalgia for the American West, I love the image of the Western desperado. It is very romantic, exactly what I should like to be were I not Sicilian."

"Well, you could come visit when I'm in Texas, and I could make you an honorary Texan."

"Ah, yes! So you don't live full time in Texas, then?"

"At the moment, no, but one of these days I may return to stay."

He smelled of pungent Italian soap, a blend of almonds and rose water. It was nothing short of a *coup de foudre* — the coiled, supple, sensual Corrado knocked her dead. It wasn't merely the excitement of his physical appearance or the glamour of the world he moved in, it was also his mind, his heart, his soul, his essence. He had dimension. He was cultured, world-traveled, sophisticated. He spoke five languages, and he had a toughness the Sicilians called *figatu*, literally meaning liver, designating a form of quiet strength.

He smoked Oxi Bithue extra suaves, Uruguayan cigarettes, very rare, difficult to obtain, smuggled through Egypt and Argentina, that exuded an irresistible aroma, the most alluring sexual fragrance that drove her wild. Tania, relishing the imaginative meeting of minds and the undeniable magnetism between them, foresaw promise of fruition. She was smitten.

She spotted him at yet another party on a revolving dance floor where peacocks strutted in gilded cages. A Palladian bridge led to a champagne and milk bar set up on the flood-lit grounds of a country home with a prize Guernsey cow tethered in front. They served turtle soup, Welch lamb and lemon soufflé. He wore a midnight blue mohair dinner suit. Although he was thin and of medium height, there was something very commanding, even imperious about him that made him seem larger. One noticed his expert tailoring, how he usually dressed in light colors, creams and greys, wonderful mellow beiges and soft browns. The sartorial signature was usually Milanese, now and then British, the total look distinctive, one of a kind. But that ever-present Nordic slut — what was he doing with her?

The instant Fiona Stonemartin-Cartwright crossed the threshold at Brown's Hotel dining room, Tania knew who she was. The lively, smart, titian-tressed former journalist had exactly the elan and esprit that Tania would have expected of someone who had tired of working with deadlines and disgruntled editors, seen a need and filled it in the form of a fabulously successful stud service for women in the heart of Mayfair.

The two chatted like old friends. It wasn't until they were midway into lunch, avocado salad for Tania, eggs florentine for Fiona, that they took up the topics of Dongs & Wongs and Balls.

"Where do you get your studs?" Tania wanted to know.

"Ducky, the men line up for blocks," Fiona confided. "It's not a problem. The unemployment situation in Britain created a natural market — we've had scores of out of work coal miners up from Newcastle, for instance, applying. Strong, well-built blokes have a natural bent. Then you have those not yet established young men who aren't ready to get involved with the kind of women who expect marriage — future physicians and barristers, for instance. But the most surprising thing was totally unforeseen — "

"What's that?" Tania asked.

Fiona leaned forward confidentially. "We've acquired a whole contingent of eager participants who are older, well-to-do established professional men from all walks of life, as well as a large body of upper crust members of the aristocracy — volunteers, almost."

"Really? How did you attract this group?" Tania asked.

"Well, ducky, you know how terribly constricting social convention can be — marriage, living together, taking a mistress, even having a girlfriend or a fling can be perilous for a man these days. Less and less can one afford risks; all relationships seem to be traps."

"I understand, Fiona," Tania said. "Most people are looking for a situation they can control, like this."

"Exactly. There's so much heavy-handedness in qualifiers to wade through, that too often a caprice that prompted desire is already killed, all the spontaneity and fun has gone out of a sensual experience before it starts. So it seems what has developed with Dongs & Wongs is that two mutually attracted people can come together without fear of consequences.

"For instance, let's say a woman wants to get it on with a particular M.P. She can request him, we'll ring him up and invite him over, he'll be paid five hundred pounds for his services, which is flattering to the man. Even in this day and age of liberated women it's still largely the man who foots the bills, so how many chaps won't jump at a chance to have their egos stroked by being paid for getting laid? A man loves the idea, brags about it to his friends, and they all want in on the action.

"Consequently, a man's participation in a Dongs & Wongs assignation has become a status symbol at all the fashionable Mayfair parties. I've had earls and lords ring me up asking to be included. And although they may not like to boast, many are even willing to offer a provocatively enticing thumbnail sketch of their assets and abilities."

After lunch, Fiona and Tania headed in a taxi over to Dongs & Wongs. The fashionable ladies' bordello was located in a six story townhouse on a quiet, sparsely-trafficked Mayfair street. Should one glance upward at its entryway, one would notice a discreet marble sculpture of two erect penises, one circumcised, the other not, small carved lettering reading "Dongs" decorating the circumcised organ, the word "Wongs" written on the uncircumcised one, with an ampersam (&) between the two. The message was subtle and tasteful.

Inside, the establishment's Victorian decor was understated. A quiet soothing atmosphere prevailed with piped in classical music (this particular moment, Ives' Symphony # 1 in D minor), the layout consisting of a series of soundproof bedrooms as well as parlors, bars, a library and billiard room, commons, and a kitchen. Furnishings included king size beds with attractive headboards of varying designs, silk and velvet-covered chairs and loveseats, grandfather clocks, and étagères. There were private elevators in addition to secret entrances and exits for trysting guests to avoid being seen. Fiona also showed Tania a connecting tunnel to the houses next door and in back.

Fiona, a distant cousin of novelist Barbara Cartwright, distant relative as well (albeit many times removed) of the royals, thus in an inside position vis à vis British society, felt it her duty to catalog information that might prove of possible interest in generations to come, regarding the physical endowments of her illustrious clientele. She showed Tania a computer program containing comments, notations and graphs on the assorted dongs and wongs of the male performers who had passed through the portals of the establishment: "Lord Pentland's dong, for instance, is rather slender and angular, whereas the Earl of Fauxhall's wong has a wart on its very tip ... and as for the Duke of Hampshire ..."

Tania was excited. She knew there was a niche market here for women who were either bored with marriage, without a steady bed partner, or merely looking for kicks, variety, and adventure. But she hadn't thought about this enterprise as also a means of screening potential liaisons, bypassing social conventions of dating, dinner and b.s.

"As I see it," she told Fiona while the two of them were sipping Harvey's Bristol Creme in one of Dongs & Wongs' parlors, an attractive room decorated in Victorian shades of puce and ashes and roses, "this can be a splendid way of circumventing social restrictions, a shortcut to avoid game playing."

"Definitely," Fiona agreed. "It's all honest and above board and nothing beyond the hour is expected. Pay the five hundred pounds and that's the entire commitment, but very often it does serve as an impetus to more, much more, that never would have happened otherwise. Most people are not interested in getting caught in a net, and the fact that they're free to indulge their fantasies without entanglement is very attractive."

"So they can get entangled in spite of themselves."

"Yes, they can."

"Hmmm — "

"I see your mind working, Tania. Let me guess. You have a man you'd like us to ring up for you?"

"How did you guess, Fiona?"

"I've been in this business long enough to spot all the signals. Who is he?"

She told Fiona about Corrado, how he had affected her in the deepest sense. "He's been seen all over London with a German or Scandanavian — shall I say dish?" she confided. "The woman looks like a hooker to me, though perhaps I'm being unfair — "

"Corrado Sofino — Italian — "

"You know him?"

"He's new on the London scene, but I know who he is. Wait a bit, luv." Fiona rang for Ali Bhutto, Dongs & Wongs' Pakistani major-domo, and sent him out to fetch "Tattler."

"I believe his picture is in this issue," Fiona explained.

"In a way you could describe this Teutonic-looking woman as drop dead gorgeous, because she's tall, striking and blond, but to me she looks cheap," Tania said.

"Those Nordic types do have that handicap sometimes," Fiona agreed, "they can look cheap. I know just what you mean."

"I wondered what an obviously cultivated man of the world, so in gamba, would want with a slutty type like that. She lacks class, but she does seem to have her hooks in him nevertheless."

"You know, now that you mention it, I believe I've seen this woman as well. She's about 30, with a big chest, and I agree, she does look like a hooker. Italian men often go for her type, but a woman like that can't fulfill a Mediterranean man's deepest needs and fantasies. This bitch shouldn't pose a problem."

"Fiona," Tania said, her insides churning with hope and anticipation, "do you think you could arrange it?"

"Why, I will personally take care of it myself, Tania," Fiona promised, "first thing tomorrow."

"So what happens? He just moseys on over, takes off his pants, then I pull out the five hundred pounds and — "

"And the rest is up to you, ducky. It's what you make of it."

Ali returned with the magazine. Sure enough, there was Corrado's picture together with a caption identifying "Mr. Corrado Sofino, noted Italian financier, taking luncheon and sherry at 41 Bishopsgate," among the ancestral paintings and Windmill & Whiteman grandfather clocks with the venerated partners of Hambros. Corrado was quoted as saying he was delighted to be continuing an old tradition, since after all, Italy's relationship with Hambros dated to Cavour and the Risorgimento. The article also noted how Corrado had been entertained recently at several staid old clubs, among them White's, Brook's and Pratt's. It left no doubt of his acceptance in the uppermost reaches of City finance.

CHAPTER 9 - CORRADO

Admittedly, this was crazy. But from the moment she laid eyes on Corrado, something just welled up inside her, this immense feeling of longing and need, so that everything else receded in importance. All that mattered was connecting. And now that Fiona had arranged it, Tania was nervous.

Fiona told her to put the other woman out of mind. "Men all have their security blankets, they all have to have a mother/maid/hearth figure at home, and if they're rich enough, an accoutrement on their arm for public appearances, but nine times out of ten neither woman is what he truly wants — men are always looking for something other than what they have. You, Tania, can be that something else to him, that point of happiness, that satisfaction of his deepest fantasies."

The accommodations were comfortable and inviting — cut velvet red flocked wall covering, four poster bed with red velvet canopy and drawable portières, huge armoire and armchair, private bath with bidet, large tub on golden legs. Prokofiev's Suite from *The Love of Three Oranges* sounded from the stereo. As Tania waited, she wondered if she'd made the right decision to wear her Victoria's Secret pushed up bra, garter belt, black hosiery, black velvet choker, high heels and satin lounging robe for the occasion.

Checking her appearance in the mirror for the dozenth time, she jumped upon hearing his knock. He stood at the door, smiling, kissed her hand and said, "Hello, my Texas rose." She admitted him and he took a seat in the armchair. Tania sat down at the edge of the bed.

If he felt this rendezvous was unusual, he gave no signs. Just what was going through his mind? Had he ever done this before? Did he really want to do it with her? Nervously, Tania tugged at her Phi Beta Kappa key.

He was wearing a tasteful mocha brown suit, purchased, he said, at Blades, a fashionable tailoring outfit at the end of Saville Row. He was sunny, playful, witty. Like so many Italians, he projected lightheartedness on the surface, with a deep tragic sense of life grounded underneath. She envisioned a whole adventurous new world opening up.

"Your suit is divine," Tania said, "so beautifully fitted. Your being a `man in the mocha brown suit' reminds me of `J. Alfred Prufrock' — you know, T.S. Eliot — "

"Yes, I know." He smiled, rose, and came to the bed. Tania quickly reached inside her push up bra and offered him five hundred pounds. He took it with a sly grin and tucked it in his shirt pocket.

He said, "I am your willing and eager stud. I will do everything you wish. I am here to gratify your every desire."

When first he took her in his arms and held her, she emitted a long, deeply felt sigh and began to tremble. It was all so reckless yet so utterly right, as if she had been waiting for him her entire life. She wanted to swiftly grasp this moment and never let go.

It was beyond anything she had ever dreamed. At first it was pure lust, but then how much more. The wildness turned to tenderness, her soft tears flowed unbidden as if from the river of life, from a source never before realized, a depth of longing, a place long hidden. It was as if having known one another in many lifetimes they were now reunited after centuries apart. What was this feeling of need and desire she had harbored forever, not knowing who could satisfy it, only faintly imagining him in the deepest recesses of her soul, almost a fleeting image, scarcely a recognition, finally connecting.

But there was sadness too, a thought that though they were destined to be together, something might prevent their realizing the ultimate destiny together. What was this force she didn't understand, the terrible longing for this man?

The sex was too amazing to describe; the release, when it came, of such an astonishing order — exalted, melted down. Afterward, he too seemed overcome by the experience.

He invited her for lunch the next day at Alvaro's Restaurant in King's Road, Chelsea, where they dined on poached salmon, potato cutlets and loganberry ice cream. She dressed for the occasion in one of her best colors, teal blue. During lunch, he daringly reached his hand down through her skirt till his finger found her vagina. She liked an adventurous man. She liked everything about him. She loved him madly.

In that first erotic luncheon together was the seedling of what he could become in her life, with the imaginative meeting of minds, the promise of full surrender to a man who would put his kingdom on display for her. She was so utterly drawn to him, touching hands, holding eyes, as he spoke about his native Sicily and the supple, angular Mediterranean face creased into a smile. "You will like Sicily, it is very beautiful," he said. "It is a land of contrasts — of orange blossoms and lava eruptions and mysterious cliffs and grottos, of elusive people. A closed society, often dangerous."

She smiled and raised her glass. They drank each others' essences. He took her hand and guided it to his crotch. How had he known she wanted it there at that very moment?

After lunch, he said, "I want you."

"I want you too. Have I spoiled you? You should have another five hundred pounds, of course. But wait — I'll double your fee, that's how wonderful I think you are!"

So it was Dongs & Wongs again, a different room, this one decorated in rococo style, with ornate gold putti swooping down from all corners. The experience of being together surpassed even the previous time in excitement and fulfillment. 900 pounds in two days and worth every last farthing. Never, never in her life had she experienced a man like this one.

They would meet again soon when he was next in New York, where he kept an apartment at the Pierre. She would be hearing from him. He would phone. Flying home, Tania settled back in her seat, feeling relaxed and content, evoking Corrado, with Jack seeming a million miles away, gone out of her life forever, almost as if he had never existed ... how could there ever have been anyone but Corrado?

She didn't expect Jack to be home at two in the afternoon, figuring he'd be out at the track. Unfortunately, she thought wrong. He waited almost as if he knew she was coming.

"Where were you?" he demanded. "I've been so worried. I phoned London, they said you'd checked out — I was frantic."

"Business took longer than planned," Tania said, annoyed at his prying. "I had to change my flight."

"Why didn't you call? You should have let me know."

"I was tied up. I couldn't."

"Doing what?" He acted like it was his right to know, like he ought to be keeping tabs on her.

"A financial deal," Tania said evenly, and went to the bedroom with her hand luggage.

Jack followed. To her surprise, of all things he was in the mood for sex — said desire had returned full force. "Let's go to bed, baby," he murmured softly, holding out his arms.

"I — not now, Jack."

"Honey, I've been going out of my fucking mind I was so horny. God, did I miss you."

"Did you win at the track?" Tania asked.

"Yeah, how'd you guess? Listen, baby, I apologize for what happened. I don't know what got into me. I'll make it up to you — what's wrong? Aren't you feeling well?"

"I'm tired. I've had a long trip." Freeing herself from his attempted advances, Tania started unpacking.

"Well, ok; we'll save it for tomorrow, then," he said, disappointed.

Sooner or later she'd have to come clean; maybe better plunge in now. Tania said, "Jack, I really think we have to re-assess our relationship. A lot's missing, I need time to myself, and —

"Listen, relationships all have their strengths and weaknesses, but you look at the bottom line."

"I've looked, and I believe I know what's the right decision." Tania paused, trying to ease the blow. "For now, I need to be on my own, and I'd like to live here in this apartment by myself."

"Of all the nerve. We're only living here because my friend gave it to me. If we break up, and I hope we don't, I stay. I want the apartment."

"What makes you think you'll be able to afford the rent? Then we'd both lose out."

"You want to leave, you leave," he said. "I'm not budging. I don't understand what's happened to you. What could've gone on in London to change you so drastically?"

The next day, Tania signed a short term lease on a two bedroom furnished apartment on Park Avenue in the 60's. It was a relief to be in control of her destiny again. Amazing how stultifying the relationship with Jack had made her feel. Just to be alone again seemed a luxury.

She was flipping through some Italian magazines when she spied, splashed across one cover in prominent red lettering, the words "Dossier: Mafia." It was a special report dealing with the Italian mafia and their American counterparts. Her eyes nearly popped out when she noticed in the centerfold layout a photo of Corrado! Mafia?!

Corrado Sofino was the most feared and powerful man in western Sicily, a member of the "high mafia," the strongest mafia force in Italy, said the article. The members of this mafia, anonymous and untouchable, were seldom identified.

When his father died two years ago, Corrado had ascended to the head of his family, assuming control of a very large chunk of the island of Sicily. All the visible old mafia bosses from the region answered to him now. Corrado was on his way toward making the cosche, or Sicilian mafia groups, a major international financial force. Branching out from his family-owned Palermo bank, having already gained a reputation for being the Sicilian gnome behind Roman and Milanese deals, he was assuming prominence on the City of London money scene, kicking up his heels in the New York markets, and had just become the official outside investments counselor to the Vatican. To make a long story short, Corrado was the secret power behind all the capos pictured on these pages, and he was out to change the honored society from a local phenomenon into a giant global empire, with himself as its leader.

The Italian magazine said that in London they were unaware of his shady Sicilian connections, that he was leading a double life. Tania put down the magazine and remembered his tenderness, the passion they had shared, and was overtaken by a strange new thrill, a complicity that she was part and parcel of an enormous clandestine force.

So they had more in common than she'd even suspected. Corrado had stirred her as no other man had. He was ever so much a part of her. Now she understood him better. It was meant to be.

CHAPTER 10

1

Laura's underboss Kami Raines' policy game was now raking in dollars hand over fist; profits were being recycled into legitimate business, and everything was shaping up fabulously well financially.

Just as Kami had said, the key to a numbers game's success was finding the right personnel. For this Kami had first turned to the reliable Harlem locals, then moved beyond. When Kami suggested using an underground communications network known as the Hustler's Grapevine to go talent hunting at the Annual Pimps' Ball in Charlotte, North Carolina, out of curiosity, Laura tagged come along.

The Pimps' Ball was a yearly must for all the big time black macs in the country who convened to compare notes, discuss business, show off their best whores and project improvements in the hooking trade. Seventy-five pimps descended from New York alone and a large number from every other corner of the US.

On the agenda was a pimps' fashion show with the latest attire for the clothes-conscious procurer, modeled by slim-hipped, jive-assed dudes in tight gold and silver lame pants and feather trimmed wide brimmed hats. "Pimp of the Year" award went to a flamboyant Texan duded up in magenta-piped eelskin boots, batwing chaps, 18 karat gold spurs, honkey-tonk shirt with rattlesnake stitching and custom-creased Stetson decorated with a cluster of marabou feathers. His gaggle of prosses, half a dozen strong, were driven by smartly attired liveried footmen-chauffeurs in shiny, rainbow-hued donut-tired Eldorados with horns blasting "Deep in the Heart of Texas."

From this environment, Kami signed on several flatbackers to groom for operations. With the Italian organization's pizzo and another hefty sum turned over to the New York City Police Department, the numbers game still came out making in the five figures a day at inception, with a take that was rising fast.

You couldn't keep all that money lying around, so they got a big portion out on the streets to keep it working. Mafiose like Barby "Paint Brush" Porter, Kim "Three Shoes" Sutherland, Babette "The Nose" Landers and Mary Ann "Knickers" Wilson were some of Laura's most capable shylocks.

Laura's branch of The La Femmina syndicate looked in all directions for venture capital, and several interesting avenues materialized: Chinatown underboss Eleanor Lee Wong nailed down her neighborhood fong (cooperative banking organization for Chinatown residents). No means was overlooked. Even the US government unknowingly sponsored some La Femmina expansions, through MESBIC (Minority Small Business Investment Company) loans, and also through the Bureau of Indian Affairs, a part of the Department of the Interior, which guaranteed funding to Native Americans. Through this channel, Laura's captain, authentic Cherokee Indian Roseanne Silver Cloud, opened an import-export company which was in reality a narcotics cover.

Laura's lieutenant Deborah Cook masterminded a public underwriting for loansharking -- all strictly legal. Gaining control of a shell, the LFM partners restructured it, then from a public offering raised $2,000,000. From this they spun off a number of lending corporations which in turn borrowed from the original restructured shell at the highest legal rate.

These funds were then lent out to loan sharks at a point a week wholesale, 52 percent a year. The La Femmina group took 27 percent profit, and pumped back 25 percent into the shell to pay off the loans. The shell was projected to grow at the rate of 25% a year compounded, causing the stock to be worth ten million dollars in five years' time.

"There's no way this can backfire," Deborah assured, "because it's done through a public company. The only thing we have to worry about is that nobody backdoors us. We have to have the box, that's the whole secret, that and controlling the buyers." Furthermore, this vehicle was enabling them to control any number of shylocks around town, increasing their clout in the underworld.

Through Deborah, Laura had a lot of other action going on Wall Street. Stocks didn't just go up, they were pushed up, and Deb knew how to move the pieces of the game. It was all in the marketing. Working insider and unregistered stocks, parking shares, utilizing the obligatory grace period to maximum advantage, selling the same certificates several times over to different parties, Deborah and her financially savvy team were using every gambit. They'd acquire stock in floundering companies for small amounts of money, report fictitious sales, then sell shares to other broker/co-conspirators at inflated figures. The whole secret, Deborah knew, was controlling the box and buyers. Through Deborah's maneuvering, Laura and her LFM group made big profits for themselves and selected relatives and friends. The only losers in the game were other greedy Wall Street brokerage firms left holding the bag — but they'd pulled the same stunts themselves, in spades.

As you became more aware, you realized that the mafia, since its inception, had been doing very little that the Fortune 500 didn't think of first; the real marketplace for O.C. was big business. So if this was the ethics of our society and you couldn't lick 'em, you joined 'em, right? You had to, out of self-preservation.

Thanks to Deborah and others like her, letters of credit on behalf of Laura's LFM interests were being juggled, pyramided and parlayed left and right, and her financial advisors were kept busy channeling racket cash into smart legitimate investments. Deals proliferated. Laura had a hidden ownership in a City Island marina with her lawyer, a former assistant D.A. There were construction projects on the drawing boards, businesses were being bought and sold and fronts tied up, as their sheet grew in size by leaps and bounds. Laura's schedule was crowded with meetings with legal counsel, accountants and partners. In addition to her numbers operation that was making a fortune, the prostitution, handled by her underboss Nancy Jo Corcoran, was also booming.

Everything was coming her way now, Laura thought. That is, everything but her personal life. What had gone wrong with Frank? Why did she have the feeling something about herself had spooked him, turned him away? Maybe it was the past they shared; she might be his bad conscience, in a position to betray his sleazy origins. She represented a background he wanted to forget. The world he had attached himself to was the antithesis of the one they'd both come from, and she was one of the few people who knew that.

Then came the shock to end all shocks. Frank Gantry got married. His new bride was five months into a pregnancy when they tied the knot.

"I don't understand what he could possibly see in this woman," Laura insisted to Kami, tossing a copy of the New York Post with photos of the newlyweds on the table for Kami to look at.

"Hmm - Wendy Wagstaff, former debutante of the year --"

"Spoiled, arrogant Park Avenue socialite, heiress to a vast fortune -- does he really think she can make him happy? Kami, my dream is dead. Why? I so wanted to belong to this man, you can't imagine."

"Laura, let's put this in perspective. It's painful, but you'll handle it; you'll move on."

"Sure, eventually I will. But I've lost out on a whole wonderful life I might have had. The man I fantasized marrying all these years - how could I have misinterpreted the signals?"

"It happens, hon."

"You worship someone your entire life, love him with your entire heart, soul, mind, body and being -- then this. What do you do? Order yourself to stop loving him? Or tell yourself that some day he'll see the light?"

"Why not? Give him enough rope, let him find out the ugly truth for himself," Kami advised. "Look, 35% of all marriages end in divorce, and of the remaining 65%, more than 75% of that group of husbands are unfaithful to their wives, vulnerable to the right woman. So as I see it, eventually, if you really want this guy, it could definitely work."

The wife Frank had chosen was all wrong for him, Laura knew. Obviously this was an expedient union that made sense only in the light of ambition, money and image. And the woman in question had gotten pregnant besides, probably to force the issue. Kami had the right take on it. Just give it time. Laura was hurt, she was outraged, but she wasn't going to let it destroy her life; she would channel her anger in a positive direction.

Initially financial problems had propelled her to hustle, but now that she was entrenched and doing so well, her motivations went well beyond that. She really wanted this life of crime; crime was her choice. It gave her something to fight for, and maybe even something to make Frank think twice, one of these days.

His ill-conceived marriage couldn't possibly last. She was nothing if not patient. He'd end up sorry. Then her turn would come.

CHAPTER 11

"Rose: I love the idea of buying into that cute professional boxer. Let's discuss."

Victoria was dictating memos to her lieutenants and captains Legs, the Pelvis, the Cow and others into a microcassette recorder. Her secretary would type them up; later, the documents would be put through a paper shredder after they'd served their purpose.

"By the way," Vic continued, "next trip, please grab as many crates of Marlboros as possible. Have new outlet, can lay off in Europe all the filter-tips we can get. Arrangements being made for shipping to Naples. Hurry — this one's hot.

"Cow — what's doing on the precious gems? Have a new way to go with rubies, sapphires, emeralds, opals — to be used as collateral through a savings and loan in Arizona. These people are well-connected politically, wired into the US Senate.

"Georgia: follow up, please. I have buyers waiting. A hotel chain is interested in purchasing large quantity of our cut rate made in Malta scotch whiskey. Can you provide immediately? Also need inflated balance sheet you promised on the coffee deal. "Shelley: Is the prospectus ready on the Panamanian shell? And please get me info on your new source for renting certificates of deposit pronto. I can place these immediately either as collateral to establish a trust account or to create letters of credit and loans, or we can always go abroad for resale. Shelley, this is a great gimmick. Practically the entire Costa del Sol was financed via this means. We should get more active in this outlet.

"Deborah, Laura's lieutenant, advises we can set up shop as a brokerage firm at a cost of only 5 grand or with an investment of 50 thou, make it into a deluxe operation, then we open a boiler room. We're also negotiating for a transfer company to facilitate transactions. Girls, let's be ready to discuss all this and more at our weekly gathering."

She had a million deals cooking. If you entered her phone room, you'd hear dialog like: "I've got some great South African wines. A Fortune 500 company in Jersey City has it in their inventory and they want to unload it. To the connoisseur it tastes like vinegar, or like shit. But the uninitiated will never know the difference. Especially if they get drunk first. Think you might be able to lay this crap off for me?" Or: "I'm looking for a guarantor on a 50 million dollar loan, the collateral for which is 180 million tons of coal I'm taking an option on." Or: "I've picked up a couple of central bank guarantees on some construction loans and equipment leasebacks, I've just taken over a nursing home and backed a pirated bestsellers on cassettes situation. I'm also negotiating to take over a brewery and bust it wide open."

On some of her commodity deals you used "funny banks" for swing money. You bribed the officers to swing short term interim financing, sometimes merely overnight, till you could kite things in another direction and get the deal to consummate elsewhere along the line. Often these situations were held together by a hairbreadth. Sometimes you might use counterfeit securities to obtain loans, which was no different from the way big business operated, or you secured semi-bullshit Cayman Island letters of credit for up front fees. There were at least a half a dozen ways to skin a cat.

Another live deal Vic had going now was a Medicaid factoring gimmick she was milking to beat the band. You paid doctors at a discount of their claims, then collected the full amount from Medicaid. The belt was your profit, the doctor got his bucks right away, that was the edge for him. There were a bunch of doctors running Medicaid mills, particularly in the Bronx and also a group in Massachusetts. She was joint venturing this deal with Ayla Kalkavan, leader of the New England LFM family. Ayla liked it so much she was talking about doing an IPO and making it a turnkey operation. It was sort of a variation on the old loan sharking theme.

After getting her period at the Anthony Zino Angus lunch, then executing the stunning St. Patrick's Day caper, Vic had waited a few days, then tried phoning Zino but had trouble getting through. Her messages went unanswered. She looked for him all over town at his usual haunts — the Little Italy and Queens social clubs, the San Carlos Hotel, the Luxor Baths, the Mannequin, the Bull & Bear, the Black Angus, the Round Table — but he was nowhere to be found. Must have been keeping a low profile because the LEOs were on his tail. Then Jasmine returned from South America and the two were seen together again.

How to get this guy back to the point he was at that luncheon at the Angus? She'd been waiting for a pat on the back or the toosh, or better yet a hot session under the sheets, but temporarily, at least, her plans seemed checkmated. She would have to concentrate on other horizons for the time being. Who else could she corner, get in thick with?

It was late in the day. Vic and Harry were noshing on ham sandwiches at the Carnegie Deli. "I need a mentor, Harry," Vic lamented. "Now that you turned my thinking around, I'm wondering — how and with whom? I counted on Zino."

That was when the idea of Judge Casey first hit. Harry took a swill of Bud, wiped the foam off his mouth, then raised the ham sandwich to his mouth and said, "Ham sandwich! That's it!"

"Huh?"

"The government can indict a ham sandwich!"

"What on earth are you talking about, Harry?"

"An old saying around federal courtrooms, honey. It made me think — there's that judge — Robert Francis Casey — he could be useful — hell, he's the top judge in New York State — and you told me he came on."

The Honorable Robert Frances Casey, Chief Judge, New York State Court of Appeals, was rumored to be a leading contender for governor. They'd met recently at a drop-in breakfast sponsored by the Academy of Motion Picture/Television Arts and Sciences at the Marriott Hotel, where Casey was lecturing on the topic "How to Assert Your Opinions and Avoid Libel."

His Honor was chomping at the bit. She could see he was taken with her, and this was 8 o'clock in the morning. Now if a man made a play at that hour, you knew he was serious, and Casey was definitely frothing at the mouth, while casting furtive side glances at his frigid-looking wife. She understood how like so many members of his profession, the guy loved to take chances. Amazing, wasn't it, how many political and judicial types were sexual deviants and sociopaths. The problem was creating the circumstances so Casey would put his money where his mouth was.

"Judge Casey definitely wanted to get it on with me, I could tell," Vic said. "Making that initial follow through, though, is the problem. I need a hook."

"I'll look into the matter and see what I can accomplish," Harry said.

"What could you do?"

"I have a connection. Let me work on it for you."

"Be my guest."

"We'll try the Casey angle, but let's not give up on Zino. Jasmine doesn't have exclusive rights, we know this from the surveillance and wiretaps. We know both of them are getting action from other directions. So that should leave a slot open for you. No reason on earth the two of you couldn't become fuck buddies. Hell, what's Jasmine got, for Christ's sake, a pair of tits and a cunt? You're not only fine in the tits and ass department yourself, you've got it all over her in every other area as well."

"You think?"

"Damned tootin'. Unlike Jasmine, your brain doesn't happen to be between your cleavage, or your legs."

"The problem, as we've noted, is guys like this don't appreciate a good piece of ass when it comes their way, they've got so much pussy thrown at them they lose all sense of proportion. Well, everything will have to wait till after Lebanon. Let's hope I can move the drugs forward on another front from there."

Vic was counting heavily on this Beirut trip to change the course of her life.

CHAPTER 12

Nine La Femmina capos, Victoria, Tania, Laura, Jasmine, Carole Curtis, Deborah Cook, Lily Wyszowsky, Ayla Kalkavan, and Dove Cameron shared a table under a shaded trellis at a secluded outdoor cafe fifteen kilometers outside Beirut. Their faces, dappled from the sunlight that shone through trees and vines, were intent on conversation. A soft sea breeze and the odor of bay leaves wafted up from the Mediterranean, and a Nana Mousskouri song sounded from below.

The socko impact of Dove Cameron's fabulous looks struck like lightning from across a crowded street. Perpetually suntanned with a mane of topaz hair, long, shapely legs, a sultry walk and high rounded breasts, Dove never failed to command male attention. At the tender age of twelve, she had been a recognized child prodigy from Nashville, a prize-winning organist performing to critical acclaim at New York's Radio City Music Hall. By fifteen, she became the mistress of a famous Pacific Rim dictator, at eighteen was ousted from the regime by the tyrant's jealous wife and nearly killed in a resulting fracas. Eventually her protector installed her in Beverly Hills, where he bought her an expensive house his ruthless wife later succeeded in confiscating.

Sobered by brushes with death and by having been outwitted by the dragon lady, Dovey rose to heights as a syndicate leader. Her portion of the La Femmina pie encompassed a slice of territory south of the Mason-Dixon line, but her chief area of expertise remained the Pacific bases with which she was so familiar.

Dove was telling the group about an offshore gambling deal she had in the works. She would own the major portion, the other crime chieftains would each have a smaller piece. Through one of her connections Dove had been able to obtain at bargain prices a lease for Netherlands Antilles beachfront property from the Dutch government, which came with a guarantee to be able to build a casino. Though normally a hotel must be constructed before the gaming license was granted, the rules in this case were waived by a special permit.

"The Dutch government will cooperate — we get the land cheap. His Royal Highness the Prince of Holland is very eager — " Dove winked knowingly. The Netherlands Queen's consort was notorious for his roving eye and taste for delicacies that lay under a skirt. "Thanks to the Prince we're going to be able to lease 500 prime beach front acres at only $500 a year for the next 99 years. The ultimate decision makers for the Dutch government here are the Prince and the Minister of Justice of Aruba. They're both in our corner. A corporation is being formed right now, and development is the next stage."

Victoria plucked a fresh fig from the silver epergne in front of her, split it in half and dunked it in cream. She asked, "Why is the prince being so generous? How come we're getting this deal so cheap?"

"Friendship and trust," Dovey winked. "In exchange, we promise to invest American money in furniture and fixtures. They'll even guarantee a government loan to build the hotel. Preferential treatment all the way."

"Having one of these offshore places is a license to steal," Jasmine said. "I think we should set more horizons in this direction."

"Definitely," Carole Curtis, partner in a prestigious Washington, D.C. law firm, one of the nation's best loophole lawyers, and head of the Beltway branch of the LFM agreed. "The smart money's offshore. The couriers are hauling it away by the barrel load." Carole was tall and wore little makeup. A bump on her aristocratic nose gave her a distinctively memorable air.

The topic switched to the agenda nearest and dearest to Vic's heart, narcotics. Jasmine said, "Our retail outlets need more merchandise, and we need a bigger, cheaper supply. We're getting gouged right now."

Laura said, "At present there are eighteen steps from growing to distribution ahead of the point where we enter. Eliminating just a few of these middlemen will bring enormous profits. Economically we want to plot a better course." She shuffled sheets of paper and picked one from the pile, held it up and began consulting her figures.

"We're told that opium purchased for not more than $100 at the first round will eventually escalate to five million on the street in western sales, having been cut again and again. One estimate says the Corsicans buy their raw opium in Turkey for around $25 for ten kilos. When they transform it in their labs into one kilo of morphine, it's then worth $5000 FOB. After it becomes heroin, they get not only their wholesale price but a kickback on sales of final product. 5-6000 or 7000 kilos a year can supply the US market, around 12-15 tons. The Corsicans have got 80 per cent of this traffic. In addition, their product is superior."

"In what way superior?" Dove asked.

"Other heroin producers can manage only about a 90% purity, whereas the Corsicans can go between 97-99% pure, and that's in big demand," Jasmine answered.

"Think if we didn't have to pay the Corsican markups, if we could bypass or knock the Corsicans out of their monopoly... too many steps, too many middlemen," Laura said.

"Streamlining would entail a big initial capitalization, but in the long run would pay off handsomely," Turkish-born Ayla Kalkavan remarked.

Until now the Corsican network had been providing the LFM and most of the other American underworld retail systems with all the heroin they could use. Now the LFMs wanted to explore alternative methods which could provide a more profitable artery with less intermediaries.

Ayla's slanted slate-colored lynx eyes were fringed with a thicket of dark lashes. Five years of struggle as an architect had led her to look to the LFM for her fortune. She'd made a great success from her Boston stronghold, and was now also dating the governor of Massachusetts, a widower with twelve children.

Ayla continued, "We believe that our present $60,000 kilogram buying price can be reduced to a tenth that amount. Multiply that by the tons, you start getting an idea of the profits. Just take an 8 ton per year figure, estimate a conservative one million a kilo street price and you don't need a pocket calculator to tell you we're talking about billions. And in addition, control. Control's the key element."

One idea under consideration was to start their own Turkish operation. The plan involved going into Turkey on reconnaissance. Several intermediaries would be necessary to buy opium in small lots direct from Turkish peasant growers, each of whom would supply 3-5 kilos.

Ayla, as a native Turk, was a natural to take charge of investigations. She proposed a broker buying up the lots for an account designated by a La Femmina financier in Istanbul or Ankara. The goods would then be smuggled to Syria along little known paths, facilitated through customs officials and ex-soldiers who would guide the caravans through Turkish government-laid mine fields along the border. In Syria, the consignment would be delivered to the party responsible for the transformation of the chocolate covered opium into base morphine. The morphine would be shipped from Aleppo to Beirut, the latter being a free port, not subject to customs, in addition to being a center for banking secrecy. With bribery of the right officials the wheels could be set in motion for the growing, processing and smuggling stages.

Jasmine was still claiming she was going to draw her French financier friend Maurice Hirsch into the picture, but the situation was still on hold.

Vic said, "I can see all this as possible over the long term, but we need a good pipeline for the short term. There's no reason we can't double or triple or present capacity immediately. Now is the time to move, before the competition gets any stronger. I have a few ideas in this direction. If I can come up with a solid immediate heroin plan for increasing our profits, do I have everyone's cooperation?"

"Of course," Laura said. "We're always looking to make money."

Already plans were in the works for an offshore fund named Second General, from which they would be able to borrow huge amounts once it was set up. Deborah Cook, official money mover for the group, described the venture.

Deborah, whose face evoked the lingering beauty of a Picasso line drawing, had faintly sucked in cheeks and an expression that seemed always to be sheltering a smile. Auburn hair framed her pleasant heart shaped face. Deserted by her husband after the birth of twin sons, soon afterward Deborah had become secretary-mistress to the head of a Wall Street brokerage firm specializing in new issues. Her former lover taught her the inner workings of the securities business, practices she put to work on La Femmina behalf. At the outset, Deborah tapped into brokerage house excess funds accounts, generated revenues for nonexistent customers, and after that, there was no end to the other schemes she came up with. Her expertise was crucial in laundering and hiding funds.

Deborah said, "We've discussed this Cayman Island reinsurance situation previously. Now we have a more coherent picture." The scent of Deborah's sweet smelling perfume competed successfully with the fragrant and profuse wildflowers.

Deborah turned her attention to a sheaf of papers concerning the fund deal for which the La Femmina organization was seeking ten million in startup capital. "Income will accumulate offshore without any current or future taxation," she explained. "We've designed this so on paper it will appear to be controlled by foreigners or anonymous US shareholders, thus eliminating all taxation in the US under Subpart F rules."

Lily Wyszowsky, quiet, unassuming holocaust survivor with a degree from Queens College and an Advanced Professional Certificate in Accounting from NYU, was the outfit's double and triple book accountant. Lily said, "There's literally no practical method by which the IRS can police a transaction involving two foreign reinsurers, because this would violate the privacy acts of the Cayman Islands."

Carole picked up the ball. "Second General has a very solid working relationship with one of this outfit's best people, Michelle Palmer, subcapo with the Susan Goldman regime in Los Angeles. Michelle runs a general insurance office in Glendale. A combination of premiums we'll have coming through Michelle, plus what Second General brings with them will start us off with nearly 20 million in gross premium writings, and with reshuffling we should triple the existing investment income in the first year. As an international service corporation, the insurance company can pool multinational exposures of any company. It will operate directly as well as in major countries, through service brokers or consultants or through domestic fronting companies."

"This deal has got to be the greatest moneymaking gimmick in decades," Laura enthused, intent on business at hand. "And the beauty is everything we need to make it fly is right here in Beirut."

"Ten million," Tania said. "We already have two or three good possibilities. We should have it settled by the time we leave."

Vic knew Tania was probably right; you could do anything here. Pre-civil war Beirut was a fabulous place to be, like nowhere else before or since. The city was crawling with entrepreneurs, industrialists, sheiks, maharajahs, bankers, oil men, movie people. You could close any venture here, including all manner of clandestine operations, such as the item nearest to Victoria's heart, narcotics.

Two large oil pipelines, the Trans-Arabian terminal in Sidon and the Aramco Tripoli pipeline, had put Beirut on the map, bringing to it an influx of the world's financial corporations and turning it into a dynamic multinational society. Visitors flocked to this al fresco paradise, where nine months of the year business was conducted at waterfront cafes and on the broad white sandy beaches.

The city's heart, "Ras Beirut," was a hilly peninsula nestled in the Mediterranean. On its seafront ran the Avenue de Paris. At the Sabbagh commercial center on the Rue Hamma, a blustering area overflowing with cafes serving exotic cuisine from all over the world, patrons lingered for hours, wheeling and dealing while enjoying the atmosphere in which old mingled with new — clusters of ancient stone houses stood smack against tall modern skyscrapers, and there were cedar stands with trees over 1000 years old. The elegance and beauty of Lebanon's great capital captured the imagination; the style fascinated: elderly men in fezes puffing on water pipes, *shawarma* vendors everywhere. In this city of languid sunsets and golden light, clad in a bikini, you could conclude important international affairs under the appreciative stares of admiring males from every corner of the globe.

Since their arrival, days and nights had been a never ending round of meetings. At the harborfront cafes of Tyre, Sidon, Byblos and Tripoli, and at the mountain casinos, the La Femminas had already negotiated apartment complexes in Florida and Spain, Brazilian emeralds, Israeli diamonds, sugar and coffee deals. On their agenda was also a major project afoot to develop the Algarve coastline of Portugal into a resort area with hotels, casinos and a marina.

Beirut was unparalleled as a source for loans, laundering, lines of credit, moving counterfeits — in short, for anything a scheming La Femmina criminal mind could conceive.

The LFM party was staying at the sumptuous Hotel le Bristol, where the sea below spread out from the curving green land like blue silk, calm and peaceful. In the hills surrounding the city, some of the richest men in the mid east maintained stucco residences rivaling sultans' palaces.

Beirut's fabled nightlife never disappointed — the wild, legendary Le Tabou, where American oil drillers played poker for $1000 hands; the Caves du Roy, alive with the sound of English pop groups; the Arab shows of the Casbah, where dazzling sequined belly dancers contrasted with sober dark suited musicians.

Evenings, they explored the wonders of Macumba, a popular night spot located under the Palm Beach Hotel that boasted Italian music, papier-mâché parrots, rum bottles on walls and ceilings, an aura of privateering on the Spanish Main, and an impressionist in a ten-gallon hat doing an imitation of American cowboys in French and in Arabic with a Texas accent.

Drinks here were served by robust golden-tressed Valkyrie maidens, recruitment potential for LFM soldiers. In addition, Victoria rescued three peasant girls from Marika's, a famous local bordello, offering them training for impending expanded narcotics operations.

"So Maurice can't make it this trip?" Victoria fell in step with Jasmine, as they moved on to the Kit Kat, a nightclub situated at the end of the Avenue des Français, across from Anzak Harry's Bar. From somewhere nearby, you could hear mixed strains of Edith Piaf and Dalida recordings competing.

"You know how busy Maurice is. But it'll happen, not to worry. Meantime, I like Dovey's deal," Jasmine was saying. "I'd like to expand that end of operations, find other casino situations, own a bigger piece than we do on Dove's deal."

"Get the drugs moving, get more laundered money and we'll be in a position to do anything," Vic said.

The Kit Kat terrace opened to the sea. From this vantage point one could see both a fabulous floorshow that offered the most tantalizing fleshpots of Lebanon, as well as the glowingly lighted ships across the way in Beirut harbor. A transatlantic ocean liner, anchored offshore, was ablaze with twinkling luminosity. A shimmering moon gliding across the water, coupled with the warm soft breeze, was tropical and romantic.

It was the golden age of Beirut: omnipresent Saudi and Kuwaiti sheikhs sent out swarthy procurers in long American-made limousines to tempt willing European adventuresses to visit their hillside villas. The young ladies, heedless of warnings about white slavery and Arab sado-masochistic practices, jumped at the chance and were financially well-rewarded.

At the Aley on the Damascus Road behind Beirut, mideast potentates pegged their prizes with leis of jasmine blossoms. Choice female specimens were then escorted to the sheikhs' palaces in air conditioned Daimlers, where they extracted a minimum wage of $1000 a night and up to $10,000 per screw, together with the guarantee of an old age pension.

Just the other night at the Bar Les Troubadours, a disco converted from an old crusader warehouse, people were pointing out a voluptuous blonde "dancer" who had recently scored $300,000 in cash and a home worth half a million in exchange for exotic "dancing" at a very private party at the Al-Bustan Hotel in the hills of Buomana. It was like a different world. This was a philosophy diametrically opposed to La Femmina mafiosità.

Midway through a shot of ouzo, Victoria caught sight of someone who'd stopped to chat at a nearby table. The guy was like an apparition, an arctic flash in a white suit, icy and in full command.

"Who is that divine hunk?" she asked, intrigued.

"Charles Cestari," Laura said, "the Corsican Romeo, numero uno in narcotics himself. Are you ready for that?"

Ah so. Vic sized him up. He was goodlooking in the extreme, his pretty boy features masking a rattlesnake quality that lurked underneath. An inner perniciousness fairly seeped out of his pores, giving him an intriguing appeal.

As he moved on, Victoria, followed him with her eyes until he was out of sight, and felt an alternating tightening, then loosening of her anal muscles. It always started that way. The ass snap was a good sign. She had the feeling this man would somehow occupy a key place in her life. And then he just breezed out, leaving her wondering when she'd see him again. Cestari was the man to get to.

After that sighting, she looked for the Corsican everywhere, at the Kit Kat, Macumba, le Tabou. He was supposed to be highly visible on the Beirut scene, but except for that brief flash, he had eluded her. She went to his casino, the Des Collines, and was told he left town unexpectedly and would be gone at least two weeks. Would she like to leave a message?

No, thanks, Vic said, feeling a sinking sensation in her stomach. Well, she hadn't solidified the connection this time around, but now she knew — she was going to get to this guy if it was the last thing she did.

In the meantime, she'd decided to make the trip to Turkey.

CHAPTER 13

It was the strangest thing: Jasmine, Ayla and Laura had been set to go to Turkey but canceled the trip. Their reason for backing off, they said, was that the original idea of trying to get a large supply of heroin direct from in Turkey no longer made sense, Ayla's further investigations having convinced them they would be unable to obtain enough product there to operate successfully on a big enough scale.

Supposedly the Corsicans had things wrapped up; the natives were neither able to fill additional orders nor refine the heroin effectively. Vic didn't believe it. Her feeling was if you were persistent enough you could accomplish anything. The others were focused elsewhere.

"I think we're missing a golden opportunity," Vic dissented. "This is such a natural for us."

"There's still time — "

She didn't like the sound of it. Having been screwed once too often, she couldn't have this be a repeat of the cocaine story. No doubt, as usual, the others had something up their sleeve. She'd just have to take matters into her own hands.

She spoke to Ayla, who stuck to her guns, insisting that based on new information the plan wasn't sound. But Vic didn't want to accept someone else's word for it, even Ayla's. Now just suppose if she went into Turkey and brought this thing off herself, showed everyone they were wrong, that the deal could be made. Everyone here, all these self-styled *pezzo da novanta* types, would they be surprised. Laura had said they would invest if there was a way to go that made sense. Well, she'd give them that way. So through Ayla, Vic arranged to connect with somebody trustworthy in Turkey, and caught the next flight out.

It was drizzling when they arrived at immigration at Yeshilkoy. She was met by a guide and interpreter named Nazim. They drove along the Kennedy Caddesi by the Marmara Sea, past the fishing piers and outdoor cafes along the Byzantine city walls.

Nazim pointed out the sights, as the car passed a green canyon of cedar trees, willows, tamarisk and Russian olive. The countryside was full of yellow daisies and ground lupins. Overhead flocks of red breasted geese called *ankaz* were heading for Arctic migration.

Vic was sure this potentially more profitable artery involving less intermediaries would work out beautifully. Of course she still intended to connect with Cestari — from the brief glimpse she'd had of him in Beirut, the guy was too incredibly appealing to pass up. He might even be so impressed with the way she zeroed in for the kill, he'd invite her to join his operation as an associate.

In Turkey you could do nothing alone; you needed references. It could be dangerous without protection, and bribery was the name of the game. Vic was prepared. She had confidence in Nazim to explain everything necessary to make this deal.

They passed 12th century yellow granite castles whose medieval towers flew the white crescent Turkish flag. Music from the Turkish hit parade was blasting over radios everywhere, until thorough the town loudspeaker the muzzein chanted his call to prayer. The weather cleared. They paused for lunch at a crowded smoke-filled tea house where men were pitching backgammon dice between swills of spiked tea from tulip-shaped glasses. Outside, the townswomen went on endlessly weaving rugs, tying knots on vegetable dyed yarn and silk. It would take two years to finish a rug that would sell for $200 a square yard.

The journey continued. Opium was cultivated in areas removed from the frontiers, originally in twenty-one provinces, later in sixteen and then it was cut down to only four provinces, Afyon, Kutahya, Isparta and Burdur.

A thousand foot high mountain jutted up in the center of the town of Afyon. The local farmers called this town the "Black Citadel of Opium Mountain," and for over one thousand years it had been the capital of opium growing in Turkey.

In summer the region was stark, baked dry; in winter icy winds blew off the steppes. The poppy was the staple of village life. In spring the brilliant flower bloomed with white and purple petals. Weeding and hoeing took place in March and May. In late June and early July, poppy pods emerged and gum oozed out, remaining on the pod overnight to congeal into a substance with the consistency of clay, which was collected the following day by scraping. An acre of poppy yielded twenty pounds of dark gum, to be shaped into loaves and stored.

In guarded mountain caves, armed men kept watch over what was estimated as at least 200 tons of opium base. Base was also kept in small amounts in assorted private cellars, barns and warehouses, often used as dowries and as insurance against inflation. When changed to morphine base it became an easily smuggled powder.

The illegal market price for a pound of opium in Turkey was ten dollars. Enough gum to manufacture a kilo of heroin that sold on the streets of New York for hundreds of thousands of dollars could be purchased in Turkey for a mere $220. Or you could purchase a kilo of morphine base from the Corsicans at $5000 FOB. If on the other hand you opted for finished product, pure white #4, you'd have to pay between $50 and $60 grand.

The trick, of course, was to peg supply, purchase enough base, then get the manufacturing done cheaper than the Corsicans could do it. She'd worry about supply routes later. Thanks to her shilly-shallying LFM partners, she'd been held back long enough. It was time for action, and she was ready to deal.

At 4:30 a.m. the next day, Vic breakfasted on the Turkish steppes on hard bread, cheese and tea, hot milk boiled with sugar, slices of unleavened bread and tarhana soup, a mixture of boiled wheat, yogurt, butter, tomatoes, chicken entrails and green peppers. Nazim, who would be escorting her straight to the poppy fields, entertained with jokes, bawdy songs, magic tricks and imitations of Turkish pop singers.

Some of the villages in the Afyon province were accessible only by donkey ride up tall mountains. The village of Degirmendere was one of the opium growing areas that radiated from the Opium Citadel.

The women toiled in the poppy fields. In fact, all the work here was done by women, while the men played cards, drank and loafed. Although wearing the veil had been forbidden by the government since Ataturk's reform, every woman in the village over the age of fifteen wore one. The women also had to wear long sleeved blouses and pantaloons regardless of the heat, so that men would not become sexually aroused. The men claimed it was always the woman's fault when crimes of passion occurred, so females must obey, cover up, toil as beasts of burden and hope for the best.

Midmorning, the hospitable peasants served poppy seed bread and small glasses of Turkish tea. Through Nazim interpreting, Vic learned the peasants did not understand why the United States made such a fuss about drugs, that the big problem was the junkies who were using opium the wrong way. "My thinking entirely," Vic concurred.

At a local cafe she met Şefik Ekmekçy, an agricultural agent who headed the squadron that assured farmers sold the required percentage of their legal crop to the government. On the side, Ekmekçy owned parcels of land which he rented out to growers in return for half the profits of the opium crops sold illegally. Many Turkish legislators came from the poppy growing region and countless deputies and their families were involved in the black market.

Over vodka and warm Pepsi, they discussed planning and financing of large scale smuggling operations that would make her one of the biggest importers to the United States of heroin. This could be arranged, Ekmekçy said. He would require as payment either small arms, gold or Swiss francs. His cousin could transport, his nephew convert to morphine base.

The base could be smuggled in TIR trucks so that Customs after leaving Turkey would be unnecessary, shipped across Bulgaria to Munich, where it would be stored. His fee would be $7000 for 100 kilos of morphine base, a big break in price from the Corsicans. Another way he liked to do the job was to wreck a car; the authorities seldom checked wrecked cars.

After lunch, Nazim stayed to talk and fraternize with the locals, while Vic went to a hotel to make a phone call. She was excited and couldn't wait to tell Harry how well things were progressing. After their conversation, she wandered around outside, noticing that the peasants had retired from the fields to take an afternoon siesta. She'd eaten a heavy meal and suddenly felt like napping, herself. From the car she retrieved a blanket and placed it near the deserted poppy fields to lie down.

In the warmth of the sun, Vic contentedly basked in pleasant sensations. Everything was coming together beautifully. Funny, though, she really missed

Harry. She'd been thinking about him a lot this trip, about what a great person he was. He kind of reminded her of the words of the old song, "Just my Bill, an ordinary guy; you'd meet him on the street and never notice him." That was Harry — you wouldn't notice him, either. He was a chubby tapioca blob of a man with the look of a past-his-prime NFL linebacker. His washed out appearance sort of blended into the scenery; there was a greyish cast to his face, like he'd spent the winter holed up in a dingy basement. A severe, short haircut made him resemble a skinned rat, and his dishwater colored eyes were ringed with yellowish circles, like two almost-healed black eyes. His bite needed fixing, and when he smiled he showed blunt edges of worn down, tobacco-stained teeth. An Adonis Harry wasn't, though he did have a certain animal appeal. Regardless of anything, he was the most unusual man she'd ever known. An aficionado of gun magazines, covert newsletters and police bulletins, he was also an avid daily reader of the Wall Street Journal. And there wasn't a cleaner man in God's creation; compulsive about personal hygiene, he usually took two or even three showers a day.

Vic was looking forward to getting home. Gazing up at the sky, feeling satisfaction at a job well done, she fantasized the reunion she and Harry would have in just a couple of days, and dozed off with her mouth open. Nobody ever told her that this area was legendary for its small snakes that loved to crawl down human throats and lodge in human stomachs.

Just minutes later she awoke, screaming and choking, with a mouth and esophagus full of reptiles. Already, tiny, odd microscopic organisms from the snakes were attacking her immune system. She was rushed to the hospital in critical condition.

Several weeks of recuperation would be necessary before she could be moved and allowed to fly back to the States.

CHAPTER 14

Nick Condon, junior Senator from California, had all the earmarks of a future President of the United States, Jasmine thought. They met in Palm Springs. Nick's eyes were darkly sardonic as he slowly puffed on a briar pipe. He smiled; their eyes met. He was a subtly attractive man, dark haired, olive skinned, charismatic.

Their dialog was demure and suggestive. The Senator said, "You smell so good. Are you as dangerous as I think you are?" And when Jasmine replied, "More dangerous than you can ever imagine," his answer was, "I don't care! I have the feeling you can do things to me no other woman ever has."

"What kind of things?"

"The hell with telling you. I want you to do them."

Jasmine said, "Are you sure you know what you're getting yourself into, Senator? After all, you're talking to one of the world's leading criminal minds."

"Really? How interesting," he laughed. "What crimes have you committed? I can think of a couple of acts considered felonies in several states I'd love to have you do with me."

"Well, them, perhaps we could explore this further, if you're interested."

"I am interested. Very interested. But you still haven't told me the crimes you specialize in."

Her voice soft and breathless, Jasmine told him she was involved in "a wide variety of criminal acts ... paper crimes. narcotics, gambling, numbers, prostitution." Her voice was a low whisper. "Would you like an entire listing of my dossier?"

"That won't be necessary," he said. "I expect I could run an M.O. on you."

"You could," she said, "only law enforcement hasn't caught up with me yet."

"Ah, well, then I guess I'll have to accept your word for it — that you are indeed a dangerous woman."

"Now that we've got that straight — "

"Baby, I have to see you. Tell me when?"

It was his choice to believe she was joking.

While still recuperating from her Turkish nightmare, through surveillance, Vic learned about Jasmine's new VIP lover. Senator Condon could be useful to the LFM, both for his political influence and also as a target of potential blackmail. They'd keep especially close watch here.

Nick rang the doorbell at Jasmine's East 63rd Street townhouse. Jasmine admitted him to the marble-tiled entrance hall. He was carrying flowers and a bottle of wine wrapped in a brown paper bag, and his erection was already protruding from his pants.

The entryway opened into a curved foyer containing myriads of dogwood branches suspended in lucite boxes against beige linen wall covering. Nick was no sooner standing there, having handed over his gifts, than he made a grab.

"Nick, Nick -- this is so abrupt."

"We don't have all that much time, and I've thought about you constantly —"

Jasmine insisted on small talk first. Dutifully, he admired the bleached pickled oak flooring and modular units upholstered in grossepointe, the bessarabian carpet and French art deco chairs in the living room. Near a melon-colored velvet couch, huge vases of calla lilies and apple blossoms were displayed on chrome and lucite tables. Softly, Liszt's Transcendental Études, *allegro agitato molto* in F minor # 10, Van Cliburn at the piano, played in the background.

"This is your family's residence, I presume?"

"No, it's mine," Jasmine said. She offered him the wine he'd brought. "This is the house that cocaine bought, and it's mine, all mine. I did alert you to my criminal tendencies, remember?"

"I remember."

After jockeying and positioning, they finally ended up in the bedroom. It was furnished in luxury, the piece de résistance being the empire Malmaison bed strewn with cushions in soft earth tones. Nick dropped his pants immediately, and they went at it. Later, they luxuriated in a tub of warm, perfumed water together while she fed him crushed strawberries with sour cream, rubbing the mixture over his body while simultaneously popping the delicacies into his mouth.

He wanted to know, "What are you doing all over the world — Asia, South America, Europe, everywhere? Are you independently wealthy? Do you have a rich boyfriend? You're a woman of mystery. You truly fascinate me."

"Do I?"

"You have beautiful clothes, an affluent life style, a fabulous home at an exclusive address, you stay in pricey hotels — you come and go as you please. What enables it?"

"Tell me, Nick," Jasmine asked, "would you go to a man's home and ask him how can you afford this? Do you have a rich girlfriend? Is your family wealthy? Did you inherit your home? How do you pay your hotel bills? Where do you get the money to buy your clothes?"

"I'm sorry," he apologized. "I didn't mean it the way it sounded." He seemed genuinely apologetic. "But what exactly is it do you do?" he persisted, "other than the obvious?"

"My primary work is with the mafia," she answered, popping another strawberry in his mouth and planting an ardent kiss on his lips.

"Of course. Anyone can see you're a made woman." Obviously, he didn't believe a word she'd told him.

"When you think mafia with me, Nick, get the idea of LCN, La Cosa Nostra, out of your mind. My alliance is with another order of mafia altogether ... a female mafia. We're nationwide."

"A woman's mafia — an idea whose time had come," Nick said, laughing at the thought. "I love it, I love it! It must be very profitable."

"Very. My people and I import cocaine, enabling other aspects of my life to function, my legit ventures, for instance. I'm building a catalog business, my designer licenses are taking off, I'm opening a boutique on Madison Avenue soon. I have my own legit designer line, Jasmine Jeans, and then I also manufacture knockoffs, counterfeit designer clothes, fake Guccis, Vuitton luggage, Omega watches and other name brands."

Vic couldn't believe her ears when she heard Jasmine even confide that one of her narcotics covers was an import-export firm specializing in furniture, fabrics, rugs and jewelry, and that her consigliere, Sandra, also operated under cover of a South American powdered milk firm that exported dehydrated milk products to the US and Canada — perfect for the narcotics smuggling operation. Nothing like letting the entire cat out of the bag.

Only Nick didn't believe any of it. He was really getting a kick out of this. "But tell me, allocation of capital is strictly controlled, only a small segment of society has access to that market, most people can't get a foot in the door. How did you qualify? Through bank robbery?"

"No, that's one thing we don't do, at least not with a gun. We do it in more subtle ways -- often using rental or counterfeit collateral, kiting, that sort of thing."

"I should have guessed. Well, what's wrong with that?"

"Nothing. As far as counterfeit collateral is concerned, the Treasury Department figures there's at least fifty billion or more in bogus collateral floating around the nation's top corporations. Spain's entire Costa del Sol was built on counterfeit collateral. Just a minor deception to make the banks feel better."

"Makes a lot of sense to me."

"Anyway, so-called crime is dependent on definition, on what current laws are on the books, who's your lawyer and accountant, what judges you have in your pocket. Almost anything can be rationalized, including conspiracy, fraud, and obstruction of justice."

Jasmine was massaging the strawberry/sour cream mixture into his scalp now. She said, "This is very good for your circulation, and it will help make your hair grow healthier. So now that you know all about me, about my life of crime, how do you feel?"

"I love you with all my heart," Nick said, his eyes closed in mellow relaxation. "And to tell you the truth, I'm wildly jealous. I wish I could join the female mafia myself."

"A number of men have said that, but obviously you can't — not ours. Anyway, you already have a mafia of your own, the Beltway Mafia. All you Washington hotshots are mafioso as hell."

"You know, I think I'm falling in love with you," Nick said, turning to her and looking at her with a suddenly startled expression.

CHAPTER 15

Now that Jack and she were no longer together, LFM business was occupying Tania's total energies. Plans for Balls were progressing, she'd hired renovators to knock out walls and replaster. She was still consulting with painters and decorators and looking at fabrics and furniture, although an overall theme for the décor still had not taken shape in her mind.

In addition, she was involved in heavy meetings with her attorneys and accountants regarding a number of offshore shells out of U.S. jurisdiction, hence not subject to regulation, in which money could make more money through simple manipulations like inflated balance sheets, rented deposits from money brokers, dead collateral and so forth. These in turn were juggled to obtain loans to finance other projects.

Corrado occupied her thoughts on a constant basis. While she hadn't heard from him, no doubt his travels the world over could explain the lapse in communication. She envisioned him transacting important deals among the mahogany parlors, staid oil paintings and Victorian atmosphere of British finance.

This man stirred her blood as never before. The rapport was fantastic, magical, beyond anything she had ever known. She dreamed of melting into his being, their pelvises locked in belonging. In her fantasies, he lifted her buttocks onto him, his body started to slowly thrust inside her as he murmured in her ear and then finally they reached a climax together of such proportions the very earth shook on its foundations.

But what about the woman he'd been seen all over London with? Somehow, at the back of her mind it troubled her.

In a transatlantic call with Fiona, Tania asked if Fiona could find anything about Corrado's consort. The next day Fiona rang back to say the woman's name was Ingeborg Kessler, she was German and a big time operator on the international whoring scene, specializing in rich, powerful men.

"She's led this life, ducky," Fiona said. "She's definitely in it for the money. This Ingeborg is notorious. She's had some pretty lofty males in her day. For some reason, many of them have passed her around, and she keeps trading up. But get this, an unusual twist — Ingeborg Kessler is an identical twin, with a sister, Ingrid Kessler. They often work together. The men go wild."

"Oh, God, don't tell me."

"I'm afraid so. The sisters are both models based in Munich, but the pair has worked New York and Los Angeles too, London, Paris, Rome and Milan, up and down their native Germany, Spain, the middle east, Hong Kong — they're highly skilled and very expensive and they always get what they want."

"Oh, God," Tania groaned.

"These Nordic and Teutonic cookies are all so cold and calculating," Fiona said. "Yet men don't seem to know the difference ... it has to be an ego thing with him, that's all."

"What shall I do?"

"Darling, you ought not to worry, truly."

"How can you say that, Fiona?"

"Because it's obvious you really love this man and she doesn't... or they don't. And as long as you get exposure to him, he'll discover the difference. He'll come to realize what he's got going with Ingeborg — and to a lesser extent Ingrid — is superficial by contrast to you. Men aren't total dummies, you know, though it may sometimes seem that way. Eventually they catch onto a woman — women like this."

"Are you sure?"

"Trust me, Tania, this German bitch is a flash in the pan."

"How long has it been going on thus far?"

"Maybe on and off for about five years."

"Five years! A flash in the pan?"

"Ducky, she is not important to him. Believe me, he could be very easily persuaded to leave her flat. It won't take much."

"Yes, but five years — "

"Some men are creatures of habit and lazy about extricating themselves. They settle in by default till the right woman convinces them they have reason to switch."

Tania was brooding over the new information, when (magic!) she connected with Corrado. She knew he kept an apartment at the Pierre, and as luck would have it she happened to phone there at the perfect time. He'd just arrived from the airport, he was on jet lag, in town for only 24 hours, but said he'd love to see her. She was on his doorstep in ten minutes flat, brazenly throwing herself at him, rushing into his arms as if they'd never been apart. How to describe the wild lust, the tenderness and immense passion, the deep connection on all levels — oh, God, to hole up with him forever and never let go!

The next day it was La Caravelle for lunch, Romeo Salta for dinner, more lovemaking — lord, it was crazy, loving a man who could made the adrenalin course through her veins and activate currents she had never felt before. Then in a flash he was gone once again, off for Hong Kong, and she was feeling empty without him.

No doubt he meant it in jest when he casually said, "If you were my mistress you would come along with me to Hong Kong."

It didn't sound like an offer and she didn't take it as one, but why had he even thought of her in such a secondary, essentially dishonorable role? Why hadn't he said something about considering her for his future wife? When Tania objected to the term mistress, Corrado explained it sounded more agreeable in Italian.

"In Italy, we call the two people friends. The woman is a man's *amica* and he is her *amico*. It's all very natural. It's you Anglo-Saxons who've complicated this thing."

"Well, in any event," Tania said, "I've never been any man's mistress nor do I ever intend to be. I'm an independent woman who would never want to rely on a man's handouts, and I should think any man would prefer a woman who chooses not to be a mistress, so that he could be certain she loved him for himself. And besides," she teased, "it's I who should be asking you to be my gigolo, my stud. That's more my style."

"I'm flattered by your offer," he said. "You are the first woman to ever ask. I would have expected I was too old to qualify. After all, I'm getting close to 40 — I'm 37, practically an old man. Are you sure that's not too ancient to be your stud?"

"It's perfect," Tania said winding her arms around his neck and kissing him. They made love again, after which he said, "We can be together, and I will be your stud forever if that's what you want."

"What about that big blond?" Tania asked, in spite of herself.

"Ingeborg, you mean? But it's nothing serious. She's just a friend."

"Your *amica*?" Tania prompted.

"My *amica* -- of sorts."

"If you already have a mistress, why did you suggest, even indirectly, my playing that role in your life?" Tania said, hoping he would list any number of reasons.

"Whoever said a man should be restricted to merely one mistress?" he asked.

"I couldn't imagine — " Tania searched for words. "Who would need — "

"But this is only normal," Corrado protested. Then he opened up more, elaborating on his personal life, on things she had no idea of and could never have imagined. As he spoke, Tania became increasingly alarmed. She almost could not believe it when he told her that his crippled wife of ten years, whom she had never heard of before this instant — Valentina was her name — was now confined to a wheel chair, the result of a hunting accident. They had two children, a boy and a girl, ages seven and nine. Wife! Children! She had never thought, never suspected ... it simply had not occurred to her that he might be married. First a mistress with a twin who was also a part of his ménage, and now this wife —

And then he was off again, in town again, out again. It was bad enough about the twin mistresses, but on top of everything else he pulls this crippled wife out of a hat. Where was the future in this for her? And what was the alternative? Tune him out? She was in love with this son of a bitch, dammit all.

Could she cure herself of an addiction like no other she had ever imagined in her life?

CHAPTER 16

Vic's hidden camera was grinding as the towel around Nick Condon's waist popped open and his erection jutted against Jasmine's crotch. The video caught his hands easing under her buttocks, her pelvis arching up to meet his, and her legs moving along his thighs.

Later, in a post-coital twilight zone, Nick told her, "I'm afraid of falling in love with you! I fear being vulnerable! And yet, I can't help myself." He sighed. "I know it sounds crazy," he said. "What can I expect, what can I offer? What do you want that I have to give? Why am I thinking about you day and night? Why can't I get you out of my mind? Why are you the one thing that makes me feel happy?"

"This guy's got it bad, Harry," Vic said.

Nick still wasn't satisfied about her lifestyle. "What do you do on all these trips? What other life do you have, apart from me? I've tried to fantasize it."

"I told you," she replied. "I tend to my mafia business."

He laughed, still taking it all as a joke. Then he said, "I'm curious about your other men. Who do you fuck?"

"Whom do you fuck?" Jasmine corrected the senator's grammar, and then answered his question, "Nobody important. Nobody in your league."

CHAPTER 17

Jack's uncle, Thomas Kelly, gazed at Tania from across his sprawling desk. He was tall, thickset, broad faced, and at sixty plus years of age still maintained his loading dock physique. His hair was only slightly greyed, his skin youthful and tanned. The walls of his Madison Avenue longshoremen's union headquarters were decorated with certificates and gold plaques commemorating his distinguished career as one of the most powerful men in the international labor movement.

Victoria had hounded Tania for a long time to meet Jack's uncle, Tania had begged Jack over and over to introduce them and he'd kept putting it off. Now that she and Jack were a thing of the past she hadn't expected to ever meet him, but Kelly had phoned her himself, requesting this meeting in his office.

Kelly wanted to talk about his nephew. "Jack is a good-hearted boy," Kelly said in his faintly lilting, leprechaun voice, rubbing his index finger over the thin sprinkling of freckles that covered his forehead. He was silent a moment. Tania's gaze wandered to the wall testaments to Kelly's life in public service — he'd even been the Honorary Grand Master for the Ancient Order of Hibernians.

Kelly swiveled in his chair to face St. Patrick's Cathedral rectory, directly at his side below. Thoughtfully, he allowed his fingers to temple, almost in an unconscious prayer directed at the Archdiocese below. "I'm going to ask you a favor, not for myself or even for Jack, but for Jack's mother, my sister. My sister is a widow, and as you know, Jack is her only child — "

Kelly went on to say that Jack was going through a bad time, and that he was afraid if Jack lost Tania at this crucial time it might send him over the edge.

"When Jack met you we both agreed, his mother and I, that from all reports this was the best thing that ever happened to him." His gaze wandered to a Cystic Fibrosis Man of the Year award, and returned to her. "Now that you've left him we're afraid." Kelly leaned forward for the final pitch. "Jack is devastated over the breakup. He needs our help. His compulsive gambling is a disease, and it can be cured. If you could see your way to hanging in with Jack for just a short time longer, even just a month, this will give me time to work on him, get him into a program like Gamblers' Anonymous, and possibly be seen by a competent therapist."

"You're asking me to reconcile?"

"If you'll do this favor I guarantee to be eternally in your debt. Anything you ever want, just ask, and if it's within my power, consider it done." Kelly could deliver on that score. He could be a formidable ally.

Tania said, "I've heard you're supporting Robert Francis Casey in the gubernatorial race, and that in great measure thanks to your influence and backing, Casey's a shoe in."

"I'm known as a man of my word," Kelly smiled assuringly. "In fairness, Casey has a good chance, with or without my support."

"Regarding Jack, you're asking for a miracle," Tania said. "Furthermore, I'm not sure I could do what you ask, considering the state of affairs between Jack and me at this time. You're expecting a lot."

"A miracle, as you put it. But one miracle deserves a miracle in return and I'm prepared to do just that. Please, for Jack's mother's sake, go back, stay just one month — don't rock the boat. The return favor will be commensurate with your sacrifice. This I promise, and I will personally guarantee Jack gets help."

Tania was thinking about Corrado too. Could she rationalize that maybe he was too busy running around the globe on business to return the messages she'd left, or should she just accept the painful alternative that it was a wild fling that didn't fit into real life? He was a man with a wife, a mistress and a girlfriend, so why was she in this emotional maze? Had she used bad judgment to fall in love so wholeheartedly and ingenuously? But she couldn't help it!

Corrado and she had no formal commitment. She didn't know when or if he'd be phoning her again. She didn't want to go back to Jack. But was it asking so much to do as Kelly requested to help for just a month? One month was only a short time. Despite their differences, she still felt affection for and yes, responsibility toward Jack. As much as she'd wanted it over and finished, this would be for only thirty days, and after that... no, it wasn't long ... just for now ... then everything would straighten out, they'd be out of the woods, and maybe by then Corrado would have altered his lifestyle and ...

"All right," Tania finally promised, "I'll go back to Jack for a month."

"I'm very grateful to you," Kelly smiled, shaking hands as he showed her to the door. "Everyone who knows me knows I'm a man of my word. I'm at your everlasting disposal — just as long as it's not illegal or immoral," he added, laughing.

Tania shook hands with him, hoping she hadn't made a bargain she'd regret.

CHAPTER 18

Several months back, two La Femmina chieftains with far east connections, Eleanor Lee Wong and Dove Cameron, had made reconnaissance missions, setting up an intricate system that would yield the organization annual profits well into the six and eventually seven figures per annum. El and Dove had checked out Asian circuits where an inexhaustible black market in gold existed. In Japan, India, South Korea and the People's Republic of China, the going gold rate was double London fixing. A sales force of La Femmina carriers had swung into action as couriers, with Jasmine's jobbing firm providing special suits that featured carefully constructed pockets sewn to hold gold bars. Puerto Rico and Santo Domingo were bouillon pickup points.

Supervising a new round of this operation, Vic had delegated her captain Georgia Jensen to go out on the next trip. Georgia, who would be leaving with her group for the Caribbean in the next couple of days, stopped by at 1 o'clock for a meeting and to leave her dog Marlene Dietrich with Vic. As business was winding up, Vic said, "I almost forgot, Georgia, there's something I need you to get for me — I want you to take a side trip to the Dominican Republic and pick me up some Pega Palo."

"Some Peg-a-what?"

"I'll write it down so you don't forget. Here." Vic handed Georgia a slip of paper.

"What is it?"

"Honey, Pega Palo's a small bottle of incredible stuff with the ability to keep a man's cock hard for three days straight, minimum. In fact, it's also a great weight loss technique — for obvious reasons."

"Maybe I should try some myself. All that fun, and I'll lose weight besides?"

"Sure, but you'll have to screw 36 hours straight to do it."

"What's so bad about that? Tell me more."

"Christopher Columbus first discovered it when he sailed into Hispaniola. As you may have heard, those old Spaniards fucked up a storm in the Caribbean, and Pega Palo is the reason why. Barbara Hutton said Pega Palo was the secret of Porfirio Rubirosa's virility — he could go for hours without coming, stay harder longer than just about any man alive, Barbara Hutton said. It's wild stuff."

"Why are you so anxious to have this stuff?" Harry wanted to know after Georgia left and Marlene Dietrich had settled under his feet.

"With networking taking on interesting dimensions, you just never know when it could come in handy," Vic explained. "Some people require enhancements."

Harry understood perfectly. He always did.

CHAPTER 19

Tania kept her word to Thomas Kelly. But at the end of a month's time, Jack had shown only mild improvement; he was still gambling, the same problems existed, and Tania decided to move back to her Park Avenue flat.

Despite herself, her thoughts were filled with Corrado. She managed to track him down in Singapore. He returned her message, saying he'd tried many times to reach her without success, and suggested if by chance she were going to be in London the following week that they meet there. Tania needed no persuasion. Was she chasing this man shamelessly? So be it. She was chasing this man shamelessly.

Immediately upon arrival, she phoned him from the Dorchester and they started talking dirty over the phone. He was very uninhibited in English, although strangely puritanical in Italian, didn't think she should use words like *cazzo, figga, culo, chiavare, scopare*, and so forth — too vulgar. But in English it was anything goes and their talk made her wild with desire. He said he was expecting a phone call and couldn't come to her hotel. So she rushed right over to his, to the Connaught.

He took her to the Other Club, the exclusive dining place founded by Winston Churchill. For the next several days, London was a blur of restaurants and romantic trysts, at White's, the Savoy Blue Room, Anabel's and Mirabel's in Curzon Street. They wouldn't let him in Anabel's because he was wearing a pale colored suit, Anabel's in Berkeley Square stipulating men must wear dark suits and ties. Then it was Quaglio's Restaurant off Jermyn Street, and Pratt's Club, in a basement off St. James Street.

He said so many seductive, charming things. Oh, the irresistible Italian male! This one more so than any other. She knew this man could bring her everything she had ever wanted. At first she avoided asking about Ingeborg. Then, "Where is your mistress?" she finally heard herself ask, and he replied she was visiting her mother in Germany.

Corrado continued uttering his sweet nothings, and she continued eating it up. "With you I have the feeling that we have known each other before in many lifetimes and that in this life we must come together for completion," he said.

"Forever?"

"Yes, forever, my dear." He smiled. "It is destiny that we came together."

Everything was beautiful. She was sublimely happy, she was delirious. She asked no more. Even so, something was gnawing at her, something was wrong. All of a sudden this feeling had come upon her in which she no longer felt like herself, but rather as if some outside force had entered her. She had lost her appetite. She became tired, she was urinating like crazy. And her period was late. It dawned on her in a flash. She was pregnant.

Pregnant! How could it possibly be?

When she told Corrado, he looked puzzled. "But that's impossible," he said. "It's too soon."

Tania hastened to assure him, "It's not yours."

He asked, "What are you going to do?"

"Marry the father," Tania said.

Of course marriage was the best solution. She was madly, passionately in love with Corrado, she'd sworn never to go back to Jack, but it was as if the hand of fate had intervened and played a cruel trick. Besides, what could Corrado offer? His life was tied up.

"You're sure marrying Jack is the best decision?" Victoria asked, at the meeting of the New York crime chiefs at Spark's Steak House, where Tania had just announced her pregnancy.

Tania sighed, "Do I have much choice?"

"What kind of a father do you think Jack will be?" Laura probed.

"Don't bother to ask," Vic said. "She can always divorce him."

"A healthy attitude to walk down the aisle with," Jasmine said.

"Face it, if Jack continues on his present course Tania won't want to stick a marriage out," Laura said. "But at least the kid will have a name."

At the others' suggestion, just to be certain, Tania went to the drug store and bought a pregnancy kit. Sure enough, the results were positive. So that confirmed it. Jack was thrilled about the baby.

This child was being sent to her for a purpose, Tania knew; it was meant to be. As she felt new life growing within her and moved toward her biological destiny, she knew things did have a way of working out for the best — because now, miraculously, Jack really seemed to have reformed — he hadn't placed a bet since she'd given him the glad tidings. So the hand of God could work in mysterious ways.

She was sad about Corrado, though, although she was weary of the emotional roller coaster. She believed Jack when he said this baby would change everything. Certainly, fatherhood had been known to change many a man; it could change Jack. Corrado couldn't offer marriage, stability, a home and children, and there came a time when certain things took hold of one's life. The decision had been made for her. It was time. She would settle her life, get on with it.

Jack was a willing bridegroom, and there was no question of her love for him, although it was a different kind of love than she felt for Corrado. The Greeks didn't have just one word for love, they had four: philos, storge, eros and agape. C.S. Lewis had even written a book about the subject, The Four Loves. Well, the particular kind of love she felt for Jack was called storge. Storge was an attachment for the familiar, occurring when one was accustomed to being around someone, used to their presence and habits and to the pattern of a life together. With Corrado, on the other hand, it was erotic love. Eros was much rarer, an all-consuming force, that depth of flowing, that overpowering giving of energy from the bottomless depths of ones being, and in like kind receiving from the other.

Eros was full surrender to a great, incomprehensible power. It was finding a missing link. She had never known it with any other man.

The marriage ceremony was held at The Little Church Around the Corner. Tania's sister Emily flew in from Ft. Worth to be her maid of honor. The reception was held in Little Italy at Laura's club the Tiro a Segno.

Hearing the strains of *Lohengrin*, Tania smiled softly as she went forward to meet Jack. She was renouncing eros for storge, and her life was taking a whole new direction now — for better or for worse, only time would tell.

CHAPTER 20

Vic studied the video as Senator Nick Condon removed his jacket, loosened his tie, doffed his pants and joined Jasmine in bed. He took hold of her gently at first, then forcefully. She straddled him, lowering herself onto his stiff, throbbing penis. He groaned and their gyrations continued until the floodtide.

Afterwards, he was telling her about his life, his past, his hopes and dreams for the future. Southern California born and bred, he was a product of Eastern schools, Exeter and Harvard, with an interlude as a Rhodes scholar, then Yale Law School and Law Review, followed by private practice in Los Angeles.

"Have you thought about running for President?" Jasmine asked.

Nick laughed. "I guess at the back of every senator's mind there's always that idea. Of course, I'm still only in my early 40's, so I hadn't considered the immediate possibility."

"I think you should start thinking about it," Jasmine said.

"Now what makes you say that, darling?"

"My consigliere, Sandra Martinez, says you have a great shot at it next election."

Every time she mentioned anything connected with the female mafia to Nick, it invariably evoked a smile, chuckle or hearty laugh. This time he chuckled. "And what would your — consigliere — Sandra be basing her information on?" he asked, amused.

"Sandra's amazingly psychic, a good 85 to 90 per cent accurate. You've seen her cable show, of course?"

"I've never heard of her," Nick confessed, smiling indulgently. "Does she do astrological charts too?"

"How'd you guess?"

"It figures."

"Well, in any case, you definitely should start thinking about it," Jasmine repeated.

Nick said, "I must say, I feel sorry for the guy who runs against Herbert Tree — he's one of the most popular presidents in history, a sure bet for reelection."

"Don't be so positive," Jasmine said.

"Don't tell me — something's going to interfere with Tree's ratings in the polls, he's going to slide downhill — Sandra says so."

"In fact, Sandra does say so."

"For my party's sake, I hope Sandra's right. At this point nobody wants to run against Tree. But when the time comes, there are other candidates better positioned than myself, so I don't think now — "

"But that's just the point," Jasmine said. "These would-be candidates are going to find themselves left at the post — it will be too late for them to mount an effective campaign. The thing for you to do is announce your candidacy early, then just sit and wait till Tree hangs himself."

"Sounds like a good idea, darling. Thank Sandra for her consigliering. Should I have a reading with her?"

"That's up to you."

"Well, I don't know — she might find out about us, and I wouldn't want that. The secrecy of our affair makes it more stimulating, don't you agree? If it weren't secret, do you think it would be as erotic?"

"Let's not talk rhetorical situations, Nick," Jasmine said. "Let's deal in the definite. You are definitely going to run for President of the United States, and I am definitely always going to play an important role in your life. Agreed?"

"Agreed. I wouldn't have it any other way, my darling."

Vic had three women on the payroll whose jobs consisted exclusively of listening to wiretaps and watching surveillance videos, then reporting back with noteworthy passages for her reference. She had bugs on well over two dozen key people now. Via this means she was keeping updated on the increasingly provocative Jasmine and Nick Condon relationship.

Vic had now fully recovered from her Turkey mishap, but there was something chillingly upsetting about the whole experience that still disturbed her. Ok, maybe it was all an accident, but nevertheless she was convinced it was a bad omen. She understood now that Turkey was a lost cause, that it would be impossible to get a dependable heroin deal going there in large quantities. As cooperative as Nazim, Şefik and others had seemed to be at first, they changed their tune, eventually backed out, either couldn't or wouldn't make good. It was all very weird. Ayla said it was her understanding the Turks had been paid off, that due to their formidable network of spies, the Corsicans had found out and nipped her plans in the bud.

The greater wisdom for the present was Charles Cestari. She was going to get the heroin deal going by hook or crook and it would be her deal; the others would have to do things her way.

She retained the image of Cestari in her mind. Sexy guy. She'd like to get into his trousers for a night or preferably a whole string of nights, but it seemed that one thing after another was keeping her chained to Gotham. There was just so much going on in the mundane day-to-day bullshit with managing her troops, overseeing rudimentary chores, legalities and keeping things running smoothly, she hadn't been able to pull herself away again yet, even though she was itching to get moving and wanted the heroin so bad she could taste it. That combined with the haunting memory of Cestari was making the situation grow in urgency.

Then she heard via the grapevine that Cestari was due in the city in a few weeks. Good. She could be patient, work something out with him right here in Manhattan.

In her mind, she settled the details of how it was going to be when she nailed him. So certain was she that they'd lock into a deal that she even repeated to the other capos, "Look, I may have an angle on a narcotics situation. If I can put this together, would you be willing to invest?"

"We're always looking to make money," Jasmine said. "What kind of drug deal?"

"Heroin connection."

"As you know, we have long term plans under consideration, but if you come up with a viable way to go first, I'm sure everyone will be interested in pursuing it."

So of course the others would invest. She'd soon conquer the head of the Corsican mafia and that would cinch it. In the meantime, she had work to do here on the home front.

She said to Harry, "After nothing but setbacks and obstacles, I need to adjust the balance. I'd like to spread some good will around while I'm waiting for Cestari to arrive."

"Honey, I've got just the guy to help you do it," Harry said. "That big Judge, Robert Francis Casey."

"Yeah, you said you had an idea on that subject."

"I've been working on it. I hope to have news soon."

"What kind, Counselor?"

"Listen, baby — if things go the way I think, the La Femmina Mafia Organization can own this fucker."

"The hell with them — I want to own the fucker."

Harry was cleaning his AK-47 assault rifle in the trophy room, Vic was filing her nails, and they were discussing Judge Casey again.

"Just what specifically can this judge do for me?" she asked. "Do I have a case in his court? Do any of my people?"

"You probably will have soon, baby — one of your girls, Ilona Maxwell, is probably gonna try to get her case heard there. And then we have the Cynthia Simmons appeal coming up."

Simmons, one of her captains, had been sentenced to 15 years in prison on a counterfeiting charge. "Cyn Simmons? That was federal."

"Yeah, but no matter what, the guy has tremendous influence with the bar and with judges in other jurisdictions — local, state, federal, whatever. You want him in position for the future. He's a powerful guy with a long arm — he can be useful, believe me."

"And I have to play the hooker with him, you say. You're sure I have to go that route?"

"It's the best way to his heart, soul and mind. Trust me. You gotta use what works."

Vic was on her way from a sitdown at her social club in Little Italy, uptown to the Woodward, with Harry at the wheel of a brand new green BMW, a gift from her captain Millie "Bug Eyes" Newins, who ran the Bronx car theft ring. Some of Millie's people had found the vehicle sitting on St. Nicholas Avenue in Washington Heights and helped themselves. Probably belonged to some Dominican drug dealer, Vic figured. No more. Well, tough shit, Juan or Pablo or Jose or whatever the fuck your name was.

Harry had connected. He was explaining, "The thing you have to realize about guys like Casey is they all operate from the background using pimps and beards, they never go direct to a chick. Casey's key man is Johnny Pabst, who excels at getting Casey all the pussy he wants. What's the matter?"

"This is so beneath me it's ridiculous."

"Yeah, but there's a decided method to the madness. Trust me. You do things his way, and he doesn't realize he's playing right into your hands. He only thinks he's getting his way. Little does he dream you have a plan — "

The Honorable Robert Francis Casey was a mid-50ish, fair-complected fellow with a pleasant kennedyesque schoolboy face and blond hair that fell casually onto his forehead. His power base was in Nassau County on Long Island's Gold Coast, the North Shore. Not only was he increasingly rumored as the state's next governor, he was also on the President's short list of Supreme Court nominations.

On the personal side, he was your typical idol with feet of clay, looked clean, played dirty, known as a guy who lived through his gonads and his fantasies, and for being a frequent visitor to Belle de Jour, a La Femmina-owned S & M parlor in Soho, where he often went for bondage.

"We're working out the logistics," Harry said. "When you get the chance, be sure to play up to him. Remember he had eyes for you."

"What am I supposed to do? Plop my bod in the lobby of the Carlyle where he lives and pull my pants down when he walks in, assuming he ever does?"

"Listen, I know a guy, a bouncer at a club in the Village. He told me Johnny Pabst, the guy I mentioned, is Casey's chief pimp, comes in there all the time."

"Pimp? What the hell do you think I am?"

"Now don't get excited."

"Harry, this is going too far. I won't degrade myself. I don't need crap like that."

"I respect that, honey. You got integrity with a capital `I.' But you gotta look at the bottom line."

"I have my principles," Vic insisted, "I'm not a whore, and I will not be insulted. I draw the line somewhere. We've been through this before, Harry."

"The way you get on your high horse, you'd think you were one of those rich bitches around Casey, and none of them has any compunctions when it comes to fucking around."

"Yeah, their shit don't stink, right? Well, my nose is not in the air, it's too busy being to the grindstone."

"Just the point. Get cozy with Casey, the road could be a helluva lot smoother for you. Think of the future, of the potential of getting a case fixed in any court in New York State."

"And why should Casey want to do that?"

"Because we make him an offer he can't refuse."

Subservience was against everything she stood for, but Harry was right about Casey being prime meat.

"A cunt is a valuable thing to waste," Harry paraphrased the NAACP ads, reassuring her, "It's no big deal. Guys do the same thing, so don't feel bad. They angle, marry rich women, fuck them, climb."

"Yeah, I guess," Victoria conceded.

Homework was in order, so they went to the library to learn all they could on Casey's family background.

On the surface, Camelot-type publicity might lead one to believe Casey came from an impeccable social background, a family of four generations of public service, but probe a little deeper, you'd find another story. There was his great granddaddy, son of a shanty town mobster of late 19th century Boston, a brothel and tavern keeper who bought his way into the corrupt Back Bay political machine that had its roots in opium trading.

Gramps Casey obtained a seat on the party's ward committee, gave up his tavern, went into the wholesale liquor business, and was elected to the state legislature. The secret of his success was control of the local crime group, the McGuire Gang. In 1916, the family bought a drug company from Hudson's Bay and profited from a loophole in the War Measures Act that permitted distribution by pharmacists of alcohol for medicinal purposes. The family kept their hand in prostitution and were brothel keepers in and out of Massachusetts, New York and Canada.

They pushed cheap rotgut that paralyzed and killed thousands during Prohibition, a period when both Casey's father and grandfather made millions by being in cahoots with gangsters. During this same period, the Caseys also made a killing in the stock market through insider trading. After that they cleaned up their act to become huge, eminently respectable liquor distributors worldwide.

Needless to say, Judge Casey's curriculum vitae made no reference to how he got his start in life, and it was generally perceived he could do no wrong. Ditto his wife, a descendant of a noted Philadelphia Quaker banking family who allied themselves with dope trafficking in the early days of the American Republic. All very interesting, but Vic wanted some information of a more personal, intimate nature.

Why didn't she think of it before? The LFM's own Nancy Jo Corcoran. She must talk to Nancy Jo.

CHAPTER 21

Nancy Jo Corcoran, one of Laura Lo Bianco's underbosses, was running three LFM bordellos, including Belle de Jour, the S & M parlor downtown which Casey patronized. If anyone would know the entire poop scoop, it would be Nancy Jo. Vic arranged to meet her uptown, where she presided as madam at the La Femmina's exclusive brothel located in a Calvert Vaux-Frederick Law Olmstead Victorian gothic brownstone in a fashionable section of the East 90's.

Pale skinned, mahogany-haired, mother of three and a former Miss Wisconsin, Nancy Jo had married a lout and was rearing three kids on next to no funds when the LFM prostitution management gig fell into her lap. Lately the racket had been paying off so tremendously that her former spouse was trying to woo her back.

Nancy Jo answered the door herself. Friendly and warm, she extended a firm handshake to Vic, at the same time offering kisses on both cheeks, European style. Nancy Jo wore a simple blue cotton jersey dress that clung to her curves and emphasized her pointy, architecturalized breasts. Her most anachronistic feature was prominently displayed on her forearm: a colorful tattoo of the flying horse Pegasus, surrounded by a snake swallowing its own tail.

Vic was impressed with the ambiance here. There was an indoor swimming pool, a bouncer in a top hat and tails, a stable of young girls all about 18 years old running around in bikinis and lingerie, all with glamorous long hair and dragon lady red nails. Each boudoir was done to perfection. Piped in music, Luigi Boccherini's sonata in A major for cello and harpsichord, soothed savage nerves.

Vic said, "This is a class act, Nancy Jo. I have to hand it to you."

"Thanks, Vic. I'm pleased you could pay us a visit." The two were sipping Oolong tea from Rosenthal china cups in the tasteful parlor. "The man you're interested in knowing about, my client Judge Casey, prefers my place downtown. In general, most people in the criminal justice system frequent there rather than here, the reason I believe having something to do with their interest in and psychological bent toward guilt and punishment."

Nancy Jo, Vic remembered, had been a psychology major at the University of Wisconsin. "Maybe I'll get to see that place too sometime," Vic said. "For now, I just wanted to get a little background information."

"Glad to help, Vic."

"I'm sure we both agree, Nance, that the way to a man's heart as well as his wallet is through his cock and balls, plus in some instances his mind, if he has one, which Casey, I understand, does. So I want to know what's in your trick book. What can I learn that could be of use? What turns this guy on?"

Nancy Jo said, "Casey's pretty eclectic in his sexual tastes. Has a few scatological hangups -- but generally, to start from the concept that illusion, teasing, and sexual banter can be a real turn on for many men, in this respect, Casey's no exception."

"Interesting, isn't it? I've always felt one reason that's true is most men are so pedestrian; they want the woman to stimulate their glands, their brains and their cocks. Left to their own devices, men can be pretty lazy and unimaginative."

"True, very true. And a propos of Casey, I can tell you he's a Cancer, so he has his moods. I've had him on my floor -- bound and gagged, I've had him stretched out on the rack -- one of my girls had him in a special contraption, this iron mask type thing where we put his cock under lock and key for six hours and make him beg for release -- "

"God, I assumed he was kinky, but I had no idea the sonofabitch was that kinky."

"Being a Moon Child, he fluctuates, but you should definitely be prepared for strange requests. Remember, this man is in a position to buy all the sex he wants of whatever variety he chooses, kinky or non-kinky. If he doesn't get it from you he'll get it elsewhere. He's moody and he's impatient. He expects to be serviced."

"How about verbally? What are his verbal requirements?"

"Keep the dialog flowing. Banter with him. He finds sexual banter very appealing. Let him guide you into it," Nancy Jo counseled. "You know what to say — the usual dialog about cocks and cunts and fucking — you have to explore that whole dimension with him."

Vic nodded, making mental notes.

"See, in my opinion, my customers are sick," Nancy Jo said. "They don't think so, so I act like they're not. But keep it in mind. And you should be aware Casey's not the most generous man in the world — I know your motivation is other than monetary, which is as it should be, because he can be stingy."

"A real anal retentive type. I thought so."

"He likes to take chances. What he finds most sexually exciting is flirting with danger. You have to be tacky with him, he likes his women down and dirty, yet high class at the same time, if you get what I mean. He's looking for a lady in the parlor bitch in bed type — basically he wants to degrade women — "

"Great."

"I mean, he wants a classy slut, not a sex goddess. That's how his sex center functions. I know you can comply."

"Comply?" Victoria shuddered. "I loathe that word. It's not in my vocabulary."

"Well, honey, start learning it," Nancy Jo said. "Just keep your mind centered. On another tack, gossip is that one mistress Casey had a couple of years ago really got to him. She cut up all his clothes, all his expensive suits, his entire wardrobe, and he loved it!"

"How'd she do it?"

"Broke into his apartment at the Carlyle when his wife was at the hairdresser, and just went to town. I tell you, Casey's a glutton for punishment. That's his aberration. The lady who did this bit, incidentally, was Wendy Wagstaff, who's now married to the guy my boss Laura Lo Bianco is — or was — in love with, Frank Gantry."

"Wendy Wagstaff a mistress? Come on, Nance, Wendy can buy and sell the U.S. Mint. Rich women aren't mistresses, darling."

"I beg to differ. Wendy and Casey had a fling, and Wendy, as rich as she is in her own right, got into Casey for seven figures. By the way, Casey thrives on danger. A lot of these law and order and political types are like that. And another thing about them -- most of these guys dig bondage."

"Well, I just hope I can pull this off."

"Oh, you can. And if you really want to get him where he lives, crap on his belly. You know, lay a nice little mound of turds on his gut. He'll freak; he'll adore you for it. He'll even analyze them — he'll do a whole number."

"Disgusting."

"You just have to look upon all this as a game and take control. Control's the secret, Vic."

"Suppose I have a problem in production?"

"So take a laxative."

"That might be a turnoff. It could thin out."

"You're right. No, you prepare. Diet's important. Your shit has to come out smelling like a rose."

"It would have to be timed just right, wouldn't it? Because how many people can produce exactly on cue?"

Shit! She knew a lot of legal, judicial and law enforcement types were into S&M, especially the M part, but crapping was going too far! You had to draw the line somewhere.

"I just wonder out of curiosity what time of day — or night — he expects this service?" she said later to Harry. "You know me, I'm pretty regular. Off schedule, I wouldn't be able to manufacture. You know the particular hours I'm geared toward crapping, Harry."

"We'll work it out."

"You just wonder how a man in his position manages. Psychiatrists will tell you these politico womanizers are thrill seekers with a death wish who need to see how far they can push their luck. They're addicts, compulsive types. Something happened in the toilet training stage of their upbringing. If they're rich, they have an even bigger problem, since they were probably potty trained by a nanny, so they have a mother identification problem as well."

"Well put, pumpkin. That's what you have to contend with, with Casey."

"This can also make them cheapskates. Money and feces are very interrelated, Harry. Not many people realize this. From what I gather, Casey's even had film stars crap on his belly."

"Some women will do anything -- and for nothing, too."

"You can't imagine how I loathe being thought of as a trick, Harry. Me, of all people — an international businesswoman and entrepreneur, one of the most powerful women in the city — or the country — the world, even – and I have to go this route?"

But Harry was right. It was a great connection. The opportunity was just too good to pass up.

CHAPTER 22

Casey's Carlyle abode was a done in asexual upper crust Wasp decor, the living room displaying a photographic rogue's gallery of silver-framed Casey family members, along with the de rigueur Alexandra Schumantoff portrait of Mrs. RFC over the marble fireplace. Vic and Bob sat on a peach-colored couch by the fire across from the portrait, and he'd turned on some obscure Broadway show tunes as background music.

His bringing her up here was probably either the ultimate nose-thumb at his wife, or else a testament to his pathologically sneaky nature, or possibly both. The wife was in Europe, he told her, the kids off doing their own thing. According to likenesses, the wife was slender and blond with aristocratic bones, and the four kids were of similar hair color, all with typically prominent Casey teeth. You could practically hear the sound of his wife's Locust Valley lock jaw.

Vic wanted to open her coat. It was hot as blazes. But Harry had told her to keep it on; he said Casey wanted it that way in the beginning.

The first thing Casey'd told her was, "You'll do everything I say. Listen, and pick up your cues." Then when they were seated side by side on the couch, the judge opened his trousers and asked, "Do like my prick?"

"I love it," Vic replied. "It's one of the all-time great cocks in creation, believe me."

"You think so, eh? Tell me about some of the other cocks you've known."

"Oh, my heavens — pricks — cocks — yes, indeed, I could tell you a few stories, Judge — "

Could she ever. Pricks, cocks, schlongs — she'd seen a cross-section of them, a wide variety — long and thin, short and stubby, solid, sturdy, utilitarian; pink, white, blue, red, beige, peach, apricot, yellow, purple, brown, black; plastic and elastic, surgically lifted and implanted, some encrusted from improper cleansing, general neglect and poor urethra control; and so on and on. She'd seen so goddamn many of these tools in her day it could make your head dizzy. She told him about a few of the standout organs she'd run across over the years, to which he listened with interest. Then he pointed out an unusual feature of his own pecker.

"See, my cock bends. Watch how my prick springs."

"So it does. Amazing." It listed to the left.

A bead of sweat had appeared on his upper lip. "I want you to suck my dick," he said. "I want you to sit on it, baby, and feel it bulging inside you."

"I can't do both at once," Vic pointed out.

"We'll make time for everything."

Next, as a getting-to-know-you device, he wanted to play the where-have-you-done-it game, also known as the I-have-fucked game. This was one of his favorites. It centered around the litany "I have fucked." I have fucked, I have fucked, she recited, and it was actually half true — I have fucked on the Staten Island ferry, LIRR commuter trains and PATH trains, coast to coast jet planes, boat trips around Manhattan, the merry-go-round in Central Park — "

"Where else have you done it?" he inquired, turned on.

"I have fucked in a box at the Metropolitan Opera ... I have fucked on the tracks in Grand Central Station ... under the clock at the Biltmore ... I have fucked in the Saks Fifth Avenue parking lot in Palm Springs ... I have fucked in St. Patrick's Cathedral ... and I have fucked under the 59th Street bridge — "

"No!"

"Yes!"

"You must really need it."

"Yeah. Like crazy. I can assure you I'm the hottest fuck you'll ever have, baby."

"Tell me, which would you rather have up your pussy, my cock or a huge big black one?"

"Yours."

"Come on, you're bullshitting me. Seriously, how about it? Ever balled a black?"

"Never have, never will."

"I bet you have."

"Honey, you don't know me. Mysegeny's not my thing."

"Why not? Prejudiced? Don't tell me you're a racist."

"Damned right I am, and proud to be a first class white supremacist. Listen, Bob, I'm an old-fashioned Southern girl, a genuine Florida cracker, and you can bet your ass I wouldn't be caught dead in bed with a person of color."

"Ever think you might be missing something?"

"Must I share your liberal politics just because I fuck you? Must I vote for you for governor?"

"Who said anything about politics?"

"You're a politician, aren't you?"

"Jurisprudence is my line. And from my extensive life experience — on and off the bench — I know you'd definitely enjoy balling a black. How about my arranging it for you?"

"And you'd watch?"

"I'd love to watch," he said, drooling.

"Well," Vic conceded reluctantly, in an effort to please, "that chocolate-skinned Reverend from Brooklyn, the one who's on TV all the time — he's a little chubby but he is kinda cute. And I hear he fancies a good piece of white-skinned poon tang now and then. Think you could set us up?"

"You're evil. I love it."

"But I want you to know that I'd rather fuck you, Bob, any day of the week."

"Aw, come on, Victoria, I bet all your life you've had a secret yen to take a good, stiff black cock between your legs. Or in your mouth, as the case may be. Admit it. You've repressed it all your life."

"Ok," Vic said, lying to shut him up. "I would and I have. I confess I did do it once -- it was on the # 7 subway between Grand Central and Long Island City. The train was packed."

"How black was he? Was he a genuine darkie, or a hi yeller mulatto? How big was his cock?"

At this point sexual banter had turned the judge on to such an extent that he was guiding her head toward his lap. In response to his urging, Vic ran her tongue lightly over the glans of his penis and onto its shaft, taking it slow at first, then increasing the scope and breadth of her flicks. She swallowed 3/4 of his cock, then came up for air and planted a series of long hot licks on the organ's surface. For variety she rubbed his cock on her nipple and stroked him lightly. He was getting stiffer by the minute, or as stiff as Casey was apt to get.

After that he gave her a whip, a silken rope, a pair of handcuffs and a saucer filled with milk. The game involved tying him up and handcuffing him, then, with threat of whipping, ordering him on his haunches to lap up the milk from the cat's dish. The china was Limoges, she noted; nothing but the best for a Casey cat.

Although she'd never done anything like this before, Vic proved an able dominatrix. And then it was time for scatology. Just as Nancy Jo predicted, the judge wanted a neat pile of turds dumped on his belly. Vic obliged and was pleased at her ability to fill all requests to satisfaction. The man was obsessed with feces, kept asking her about her toilet bowl habits, if she generally produced "floaters" or "sinkers," about their length and diameter and other such nitty gritty details. No doctor had ever been as thorough.

Casey said he wanted to see her again. "I shouldn't, you know. It's dangerous. We could be caught."

"Come on, you know danger's the name of the game for you. It's what makes you tick."

"What do you mean?"

"Honey, you love the idea of being caught, don't you? You politicians are all alike, you all have this Russian roulette factor going vis à vis the sexual. You actually dare people to catch you with your pants down," she told him and he ate it up.

"I'd like to send you a thank you note," the judge said. "Where do you live?" He had a pen in hand.

"The Woodward," she replied.

"What's that? Never heard of it."

"A very fine establishment — 55th just off Broadway."

He frowned, as though the Woodward was beneath contempt, which compared to the elegant Carlyle it certainly was.

"And what's your phone number, in case I want to call you?"

Vic gave it to him. Then he peeled off twenty one hundred dollar bills and gave her a four fifty spot tip on top of it.

Casey was a case. Actually, if the truth be told, she even kind of liked the poor fucked up sonovabitch. He had a certain charm. Probably the Irish in him. But if she were a psychiatrist she'd have a field day with this guy. He was an addict, for sure, testing to the limits. In a way they were a lot alike. What he failed to realize was he was being controlled.

Two days later, the promised "note" arrived, a raunchy pornographic card minus a signature. Following that, it became official. He was definitely running for Governor.

The crank calls started around then too. It wasn't hard to figure out who was making them, even though the judge was using a voice altering device. Harry had a trap on the phone that proved the calls were originating either from Casey's home number or from the phone booth directly across the street from the Carlyle.

"How's your cunt?" the calls usually began, or alternately, "How's your pussy?"

"Do you suppose Casey walked into Hammacher Schlemmer to purchase that voice altering device himself, Harry?" Vic asked. "And by the way, what the hell is the Chief Judge, New York State Court of Appeals using a voice altering device for in the first place?"

Harry shook his head. "Un-fuckin'-believable."

"Tell me, Harry, do you attribute this behavior to on-the- job stress, or is this judge meshugge?"

"Maybe a bit of both," Harry said. "One thing's sure — if the SOB ever lands in trouble, insanity's gonna be his defense. And after the courts let him off the hook, just watch his mental health improve."

CHAPTER 23

After that, Harry, using surveillance techniques at Belle de Jour, got some interesting footage there; he also penetrated Casey's Long Island Gold Coast fiefdom, a 40 room castle out in Oyster Bay Cove inherited from his rum running forebears. Some spread. The façade was all handcut stone. An ornate bronze staircase led to the second story. The mansion had bathrooms with heated marble floors and gold plated towel racks, bathtubs of single slab Carrara marble, indoor tennis courts, a glass enclosed indoor pool, orchid house, herb garden, amphitheater, and custom made air conditioned dog kennels for Mrs. C's prizewinning Rottweilers, as well as a greenhouse for her award-winning flora.

There was a two way mirror on a pole in front of the house, so vehicles entering or exiting could be observed and photographed. All windows were wired with a burglar alarm system; all of them had photoelectric eyes, so that merely walking close by could set off an alarm, and there were searchlights at every inch of the grounds. Harry said none of this would pose a problem, he could circumvent, not to worry. Vic had the feeling she was laying the groundwork for something big.

With his wife still in Europe, the judge invited Vic out to Long Island for a Saturday evening's fun and games. Thoughtfully, he ordered Chinese dinner sent in from a local eatery. They'd chowed down, played house a couple of times and were resting after one of their longer sex sessions. Casey was downstairs and Vic was in the upstairs study, when she happened to notice the phone was lit and picked it up to listen. She was surprised to hear Anthony Zino's voice on the other end.

Casey said, "I told you not to call me here."

"Something's come up," Zino's abrasive baritone at the other end countered. "We wanna meet you at the Roosevelt place."

"You can't be serious. We can't be seen in public."

"You won't be. We meet upstairs at midnight. The place closes at 11."

"The Roosevelt place" was a rib joint, Vic knew, formerly an Italian restaurant called the "Casa Bianca," so named because it was situated not far from President Theodore Roosevelt's home, Sagamore Hill. The restaurant was once Teddy's law office, used as a sort of "Summer White House" back at the turn of the century. After the mob took it over as a restaurant, they began using it for summits with union bosses and mafiosi like "Tony Ducks" Corallo and others residing in the Oyster Bay area.

Listening, Vic heard a sound that was a muffled sort of whoosh that seemed to be coming from a desk drawer. Fortunately, a key was visible, it worked and she unlocked the drawer. What she found was a tape counter winding, recording the entire conversation. She was onto something. She would have Harry investigate further.

A week later, Vic accepted Casey's invitation to fly by helicopter to Montauk. Together with pimp Johnny Pabst acting as beard, they had a lobster dinner on the pier. When Vic returned to the city, another couple of thousand richer, Harry told her he had Casey's scene figured out.

"There's method to this guy's madness. The son of a bitch is a not so subtle blackmailer."

"What are you talking about?"

"While the three of you were enjoying your quiet tête à tête à tête dinner on the Montauk wharf, I snuck in to the Casey Oyster Bay Cove compound and what do you suppose I found?" Harry held up two tapes.

"Dynamite," he grinned. "Baby, I do believe we have succeeded in getting to the bottom of what Judge Casey's up to and how he goes about it. Honey, this guy's bugging every major political figure in New York State. His game is storing potential blackmail information. He's gonna have so much shit on everybody they'll have to give him the support he wants when he goes after the gubernatorial nomination, and nobody opposing him will have a prayer."

So they decided to give Casey a taste of his own medicine by bugging him. Harry, assisted by Vic's soldiers, set things up so that they could not only duplicate Casey's existing tapes for their own use, but also keep track of all his future tapings. Harry worked it so that via remote control, they could get everything, past, present and future.

"Anything Casey has we have," Harry said proudly. "And believe me he has plenty. He's leaving nothing to chance. Nor are we."

"How's your pussy?"

Casey again. This time he was using his own natural voice, no altering device. Vic made a face and held out the phone for Harry to listen. The call was recording automatically.

Casey continued. "Do you know who this is?"

"Of course I do. Hello there, Judge."

"Don't say my name. Don't say anything."

"Where are you calling from? From a strategic spot?"

"From a booth. But speaking of strategic spots, you didn't answer my question."

"What question?"

"How's your cunt?"

"That wasn't what you asked, honey. You asked, 'how's your pussy?'"

"So you do remember. Well?"

"My pussy'd be in a lot better shape if you were here to give it some attention," Vic purred.

"I'll do that, baby. Soon. Meantime, tell me you like my cock. Tell me your pussy's wet, it's hot, and you're hungry for my cock."

Vic obliged. Then Casey asked, "Are you horny now? Are you playing with yourself?"

Vic asked Harry, after hanging up, "Can't you see the s.o.b. jacking off in that Madison Avenue phone booth?"

"He who laughs last laughs best," Harry said. "Some day all this will pay off."

"Sure — we'll have all the evidence he has, and the goods on him besides. We'll be sitting in a good spot."

"Casey's a nice, steady piece of action," Harry said. "It's an investment in the future, quick work, over with in a couple of hours, and you get to pick up chump change to keep you in bagels besides. Did I tell you that pussy of yours was a gold mine?" He grinned. "All it takes is using it wisely."

"I think I'm doing pretty well, all things considered."

"Honey, you're only one person, you can only take just so much action. But you can send out other chicks on the team to work in this same direction. Think about it. Ten cunts are better than one."

"I have to hand it to you, Harry. Your head, if you'll pardon the expression, is in the right place."

Harry smiled. "Problem with most women is they lose sight of the long term, they don't realize the gold mine they got going for them with their cunts. A cunt is good only so far as it's out working for you. But gradually, things are all coming together. You're catching on, baby."

Recycled La Femmina gambling, shylocking, numbers and narco-dollars were circling the world through wire transfers and SWIFT wires, passing through offshore banks and corporate fronts, purchasing hard assets, being converted back to cash and letters of credit for reinvestment. Syndicate strength increased as more women came into the picture, locating in cities all over the US. The pad was growing in size. There were bigger moves into counterfeiting, gambling and drugs; money was out on the street working via lady shys, and legit ventures were flourishing as well.

Operating behind the scenes was their new company, OFF, Offshore Fiduciary Fund, a mutual fund based out of US jurisdiction, not subject to SEC rules. OFF bought stock for anonymous customers and there was no way law enforcement could tell who they were. Offshore Fiduciary Fund's office in Nassau made it possible for laundered money to reappear as loans anywhere in the world. These loans would be used for LFM enterprises in which the real owners were often controlled or hidden.

Compensating balance loans using floating instruments traveled into Bahamas corporations, Cayman reinsurance, Liechtenstein anstalts, Panama trusts, and various dummy corporations. Their operations often involved grand scale kiting or figuring out clearance dates to the hour. Sometimes elaborate deals were held together by a hairbreadth involving counterfeit collateral, bogus insurance guarantees on oil well production, diamonds, gold or inflated property, until the ante was raised, a large line of credit arrived at through financial paperwork and abracadabra.

It was pure prestidigitation — juggling, shifting, kiting — and it accomplished what they wanted. Improved financial statements were easy to come by. Any number of sources could be tapped for rented, borrowed, stolen, forged or inflated collateral. What these instruments did was reassure bankers, giving an edge that led to permission. Permission, that was the whole story of life in one word.

CHAPTER 24

Surveillance at Jasmine's townhouse continued. Vic was learning a lot about Senator Nick Condon. He'd studied in a zen monastery and once had even contemplated becoming a priest. He was a totally new kind of politician, very much with the times and of the future; he projected something that no other politician did, a genuine New Age feeling — in his environmental consciousness, his mystical reverence for Planet Earth, and his sense of mission in connecting the country to the Cosmos. His scene played well in California and it was catching on with the rest of the nation.

The couple picnicked together on Jasmine's roof garden. Thin rivulets of perspiration trickled down Nick's naked chest as he pulled a robe on over his body. Jasmine spun ice in her glass. The song on the stereo changed. She stood at the roof garden threshold, her eyes steady, and arching her body sinuously, idled over to him and slowly opened his robe to palm his bulging cock.

"Ever made love on a picnic before?" she asked.

"No, never," he answered breathlessly.

"Well, then, how's about taking your shorts off to find out how it would be?"

There was a tempestuous fury to their movements as their bodies joined.

"Oh, God, what does an absolutely drop dead gorgeous young woman like you want with a stodgy old senator like me?" Nick wondered afterwards, and Jasmine chuckled, holding him closer.

"I think you need a massage," she said. "Come."

He followed her into a small room. The lights were dim, low and soothing. The room was decorated with teak and rosewood Chinese antiques, pieces covered with exotic cloths, with sculpted handles and hinges of precious metals. There were hand painted Mandarin panels and jade statuettes, priceless crystal and porcelain and chinoiserie. Jasmine disappeared behind gently rustling jade-colored silken curtains to return with a silk Mandarin robe for him to put on that was embossed with a triple dragon emblem in jade, gold, and silver.

He lay down on a king size bed with an oak headboard inlaid with mother-of-pearl. Bartok's Concerto for Orchestra conducted by Serge Koussevitzky played on the stereo. The room smelled of sandalwood and patchouli. Jasmine rubbed his body with rare oils and herbs from South America. Her technique was derivative of shiatsu, acupuncture, and Reichian manipulation.

She came to the delicate matter of his anus. Donning a plastic glove, she applied petroleum jelly to her finger and penetrated him, instructing him to breathe deeply.

"Oh, God, God, I can't stand it, it hurts!"

"Keep breathing! Don't stop!"

"What are you doing to me?"

Her finger continued probing, in and out, up and down, around and into every nook and cranny of his asshole.

She gave him a peculiar concoction to drink — it contained damiana and yohimbe, six blends of sea food, six kinds of liqueurs, twenty herbs and spices, and other ingredients that she would never reveal, a secret recipe.

Other times she used Tiger Balm or Viks Vapo Rub. He enjoyed it when she rubbed cocaine on his genitals and they had sex again afterward.

CHAPTER 25

"One does have to wonder about these politicians, doesn't one, Harry?" Vic said, watching the video of Jasmine and the senator. "Well, my hat's off to the guy. Condon's statesmanship is exceeded only by his cocksmanship."

"What is it about these guys?" Harry echoed. "It's like an occupational disease. They're all the same."

"Lucky for us."

"Yeah, we got some sensational material here. As this guy advances in the political arena, he'll probably go for the highest stakes possible — he's sold on that already."

"The number one spot in the nation. Imagine our owning the President of the United States, Harry?"

"What do you suppose we'll want him to do for us when he makes it?"

"It's never too early to start thinking."

Vic was busy, working out a purchase plan for a chain of dry cleaning establishments in Duchess County; there was a wholesale record operation in the works; she was involved as a broker in some electronic and communications arrangements for which she expected to collect fat finders' fees; her auto repo business was going great guns; a new fertilizer she had under option was shaping up to be a winner; she was concluding a cross-licensing agreement in the field of hydraulic motors and swivel gears as a joint venture with some crooked krauts in Germany; and she was swinging deals with offshore rental collateral in addition to elaborate schemes involving bogus insurance company guarantees from fly-by-night P.O. box outfits in Colorado and Vermont.

Other mob associates, not actual members of her New York borgata, were also contributing to her success. Included in this group were Charlie, a super charged, sprightly west coast-based female geriatric with access to a great funny bank in Maine, two in Florida and three in Southern California, who was plugged into some heavy S & L people across the country; and Johnny, a black woman in Chicago's Old Town who brokered oil and had $5000 a month phone bills. Most of the people working in this capacity had large phone bills, matter of fact, but thank God Harry had circumvented that problem with a black box so that now she and her local people could call all over the world minus the inconvenience of Ma Bell sending a bill.

Amazing what you could create — it took chutzpah and leg work, but if there was one thing she'd never been it was lazy. So she could claim a lot of credit, and basically she should have been proud of her accomplishments, except that one delay after the next had plagued her as far as heroin plans were concerned.

She told Harry, "Either people aren't being straight or they're simply indecisive." She was getting antsy from the need for action.

"Honey, you're gonna have to make your moves in self-defense," Harry said.

He was right. It was essential she seek Cestari out. She'd lost several weeks first from the Turkish snakes fiasco, then after that, more weeks of waiting, expecting the guy was coming to Manhattan, only to find he'd postponed the trip.

Her people had thoroughly checked out his habits and haunts in Paris, Marseille, Corsica and Beirut. He was in Beirut now, and Vic's mind was made up. She was going over there, find him, make a direct approach, nail down a deal. If she didn't take this step, the situation could drag on interminably. After she arranged things, she'd get the others to invest.

The entire flight from New York to Beirut, she could think of nothing but Cestari, the appeal of the man himself and what she knew about him. He owned mining companies, shipyards, construction companies, a chain of restaurants and gambling casinos; he was a decorated war hero, an elected official from Corsica, former Chamber of Deputies member from Zicavo who also controlled the waterfront of Marseille. Owner of the well-known Club Haussmann in Paris, he also had a Paris bar called Trois Canards in addition to a restaurant in Corsica, Verité, and the Café de la Paix as well as a bar in Marseille called les Organdiers. One of his restaurants was mentioned in all the tourist guides as being one of Paris' leading attractions. When in the French capital he could usually be found taking late night suppers at Fouquet.

Victoria welcomed the familiar sights, sounds and smells of Lebanon's great capital. Ravi Shankar-sounding sitar music to a dervish tempo blaring, skinned lamb carcasses hung in the bazaar stalls, lovely goldsmith-fashioned jewelry on display everywhere told her she'd arrived where she wanted to be. Beirut was a fabulous city of which in a very short time she had become extremely fond; in fact, she might even consider moving here some day when she'd earned her retirement stripes. After checking into the Bristol, she waited till evening when she joined a party of Americans and taxied thirty minutes out of the city to the largest casino in the middle east.

Jounieh, a small village of stone houses with arched windows and red tile roofs, lay facing a soaring cliff whose 2000 foot summit was crowned with a white statue of Our Lady of Lebanon. A complex of theatres, restaurants and casinos was built into the mountains overlooking shimmering Jounieh Bay below. Ascending to the Casino Des Collines via funicular, Victoria and her party arrived at the impressive structure. Across the bay, the lights of Beirut flickered in the distance. The entire building seemed to reverberate with blatant raw sexuality and excitement. Arches, mosaics and chandeliers predominated inside, where a posh international clientele was dressed expensively in jewels, furs and evening attire.

Dozens of cages and goldfish bowls housed a variety of topless cabaret girls, their genitals discretely covered in skimpy g strings or black diamond and autumn haze mink merkins, the latter giving their wearers the illusion of silky pubic hair five layers thick. More showgirls cavorted nude and semi-nude in mini railway cars that passed by the gaming tables, where under the glittery lights the guests played $2000 a throw crap stakes.

She spotted Cestari immediately, going about his job hosting. She watched him greet five international concubines at the baccarat area and caught his attention. She smiled. He smiled back. The maitre d' led her party to a ringside table flanked by reflecting pools. At the center of the great room, a huge banquet was laid out.

One side of the long buffet displayed western fare: everything from truffled foie gras and caviar to lobster and beef Wellington. Cestari idled on the opposite side by the spread of mideast cuisine. Called a Lebanese *mezeh*, dishes were all artistically arranged with flowers and greens on gleaming silver and gold trays.

Attracting his attention once again with a smile and provocative thrust of her hips, Vic grabbed some dinnerware and began piling up from the sumptuous feast. From the selection of hors d'oeuvres she chose flat Arab bread, huge Damascus green olives soaked in lye, traditional Lebanese dishes of hummus, tahinah and baba ghannouj, and whatever else looked interesting. She was just spooning herself some kibbeh Aleppan style, liberally seasoned with mounds of hot red peppers, when Cestari's deep basso profundo sounded from behind.

"I see you smoke blonds," he said.

"I beg your pardon?"

"American cigarettes. We call them blonds because of the light color of the tobacco. Won't you try one of mine?"

"Thank you, but later. I'm concentrating on the *mezeh* now."

"If I may make a suggestion, Madame?"

"Of course," Victoria purred, turning slowly and bestowing on him her most dazzling smile. "I'd be delighted."

Hovering close, she sniffed out his appeal. An ineluctable aura of *homme fatale* clung, the suave matinee idol good looks and throaty speech inflections became him, yet it was the predominance of the icy, menacing quality under the facade that drew her so irresistibly. What was that unusual aroma he exuded -- a combination of musk, patchouli and yes, an added ingredient, some very secret, passionate attractant.

In a voice like velvet, he said, "You must try this delicious Egyptian caviar. It comes from the female grey mullet, called *buri*. Her o-var-ies," he caressed the word, "are dried in the sun, then pressed into long amber bars."

With a large strong finger he indicated another choice. "Desert truffles! It is the wild desert storms that give these their mild succulence. Believe me, nothing in Perigord can compare."

He insisted she try na'ud, shark boiled for many hours; *lukhmah*, purée of stingray; and above all she must not miss the tiny rare fig-pecking birds that were to be eaten bones and all, he said. Then what would she like sent to the table? A 1955 Chateau Latour, *peut-être*, or a 1947 Cheval Blanc? Or then again, possibly an extraordinarily fine 1929 Nicholas Rolin would be the most appropriate choice. His compliments, of course.

Victoria, no oenophile, decided, "Why don't you surprise me, Mr. Cestari?"

"I have the feeling that very little would surprise you," he answered. "But you must call me Charles." This guy was dangerous to her independence, a menace to dormant emotions nobody had ever aroused.

True to his word, he sent them a very fine champagne, a 1959 Château d'Yqem. Victoria imbibed, enjoyed her food, and in short order was up once more, over at the mezeh, inspecting the desserts. She felt Cestari's eyes behind her and knew he was approaching again. This time he suddenly closed an outsized hand over her shoulder.

He said, "You don't have to be afraid of me."

"Don't worry," Vic replied. "I'm not."

He guided her through the array of desserts: candied fruits and honey-drenched, sugar-dusted semolina pastries filled with creamy cheese, crushed walnuts, hazelnuts, slivered almonds and Aleppan pistachios; nightingale nests and Lebanese clementines: flower-scented custards, little pancakes flavored with aniseed, cinnamon, lemon juice and sesame seeds.

"What do you recommend, Charles?" she asked.

"*Saliq*," he replied, "is our most *recherché* dessert, a wonderful hot pudding with cardamom scented with a soupçon of *mustaka* -- that is gum arabic, the aromatic resin of the mastic tree. You may know this spice is even more expensive than *luban*..."

"*Luban*?"

"Frankincense to you. Ah, *saliq*, if you have never tasted any, is a wonderful Damascene delicacy. Of course, we order most of our desserts from Damascus. As you probably know, Damascus' Port Said Street since the time of Haroun-al-Raschid has been the sweets capital of the world."

"Haroun-al-Raschid?" Victoria repeated. The name did have a familiar ring. "Is he in the oil business?"

Cestari laughed. "I like a woman with a sense of humor," he said.

She waved her cigarette, purposely blowing the smoke in his face and relishing her power to distort his nerves and jar his judgment. She measured her effect and knew she fascinated him. She could feel his body heat traveling toward her in waves and knew he was savage with tension and desire. "You seem to know a lot about mid east food, Charles."

"It has become an interest," he acknowledged, his eyes steady.

"Among your other — interests — there's one in particular that brings me here tonight," Victoria said, seizing the opening.

"Ah, yes? And what might that be?"

"I am a friend of Maurice Hirsch," she said, using the magic name as an entre. "You understand? We — my associates back in the United States and I — are looking to make arrangements. Maurice said you would know what I mean."

"*Mais oui, je comprends.*"

"Maurice said you were the man to supply me with everything I need, in terms of large quantity at a special discount price. I'm authorized to speak for my people." Her voice lowered. "I came to Beirut alone — especially to see you."

"You say you are alone — " He stepped closer, eyeing the table where she'd been sitting.

"Acquaintances." Victoria waved the table's occupants aside. "I'm unattached — and available."

"Ah, perhaps then you would like to meet later on? Say in about two hours?"

"I'd love to," Victoria said.

Slowly she sipped champagne as the steady stream of semi-nude houris in cable cars glittered and sparkled past her line of vision. It was all sex and Sodom, larceny and flash here, sleazy and splendiferous, Gomorrah, Tangier, Hong Kong, the Casbah and the Reeperbahn all rolled into one, and she was on top. Relaxed, she poked at a few bites of the desserts, then decided to stroll through the casino to await the fated and fast-approaching rendezvous.

As she wandered by the spinning roulette wheels, the strong recollection of Cestari's scent assailed her nostrils, and she was filled with the aura of his mysterious eroticism. Her anticipation was reaching toward a crescendo.

All eyes were fastened on that small white ball bouncing its way into and out of slots. Victoria decided to play. She stayed with red even, increasing, decreasing, amusing herself trying to pin down the percentages. She played 39, placing one or more chips on every spin; at the end of an hour her number had come up four times and she had won close to five thousand dollars.

She quit while she was ahead, watched more action in the big area, then drifted over to the chemin de fer room where a rich tuxedo-clad Japanese held the bank. A sign reading "*pas de limite*" was suspended over the table. Each gold plaque was worth ten thousand dollars. There was a half a million bucks worth of plaques in the game now. She watched the cards spin out of the shoe. In three draws, the Jap broke the other players and the stickman pushed a pile of gold plaques across the table to him. Victoria moved on.

When the witching hour arrived, Cestari suggested instead of taking his usual front row table that they be seated in back where it would be more private. Here they were only peripherally aware of the flashy floor show in progress under the bright kleigs. Over his favorite late supper of plump oysters on the half shell washed down with ice cold Dom Perignon, he related something of his fascinating if checkered past.

Although he didn't mention it, she knew that because of his record in SEDCE, a special actions section of Intelligence known as the *barbouzes*, he had immunity from prosecution as the largest heroin dealer in France.

Vic had drained her champagne and was ready for a refill. Cestari motioned to the waiter. Over the rim of her glass, she gazed at him, seductive invitation in her eyes. He moved closer to take her hand and cradle it to his body. It did not seem that they were in a public place, but that they were alone, just the two of them. When she reached for a cigarette from her platinum initialed case, he lit it for her with a cheap Zippo, which she accepted as if it were Van Cleef and Arpels. Inhaling, then exhaling a long smokey zigzag, she kept her eyes focused on him for a long moment.

"Tell me about yourself," he said. "You are a fascinating woman. I want to know everything about you."

When she gave him the line on herself she couldn't help boasting about the unique organization of women to which she owed allegiance.

"*Merde*! I cannot believe it. Is all this not a dangerous life for a woman?"

"I've got a crew of enforcers to insure peace on my turf," she replied.

"*Merde*!" he exclaimed again, with admiration.

"We're always looking for worthy places to invest our money. We're willing to take big risks for big rewards. I'm authorized to negotiate and close. Wanna talk numbers?"

Picking up his cues, he had no reluctance to explain the operation of the truc blanc, the white stuff. It was very simple, he said. "Turkey point of origin, morphine base in TIR trucks crossing Bulgaria into Munich, pre-clearance at Customs, no problem through Germany. We await the order, then ship base to our labs in Marseille for conversion. *Et ensuite*, on to Canada and New York, generally using South America as entrepôt... "

Accelerated heartbeats raced inside her body. He was negotiating with her now on shipment, quantity, frequency, price, commitment -- he was even saying how he was expecting to deal with her exclusively. Victoria basked in a glow of satisfaction. Wait till the others heard who was calling the shots.

Cestari stared deliberately at the open neck of her gown and said, "Everything you require can be swiftly expedited. Before you leave Beirut we shall settle all the details, you and I."

Victoria welcomed the feeling of the cool, bubbly golden liquid slipping down her throat, forming warm circles in her stomach. She opened her Cartier case again and offered Cestari one of her "blond" cigarettes. He lit two and handed her one. For several moments they smoked silently together. Then he reached to draw her hand to his heart, so she could feel his quickening. "This is what you do to me," he whispered. And then he leaned over to ask what sounded like a non sequitur. "Do you know the opera *Un Ballo in Maschera*, `The Masked Ball,' by Giuseppe Verdi?"

What the hell did that have to do with the price of eggs? "Sure, by reputation. Never in the flesh."

A small bead of saliva adhered to his mouth. "How would you like to attend a very special private performance?" His eyes gleamed with lubricious expectation.

"Could this be something beyond a mere musical event you have in mind, Charles?"

He smiled. "This, I promise you, will be unlike any other version of the opera you have ever heard. It is *un bal masqué à partouze — tu comprends, ma petite?*" His hand was shaking slightly and his eyes shone with a wicked glint.

"My French may not be the greatest, but I'm game for just about anything."

"*Très bien*. I think you will not be disappointed, but very happy, *ma chérie*." Vic didn't know then that partouze was French for a sex show, an orgy.

"*À La Jeunesse Dorée*," Cestari instructed his driver as they stepped into a midnight blue Mercedes limo. A haze hung over the fertile plateau between the Lebanon and the Anti-Lebanon. An aroma of jasmine, bougainvillea and oleander permeated the air.

Cestari lit a cheroot. Staring straight ahead, puffing on his cigar without so much as a glance at her, he reached for her hand and ever so casually placed it on his bulging crotch. The shock of his immense swelling, its stiffness and bulk, brought an audible gasp from her lips, but still he went on smoking, as if oblivious to her reaction.

He was talking about taking her sightseeing. They would visit the ruins of Balbek, he said, and the casinos of Zahle, where there were so many open air restaurants situated along streams and waterfalls in the Bekaa Valley. You could get wonderful yogurt there, he said, and also lemonade and Arab pastry. This was a region of vineyards and cliffs. At the tip of the valley stood the ancient Temple of Jupiter and the site of a music festival where a famous American jazz artist was now appearing.

As he spoke, he was slowly opening the buttons on the fly of his white tuxedo pants. His erection, bare now, was absolutely enormous. The sudden eroticism of his unexpected exhibitionism overcame her. She had never met a man more detached yet more seductive.

"*Suces-moi* — suck me," he commanded, directing her face toward his engorgement.

"Your chauffeur," Victoria protested.

"It is two way glass," he said, the urgency in his voice increasing.

She bent over to take him in her mouth and he watched in silence, through clenched teeth, until they pulled up in front of the establishment called the Jeunesse Dorée.

The strains of Verdi's opera escaped from inside. At the entrance one's attention was immediately diverted from the imposing, huge central skylight to the man who stood under it, naked but for a feathered mask. Baton in hand, he was conducting a non-existent orchestra in a recording of the opera.

The sensuality of the ambiance and its assault on the senses overwhelmed her. The Jeunesse Dorée's high ceilinged interior embodied a certain Parisian decadence of the hôtel particulier in its eclectic decor of art deco, fin de siècle and neo-oriental. The Tiffany skylight and soft lamps blended to create subdued roseate lighting. A domed cage of latticed brass housed an assortment of multi-colored tropical birds. There were coromandel screens and Chinese paintings set in recessed Japanese paneling, and smoky mirrors tinted in variegated pastel hues. Near the bird cage stood three circular beds and a fish tank with flashing lights.

They were handed a pair of plumed sequined masks. As Victoria's eyes became accustomed to the light, she saw that an orgy was in progress, its participants, nude but for identical bird-like masks, copulating vigorously to the tune of Verdi's lilting music.

After they had been seated, Charles ordered her a liqueur called *Shaybah*, or "old man," that he said contained wormwood. Victoria drank, feeling her stomach burn as she watched the erotic gyrations on stage, where everything was becoming a blur of cocks, cunts, feathers and sequined asses. Cestari sat sipping Pernod without comment, both amused and aroused, but dispassionate. He was a tough customer, all right, hard as nails. She was drawn to the icy still inbuilt menace, to the chill of this man. Make me melt, she was telling him with her eyes, you're the guy who can do it for me.

She sucked on her cigarette, exhaling the fumes in gulps. Watching together and sipping cordials with exotic names in an ambiance of the forbidden was at once lascivious, tender, salacious and sweet. Charles' restraint amazed her. How the hell did he manage to stay so stiff-so cool, to make no move to enter into the action — what was it they called this, a *partouze*? Wild.

The pulsating pleasure of bulging cocks and hairy cunts, flashing lights, music and wormwood were all conspiring to make her head spin. Nothing equaled the eroticism of Cestari's fierce eyes sweeping over her, baleful and dangerous.

She wondered if he understood the significance and felt the symbolism that this ritual was binding them together. Their syndicates would meld, the two of them unite. She and he were the keys.

God, she wanted him. She felt her hand that was resting on his thigh collect heat from his body. She caught his seductive smile as he whispered, "We will go to my home now." It was a statement, not a question. "You will do everything I ask." That was more than a statement, it was practically an edict. A strange, moist warm thrill came over Victoria. How was it this man understood secret places, parts of her no one else had ever reached?

Ahead lay his villa, a near eastern confection of moorish arches, towers and balconies. A pack of ferocious sounding dogs was barking inside the iron gates. Cestari had dismissed the chauffeur and was at the wheel now himself. They drove into an underground garage that housed a powder blue Jaguar and an apple red Lamborghini.

Cestari led her upstairs to the mirrored, tufted red velvet master bedroom. His smile was a malevolent glint of gold against ivory. Wordlessly, he chose a Frank Sinatra recording, Strangers in the Night, and invited her to dance. Through open French doors they glided out to the balcony. It was very romantic. The air smelled of pine and palm. He pulled at the back of her dress and undid the zipper.

In just moments she wiggled out of her clothes and stood before him in naked glory.

"*Ah, magnifique*!" he exclaimed. She had totally forgotten she was wearing a small, amusing dinner hat, the same one she'd worn at the Black Angus with Zino. Charles removed it. "You do not need this," he said, then took out her combs and hairpins to allow her hair to fall loose to her shoulders. "Ah," he whispered, "*comme tu es belle*! Formidable! Remember, you will do anything I say."

Her arms, encircling his body, tugged at his trousers until they fell to the floor. She lay her face against his muscled chest, inhaling his odor. Then she sank to her knees and buried her face in his crotch. With deft licks of her tongue she teased his elephantine erection and felt him enlarge even more.

His eyes were glazed over with lust as he moved his pelvis back and forth, slamming his prick against the back of her throat. The Sinatra record had ended, and the silence was pierced only by the sound of the dogs barking and by Cestari's uninhibited whoops of pleasure.

It wasn't long before Victoria realized they were not two solitary lovers, but were being watched by someone. On a balcony not five hundred yards away, binoculars raised to her eyes, a woman of a certain age, dressed in a scarlet damask *djellaba*, was witnessing their erotic encounter. What a kinky, surrealistic touch, Victoria mused, to be sharing these intimate moments with a stranger.

"*Viens-y*, come." Cestari pulled her with him inside. Their footsteps were absorbed by the thick dark carpeting. His erection was pushing against her leg. He muttered, "You are like a leopard, ready to spring. Your eyes, like the sea, your warm skin, they drive me insane. But you must also understand --"

"Yes?" she said breathlessly.

"I am also a seeker of decay. I demand ceremony and obedience before I take possession of you entirely." He gripped her buttocks hungrily. "You are an extravagant feast, a caprice, *ma chère*, and you are my whore. Waiting for you creates obsession... it is necessary ... my nerves shiver for you ... you are cool, like a drug ... yet hot ... I would like to crack you open..." The gold in his smile glinted in the dim light. His eyes were shining, feverish, his tongue imbued with the odor of pomegranate and Cuban cigars and the taste of fresh vanilla.

Slowly he traced the outlines of her breasts with a slight fluttering of his tongue, till he commanded, "*Viens-y. Suces-moi*," and once again thrust his throbbing tumescence in her mouth.

Just as he asked, she would do anything he wanted, even things like *leches mon cul* -- lick my asshole. At the same time, tension was mounting. Something out of the ordinary was going to happen.

She was watching them in all the mirrored panels, a thousand erotic images of their copulating. "You like mirrors?" she whispered in his ear. "I love to fuck in front of them." Saturated with moistures and fluids of desire, she was thirsting, begging for more.

He did not reply but with his knees rammed her legs apart and heaved his body on top. Gripping her hips, he bent his legs to thrust deeper, deeper into her, and when his fingers dug into the tender flesh of her breasts, she cried out in ecstasy. There was the furiously hard slow tease, the filling with him. Then suddenly he caught her arms and twisted them behind her back.

Her mouth opened with the pain of his hold. His body was like a tank now, crushing, devouring, touching her off again and again, controlling her as no man ever had. In the knocking and thumping together and in the frenzy of sliding wetness an energy was building, until a series of small explosions dissolved the walls in her and she succumbed to the full furious passion of his power.

A voice warned her this man was dangerous enough to kill, but as she strove again and again toward apex, she was compelled to go on, no matter if this could mean her very life. She was his slave, and if he wanted her death she could not resist. He was melting her away, ripping into her core, and she was willing to die for him, to die for sex. She loved him and she hated him, but she must obey him.

"*Oui, baises-moi, encore, encore, donnes-moi, comme tu es magnifique ... encore...*" Sounds that began deep inside spiraled up through his mouth, emerging in animal utterances, sending them into passionate writhings until it hit her, a wet hot flush-rush that melted between her legs, inside and outside herself, and she heard herself cry yes yes ...

Later she smoked, languidly sucking from her slender platinum holder, staring at the narrow stream escaping from her cigarette.

"*Ma petite fleur du mal,*" Cestari murmured. His eyes, his teeth, the outline of his face and body, looked satanic, depraved, fascinating.

A propos of their impending deal, he said, "Your group will be getting the best product available, never less than 97% purity, up to 99%. You must realize that no one else can duplicate this. It is very difficult, but our chemists have spent years perfecting their art. As soon as you are ready, we will begin. We have sealed our agreement, *toi et moi.*"

"Excellent. 400 kilos a month, five year contract, with a fifteen percent discount over what you ordinarily charge."

"*Merde!*"

"Why do you say that?"

"It is a very large shipment, 400 kilos per month. This is over 5 tons per year."

"I know my metric system, darling."

"Ah, yes, and do you also know your market? You can really use this much product?"

"You bet I can. Listen, Charlie, I intend to saturate the entire eastern seaboard with this stuff. We've got captive clients already and we'll get more. I have a fabulous promotional gimmick to make heroin become practically the national pastime of the United States. We'll haul in the additional customers, don't you worry."

Victoria was elated how everything had swung her way. She had negotiated where no other LFM leader had dared. She had gotten a great price, fabulous terms. People would listen. And on top of that, there was the bonus of Charles himself. Far more than she had bargained for.

"*Ma fleur du mal*," he repeated, and Victoria smiled to herself.

She awoke the next morning full with swelling, mellifluous pleasure, warm and voluptuous. Christ almighty, that was some workout Cestari had given her.

She had finally done this and done it alone. Cestari was eating out of her hand. She felt like she belonged here in this ancient biblical land, that she had an affinity with the notorious ladies whose domain this once was — Delilah, Jezebel, the Queen of Sheba, Salome, Bathsheba. She felt particularly akin to them this morning. Maybe Charles was right, perhaps she was a flower of evil, now blossoming in native soil, planted, well-fucked. Moreover, there was something in this atmosphere that empowered a woman. That was why those old fart biblical patriarchs were so down on women, always blasting houris, harpies, harlots, hussies, harridans, whores, she-wolves, concubines, courtesans and adulteresses. Well, she knew the full range of her power now, and she was using it to the hilt. But she'd be on her guard, lest anyone guess her secret. Cestari thought he was in charge. She'd keep it that way, let him think he had the upper hand. She knew better.

When she arrived back at the hotel, an urgent message waited from Harry. Vic rushed to get back to him and they arranged a phone booth to phone booth conference.

"The shit's hitting the fan all over the place," Harry said. "Your lawyers and accountants are calling every hour on the hour. You have to come back."

"What's the problem, Harry?" Vic asked.

"What isn't the problem? The IRS is descending, I think some son of a bitch must've reported you to them, there's a small matter of your being subpoenaed to a grand jury hearing that can't wait — maybe your friend Casey can get it quashed, but there's also about a million other things — you have all these documents and notices — shit, I can't figure it all out, honey, but it sure looks like trouble. You can't trust these lawyers to handle things. They screw up, you're the one who suffers. Sometimes I think they fuck up on purpose, just to get fatter fees for straightening things out. Anyway, they're telling me you gotta get your ass back here."

"Okay, okay, all right already ..."

"You gotta come now. I don't like this IRS business or the grand jury subpoena -- there's too much crap going on -- to say nothing of your crew that needs you to run things. You gotta keep everything in line."

"Jesus, I go away on a well-earned vacation and all hell breaks loose." Victoria consulted her watch. "All right, Harry, I'll be on the next plane. Meet me at Kennedy."

CHAPTER 26

A baby on the way made all the difference. Miracle of miracles, Jack had quit gambling! The marriage was going well and they were happy together. As an expectant father Jack had become solicitous, ready to cater to Tania's every need. He sympathized with her constant morning sickness, didn't mind going out at all hours of the night to fetch kosher dill pickles, butter crunch Hagen Daz, peanut brittle, rhubarb, kippered herring and whatever else she craved, and he worried like a mother hen over her other symptoms — frequency of urination, sleepiness and fatigue, increased sensitivity, subtle mood shifts. Eagerly, he went along with her on shopping jaunts for layettes and baby furniture, and was even an enthusiastic party in plans to turn the second bedroom into a nursery. He was really looking forward to fatherhood, so much so that for the first time it seemed Jack had found something that could mean more to him than poker, gin, football pools and the track.

Tania still thought of Corrado, but to put it in perspective, what framework could such a reckless relationship ever really have occupied in her life? He was a heartbreaker and probably she'd never get over him, but she had a full life now, looking forward to motherhood and being kept busy with her usual business transactions, plus all the preparations for Balls. The renovation of the townhouse would take several months. It was likely she would give birth to both a new a child and a new business at the same time.

Funny how things had a way of working out for the best, wasn't it?

Since her return from the middle east, Victoria had scarcely had a moment to sit down to work out the full details of her exciting heroin deal, due to a host of annoying operational concerns. There were numerous facets of her borgata in need of attention, not to mention the grand jury proceedings, and last but not least, Internal Revenue was closing in.

The whole IRS thing was grossly unfair, caused by a bureaucratic fuckup which the government seemed incapable of rectifying. A decade ago, she'd filed one lousy federal return in California, then moved east. Other than this single example, all correspondence from the IRS for the past ten years had been coming from the New York Service Center in Holtsville, but suddenly for some inexplicable reason probably originating with a computer error, the IRS started sending her tax notices from Fresno, California, none of which she ever received.

Since the IRS didn't hear from her they began proceedings to put liens on her bank accounts and real property, garnishing everything in sight, making claims on anything that was nailed to the floor and then some. Deficiency judgments were coming at her left and right. She would have to fight them in court. It was a complete fiasco and it was lousing her up royally.

Trying to solve her tax problems had become a constant source of frustration — bureaucrats didn't answer phones, the mails were undependable, everything was going haywire, her business affairs were in total disarray. No matter that she hired the best accountants and tax attorneys, she still got nowhere. Everybody was incompetent and charged an arm and a leg for their dubious services. This was the thanks she got for playing it straight and filing a fucking 1040. Never again, never again.

Nor were the IRS and the grand jury her only complications. She also found that due to the activities of one of her underlings, she was under stepped up federal surveillance, hardly the ideal climate to go in and nail down the heroin. So given the circumstances, steps she would ordinarily have taken on the drug deal were currently outside the realm of the possible.

What a time for her LFM supposed allies to hit her below the belt.

At a meeting of the capos of the four families, Vic described the fabulous deal she'd made with Cestari. She told Laura, Jasmine and Tania how she'd committed to 400 kilos a month of the purest #4 white heroin available in the world over a five year period at a 15% discount. This deal wasn't merely good, it was great, so naturally she'd expected they'd love it. Amazingly, the others reacted negatively.

"400 kilos a month?" Laura repeated. "Do you realize that's more than half the present U.S. annual consumption rate?"

"Not to worry – we'll be needing even more merchandise than this," Vic predicted.

Skeptical, Laura said, "We could get stuck with a surplus, and where would we warehouse the excess?"

Jasmine said, "The price, granted, is cheaper than we're paying now, but not cheap enough for the quantity, and considering projections of what we can accomplish via other means."

"We've talked about working out a long range grand design to circumvent the Corsicans, Vic," Tania reminded.

"Right," Jasmine said. "We aren't ready for a big move yet, and if we were, Cestari wouldn't be the way to go."

"We've had several bad reports on him," Laura said. "I don't think we want to do business with him."

Shocked, Vic said, "I went ahead and made a deal with this guy — "

"You shouldn't have without consulting us," Laura said. "Furthermore, our distribution network isn't sufficiently in place to handle such large amounts."

"The market's ripe for the picking," Vic protested. "New immigrants are coming into this country in droves. New York's a welfare city, these people are crying out to be picked off. Besides which, there's a slew of middle and upper income people to whom we have access as well. These people have bucks. They'll become our clients."

"Right now we should keep a low profile, not attract federal heat," Laura explained. "This is one of those particular times when Justice has decided to showcase their talents for the public's benefit. Give it another year — "

Impatient, Vic said, "Fuck Justice. Our operation is so layered they'd never get wind of us." What the hell was wrong with these lily livers?

A system of LFM payoffs was continually being implemented; a special branch of the syndicate maintained a sizable sheet of officials being greased. Layers of insulation had been carefully worked out, with buffers linking the chain of command so that the top would always be safe from scrutiny. Ranking La Femminas were busy cultivating political influence in City Hall and friendships in police precincts, other La Femminas maintained important contacts with the bar to keep abreast of pending legislation that might prove useful in protecting and expanding the family. Indirection, insulation and high level graft enabled them to remain at a safe distance, away from the heat. They were clean, above suspicion. Why should they worry about a federal witch hunt?

"Vic, you made this deal without consulting the rest of us," Tania reminded.

"You said you wanted something like this," Vic said. "I even put a down payment on it — 60 grand, cold cash. Listen, we will virtually own the biggest heroin supply in the United States, everyone will have to come to us, I'm handing you this on a silver platter. I gave my word, and this is your attitude — "

"If you believe so strongly," Jasmine said, "by all means, honor your commitment. It's your deal."

Vic was incensed. "So they leave me holding the bag. Can you believe this?" she griped to Harry. "I say to them, you realize what a jerk you make me look like, and they go you're the one who stuck your neck out, not us. So they essentially renege. It's unfair."

"Who needs them? Do the deal yourself. Make them come crawling. They'll be sorry they didn't get involved."

"But where am I going to get this kind of cash up front, considering all the shit that's going on right now? I was counting on the others participating."

Lesser events could cause mattress wars with the male mob, for God's sake. She hadn't expected to be knifed in the back. How was she going to work this out alone and quickly? If she went back on her word she'd look like a flake.

Harry said, "The best thing you can do is bond with this Corsican, then play on his sympathies. Don't be intimidated. He's a human being who eats, drinks, pees and craps like every other normal human being. He can wait. As soon as problems here clear up, get your ass over there. Spend time with him, butter him up -- hey, the guy's a man, isn't he? Go for it."

As incredible an experience as it had been with Cestari, it nevertheless seemed that the extension of their personal relationship depended on her involvement with his product and services. Harry was right; she must get him to agree to a delay. Tracking him down abroad, she reached him by telephone.

"Charles? Hello, luv. It's me, Victoria ... I just wanted to let you know I'm on top of the situation ... I've run across a few snags, it may take me just a wee bit longer to work things out, but not to worry, in short order I should have it all together ... I'll keep you informed, *chéri* ... be talking to you soon ... I can't wait ..."

CHAPTER 27

It came as a shock to Tania to learn Jack had started betting again. The first clue was when she returned late one afternoon from a meeting with her lieutenants to find him on the phone in the bedroom with the door ajar, talking to a gambling crony.

"You can be hitting rock bottom and just five or six passes can make you well again," Jack was saying, unaware she was listening. She could see he had a dice cup in his hands. "You got a good chance, and not just an outside chance. Thirty-six possible combinations ... if the dice throw the mathematical pattern, you oughta throw craps every nine rolls, playing the percentages. .. it's that fucking seven that can make or break you, though..."

Shaking the cup, he tossed the ivories out, gathered them up and rolled again. He said, "I dropped an even thirty on that fiasco the other day. I've been losing big this round but it's gotta reverse soon ... Holy shit, like I say, everything's haywire. Think I'll go look for a good poker game... ha! Better still, the track. That's the only place you can get any real action."

At that moment Jack caught her reflection in the mirror and his mouth dropped. Abruptly, he cut the conversation and hung up. Gathering up the dice with a sheepish grin, he reached in his pocket for a cigarette and lit it, cupping the flame with yellow tobacco-stained fingers.

Shaking her head in disbelief, Tania glanced to the corner of the room, where a bunch of Jack's Turfs, old racing forms, tout sheets and material on betting systems were piled. In the time they'd been together, the stack had grown by several inches, seeming almost like a yardstick of all that had gone wrong with their relationship. She'd been so sure the baby had changed Jack, only now his conversation showed how wrong she was.

He said, "You're my wife. You could have arranged financing, but you turned your back. What was I supposed to do? I need a way to recoup. It's not my fault."

The next day he sat her down and tried to reason. "All I need is time," he begged. "Look, I'll offer you another 25% of our joint concessions, one half of my 50, if you'll pay off these debts for me."

"I can't believe how irresponsible you are," Tania shot back. "An expectant father. It blows me away."

"Shit!" he muttered under his breath. He was pacing in tight circles, taking nervous puffs on a cigarette. "You know I'm whipped. I have respiratory problems. Who knows but what I could die at any moment?" He was coughing, clutching his chest, trying to play on her sympathies. "And there you sit, refusing to help when my health is on the skids."

"You smoke too much," Tania said, going to the window and opening it. "Listen, you haven't even paid me back the money you already owe— and you have the nerve to ask for more?"

"What is this bull shit? You know the shape I'm in, yet you're hounding me like some lowlife shylock. Can't you see I'm down on my luck? It's not my fault!"

In a matter of a mere couple of weeks, Jack was a totally changed man. He was having anxiety attacks, his nerves were cracking, he couldn't sleep, some days he didn't bother to shave or eat. When she removed her money from their joint account he became incensed. "I thought we married for better or worse," he ranted. "Why are you being so shitty to me?"

If she weren't expecting a baby, it would be all over. More and more, in her mind she was reaching out to a desperate dream of Corrado, as if her fantasies were an escape hatch from real life horrors with Jack. Even though she knew her fantasies were unreal, she couldn't help it. If only Corrado were a part of her life, everything would be different. She'd tried reaching him all over the world, to no avail. If only they could be together, he could adopt the baby, it would be just like his own child. Then ...

CHAPTER 28

Victoria and Harry had learned from surveillance and wiretaps that Jack was in bigger trouble than ever before, into some very heavy shys and layoff people around the country, and owed a million dollars. Anthony Zino, Master of the Sitdown himself, arranged a deal whereby Jack's debts could be worked off while his LFM joint venture gambling and bookmaking operations continued to run and pay off. The mob would take Jack's cut. The vigorish the mob was extracting bordered on extortion. In addition, the mob was putting its own men in to oversee operations and assure all was kosher.

"This is beyond belief," Victoria said, furious. In essence, they were losing control of their own gambling operations because of Jack's fuck up, just because he was their partner. There had to be another way. When Vic took up the matter with the others, they said they were powerless to do anything.

Laura said, "The LCN is dictating. We've no choice. They're letting us stay in business, they're continuing to provide protection. Without them, we have no operation at all."

"The mob's leaning on us," Jasmine added. "They want our balls."

Disgusted with this turn of events, Vic was thinking more than ever before about her drug deal and feeling the urgency to rid herself of obstacles to get on target as soon as possible. So many things were hanging in the air, so many nuisances remained unsolved. She began thinking about Anthony Zino as a possible facilitating factor.

Since the corned beef caper, he'd been tough to reach by phone because the snotty switchboard operators at the San Carlos sometimes wouldn't put her calls through. She'd pitched Zino any number of potential business endeavors, but aside from Hudson County loansharking, nothing had come together. Either he wanted an arm and a leg for his cooperation or simply wasn't interested in her proposals. In fact, Zino and she had not had a face to face meeting since the Angus lunch. Due to those unfortunate circumstances, he'd probably branded her unfuckable, then filed her away in his mental wastebasket. Harry was right. If only they'd gotten a sex thing going it would be a totally different story. But maybe there was still a chance of it clicking. Still, no harm approaching him on the dope. He just might go for it. Although she felt on weak grounds, she nevertheless had to take the risk.

At noon on a sunny day in midtown Manhattan, Vic approached the sidewalk, as Zino, assisted by his driver, exited his Lincoln Town Car in front of the Bull & Bear. Ignoring his ever present punks, she cornered him, prepared to make her play. Zino squinted and fastened his gaze ahead, apparently not even recognizing her, the bum. Maybe it was his nearsightedness — she knew he was too vain to wear glasses and was allergic to contact lenses.

"Remember me, Tony?" she smiled, assuming a provocative stance, leaning one hip outward, her hand poised on her toosh.

"Oh, yeah — the chick from the Angus. The gal with the hat." He displayed recognition with a characteristic facial mannerism, lip curling inward, baring gleaming bone white teeth. Then briefly turning to face her, he said, "Hi there."

"Don't you know my name?"

"Vicky, right?"

"Victoria, if you please. Vicky sucks."

"Sorry, Victoria. So how's it going, doll?"

With that casual remark and a nod in her direction, he was ready to head for the door, but before he could escape, Vic launched into her spiel. Coming to the heart of the matter, she said, "Listen, Tony, look at it this way, those shylocks who advanced Jack money were wrong too. They knew they had a deadbeat, but they went for it anyway. This arrangement is bad for my business, but I have a way to recoup and put the whole mess behind us. See, I've got this drug deal — I need your help — I'll cut you in..."

"Whoa! Hold it!" Zino held up his arm. "I don't do drugs. *Capisa*?"

Although he looked annoyed, she persisted. "That's what all you LCN guys — youse guys — say. But you all take your cuts, sub rosa. Ok, my pipeline's opening, I've cornered great supply, my product and people are the best. I had nothing to do with this whole Jack fuckup. Don't take it out on me."

"Listen, my ass is on the line with that dick. I vouched for the sonofabitch."

"Who talked you into it? Jasmine? Blame her. Listen, Tony, with this deal of mine, Jack's debts can be paid off easily, with plenty to spare. All I need is cooperation, protection, routing services — "

"Not from me, baby. I keep the hell away from felony crimes."

"Ok, have it your way. You don't do drugs. You stay in the background, let me do the work, and you clip coupons." She stepped in closer, so close her tits were practically in his face, as her tone became confidential. "I'll take the risks and give you the profits. You don't know about it. All you know is money in your Swiss account. Think about it."

"Let's go, Tone. People waiting." One of his bodyguards was making a motion toward the door.

"Yeah, right — gotta split now." He nodded goodbye and with a puzzled look, escaped into the restaurant. Vic smiled to herself. So let him mull it over. She was handing him a great deal, and sooner or later he'd realize what she had to offer. Not to worry, she'd get the sonofabitch where she wanted him yet.

CHAPTER 29

Jack came home choking, trying to catch his breath, clutching his chest. He said, "I'm beat. I'll be brief. I'm in trouble, on my ass. I need money." He held up his arm to silence Tania's objections. "No recriminations, please. You've been acting like I'm some kind of thief, your own husband. This whole trouble started when the fucking bookie in K.C. screwed me, but never mind — I think I've found a solution — "

"I don't want to hear this, Jack," Tania said, as if tuning him out could cancel reality.

Jack persisted. He confessed that despite the Zino-engineered arrangement to pay off his debts, troubles had escalated to the point that something even more drastic was in order. This time, however, he was ready with collateral in exchange for cooperation. He said, "I just remembered I have something that can save my life and make yours along with it. I don't know why I didn't remember sooner. Honey, this paper is your ticket to millions, billions. I'm willing to turn over this valuable item in exchange for getting bailed."

"What is this paper?" Tania asked, immediately suspicious.

"A company whose assets are in mortgages and gambling licenses in the Caribbean. A guy welched on a debt and I took this in lieu of payment. This goes back a couple of years."

"Where's it located?"

"Sapphire Bay. Fantastic location. The mob would love to get hold of it. You and your wise gal pals could develop it into an incredible offshore situation. And with my expertise to help draw customers, run the junkets — "

"How come you have it just sitting around?"

"I won it in a poker game from a guy in the paw paw business in Barbados, put it in a drawer and forgot it till now. Then suddenly I thought eureka, this paper can turn things around."

"How do we know it's for real? The guy could have been a con artist."

"I checked it out. You're welcome to verify for yourself. Be my guest."

The company came with a certificate of exemption from the governor of the island entitling it to some gambling licenses; however, it turned out there had been problems over improper land surveys, a key document had been stolen and destroyed as part of a conspiracy.

"Not a problem." Jasmine, delighted at the thought of a potential casino opportunity, waved objections aside. She'd been looking for something like this since Dove's enviable Aruba deal with the Prince of the Netherlands. "With Lucille's help we create a fake deed, take Jack's xerox copy, from which we create an original — and with a few bribes we get a recertification."

Further investigation revealed there might be additional troubles. The company had lent money in stock promotion deals over which a scandal developed, because the loans were illegal in Florida. The company's assets were then put on the auction block, a shell belonging to the same owners bought them and rented the facilities back to the original entity, now restructured and renamed. The company then bought up several hundred acres of land to develop, but due to a liquidity crisis was now strapped for its mortgage payments.

"The land and leases are going to be confiscated unless we step in, iron out the kinks and take over. It's very promising, because all we'll need to start moving after this will be construction money."

So many question marks. Vic said they should pass. Jack's "collateral" shouldn't be dignified with that name. What good was it if it had no cash value, had nothing but liens and encumbrances? How could this be called an asset? It was a liability, for God's sake, illiquid bullshit at best, not worth the paper it was written on. Why even give this stuff attention?

"We can make something out of it."

"A silk purse out of a sow's ear? After pumping in countless millions, maybe."

"This is an opportunity we may never see again."

"Opportunity? We have to nail down financing to the tune of eight figures, it doesn't solve Jack's immediate problems and it only adds to ours."

"The unions will eat this up." The ever-stubborn Jasmine was resolute.

To sweeten the pot, Jack would turn over a piece of Nevada real estate with a resale value three times its original cost. Prime Vegas land. "Look," he said, "this land is worth conservatively in the area of eight hundred grand. People out in Nevada are looking for a spot like this to put up a fronton and would pay through the roof to get it."

"Jack keeps coming up with these schemes," Vic said, "and they keep getting more off the wall." An initial investment would be needed to start the ball rolling, money that could be going to support her heroin project. And her stuff was real, not pie in the sky.

"Vic, you know we're between a rock and a hard place," Jasmine said. "We have to get control of our concessions back, and we have to find a way to pay back Jack's debts."

"Long term capital investments are hardly the way to do either one. On the other hand, a drug deal pays off in a matter of a few weeks."

"Casinos offer great opportunities, what with the skim. A casino's the goose that laid the golden egg."

"Let me repeat: there's no short term liquidity here to take care of the pressing issue of debts."

"No problem. We'll get that million plus for Jack. We'll work it out."

"Why casinos now? Why not get an expanded drug scene moving, bring in quick, steady cash with a minimum of bookkeeping and accounting, instead of a long range investment and the headaches that go with casinos? There's a lot of legalities en route to the skim. Aren't we doing things ass-backwards?"

"Jack is offering us something we may never see again. The Vegas land is real; Sapphire Bay is bona fide. We have numerous loan channels, special situations where all you have to do is show the right balance sheet."

"And how do we do that?"

"You know how — inflated paper, rented collateral, straw borrowing, compensating balances and nominee loans, financial legerdemain, hocus pocus and various other means we're all acquainted with."

"So we have this alleged license — where does our initial financing come from?" Victoria challenged.

"A mere ten grand apiece, plus we use our ICC investments."

"That's a shell. It owns no assets."

"It'll look healthy when we get finished doctoring it up. We use it to get swing money. We take both of Jack's collateral and keep them, we don't resell. We put a package together and pitch it to the Teamsters."

Jack swore up and down he owned the Vegas land. But when the lawyers looked at it, the paper on it proved elusive.

Carole said, "Jack didn't read this right. It's only an option, not outright ownership. We have to clear up title, and for that we need another big cash outlay."

"How long is the option good for?"

"A couple of more months, is all."

"That's not much time. We have to move fast, square off Jack's debts, move on the Vegas situation, and also make the Caribbean thing a go."

"It's a big order."

"We can do it," Jasmine said. "Believe me, we can bring it off."

"Once again," Vic asked, now close to the end of her patience, "where do we get the million plus for Jack's debts quickly, then after that the money to pay off the option, and following that, how can we be certain of the financing to develop these projects? And while we're at it, what about Second General, the deal we were discussing at the summit in Beirut? Wasn't that supposed to be a fund we could borrow from?"

Laura explained, "Second General isn't in working order yet."

"We need forty thousand immediately," Tania said. "This will take care of obtaining swing money, which in turn will go toward payoffs, upfront fees, bribes to the right sources, and so forth."

"So we're asking for ten grand earnest money from each investor for a piece of the action," Jasmine said. "Each Four Family head will kick in for one unit. Are you with us, Vic?"

"I'll have to think about it," Victoria said, sulking.

Counterfeit securities and bogus loans would be used to float the swing money. They had a Caribbean connection, Shirley Bennett, whose family owned a troubled Bahamas bank that would honor the bogus paper in exchange for the forty thousand in cash under the table, then lend the swing money to advance to a brokerage house, which in turn would enable them to assume heavy up front costs to get the deal moving. Meantime, the exact method of taking care of Jack's debts remained to be solved; a modus operandi would be announced in another few days.

They were going to do this flakey casino deal, and close out her heroin situation? Unbelievable.

"Why?" Victoria asked, incredulous. "The money you're putting into this could cover my dope deal. I don't get it."

"Do you want in or not?"

Vic hesitated. Were they trying to set her up? Like she said, she'd have to think about it.

CHAPTER 30

"They want me to ransom my fucking soul to get money for Jack's cockamamie casino bullshit," she told Harry, "and the hell with my losing credibility with Cestari. I could cough up the lousy ten grand even with the IRS on my tail, it's not that. I have no faith in this project. Forty grand to pay up front fees — it's a rip off ... that kind of bread's always grabbed by the lawyers and accountants and greedy officials standing in line with their hands out ... you could lose it all on a b.s. deal like this. Besides, there's more than one deal, and none of it sounds kosher. Who needs it?"

The more she thought about it, the more Victoria was convinced she had a gripe serious enough to convene a meeting of the La Femmina Mafia National Commission. It was better to work things out before grievances accelerated to a point of no return, where maybe only a mattress war would be the radical solution. New York's Four Families had lived in peace up until now. Anyway, she had her interests to protect. So she lodged her complaint that the others were dissing her by giving favored treatment to Jack, an outsider, and that due to callous disregard of her concerns, her carefully nurtured reputation was at stake.

The *udienza*, or formal sitdown of top LFM bosses across the country, convened in a private room at the Peking, a fashionable Chinese restaurant downtown. As Vic approached the Peking's gleaming blue vitriolite facade, she could hear the click of backgammon pieces on inlaid tables inside. She liked this place: the decor was all Chinese silk scroll paintings and handcarved screens, Ming porcelain and priceless K'ang Hs and Ch'ien Lung porcelain. She was ready to state her position.

Mafia ladies present, in addition to New York's Four Families' capos, included Philadelphia's Candace Hastings, Susan Goldman of Los Angeles, Kathy Sanford, and Ayla Kalkavan.

"If it's risk you want, throwing craps in Vegas gives better odds," Victoria said, mixing chicken with garlic sauce along with shrimp with pea pods, "even with the vig involved, compared to this casino deal. On the other hand, my drug deal is risk-free and solid."

"Jack's offering us something solid too," Jasmine said.

"What's solid about a slip of paper that requires millions pumped in, that may or may not be worth the ink it's written with?" Vic reached to pour herself another cup of green tea.

"Potentially the value is a fortune, once we get it going."

"If we can get rid of the problems. If, if — if my aunt had balls she'd be my uncle."

Jasmine persisted. "Casinos might be long term," she admitted, tossing Chinese vegetables with her chop sticks, "but the deal is totally legitimate, a great way to launder money, we can get loans to finance it and create a gold mine."

Annoyed, Vic pushed her food aside and reached for a cigarette, lighting it with a Tiffany lighter and clicking shut the silver case with impatience. If they could put together the Jack deal, they could do hers, goddamnit. Why was this guy receiving favored treatment?

She said, "Let's get one thing straight: Jack is not one of us. All of us here are made women, owing allegiance to this thing of ours. Each one has taken her vows, made her bones. We owe each other, but we don't owe outsiders. This is my complaint."

Laura said, "Jack's expertise sent a lot of cash our way... If it weren't for his initial push, our organization might not have gotten off the ground."

"Bull shit," Vic retorted. "If you help one guy, you establish a policy. We don't take men in our club, ladies, remember? Men, bless their little black hearts, are subordinates. Every woman in this room has a guy in the background, where he belongs. But staking him if he fucks up is tacky, it's casting couch mentality, reverse discrimination."

Fragile, Meissen-eyed Candace Hastings' thick chestnut hair swirled forward to frame her face, enhancing her madonna quality. Thick brows, doe eyes and a beguiling raspberry mouth added to the coltish charm of her appearance. She looked ravishing tonight. "You have a point," Candace said, biting into a sweet and sour spare rib. "This is an organization of women."

"Can't we look at this not as helping somebody," Jasmine said, "but simply as a good business proposition?"

"Right," Tania chimed in, "this is an independent deal. The two situations we're discussing should be separate, Jack's collateral and Vic's narcotics."

"I disagree," Vic said, "If the money wasn't going for Jack's collateral, it could be freed up for my drug deal. I'm being thwarted because of Jack's problems."

Cool green eyes level behind brown-tinted glasses, Susan Goldman declared, "I agree that the two situations should be separate, not linked. The organization shouldn't be responsible for Jack's debts, per se; if Laura, Jasmine and Tania want to get involved in his collateral, that's a personal decision, having nothing to do with whether they will or won't invest in Vic's deal. However, there should be a way to resolve both things."

Susan removed a slim cigarette case from her Fortnum and Mason bag and leaned back. A tight fitting body-sculpting purple dress showed off her slender, well-defined frame to advantage. The soignée Susan's face was open and chiseled. Ash blond, discretely frosted, she was a bold measure of sensuality and charm.

Ayla Kalkavan contemplated her pan fried noodles and concurred, along with Candace and Katherine Sanford, a petite young woman with expressive indigo eyes and bronze colored hair who headed LFM upstate New York operations.

Kathy said, "It appears that Laura, Jasmine and Tania may have given the impression, however unintended, that they'd be interested in a narcotics deal at a cheaper price, and Vic did come through with that, although the terms may be off base. Inasmuch as Laura, Jasmine and Tania didn't give Vic carte blanche to negotiate terms, my suggestion is why don't we all put our heads together, try to work out alternatives that everybody can live with. Then Vic can go back to her man in Beirut, and see if they can make an alternative deal."

Candace wanted more details on how money would be spent to develop Jack's collateral.

Tania said, "We pitch the package to the Teamsters Central States Pension Fund to get construction money for both Sapphire Bay and Las Vegas. A gambling license in Nevada requires depositing a million with the Gaming Commission. On Sapphire Bay, we have to pay off the option, clear title, and allow for bribes to judges and politicians. This we have to front ourselves."

"Other than the Teamsters, the brokerage house and the Bahamas bank, how do you figure on obtaining additional financing?" Susan asked. "For instance, how will you raise the million for Jack's debt?"

"We take counterfeit paper abroad," Jasmine said. "We get 10-40% of face value, depending on what the market will bear at the time. It's the quickest thing we can do without hasty liquidations."

Laura said, "This will clear us up with the male mob, they'll be off our backs, and we'll have complete control again."

"So all in all," Jasmine said, "we'll need three to four million, as soon as possible. And we're confident there won't be a problem getting the financing we need."

Believing it was totally meshuggeh, Vic had talked herself out of Jack's Caribbean casino situation. But now, according to wiretaps and surveillance, it looked like the deal might be a lot more realizable than she'd thought.

Jasmine was overheard saying, "We agreed to assume Jack's debt in exchange for the collateral. I knew that collateral was golden. Already we've had great response. The Teamsters pension board meets at the end of the month, and we shouldn't have any trouble getting this initial loan. It's in the bag."

It appeared Zino was hot for the deal and it was his say so that was going to sell the Teamsters. Either Vic would have to get herself reinstated with the other La Femminas, or else plant doubts in Zino's mind, or better yet, both, and thus hedge her bets.

Another time on the wiretap, Jasmine assured Tania, "Zino says we'll absolutely have the money as soon as the board meets. The Teamsters are in the midst of legal problems, but Zino's man sits on the pension board, and he guarantees the loan will come through."

Harry advised Vic, "Cover your ass. Get yourself reinstated."

"How?"

"Tell them the check's in the mail. It got lost. You sent it in good faith. They'll have to let you in again — just in case the deal flies."

"Well, I did actually more or less hedge. I didn't say no, I didn't give my final word. So I could bend things."

"At the same time, you gotta try and get the deal put permanently on ice. When Zino talks to the unions they listen. He could get it killed — killed or done. So you gotta give him a push."

"Yeah, sure — but how?"

"If only you hadn't gotten your period at that Angus lunch," Harry lamented. "Shit, it was all set up, it was perfect."

"I know. It was a goddamn jinx. Not for nothing do they call it the curse. Now what?"

"Well, no use moping over past errors. Like I say, you just gotta get the SOB in bed, via whatever means possible. It's a sexual bottom line and it's urgent now."

"I'm game, Harry, but you know the problem is the asshole doesn't know what he's missing. How to wake him up?"

"He has to be put in a position where he can't refuse. We'll have to come up with something — Listen, I may have an idea."

CHAPTER 31

"You're sure this device works, Harry?" Vic was apprehensive as they attempted to tail Zino's Town Car on the New York State Throughway. They'd lost sight of him at the toll booth, but Harry insisted there was no cause for concern. He'd planted a beeper device on Zino's car, so if it disappeared in traffic they'd be able to locate it again within a ten mile radius.

He was right. Just a couple of minutes later they sighted the Town Car once again. Zino was heading north with his two sidekicks Al "Sugar" Zucchero and Fred "Red Eye" Barbi, as well as his billiard ball-headed mob attorney Duke Poulter, with driver Ronnie Vasco at the wheel.

"Where do you suppose they're headed, Harry?"

"My guess is the Catskills."

"The Catskills? That's a Jew joint."

"Everybody thinks of the Catskills in that manner, but the guineas have their spots there too."

"Really? I didn't know that."

Harry was right. The Town Car pulled into a fancy greaseball hostelry in the town of Wurtzboro called the O Sole Mio, Harry following immediately behind. Three smartly uniformed attendants jumped to attention under a gilt-edged porte-cochere. Ronnie Vasco turned the Town Car over to the hotel staff as Zino and his cronies exited.

"*Volare, Oooo Oooo! Cantare, Ooooo! Oooo! Nel blu, dipinto di blu, Felice di stare qua su*!" The sounds of Jerry Vale blared over loudspeakers. This was Zino's kinda place. The plan was for Vic to lay low and keep her fingers crossed that the fellas hadn't hired hookers for the weekend. So she and Harry surveyed the scene from a corner luncheon table. The restaurant walls were painted with murals depicting tourist attractions in Italy, the leaning tower of Pisa, the Colosseum and St. Peter's, Vesuvius, Michelangelo's David, Venetian gondolas, and so forth.

The establishment catered to a typically low class element, pot bellied plumbing and heating type males decked out in gold lavalieres sporting pinkie rings with shirts open to the sternum, and wives — well, forget the wives. These were all second and third generation Americans whose families had immigrated from southern Italy — Sicily, Naples and Calabria — good natured mangia mangia types. You heard a predominance of New York accents, Queens, Bronx and Brooklynese. The decor was flashy, the food fabulous — the chef's mamma mia spaghetti *alla putanesca* almost as good as Harry's.

Vic, in cognito in a long, corkscrew curled platinum blond wig, sunglasses and huge picture hat, was dressed in black from head to toe. She'd bought Harry some new duds for the occasion and together with recent expensive hairstyling and some long-needed reconstructive dental work, he was looking better than ever. No one would ever suspect that concealed in a shoulder holster under his snappy navy silk linen Armani blazer he packed a Colt Cobra Chief Special. Carefully, they surveiled Zino and crew from across the room. All the waiters were bowing and scraping. Zino was a hero in this place.

The grinning, glabrous-headed Duke Poulter was your typical Foley Square $2000 suit/gold Rolex watch type with a St. Regis barbershop shave and year round indoor tan. Driver Ronnie Vasco, a retired auto mechanic, was beefy, beetle-browed and simian eyed with a flattened nose. Despite a wardrobe of fancy clothes — shantung initialed shirts and silk designer trousers — he still exuded the aura of a cheap punk.

Fred Barbi lumbered over from the bar to join the Zino table. He was short, burly and barrel chested with a granite head and a penchant for guinea stinkers. Once a bit player in Italian films, the acromegele-faced Barbi's credits included featured player with such Hollywood on the Tiber stars as Guy Madison, Fay Spain, Steve Reeves, Lex Barker and Jack Palance. He was a eunuch in "Sappho, Venus of Lesbos," starring Tina Louise, and also appeared with Elke Sommer in "The Girls of Parioli;" other outstanding Hollywood-on-the-Tiber successes included "Barabas, Friend of Jesus," "The Pillars of Hercules," and "Hercules and the Rape of the Sabine Women." His biggest ambition was to produce a film on Lucky Luciano, his hero.

Like his mentor, the hollow-eyed, grimy Al "Sugar" Zucchero was born over an East Harlem sausage kitchen. Dark and swarthy with a face faintly flecked with pock marks, Sugar's claim to fame was having known Three-Finger Brown. A former Golden Gloves boxer-turned-bouncer in a Greenwich Village dive, he now held down a no-show job in sanitation and one in construction, and served as a race track tout as well.

Sporting a freshly brilliantined haircut, Zino was looking slick and fit, his appearance today being that of a man who had recently emerged from several hours in an herbal wrap, followed by a long session in his Turkish bath.

Later that afternoon when Sugar, Al, Ronnie and Duke were watching a ballgame in the lounge and Al was grumbling that his favorite player, Pee Wee Reese, never made Hall of Fame, Vic and Harry decided it was time to move in on Zino, who had retired alone to his cabin. Vic doffed her disguise then, and Harry locked her stuff in the trunk of the car, along with the gun collection he kept stored there in a heisted Gucci suitcase: his Kalashnikov and .9mm Parabellum, the Uzi, the Thompson submachine gun and the AK-47 assault rifle.

When Vic knocked on the cabin door, Zino answered "Yeah?" and opened it right away. A swift expression of distrust swept across his face, despite the snarling smile that bared teeth on one side of his mouth. "Whadda ya want?" he demanded in his deep gruff voice in a tone that was intimidating.

"I want your body," Vic said, leaning against the wall in a seductive pose. "Remember me?"

"Yeah. The chick from the Angus, the one with the hat. How's the drug scene goin' these days, Vicky?"

"I told you, Victoria. Aren't you going to invite me in?" she inquired demurely.

"Well — yeah, ok," he muttered under his breath, more puzzled than anything. As he admitted her, Vic noticed the rooster tattoo on his hand again.

She said, "By the way, Tony, your tattoo reminds me of a joke I heard recently. Why doesn't the rooster need underpants?"

"You got me. Why doesn't the rooster need underpants?"

"Because his pecker's on his face."

"Hey. I'll have to remember that one."

"While we're on the subject of peckers — you got away from me after the Angus lunch," she began, "and we haven't had a chance to bond since then. I've never had the opportunity to thank you or tell you that I've wanted you so much, Tony, you can't imagine how much. I've been thinking of you night and day, day and night."

"Yeah?" The curled lip and sharp, craggy wolfen teeth gave a predatory cast to his baneful, dark-complected face. He turned the radio on to his kind of music — Tony Bennett, Vic Damone, Nat King Cole — and they danced in a sweet, old fashioned prelude to fucking. Surprisingly, he was actually a romantic kind of guy.

Vic laid it on the line regarding her mission. "You don't want Sapphire Bay, you don't want Las Vegas, you do want me," she said, winding her arms around his neck and rubbing her pelvis against his pants. He responded by swiveling his hips and grinding into her. Good. Already his protruding erection was sticking way out several inches. Rubbing into him with her chest, Vic said, "Honey, do you have any idea how those Caribbean people can rip you off and produce zip in return?"

"I thought the upfront costs were minimal and accounted for," he said, swaying to the soft ballad.

"Are you kidding? Who can deal with these Caribbean crooks? Unless you're Lansky, maybe, and even so you have to be ready with a very big suitcase for the smallest favor, just like Lansky did with Sir Stafford Sands. But that was Paradise Island — and Meyer Lansky has his ways — "

"Good man."

"He's a role model for me too."

She flicked her tongue in his ear, and in a throaty voice continued, "There's a very big question whether they can deliver and if Jack has what he says."

"He's got the license. I seen it."

"Yeah, but you know these people, these Caribbean types -- *schwartzes* -- " She made a face. "What does their word mean? Besides, there's a lot of political unrest in that region, racial tension and all. The situation is volatile and unpredictable."

"I thought the joint was safe."

"It's not what it's cracked up to be. Take a closer look, Tony. I'm surprised. I thought you were a man who did his homework."

"I asked around. The reports were good."

"How knowledgeable were the sources you used, and what axe did they have to grind? Look, flakes are always trying to promote something like this. But Jack — God, he is off the wall."

"Yeah, he's pretty wild."

"It's not even worth dwelling on, it's so ridiculous. Let's change the subject to something more pleasant. Would you like to fuck me?" She grabbed for his crotch, and caught him staring deliberately at the open neck of her blouse. "Because I'd like to fuck you."

He considered a moment before a slow smile spread over his face. "Yeah," he said, almost in a why not tone. Meanwhile, his erection was practically prying his zipper open.

He was uncharacteristically timid, strangely enough, letting her take the initiative all the way. Funny, wasn't it, when these guys thought they were in charge they came on like gangbusters, steam-rolled you into the sack, and when you were calling the shots, it really put them on the spot. God, were they vulnerable and insecure. Well, they did have that added problem of erective potency to contend with -- but she could always take care of that. Didn't even need the Pega Palo Georgia had finally brought back from the last Dominican gold jaunt. She was saving that for another time, just letting this ice-breaking first fuck fly on its own natural steam.

Legend had it Anthony Z was well-hung and a great stud, and to give credit where credit was due, the reputation was deserved. The guy was exceptionally well-endowed, his dick being everything it was cracked up to be and more; in fact, if the truth be told, Anthony Zino was built like Hebrew National, added to which he had amazing endurance, so much so that the next morning Vic was totally fucked out and suffering from a sore cunt. Mission accomplished. She'd cemented the tie, gotten him to reconsider on the Teamsters, and generally speaking, pretty much had the guy by the balls.

She reported back to Harry. "He's definitely wary of the Sapphire Bay situation. I made sure of that."

"Great, hon. I knew you could turn him. How about the drugs?"

"He's resisting. Still claims he doesn't want to be involved, but just give me a little longer, he'll come around."

"How about the sex end of things? How'd that all go?"

Harry wanted a blow by blow description. Vic gave it to him. She said, "You could best describe his schlong as inordinately heavy and fat; basically, I'd label it a thick prick."

"Yeah? How big?"

"Fully erected? Nothing to sneeze at. I'm not claiming never to have seen a bigger cock in my day; but since truly outsized cocks are gross, thus a male sexual organ must land within certain aesthetic parameters, and Zino's falls right on the cutting edge. You know I've long contended that the only part of the male human anatomy that should be fat is his cock, Harry, so to sum up, Zino could actually probably win a few prizes if he ever went into competition."

"Tell me more."

She could see Harry was turned on, to say nothing of jealous. Ah, the male ego always wondering — how do I compare?

Continuing with her synopsis of the successful encounter at Wurtzboro, Vic said, "By the way, he likes my head."

"Which one?" Harry asked. "The head you give, or the one between your shoulders?"

"Actually, both. But in this particular instance, I was referring to my mind, my intellect and imagination. He digs that. Thinks I'm highly inventive."

"You are, baby, you are. We both know that."

"Anyway, Harry, to summarize: operation successful. Jasmine and Zino are yesterday's newspaper, and I'm the one in the driver's seat with Zino now," Vic declared.

CHAPTER 32

Vic, Harry, and her closest associates were discussing how they'd go about organizing the heroin situation from here on in.

"How much do we need in all?" Georgia asked.

"Two hundred grand for openers," Vic said, "followed by another payment of half a mil, and after that, even more, to make it on the scale I negotiated."

"Can't we cut the order down to a smaller size, depending on how much we can scrape together now?" the Cow wanted to know.

"My credibility would suffer if we made too big an adjustment. I'm still waiting to hear from the National Commission — we're trying to reach a compromise, and it hasn't been settled yet."

"How about using that as an excuse to delay Cestari?" Georgia suggested. "That and Internal Revenue. You have all the papers as proof."

"Sure, blame it on fucking Uncle."

"Maybe," Vic conceded, "if worse came to worst. But I'd sure hate to."

Harry said, "The question is how much longer the guy's gonna be patient."

"Yeah, " Vic explained, "I have to get my ass on over there to Cestari as soon as possible. I just don't feel I can put this off much longer. We have to make a move soon."

Vic had tried her best to get Zino to arrange clearances at the airport for her narcotics, but he was still reluctant to cooperate, saying he was under heavy government surveillance and couldn't take the risk. Also, although thanks to her negative sales pitch he'd lost enthusiasm for Jack's gambling deals, he hadn't definitively told the Teamsters to shine it on. Their sexual affair continued in a surprisingly desultory manner; on the one hand he seemed interested when she assumed an aggressive approach, but took little initiative on his own. She had the gnawing feeling he could take it or leave it.

Then, to add insult to injury, it seemed he was turning his back on her. What was this guy's problem? Then she got a clue. Harry said, "I don't want to scare you, honey, but my prick is dribbling... It sure seems inflamed, and it's sore as hell."

"Oh, God. Don't tell me." Crabs? Clap? Herpes? Syph? What the fuck could it be?

"I gotta go to the doctor and find out."

It wasn't till after Harry mentioned it that Vic discovered similar symptoms in herself. Sure enough, fucking gonorrhea, and on top of it a yeast infection to boot. "Christ," she said, "how the hell did this happen? I never got anything before in my life. I've never had monilia, trichomonas or even candida, for God's sake."

"Amazing, with the amount of action that cunt's seen."

Who gave this venereal infection to whom, Vic wanted to know. Could Jasmine have given it to Tony, who gave it to her, and she gave it to Harry? Or could Harry have given it to her (from whom?) and the round robin went in that direction? At any rate, the damned clap probably explained the rupture. She'd have to get it smoothed over with Zino to keep him on her side.

She found him at the Round Table at his customary corner spot with his punks, who wandered away to let them talk. Vic said, "I swear I didn't give you that fucking social disease. It wasn't me." Zino just looked disgusted.

"Don't blame me for something I didn't do," she persisted. "It was an unfortunate incident that could happen to anybody, and it happened to me too, don't forget. Christ on the fucking cross, you could be the one that dosed me, for God's sake — in fact, how do I know you didn't?"

Finally he came around. "Ok," he acknowledged. "We'll call it a draw."

CHAPTER 33

The swing money was late. It was supposed to be deposited by a certain date but wasn't. When Tania phoned the Bahamas and spoke to Shirley Bennett, the banker, Shirley said, "Didn't you get my message? Don't panic. The money will be there in another 48 hours. All is well."

But two business days passed and the money still wasn't in. Again Tania phoned Shirley, only this time she couldn't get through and Shirley wasn't returning her calls either.

"It looks like another phony bites the dust," Tania told the others. "We'll have to tap a different source or lose the deal."

"Where do we come up with a couple of million in cash quick?"

"Not here. The only way is counterfeit paper abroad."

"Right. We counterfeit the entire thing," Jasmine said. "Call Lucille in New Orleans and tell her to hightail it to New York on the double."

"We can do bank notes," Laura said. "Lucille is great on that vehicle. Nobody ever knows her CUSIP numbers are fake."

"Sure, bank notes can be discounted and they pay 7 per cent interest besides. Bank notes are preferable to currency," Tania agreed.

"No," Jasmine objected, "there isn't enough time for bank notes. They take more preparation. We have to research the CUSIPs so there's no foul up and nobody gets suspicious. There's a rush on this, so currency's the way to go."

At last the Cow had given Vic a clean bill of health, her plumbing was back in working order, thank God; she was ready for action again. Legal and other business complications that had been holding her up were being worked out, a deal had been struck with the IRS which should be available for her signature in just a few days, she'd paid off a few judges and LEO's, and things were calming down for the time being. It wouldn't be much longer before she'd be able to get together with Cestari again. Meantime, once and for all she wanted to make sure Zino's Teamster connections would definitely renege on getting the construction loan. With the casino distraction behind them, the LFMs would be able to devote full energies to her interests, then they'd begin full scale narcotics expansion in earnest.

When Georgia brought back the Pega Palo, Vic gave some to Harry as a trial. He couldn't believe the stuff. It gave him a hard on he couldn't get rid of the entire weekend and caused him to lose twelve pounds.

"What the hell did you do to me?" he asked. "Fuck! Jesus H. Christ!" So the stuff definitely worked like a charm. Now all she had to do was give some to Zino to raise his level of excitement to a proper pitch. He'd soon forget the bad taste in his mouth from the social disease; then she'd finalize her plans.

Cornering him at the Mannequin, she laid her bait. "I have something that'll blow your friggin' mind," she told him.

"Yeah, what's that?"

"Pega Palo." She held up a small bottle of clear liquid that had a peculiar-looking pale brown root with long silky tentacles swimming in it. "It's the hottest item in town and I am the only woman who has it."

"Never heard of it. What is it?"

"A concoction to be obtained in only one country in the world, the Dominican Republic, that can make a guy incredibly hard and give him amazing endurance."

Zino shrugged, unimpressed. "I already got all that."

"I know, sweetheart, but this'll improve on the existing, believe me. One shot mixed with alcohol and a guy can fuck without quitting for days. The last guy I used this with lost fifteen pounds balling me, with a non-stop erection over a five day weekend. Sonovabitch not only wouldn't but couldn't quit."

"Doll, in my case this is never a problem."

"Pega Palo makes a weasel into a stallion." She rotated the bottle in her hand enticingly. "Not only that, the kick is fantastic."

"Yeah?" He started to look interested. "Well, you got a real record to beat — like seventeen times a night."

"I'm from Missouri. Prove it."

"At the right time maybe I will."

"How about now?"

"This minute?"

"Why not? Got anything more important to do than exercise your dick muscles?"

"I guess not," he conceded, and requested the check.

His driver dropped them at the Woodward. "So you once fucked somebody seventeen times a night. Wanna try for eighteen or twenty?" Vic asked, as they were riding up in the elevator to the penthouse. At the built-in bar in the den she took out the small Pega Palo bottle containing the clear liquid and strange-looking root with spiny tentacles swimming in it. She mixed him his favorite Early Times straight up spiked with a strong dose of the potent solution, then turned the radio on to his favorite music, and they danced cheek to cheek on the wrap-around terrace, the way he liked before sex.

"Tell me how this stuff works," Zino said, "because I think I'm starting to feel something already."

"It causes blood to pump several times faster than normal to the cock."

"You're sure it isn't dangerous? Nothing's gonna happen?"

"Hell, no. It's purely a local phenomenon, like a natural aphrodisiac, with incredible pleasure sensations."

In a half hour's time, Zino really started to feel his oats. He became a tiger, throwing her down on the circular bed and tearing at her clothes. The fish tank with its flashing neon lights made eerie patterns on his face, giving a diabolical cast to his mouth and teeth. Who could even tell how much time passed while they were in bed. Vic counted. Would you believe twenty-five times, and no sign of quitting. Not bad for a guy of his age, or any age for that matter.

But then something went radically wrong. They were on the twenty-sixth fuck when Zino's heart must have balked or something. Maybe the strain was too great. Maybe he needed a pacemaker and hadn't had it installed in time. Maybe it was his age, after all. At any rate, he suddenly clutched his chest and in a loud voice bellowed, "Ahhwwgghh!" His torso buckled, and his cock twisted right out of her — she'd been about to come, dammit all — and then he lay silent, apparently having passed out cold. But his cock was still hard as a rock and fully erect.

What to do? Vic donned her robe and immediately dialed 911. The rescue squad was great, arriving inside of just five minutes and executing their job to perfection. Naturally, all the paramedics recognized Zino instantly, he being one of the city's greatest celebrities. Everyone remarked on the phenomenon of his hard-on and how it persevered even in the face of cardiac arrest. Next morning's tabloid headlines featured the story of the mobster's heart attack. Fortunately, Vic's name was withheld due to her influence with the NYPD. Zino's amazing priapism, however, was alluded to in the stories, while doctors at St. Luke's/Roosevelt Hospital were forced to admit that never in the history of their medical practice had they seen a coronary patient with such a giant erection that refused to subside.

So in a roundabout way, Vic achieved her goal. She hadn't willed the heart attack, but being out of commission, Zino would have to postpone the Sapphire Bay/Vegas Teamsters loans for the time being. She heard from Al "Sugar" Zucchero that Zino blamed her for his coronary, said it happened because of Pega Palo.

"That's ridiculous," Vic told Harry. "As if he weren't free, white and over 21. And he was the one who begged me to give it to him!"

"Well, honey, you'll just have to mend a few fences. Visit him in the hospital, send flowers and cards, and remember that time will take care of the rest."

"Right you are, Harry. And now that most of our problems are, thank God, either out of the way or about to be, what's next on the agenda is my finally getting over to see Cestari and mending that fence."

CHAPTER 34

"Approximately ten or twelve million to be on the safe side, in untraceable paper," Tania was telling the others, "in order to get four million cash out of the deal. We're counting on 30%, that's what it's supposed to be on the other end."

"It's the quickest thing to do, and it's a big order," Laura said.

"We can handle it," Jasmine said. "American dollars is our best bet."

"The hardest bill to duplicate is the hundred, so we could just do 20's," Laura suggested.

"Not so easy to transport. Hundreds are bad enough."

"Maybe we can do a combination."

Chinatown's Eleanor Lee Wong, Laura's lieutenant, was a big help. El said, "We have an order out of Hong Kong with a London connection. Friends of friends will pay 35% of face value, and they want to see more samples."

"Lucille can produce the entire order. And it'll be cash on the barrelhead."

"Are we certain of our sources?" Laura asked.

"Absolutely," Eleanor assured her. "The people in Hong Kong I know personally, the London people are their contacts and Hong Kong has vouched for them."

"You'd be surprised how many people don't care if it's genuine," Jasmine said. "Bills are definitely quickest. That and CD's."

"And not to worry, 90% or more arrests for counterfeiting are made on tips," Laura said. "So the fewer people who know about this the better. We keep it entre nous."

"As long as you know who you're dealing with you're safe," Eleanor said. "And as long as the product is top quality."

"Which this of course will be."

"How do we get so much cash into Britain? Ten, twelve million dollars in twenties or even hundreds — do you know how much space that takes up? What happens at Customs?"

Tania said, "I've taken care of that problem."

Just the day before yesterday Tania had explained the situation to Tom Kelly and asked for his cooperation. Now that she was his niece by marriage, they were on familiar terms. "I realize your field is maritime, Tom," Tania said, "but through the joint brotherhood of unions, hopefully you can reach out to contacts in the airlines and through them to Customs. We're trying to save Jack's hide and we need all the help we can get, so I'd appreciate your pulling out all stops."

Kelly phoned back the next day to let her know he'd arranged for her to fly out of Kennedy and into Heathrow with no hassles, circumventing Customs entirely.

Tania thanked him but also said, "Tom, I want to make it clear — I'm taking some big risks. I'm transporting and selling counterfeits, and I'm pregnant besides, so that's a further risk I'm assuming."

Kelly said, "Tania, I'm in your debt forever for helping my nephew. I repeat my previous offer — anything you ever need or ask — consider it done."

Lucille Rand arrived and checked into the Pierre to set up preliminary operations. The sixty-something Lucille, grandmother of five, was the oldest ranking member of the LFM, a onetime Time-Life photographer and counterfeiter without peer. It was Lucille who in the early days turned out all the illegal stamps used on liquor bottles from the outfit's Brooklyn still, and hatched plans to manufacture currency and securities. Later on, she moved out of Manhattan to become commander-in-chief of New Orleans, where she now wielded considerable influence.

When Lucille was ready to swing into action, the team met down at Eleanor's place in Chinatown.

"These few measly millions won't affect the economy much," Lucille said.

"So the cost is passed on to the consumer. What can it amount to, a penny a person?" Laura asked.

Sure, who could feel guilty about counterfeiting? One more sacred cow. The US government was the ultimate counterfeiter par excellence. So who gave them the exclusive right to inflate the money supply?

The paper Lucille was using was as close to the original as possible, most of it 25% rag. Anything higher in rag content, Lucille said, would feel too soft. "The 25% has just the right crackle. It's as close to the real thing as you can get."

The fix was in, it was a done deal. "Anyway, the Federal Reserve is actually illegal," Eleanor said. "It was never meant to be that way. Our founding fathers would never tolerate the Federal Reserve. So in our small way, this is a cry of protest. And think of the good that's going to come from it."

CHAPTER 35

Not pregnant? How could that possibly be?

Tania lay naked from the waist down, under a sheet, her legs in metal stirrups. Her obstetrician, Dr. Melvin Goldfarb, was removing his surgical gloves, having just given her a physical exam.

"What you had, Tania, is very rare," Dr. Goldfarb said. "It's known as a phantom pregnancy. It happens only once in 1,500,000 times."

Tania couldn't believe what the doctor was telling her. All her tests were positive, she'd had all the signs — absence of menstrual periods; weight gain, breast, waist and belly enlargement; morning sickness, frequency of urination, food cravings; she even had milk in her breasts. Now Dr. Goldfarb was telling her she wasn't pregnant?

He had reached up into her uterus to find there was no fetus – the one missing symptom. By now there should have been a fetus.

"I don't understand," Tania protested, incredulous. "I felt so pregnant — my husband felt it too — "

"I understand your disappointment," Dr. Goldfarb sympathized. "But young lady, if it's any consolation, you can count yourself lucky to discover it this early. The longer it went on the worse it would have been."

"How long could it have continued?" Tania asked.

Dr. Goldfarb shrugged. "Some women even carry a pseudo fetus to term. They actually have labor pains — "

Some women actually got on the operating table, Dr. Goldfarb said, they pushed and pushed, but no baby came out. The doctor was fooled, the laboratories were fooled, the parents were fooled, everybody was fooled.

So she wasn't pregnant; after all that, there would be no baby. She'd been looking forward to this infant so much. Tania thought about the layette, the crib, stroller, pram, all the trappings in the nursery, and fought tears, overcome by a sense of loss. She'd been so elated, so full of plans and dreams. This baby had meant so much to her, and all along it was never real.

It had been the one thing holding her marriage to Jack together. Now she had no further reason to stay with him any longer. She would keep her promise to him, take the counterfeit currency to London, do the deal, and then see a divorce lawyer.

Jack resigned himself to it being over between them. Their relationship was a truce now. He was grateful for her help in settling his debts, especially because, believe it or not, things had worsened even more for him. Just recently he'd taken a trip to California, where he'd failed to collect a marker he said was owed him. At Santa Anita, he ran into some intimidating characters from the Chicago outfit who'd roughed him up. They were asserting he owed them $200,000, on top of his other debts. He insisted these guys were claimers, and they were dangerous, they were coming after him, and he was scared.

Jack was full of these stories and they were all blending into one, the debts he owed, the claimers who were claiming, the unreasonable mobsters and shylocks, the horses with great bloodlines and nothing but class who just narrowly missed by a nose in a photo finish heartbreaker, preventing him from realizing the long shot that would have been, should have been, could have saved his life. He wiped his brow. "I can't believe this is happening. Christ, things have tightened up. It's unreal," he said.

And then there were the threatening phone calls. Tania couldn't wait to get it all behind her. She wanted to tell him, look, you knew this could happen, you knew it ages ago but you kept on, you wouldn't stop, you kept looking for impossible miracles instead of doing something to help yourself. But what was the use? Soon it would all be over and she'd be able to breathe again. And maybe there would even be a chance with Corrado? Oh, God, she hoped, hoped

CHAPTER 36

It was all set. She'd be leaving for London tomorrow, and not a moment too soon. Jack's situation kept going further downhill fast. She couldn't wait to get away.

Tania heard his key in the lock. He entered, unshaven, wearing a wrinkled suit, his shirt crumpled and soaked with perspiration. In Texas they'd say he'd been ridden hard and put up wet. He was a wreck.

"What's wrong?"

"Nothing. Let's grab some dinner."

On their way over to the restaurant, as usual Jack picked up his copy of The Morning Telegraph and a bunch of tout sheets. He was subdued at the table, poked at his food, did more smoking than eating, and appeared distracted.

She said, "The stuff you were telling me about those Chicago people — I heard rumors today, more bad news. You're in big trouble. Bigger than you told me."

He laughed. "The story of my life, at least the past few months of it." He was gazing at his drink, massaging his wrist.

She said, "I gather you already know you're a marked man."

"You exaggerate, you overreact." Jack stared into his drink. His voice was distant, and he kept glancing at his watch.

There was a lot she could say, but it had all been said already. What was the use? It was finished. "You won't face anything. You destroyed everything we had — or thought we had."

He was still staring and massaging, harder now. His jaw was set.

"You don't want to talk about it. You refused to change."

"Never mind," he said. "It doesn't matter any more. Maybe some day you'll understand." He looked at her with a peculiar expression, as if he wanted to say something but thought better of it, then turned away. "I've made a lot of mistakes," he admitted. "I apologize. It hasn't been intentional."

There was a strange finality to his words, Tania thought. He picked some more at his food and kept glancing at his watch and looking at the door.

His hand was shaking as he lit another cigarette. "I can't believe this is happening to me," he kept repeating, over and over. But he still didn't want to talk about it. Instead, he said, "For what it's worth, I really care about you, I really do love you." Tears formed in his eyes. He looked away again, glancing furtively as if searching for someone, frowned and stood up abruptly, his eyes darting in ten directions at once.

"Come on, let's get outta here," he said.

"What's your hurry?"

He was emphatic about wanting to take a route back they never took. On 3rd Avenue, he suddenly turned to her and started quarreling, accusing her of disloyalty.

"Keep your voice down, Jack. People are staring."

"I don't give a shit!" he yelled at the top of his lungs.

It happened suddenly. A man in a ski mask stepped squarely in their path and pointed a .22 calibre Smith and Wesson at Jack. Tania screamed. In a split second a shot rang out, the man scurried down the street out of sight and Jack was left clutching his stomach.

"Help me! I've been shot," he groaned. "Help, get a taxi."

Tania ran to the curb and hailed a cab. Bent over double, Jack staggered to the door. She helped him get in and tried to follow, but he held out an arm to restrain her. "I don't want you involved," he gasped. His face was white and contorted with pain. "I'm going to the hospital – I'll be ok – I'll call you."

"But — "

"Go home!" he moaned, and leaned back in the seat as the car sped away.

Frantic, Tania checked every hospital in Manhattan but could find no trace of Jack. Had he been admitted under a false name? Then the next day she received a phone call from Eddie Chang, Jack's Chinese track crony, another gambling degenerate.

"I have bad news," Eddie said. "Jack's dead."

"Oh God!" Tania cried. "No! No!"

The strange details surrounding Jack's demise were unclear. When and where had the body been located? Tania hadn't been permitted to view it even for identification purposes.

Laura asked, "Was there an autopsy?"

"No," Tania said. "The person who notified me, Eddie Chang, said he didn't think that would be necessary, since it was death from a bullet wound and I saw it happen."

"Still — "

"I couldn't face all the red tape — a funeral's bad enough."

"Tania, if there's anything I can do..."

"Thanks, Laura, I just want to put all this behind me and move on. Remember, I'm due in London — it's all arranged, I have to go."

"Where is Jack's body now?"

"I don't know..." Tania answered vaguely, "at some incinerator, I think." And she started to cry softly.

"What about burial?" Laura persisted.

"Jack always wanted to be cremated," Tania said. "Eddie said he'd take care of it."

"And you never viewed the body?"

"I wasn't allowed to, and I didn't want to anyway. I wanted to remember Jack as he was."

When Victoria heard the news about Jack she phoned Tania with condolences and offered the services of her lieutenant, funeral director Rose F. Dyson, owner of the Shady Grove Mortuary in Valley Stream. "You know my woman the Rosie the Pelvis? Rosie'd do a bang-up job on Jack," Victoria enthused. "Ro's an artist. She can take any stiff and make it presentable. By the way, are Jack's earthly remains in any way disfigured? Ro's capable of taking care of the most challenging problem that can ever happen to a corpse."

Tania told Vic how Eddie Chang had already made arrangements to cremate Jack, explaining that she was in shock and said yes to everything Eddie suggested. The best Vic could do was arrange for a memorial service for Jack at Rose's funeral parlor. But first came the funeral Eddie set up. It was a weird thing, officiated by another gambling pal, a crooked rabbi from the diamond district — nobody knew why, since Jack was Catholic, not Jewish — and Jack's ashes were scattered into Jamaica Bay, at the same spot, somebody noted, that Mayor La Guardia once dumped Frank Costello's slot machines.

It might seem a fitting end for Jack. Everyone said it was suspicious, though, that there was no death certificate, no body, only ashes. And who knew if they were human ashes? They could have come from the Jamaica recycling plant.

"It doesn't seem right," Tania agreed. "And I can't believe Jack's really dead. For some reason I have the feeling he's still alive."

"I know; death is always hard to accept."

"He was targeted by the mob. They got him. I saw it happen — but still I have the feeling he's alive."

"Death takes a long time getting used to — sometimes a year or even more."

She had to put it behind her now, get on with her life. But wasn't it a peculiar irony that her husband, the man she had wanted to escape from, was now dead, gone from the firmament.

Though she was sad about Jack's violent end, in another way she was relieved it was all over. Life with Jack had been such a nightmare.

CHAPTER 37

Vic was still having nothing but tsouris. It just seemed like one thing after another.

"I can't believe it," she said to Harry. "It's like there's a jinx preventing everything I want from happening."

No sooner had she recovered from the clap than inexplicably, she came down with another sexually transmitted disease, herpes this time, which cut into her plans and took another few weeks to cure. Luckily she still had Charles on the hook — she told him she had a virus — he was understanding and willing to wait for the deal to culminate. Over the phone she promised they'd definitely meet soon, in a matter of just a week or two.

The National Commission was going to come up with the compromise for a smaller order, and she would be working with Lucille together with connections abroad to sell a large order of counterfeit money, so even though her goals had long been thwarted, the horizon appeared promising now. She needed have to be patient only a short while longer.

It had been some time since Vic had heard from Judge Robert Francis Casey. As enthusiastic as the potential future New York Governor had seemed about her in the beginning, lately he'd pulled in his horns by seeing less of her. Could he have been a venereal disease victim as well and didn't want to reveal it? Possible. Of course Casey was a busy man, and due to his position might want to play it safe by not getting too involved with one person; or maybe you could chalk it up to the judge's endless search for the novelty of a new cunt and wanting to move forward in a new direction.

Ok, listen, she didn't really mind that much. She'd been pretty occupied herself. A few fucks was all it had taken to get the Casey situation operating to suit her ends. He'd gone to bat for her and seen to it that the New York State Court of Appeals reversed a decision she wanted fixed. That in itself was an enormous accomplishment. And in addition, her wiretaps and surveillance of Casey were yielding results in the form of potential blackmail material that at the right time would come in handy. In any event, she considered Bob Casey a friend, no matter what the status of their sex life.

After not hearing from the judge for a while, to her surprise he made one of his famous how's-your-cunt calls, saying he wanted to get together. They made a date for the following evening at the Carlyle. Meantime Georgia phoned. She said, "I'm hopping on a Path and I'll be at your place in a half hour. Wait till you hear what I have to tell you."

Forty minutes later, an excited Georgia arrived. "I thought you'd like to know about your friend, the Honorable RFC."

"Casey? What about him?"

Georgia had found out through Mike Giordano that Casey was gunrunning to the IRA. "The guy's eating out of Mike's hand," Georgia said. "Mike's also made illegal contributions to the Casey for Governor campaign and he has Casey over a barrel, practically owns the guy. The arms are mostly happening out of Elizabethport."

"That's great news," Victoria said. "I'm sure the Department of the United States Treasury would be interested to know about Neutrality Treaty violations, don't you think, Harry?"

"Definitely. The right time comes, I'd say we have some further dynamite information we can use to advantage here."

Victoria pondered a moment, then said, "I have a plan. When Casey and I get together tomorrow night, while he's in the shower I'm going to try to break into the desk in his office. I have a feeling there could be some more material to round out our already strong evidence against the SOB."

"Don't take unnecessary risks," Harry advised. "We already have plenty on the guy."

"Sure, but the more the better."

To make a long story short, Casey caught Vic rifling through his papers, became justifiably livid and threw her out. That was the last she saw of him. But the story hardly ended there.

Next, Georgia and Rose F. Dyson ended up at a cocktail party at the Carlyle given by one of Casey's fellow tenants at which Casey was a guest. They started thinking about that desk Vic wanted to get at and decided why not do the job themselves? One of them would detain Casey at the party while the other broke into his place upstairs. So Georgia and her dog Marlene Dietrich went up. Georgia had a look around, microfilmed whatever looked important to her, helped herself to a few documents, and was coming back downstairs to the party when she ran smack into Casey, who was leaving. Rose had kept him occupied as long as she could.

Call it intuition, Casey had a belly hunch she was up to no good. At the same time, with her animal sixth sense, Marlene Dietrich must have realized Casey was onto her mistress, because suddenly she leapt at Casey, knocked him over and practically mauled him to death. It was in all the papers. "German Shepherd Bitch Attacks Noted Judge: Gubernatorial Hopeful Recuperating From Dog Bites."

Of course Casey discovered the missing documents. When he found out Georgia was close to Mike Giordano, that was the coup de grâce. Right after that Georgia disappeared, and nothing was heard from her for a long time. Then at Vic's birthday bash at Tiro a Segno, the management brought out a humongous cake. Inside was a hand, a human hand, wearing Georgia's ruby ring. "That ring," Vic whispered, aghast. "Mike gave her that ring ... somebody wanted me to know it's Georgia."

Not long after that, the rest of Georgia — in the form of her bloated, nearly unrecognizable body — was fished out of the Hudson River midway between the crowded docks of Elizabethport and where the Goethals Bridge connects to Staten Island. It was a sad ending to a beautiful lady.

They held the funeral, of course, at Rose's mortuary. With Marlene Dietrich and Vic's entire borgata in attendance, Harry gave the moving eulogy.

He said, "Georgia Jensen was one of this outfit's best women. Georgia was tough. She dared to do what few women will, and it is precisely this quality we all respected so much in our friend Georgia Jensen. Georgia was doing a great job within this organization, until one person decided to fuck her over, or have her fucked over, as the case may be. Anyway, those of us whom Georgia leaves behind will sorely miss her. And I join everyone in this room in saying that we will have our revenge on the person in question."

Just who was that person in question, though? Was it Casey? Anthony Zino? Mike Giordano? Everyone had their theories. No one knew for sure yet. The thorny issue would have to be resolved.

The chapel was packed with over two hundred mourners. The LFM's were giving Georgia a great send-off: tons of flowers, organ music, the congregation joining in traditional Christian hymns like *Abide with Me*, and *Lead, Kindly Light*, Georgia's favorites. Marlene Dietrich, her head resting on outstretched paws, lay mournfully by the steel coffin that was draped in white satin and strewn with deep ruby roses and creamy calla lilies. Everybody swore the devoted animal had tears in her eyes.

Obviously, Georgia was killed because she knew too much. Vic felt pulled by a great force, an invisible power of which she was but a helpless victim. Dying happened when you could no longer withstand Powers and Principalities, when you were in their grip and couldn't get away. Now she felt nothing but anger and sorrow. No one would ever understand.

Afterwards when they were dining quietly together back in the city at a 9th Avenue wop joint, Harry checked his firearm, adjusted his shoulder holster and popped the cork off a bottle of Chianti. Sprinkling Parmesan cheese on his linguine, twirling the pasta around his fork thoughtfully, he said to Vic, "Any time you're ready we can move in on this cocksucker Casey. In my book he's the one. He arranged it. And even if he didn't, we still want to assert our power over the son of a bitch."

"No, Harry. We wait till we can make him squirm."

"Are you kidding? He'll squirm plenty right now. We can scare the pants off him."

"Not enough. Wait till his usefulness hits a peak. Maybe in the gubernatorial race, maybe even later, when the stakes escalate."

"You mean we want to let this guy to make it to governor?"

"With us pulling the strings, why not?"

"Hey, honey, you're right. We control Casey, only he doesn't know it. Casey's political star is on the rise, we let him do his thing, then call in the markers when he can do us the most good."

Harry noticed Vic wasn't eating much. She looked depressed. "What's the matter, baby?" he asked gently. "Something's wrong. Is it Georgia?"

"Yeah, I guess that's it, Harry. It just reminds me of a lot of stuff, and how unfair life is —"

They lived on an isolated island in the Florida gulf, cut off from the rest of humanity. She knew all the wildlife — the schools of fish — redfish, trout, sheepshed; the flowers and trees — saspodillas, tamarind, manila palm, frangipani, banyan, night blooming Ceres, incandescent, scarlet-blooming poinsettia, clumps of reeds and mango trees.

There was a stifling sadness in this hot atmosphere; it was a world where people seemed dead, suspended in air, hanging in a weird balance. She ached from the lack of contact with reality. She talked to animals, birds, fish, reptiles, anything that moved and breathed. Life here was strange, primitive. She was a mirage in vaporous space, falling, separate.

She used to sneak off with the sheriff's posse to the swamps and watch the fiddler crab and lizards scurrying away from flashlight beams. She remembered the musty smell of rattlesnakes and the ammonia scent of pelican rookeries, and the dense swarming mosquitoes.

Each day she went for solitary walks along the deserted shell-covered beaches and contemplated a future when everything would be different. She had it all planned. She'd leave here, head up to Charleston, then north to make her way in life. Here, the juices of life were being pressed from her. She was filled with a strange elixir with no place to give herself to, seeking some wondrous future, confronting a void. Why did no one pay attention?

She would remember all the sounds of her childhood, the poignancy and mystery of hidden enclosures, the sounds of gurgling water from the cooler in the kitchen, the never-ceasing hum of the electric fan, the clink of ice cubes in the lemonades and Dr. Peppers and Cokes she never stopped drinking all day, the sound of rain on the roof, and the hushed, oppressive songs of the cicadas.

The loneliness was overpowering, the physical heat constantly threatening to engulf her. She would gaze through salt-fogged binoculars at the coral reef, the limestone outcroppings and tangled mangrove swamps of 10,000 islands, the semi-desert isolation/desolation that was her world, and she would long to be lifted out of here into another place, where she would be recognized and rewarded.

In the nearby town of moss-hung streets lying outside the mango jungle, she watched the oyster fishermen, their backs broad from years of swinging their bulky oyster tongs. They all looked like heavyweight champs, the shrimp and oyster fishermen. She wondered if one of them might be her father, but she would never know. Where had she come from? Who were her antecedents? Her aunt refused to tell her who her parents were.

She looked with envy at the luxury of Palm Beach and Miami, feeling an aching emptiness that so much was beyond her reach. She was hungry and full of the grievance that others were getting and she was not. The power she wanted she would have, even through violence if that were the only way. A chain of circumstances drove her to the breaking point. She knew that if she were pushed to it, conditions could force her to kill.

She was engulfed by a sense of calamity when her aunt died and she was sent to an orphanage. First chance that came along, four months short of age 15, she eloped to escape. Her spouse, Herby, 62, took her to Tallahassee. Then one day while she was out shopping at the supermarket, she came home to find Herby dead. She didn't know what to do about it, who to tell; she had no friends.

She lived there with the body until it started stinking up the house. Nauseated by the stench, she had to split. Hitchhiking, she worked her way up north to the Carolinas, married again, got out of that, picked up a trucker who dumped her in Spanish Harlem, New York. Over and over again setbacks plagued her. It was tough out there. She was a fabulous human being but nobody knew it.

She began reading the Wall Street Journal and it moved her as nothing else in life ever had. This was something she understood: money. She wanted to make money, that was her answer in life. Carefully, she laid out a plan. She continued reading the Wall Street Journal cover to cover. Then when she was fully prepared, she went over to Goldman Sachs and applied for a job.

She was a bit nervous as she sat down face to face with a human resources counselor, but assuming any personnel director would be interested in hiring a well-informed person, Vic made it her business to show this bitch what she knew. And by now she knew a whole lot.

She was full of fascinating tales of the past, how dynasties were made, how for instance, the entire city of Boston built its fortunes on opium, how most of the revered brahmin families of today owed their inherited wealth to drugs. "Astor, Perkins, Russell, Lowell, Lodge, Forbes -- all of them amassed millions from the trade. But for opium, the world might never have seen the likes of a Henry Cabot Lodge or a Malcolm Forbes," she told the somewhat startled human resources interviewer.

"It was called `trade,' but it really amounted to piracy, privateering, theft on the high seas. The Forbes family, who like the others, made their fortune on opium, later invested it in railroads. Thanks to the opium trade, by the War of 1812 the Perkins family had enough money to put it to work at 18% interest. The Astors, though they started out in furs, went into opium in the 1820's. At that time opium in fact was the only profitable commodity in the trade with China. Peabody, Russell, Cushing, Appleton, Lowell, the Cabots and the Lodges, the Girards, the Sturgis family, the Boardmans -- they were all into it, cleaning up in narcotics. Thriving illicit commerce made all the great Boston fortunes. Bostonians were noted for smuggling."

Vic thought the personnel director looked puzzled, as if she hadn't a clue about the real story of America's wealth. No doubt Vic was blowing her mind. She continued, "One of the Forbes descendants, I believe it was Malcolm, wondered if in the future today's drug dealers will be as honored as his forebears?

"William Appleton was another opium dealer of social position and esteem. In his diary he wrote that his mother at age 81 had used opium for 20 years and showed no signs of wear and tear. That's because they used pure stuff back then. Perkins sold 150,000 pounds of Turkish opium a year at $7.50 a pound profit, Sturgis sold half a million pounds a year. Do you now how much money that is? All for which they were lauded and praised, and their families are at the top of the Social Register today.

"The Forbes House is now a museum in Milton, run by Dr. Crosby Forbes, an expert in Chinese porcelain urns. These people can afford to be effete. They can afford to be anything they damned please. They're untouchables, these people who bribed and skimmed all over the place and didn't pay their taxes. All of these people sent their sons to Harvard. They mingled with the intelligentsia. William Hathaway Forbes married the daughter of Ralph Waldo Emerson, for instance. In Boston there's a great tradition of mind and Mammon. It was a game only the elite could play. All the pirates and privateers became patrons of the arts."

The personnel lady glanced at her watch and asked Vic why she wanted to work for Goldman Sachs. Vic told her because she wanted money, big money. Vic talked of things the average person applying for a job at Goldman Sachs would never know, about the foundations of wealth in the U.S. and how crooked and rigged the system was.

You'd think they'd be glad to hear the truth. She'd been sure they'd welcome her with open arms here at Goldman Sachs — a woman with her mind, knowledge and abilities. To her amazement they never called her back and she was rejected for the job. It took a while to sink in. It was cronyism out there in the financial world. Women like her weren't given permission to make money. There was no way she could join the club.

Did those old Bostonians ever feel as she did, cut off from the normal routes to social and occupational mobility?

Boston, that was the ultimate mafia. One hundred, two hundred years ago, the country was full of people who took risks, people who broke the law to create the American dream. Malcolm Forbes even said so, he said it was "the piracy of doing your own thing" that made this country great. That was her ideal too, the mafia, an American phenomenon. If doors were closed and nobody was buying, what else could be done about it?

It was a league out there, the people who stacked the system against those like her. They were the old boy network, operators and wheeler dealers, pirates and pillagers, bustout artists and fancy takeover hotshots who used inflated paper, drained cash and hard assets from acquisitions into their own pockets and fucked the public. They caused inflation, over-taxation and high interest rates for everyone else and wrote in loopholes for themselves. Did anyone call them on their shit? Nobody seemed to mind. How did they steer clear of the law? Via conspiracy. They were as bad, if not worse than the old Bostonians. Her bitterness grew stronger. Clearly, the only way to prosper was outside the mainstream as a creative rebel. There was no way to join the corridors of power, they were too entrenched, they'd never let you in their mafia, so you had to start your own.

It was the ultimate feminist statement.

Time evaporated. All right, never mind, she looked great. She was aging so phenomenally well it was easy to shave off a few years and have no one be the wiser. Her counterfeit passport listed her age as 27, which was as good a number as any to be. If anyone was rude enough to ask, she'd answer "in her early 20's." Like the Gabors used to say, a woman should pick a good age and stick to it.

She must project and gain recognition for the person she knew she was and so wanted the world to certify. She had chutzpah and brains and she wasn't going to let anybody interfere with the outcome. She was a Leo, after all, a ruler.

She deserved, goddamnit, she deserved. She was eaten alive with envy. She burned to take action, do something, anything. As a woman, she was limited. Why had she been cheated? By what deceit or trickery or nefarious means did others get there? Being a male of the species helped. Having a penis helped. How to get through life without one? You had to find alternative means. Machiavelli was right. In the end the means didn't matter, the result was what counted.

Being an LFM meant demanding, then seeing the demand was met. Forget morality. Morality had no place here. You were serving a higher purpose. Life wasn't fair, it was unfair to be born a woman; ok, you were starting from behind, but you could bloody well not only catch up but surpass.

And that was just what she'd done and would keep on doing, penis or no penis.

CHAPTER 38

In the bedroom of her suite at the Dorchester, Tania gazed at twenty suitcases full of counterfeit American dollars and wondered what to do next. For three days she had remained in her room, expecting Mr. Chin's phone call. Then just minutes ago, a person in Hong Kong speaking broken English told her Chin was on a protracted trip to Singapore and India, and would not be returning to London for two months. What now?

It was her responsibility to rectify this situation, out of loyalty to the LFM. She wanted to settle the matter, be free of Jack's debt, raise the necessary cash. But how?

One possible option — Corrado, selling the counterfeits to the man she loved. As a banker, he worked with the Vatican. Grapevine said the Vatican had, in the past, whether knowingly or unknowingly, bought counterfeit securities; what better means of laundering money than through a religious channel like the Holy See? Who would ask questions? Anyone would assume the dollars came from the collection plate.

She'd been longing to see him again. So much had happened since her false pregnancy. Maybe now things could work out. Tania's heart leapt at the thought. Of course, Corrado was the answer.

After a series of calls, she located him in Sicily, where he was staying for several days. She would descend and surprise him. Perfect. She tried phoning Tom Kelly to arrange Customs clearance at the Palermo Airport, but Kelly was out of town. It was risky, but she'd have to chance it on her own. Anyway, this was Italy; even with twenty suitcases full of counterfeits, it was likely she could get through without any hitches.

She was right. Wearing short shorts, a low cut blouse, and a smile, Tania joked with the young Customs officials who briefly diverted their attention from her cleavage to compliment her on her command of Italian. "*Ma come mai che parla così bene l'italiano, signorina?*" a uniformed, mustachioed official asked in one breath, and in the next invited her for a drink.

Tania leaned over the counter, allowing her breasts to tumble, fingered her Phi Beta Kappa key, thrust her hips out, and promised to meet the Customs official at 8 pm. In answer to a request for her phone number, she scrawled the number at Corrado's office and handed it over. In thirty seconds she was out of the terminal, with her twenty suitcases loading for delivery to a waiting taxi.

Sicily! Mimosa blooming, meadows covered in yellow buttercups, almond trees bursting into white foam, wild orchids and artichokes everywhere in profusion — this was a dream come true — the sensuous atmosphere and incredible blue sea, flecks of bright sunlight, gold on limestone, the torrid air, and the overpowering aroma of wildflowers — peonies, anemones, violets, iris, pink oleander and hollyhocks among the ancient ruins, purple bougainvillea and fiery hibiscus and the smell of jasmine everywhere.

It was exactly as she'd imagined — grapevines and budding olive trees, wandering chickens and goats, wooded hills perched on rocky promontories, ornate villas colored red, pink, sienna; charming tiny villages near the railroad tracks, clusters of square houses and chicken coops, all with beautiful, blooming gardens.

"Italy is the garden of the world," it was said, and how much Sicily reflected that, Tania thought, as her eyes followed the incredible drive from her Palermo hotel to Corrado's town nearby. He lived in the tranquil fishing village of Villa Grazia della Concordia, nestled along the bottom of a mountain, at the tip of which was situated an old stone castle built by the Saracens.

She had decided to come here immediately, rather than call his office first. Better the direct approach. Parking the car near the main piazza, Tania proceeded on foot. Pale saffron sunlight fell on the town's red tiled roofs and cupolas. Most of the houses were two and three stories high with balconies, close together along the narrow cobbled roads. Winding streets and alleyways were busy with bicycles, *motoscafi*, and trappings of commerce. Townspeople sat sunning themselves in front of doorways, playing *briscola*, taking coffee at small outdoor tables near beaded curtains, from behind which emerged loud radio sounds of Mina, Milva, Modugno, and Al Bano. The women all wore black. Smartly attired *carabinieri* carried silver swords that gleamed in the sun. You could hear the endless clacking of donkeys hauling colorful carts, their panels painted with scenes of 19th century operas and plays and Punch and Judy characters.

"*Mi potrebbe dire, per piacere, dov'è la casa dell' Avvocato Corrado Sofino?*" Tania asked. A woman carrying a clothes basket on her shoulders pointed to the left.

"*Là-giu,*" the woman said, bowing her head in deference, as Tania noted the respect and awe Corrado inspired.

Following directions, Tania arrived at the impressive Sofino residence, where Corrado lived behind walls protected by electric fences, a brace of dobermans and an elaborate security system that included a team of armed guards. Deciding not to attempt penetrating these precautions, Tania left a message with one of the guards and headed back the route she had come. Only a few minutes later, she caught sight of Corrado himself. He was on foot, looking dashing in a white suit and panama hat, followed by two men, walking in town.

"Corrado, Corrado!" she called out, as he paused at the entrance to a small bar where a group of old men sat playing cards.

Corrado turned. "*Dio mio!*" he exclaimed. "What are you doing in Sicily? How did you get here?"

"It's a long story," Tania replied, wanting to throw her arms around him and kiss him, but thinking twice when she saw everyone staring.

"Come, we'll take a coffee together and you will fill me in."

They walked another block to the piazza, where they were joined by three more bodyguards. Corrado commented that she didn't look very pregnant.

"I'm not. I'll tell you about it," Tania said. "And by the way, I'm widowed now."

"My condolences. I am deeply sorry to hear of your loss," Corrado said, as they took a seat at the central café. His team of bodyguards discretely occupied another table and watched them. Under the circumstances, it was impossible to tell him much, since they were constantly interrupted by people coming up with greetings. Coffee evolved into lunch at a trattoria, listening to an accordion and mandolin, watching the tarantella.

"Is it true you're the most powerful man in Sicily?" Tania asked, "that everyone answers to you, that you're untouchable?"

"By now you know very well I am not untouchable," he said, gazing softly in her eyes.

"I remember," Tania said pointedly. "Will we get to prove that again soon?"

"Soon, yes. I want to very much. *Pazienza*. But you still have not told me how you happen to be here," Corrado probed.

Tania reminded him of his invitation to show her Sicily. "So when business reasons for this trip came up, I thought we might combine business with pleasure."

"Ah, yes," Corrado said. "I promised you lava caves, black sand beaches, baroque churches, and Sicilian hospitality. *Tu sei mia ospite. Con molto piacere per me*."

Business would wait. Meanwhile, they enjoyed the antipasto tray, followed by fresh fish served on a silver platter and with elaborate wines. More people kept dropping by — the local priest, the *carabinieri*, the tobacconist, all coming to pay their respects.

Finally, after the meal, Corrado suggested, "Let's take a coffee together by the sea."

Now she would tell him. "I'm going to be up front with you," Tania began, after they were seated at a café by the waterside. "I have twelve million dollars in counterfeit U.S. currency I need to unload. Can you help me?"

He postured at first. But when she described the situation in greater detail and intimated she knew more about his business affairs than previously disclosed, he started shifting his position.

"You needn't stand on ceremony with me, Corrado," she said. "I know who you are."

"*Davvero?*" He smiled. His eyes were guarded, somewhat uneasy.

"Really," Tania repeated. "Before we go any further, I think the time has come to disclose my own identity." She placed her demi-tasse on its saucer, looked at him squarely and said, "Like yourself, I too am mafiosa."

"Indeed!" Now he was amused.

"I am the head of one of New York's four major mafia families," she confided, sotto voce.

"I was under the impression New York had five families, and I'd also heard it said the mafia is not an equal opportunity employer," Corrado remarked.

"So it's not. Which is one reason for my group — the La Femmina Female Mafia Syndicate. Unlike the five families of La Cosa Nostra, we are four families. But let me tell you more about my counterfeits."

They discussed it another half hour, until Corrado, viewing her with new respect now, agreed to help. Later in the day he would look at the currency. Meantime, they went down to the beach, where they dove for *frutta di mare*, sea urchins, which they ate with lemon and onion on crusty bread. Then they swam nude on the deserted beach together and made love. Gazing up at the landscape, Tania thought she had never been happier.

At the end of the day he came back to the hotel to inspect the counterfeits. Apparently satisfied with their quality, he said, "Tomorrow we will take care of the matter."

Early the following day, they made the exchange. After four of his men carried out her twenty suitcases and loaded them onto a truck, Corrado handed her a certified check for 4.5 million dollars, which Tania immediately wired to the Bahamas for further laundering, to cover debts and costs. Since Corrado was advising the Vatican, no doubt it would be an easy maneuver to place the counterfeits in the Holy See portfolio, perhaps in the Banco di Santo Spirito, the Vatican Bank or whatever.

"Come, we will celebrate our successful business deal," he invited. They left Palermo's teeming streets and drove up the hills in Corrado's white Ferrari. As the car wound through the villages, men at outdoor cafes raised their glasses in toast.

Corrado said, "As a boy I liked to travel through these towns on my horse. I would ride through the hills and pastures to our farm, beyond the mountain, or swim near the old castle."

Along the breathtaking drives, he pointed out the sights: Caccamo, dominated by a grandiose medieval castle at the top of a steep hill; Cefalù, lying at the foot of a menacing rocky promontory that hung suspended as though it could fall over the town below; Roman aqueducts nestled between the palms and yellow cactus flowers. The ruins were redolent with the scent of oleander, the day luminous yellow gold, and there was a burnished sheen to the earth browns of the many *palazzi* and to the greens of the hills.

So many enormous old castles were perched on the mountain peaks. Who lived in them, Tania wondered? Then she felt a mounting excitement as Corrado slowly pulled up her skirt, and his fingers sought the naked flesh under her bikini panties. Sliding her hand down his leg to the front of his white trousers, she reached for his fly to unbutton him. Moments later, he pulled off the road, then after a satisfying sexual interlude, they continued driving.

His Agrigento flat looked like something out of another era, like a stage set from a '30's Pirandello play, very Lampedusian, not at all what she would have expected of Corrado's taste. Tania was jealous of the other women who had come here and hoped Ingeborg never had.

Suddenly, a torrential downpour began. He closed the shutters and turned to her. They made love all afternoon. Corrado said, "I want to keep you forever, *cara mia*." He told her about a place he had bought in Mexico. He said, "Some day we will go there together. We will be together always. I want to keep you forever."

He was the love of her life, everything she had ever longed for, he made her soar beyond any place she ever dreamed existed. Later, after the rain stopped, he took her to Enna, which lay in an isolated position in the center of the island of Sicily, on the edge of a plateau called the Belvedere of Sicily. Nearby, on the Lago di Pergussa, a mysterious atmosphere brooded over the oval lake fringed with eucalyptus and acquatic plants where Pluto carried off Persephone, future queen of the underworld. Quietly, they stood together on the shores.

Then they journeyed to Messina. Here, Corrado pointed out the Straits, where the Ionian met the Tirrenian Sea, called Scylla and Charybdis, symbolic since ancient times of extreme danger without hope of salvation. That night, a dynamite charge exploded by the Sofino estate.

Her LFM business continued. Every day she was in contact with family members who ran things in her absence. Lieutenants Lily Wyszowsky, Helen Portina, Bella Hamilton, Cookie Pollock, and Suzanne Coors, capos Natasha Fielding, Jennifer Reid, Louise Dalton, and Martine Ober were ably handling her gambling, escort services, massage parlors and prostitution, loan sharking, bookmaking, pornography and other ventures.

There were the projects she initiated herself and there were those she participated in, such as the numbers operation Laura had masterminded. Kami Raines, Laura's underboss, had the policy game down to a science. Not too long ago, when rumors of a mafia war similar to Dutch Schultz's problems of decades back threatened, their muscle, the East Harlem boys, brought everything under rapid control and a mattress war was averted. She also had part of the cocaine deal, and various financial ventures were proceeding smoothly. Everything was going well, and she was basking in happiness, being with Corrado.

Then suddenly, shockingly, a rival mafia faction struck. Corrado's younger brother Pietro's car was found gutted, abandoned in Agrigento. Though no corpse was in evidence, Corrado knew his brother was dead. It was no longer safe here. Reluctantly, Tania bid him goodbye at the airport, misty-eyed, but buoyed by his promise, "We will spend more time together soon ... perhaps in Mexico. We will be together, always ... ah, yes!"

The trip had been successful beyond her dreams; her heart was full of him. But she had a gnawing feeling about what might lie ahead.

CHAPTER 39

For weeks, flowers from Laura's secret admirer had been arriving every day at the same hour, always with a card reading "SS" — Santo ("Sam") Scardelli, Enforcer (Boss) of the powerful Chicago Cosa Nostra. Although they'd met only twice briefly, Sam Scardelli was phoning daily and she had an open invitation to join him anywhere -- Scardelli operated worldwide but returned to his home turf at least one week out of the month. Now Laura was going to meet him there.

Pray Scardelli would come through. Since Zino had finked out, Sam was the logical solution. In fact, he was even in a better position than Zino with the Teamsters. Sam could move mountains, and that was precisely what they needed now.

Scardelli himself waited for her at O'Hare, a crooked smile spreading across his pencil thin lips. His hair, slightly brushed with grey, was carefully groomed in an old-fashioned outmoded style. Conservatively dressed in a fitted black chesterfield with fur collar, he had a look of prominence and prosperity and radiated authority and street-wise savoir-faire. He was slim and sharp featured, and there was something intriguing about the narrow, pinched, hungry face which gave him an air of secrecy and self-control. The eyes were tiny, beady, unreadable. A long thick cigar dangled from one corner of his carnivorous, calculating mouth. Laura was attracted to his strange, perverse appeal.

"I thought this day would never happen." His greeting came from the side of the mouth that didn't house the cigar. "After all that time on the telephone." A chauffeur driven Fleetwood containing three bodyguards waited in the no parking zone.

Riding next to him, she sensed a mental space between them It was not so much a barrier as an impenetrable physical wall that placed him out of the reach of others. The space hung around him almost like a cloak. He would play a role. She would accept that role or she would be out of his life.

The car pulled up in front of the Sultan's Table, where they were greeted by the romantic strains of strolling violinists playing schmaltzy Montovani type music, and by a host of personnel falling all over them. The Gourmet Room's decor was all gold – gold carpets, gold nylon chairs, foiled walls. Even the scantily clad waitresses wore glittering lame.

In his soft, thin-soled Italian shoes, expensive continental suit and blue-tinted designer glasses, Sam Scardelli cut an impressive figure. Just barely acknowledging the staff's continuing obsequiousness, he pushed aside his wine and bent over a five inch thick chateaubriand served on a 14 karat gold plate and began carving. His smile was carnivorous, lupine.

It wasn't until their second cup of coffee and the brandies that she was ready to broach the subject of La Femmina business in need of Sam's special touch. She began telling him how she hoped he would help. "We have some real estate, and we have some gambling licenses in the Caribbean. We've been putting together a package."

She watched as Scardelli, choosing from among several brands of cigars, went to work on one. He tore the wrapper, bit off the end and spat it out. Wetting the tip between his lips, he rolled the cigar over, circling one end around his tongue, lit and puffed. He drew in deeply, pumping steadily. It was almost a sexual act, one that brought to her mind an image of them making love together, an idea that excited her.

She continued, "We'd been expecting the Teamsters Central States Pension Fund to come up with a loan. In fact, it was supposed to be in the bag. But lately our connection's been playing games."

When the entire story was out, Sam picked up the ball. He said, "Look, as a favor, I'd be glad to put in a word with the right people."

"Would you? I'd be grateful for anything you could do for us," she said.

"For you," he corrected. "Consider it taken care of." He raised his glass in toast. "Did I tell you you and I are good for each other? To a long, happy and profitable *legame*."

His choice of word didn't escape Laura: *legame*: liaison, relationship, bond, connection, with the implicit understanding of the sexual. Laura drank to it.

The cigar slipped out of the corner of his mouth and flopped. He reached for her hand. "You and I have an unusual *rapporto. Mala femmina*," he said, squeezing her hand.

Sam had booked them adjoining rooms on the second floor of the Ambassador East. Since he never used elevators, they walked upstairs, the bodyguards keeping a comfortable distance behind. At the door, a nod from Sam was enough to send the bruisers floating into the background and around the corner before Laura even realized they were gone. She was surprised when he made no move to invite himself in or even kiss her goodnight. Once again, he referred to her as a *mala femmina*, then bid her good night at the threshold and disappeared behind his own locked door.

It aroused her to hear him moving about in the next room, taking a shower, turning in bed. She was strangely relieved but at the same time irritated that he hadn't made sexual overtures. All night long she felt aroused, unfulfilled, yet ambivalent about Sam.

Everywhere they went, the sense of Sam's power was evident. He showed her the world in which he reigned as absolute king — his hangouts: the Singapore Steak and Chop House, Eros Lounge, Casa Madrid, Pepito's and the Playboy Club, the Turf Club, the Blue Moon Lounge. He was always warm and attentive but still, each time they bid each other goodnight, his parting words were, "Are you all right? Is there anything I more I can do for you?" and when she said, "*No, grazie*," he said, "Sleep warm, baby," and went go to his own room. That went on for four days.

The night before she left, he said, "I think you need somebody like me. Do you think we have a future? Look into your crystal ball. What future do you see for us?"

But he still didn't make a move. Sam would tie the loose Teamster ends together in the next few days, he promised, but elaborated little. He'd be in touch; anything she wanted, it was hers, he said, and gifted her with an expensive diamond broach just before they arrived at the airport.

She got what she came for, but Laura had a sinking feeling as she bid him goodbye: will I ever see this man again? I think I'm in love with him, I can't imagine why, I'm sure it's not a good idea, but I'm hooked; I'm a goner and I can't help it.

CHAPTER 40

Vic had gotten Charles to agree to another delay while she arranged money and transport. The National Commission had provided her a way to go. The heads of the four families each contributed up front five figure amounts, to then be followed by the required six figure balance which had been first counterfeited, then discounted, as arranged by Tania in Europe.

The initial heroin order was going to be cut down considerably, a matter which she would have to explain to Charles — the other LFM leaders insisted her plans were overly-ambitious — but at least she had cashier's checks in hand for the first two payments, $200,000 and $250,000 respectively. Vic had decided to use a Caribbean smuggling route to Florida and up north via Amtrak. All that remained now was finalizing with Charles.

She hadn't talked to him in the past few weeks, just after the last reluctant delay he'd granted, when he said he'd give one final extension of thirty days, that he wanted payment by then. "You know, I have long since placed this order, my people have filled it and are warehousing it, and want to know what is going on?" he said.

"I apologize, but it's been one thing after the next — you have no idea."

"Look, I appreciate that everyone has their problems, and contingencies do arise. But this is business, and I assumed your word was good."

"It is! I always honor my commitments."

"You had beater, because I vouched for your credibility, and now my channels are making demands, which makes me look bad."

The problem was every time in the past couple of weeks she phoned, she was given the runaround, and he wasn't returning her calls. Now she was ready to make the deal, where the hell was the son of a bitch?

"We have to do something about this Cestari business," she told Harry. "My extension's all but run out, and I can't even find this bastard."

Then he appeared in New York, at :Le Chantilly restaurant. She called his name as he waltzed past her without recognition, as if she were a total stranger. Her mouth dropped as her heart simultaneously sank. She knew his eyes were bad, but since when was he hard of hearing? She called louder. "Charles!"

He turned, an oily smile on his face. "Oh, hello. How are you?" he said in his most impersonal tone and turned away again. You prick, she thought, watching his nonchalant body language. He acknowledged someone else with a phony greeting, then turned back to her and said, "Excuse me. Nice to see you," and he was off. Weren't Frenchmen supposed to be known for their continental manners? How dare he? Where was he staying? She had to let him know she had the money, she was ready to do the deal. Later, Harry found he was registered at the Plaza. Heart racing, she phoned his room.

"This is Victoria Winters," she said.

"Yes?" As if he didn't know, the prick.

"Remember me, Charles?" she purred, feeling a knife in her chest.

"Oh, yes — Listen, I —"

He was going to try to end the conversation, tell her he was tied up, she could feel it coming. Something had thrown a wrench in this relationship, probably the unavoidable foul ups and delays. She interrupted before he had chance to say anything further. "I have the money," she said.

"What?"

"The money. Our deal."

"May I phone you tomorrow?"

"Listen, Charlie, I have the certified checks, six figures. Do you want the money, or what?"

"Of course. But let me phone you back — do I have your number?"

Maybe he didn't believe her. She wouldn't give him the option of not calling. "I'll phone you," she said evenly. "What's a good time?"

"Around ten," he said.

Intuition told her he had a woman in his bed, and that made her even more angry. Why was she so obsessed with this man? Really, who in their right mind would want someone with his indifference, a man that rude, who thought he could run the show?

On the one hand she wanted him for the sex, for his power to make her respond, but really she did not want him. What was the son of a bitch good for, except in the sack? Probably she just wanted to know she could have him and walk away — break his balls, ruin his life, make him sorry he ever met her.

The next morning she phoned at ten, as agreed. He was not there. She fumed.

Finally she tracked him down at one of his hangouts, La Grande Bide, a frog bistro in the East 60's, where he was lunching with three other people. She waited till he exited, then followed him. He didn't know he was being tailed, but she kept on him to the St. Regis Drug Store, F.A.O. Schwartz, Mark Cross, and Gucci. At every stop he made a number of purchases. Even though she hated his guts, she resented the possibility that he might be buying gifts for his mistress and hoped he didn't have one, the bastard. He was on his way back to the Plaza when she decided to corner him on the southeast side of 5th and 58th.

At first he was wary — probably still didn't believe she had the money. But when she pulled the cashier's checks totaling $450,000 out of her purse and flashed them in front of his eyes, he started changing his tune. First he made a grab for them, but she pulled them away. Then, butter wouldn't melt in his mouth.

"Won't you come to my suite at the Plaza and we will make the arrangements?" he invited in mellifluous tones. "I have only a short time. My driver is arriving at 4:30 to take me to the airport; however — "

That meant no sex. It was already 3:15 now, so fuck that. What the hell did he think she was, to just hand over checks for nearly a half a million and not get properly laid in return?

"You're going back to Europe?"

"To Corsica, yes."

"My, what a coincidence. I'm heading that way myself. Why don't we meet there?"

"In Corsica?" he said, surprised. "What brings you there? When are you arriving?"

"About 24 hours after you."

"Well, in that case, all right, then," he agreed. "Corsica it is. I am in Ajaccio, birthplace of Napoleon Bonaparte. Let me give you my number."

He wrote it out for her, and she put it in her purse with a sense of triumph.

CHAPTER 41

Although Sam had promised to help with the Teamsters, no immediate followup ensued. In Chicago, he said it was in the works, trust me; but after Laura's return to New York, two days passed with no action. Sam's habit was to phone every day, yet 48 hours had passed without a ring. Finally, he called from the far east to say the deal was definitely on. He'd been in transit, flying the 26 hour route from Chicago to Hong Kong, after which, worn out, he'd slept for the next twelve hours; that was why she hadn't heard from him. Relieved, Laura made plans to meet him in Chicago upon his return.

Laura lifted a tall crystal goblet of pale burgundy in toast, while Sam adjusted his silk tie and scrutinized her. His manicured fingers flexed. He was giving her a carefully edited version of his life story.

"I want you to hear the whole thing," he said, tugging at the cuffs of his neatly starched, grey-on-white monogrammed shirt, custom made by a fashionable tailor in Milan. He told her how his mother had died giving birth to him, that when he was only six, his father had been stuffed in a drawer in the morgue before he was pronounced dead, after which he and his brother had been shipped off to an orphanage.

"They never fed us enough, so I used to steal bread, hide it in my shirt and take it to the dormitory. They'd find the crumbs and whack me with a board." He cracked the knuckles of his manicured fingers. "Once I was so hungry I ate a whole box of communion wafers." He reached for an antacid pill and washed it down with ice water. "I came out of that orphanage fighting," he said, "but I always knew what I wanted and where I was going."

The reptilian black eyes were steady, appraising her again. He said, "You know, as a rule I don't go for Sicilian girls. But you're different. And you need a friend – am I right? So I'm offering myself as your consigliere," he joked deadpan, and took a shot of Strega. "But let's talk about more pleasant things." A nerve throbbed silently in his cheek. "You interest me," he said. "The more I know you, the more I want to know you better."

As they were leaving the restaurant, Sam said something to one of his henchmen in *baccagliu*, called `the secret tongue of the mafia.' It was strictly an insider's language, and Laura had picked it up around her father. When it dawned on Sam she understood every word he said, he did a double take. "Jesus," he said, "I gotta watch my step with you. You even speak *baccagliu*. *Mala femmina*'s right."

Business-wise, everything was working out. Sam had pushed the $160 million casino construction loan through with the Teamsters. Although he claimed to want no credit, there was an almost false modesty in the way that he managed to call attention to his pivotal role, while in the next breath denying it: "I'm not taking a piece of the action, but my payoff will come later," he joked. In spite of a small residue of ambivalence, Laura felt, inside of just a few weeks, a very deep attachment to him.

The first time they went to bed, it happened unexpectedly in the River Forest greenhouse where he grew rare tropical blooms from all over the world. Showing her his gentrified, sprawling Lake Michigan estate, he said his wife was away in Florida. The marriage had been over for years, but officially was still on the books and would remain that way. He would never divorce his wife, never. He said he felt guilty for bringing her here.

"But I wanted you to know me better — that's why we came here — so you could see this, which is such a big part of me. Come."

He took her arm and led her outdoors to the greenhouse. Cacti and creepers decorated the forecourt: rare lilies and orchids were at the far end of the hothouse. They were alone. He showed her his prize dwarf azaleas and Chinese palms that flourished under the geodesic dome. Moving down long aisles, they strolled to where vivid bromeliads bloomed. A Pablo Casals recording of Kodaly's Sonata for cello, opus 8, played on the stereo.

Tropical plant scents intensified as they went deeper down the aisles toward hotter parts of the growing area, where multi-colored flora climbed overhead and decks of lilies exuded a sweet aroma. She felt aroused by the heat, the scents, and by Sam's presence.

His hand touched the yellow petals of a tiny South American orchid. He inspected a cluster of creeping charlie, plumped its leaves and plucked a few dry ones off the plant. Then he beckoned toward a collection of desert cactuses and succulents.

She searched his eyes. Something was different now. He took her hand and led her up a winding staircase to the second floor, to a bed. They were both very excited as they tore each other's clothes off. He was inside her even before they were completely undressed. At first it was frenetic, then they slowed down and took their time. His mouth, buried in her shoulder, emitted an almost strangled sound when he came.

Suddenly a gust of wind came from nowhere. A formation of dark clouds appeared, there was a flash of lightning, splitting the sky open, another and another, each followed by low rumbles of thunder. The wind whistled through the trees. The rain rushed, roared, pounded. Laura rested in Sam's arms, happy and fulfilled. It seemed she had wanted him so long, wanted him more than she had even realized. And yet, as she drifted off to sleep, her last thoughts were of Frank Gantry.

CHAPTER 42

Victoria knew the instant she set foot on its soil that exploring "the scented isle" would be pure ecstasy. Corsica, "a mountain surrounded by sea," was a 600 mile long coastline 50 miles from the Italian mainland and 100 miles from the French Riviera, where spectacular crimson granite peaks rose nearly two miles into a seacoast fringed with pine. Napoleon said he would recognize his native island blindfolded by its scent alone — the aroma of terraced gardens and olive groves, orchards, vineyards and wildflowers — maquis, buckthorn, myrtle, rosemary, lavender and so many more. While the rest of the world was plunged in dreary winter, Corsica was wrapped in "the white spring," with flowered heath forming a dramatic rolling carpet that tumbled to the sea.

Cestari's Ajaccio home was magnificent. Nights, the villa was lit by flaming torches outside. Inside, above the entrance hall's gilded circular staircase, was a baccarat crystal chandelier thirty feet high. Thousands of soft lights glittered from its giant frame, creating interesting patterns on the floor's Chinese rugs. In back of the house, a free form swimming pool had been built around a grotto, its cascading waterfalls surrounded by large rocks and tropical plants. In the library was a glass-encased display of Chinese snuff bottles — hornbill, tourmaline, lapis lazuli; he also collected Portuguese wood carvings, Indian sculpture, Indonesian and New Guinea totem poles.

He worked out in his private gym daily for two hour stretches. But Cestari was more than just a phenomenally well-preserved hunk and more than an astute businessman, he could be a surprisingly good listener and advisor, she discovered. Despite not trusting him, she was nevertheless comfortable with him and valued his opinions. His point of view, in contrast to Harry's, was sophisticated and worldly.

It was a load off her mind to have the heroin business arranged, since she'd been thinking about it for the better part of the past year. Her life was really on track now. The first 100 kilo load would be shipped from Germany to Puerto Rico next week; she'd given Charles the initial payment. Still she was on her guard, given his strange performance in New York. His explanation was he was being watched and didn't want to draw suspicion to her, it was for her own safety he'd treated her like a stranger. He swore there never was a problem. Vic remained wary.

They were dining at a local hangout on delicious blackbird paté with ham and sausage made from chestnut fed pork, smoked over the fires of aromatic Corsican shrubs.

"You mean you couldn't even say a decent hello in that restaurant?"
"It was my poor eyesight. I apologize. I didn't know it was you."
"Some excuse, fucking and forgetting," Vic grumbled.

Still, she must have been doing something right, because after Corsica he invited her to his villa in the Aubagne section of Marseille, where they spent several days together. Or maybe it was because he wanted the second cashier's check, while she was still withholding it, pending clearance of the first shipment. He knew better than to push, so he was treating her very carefully now, catering to her every need.

Like Ajaccio, his Marseille spread was unbelievable. The heart of the house was not on floors visible from the street, but in a concrete bunker below. The living room was an exotic jungle paradise lit by special simulated sunlight, with an aviary of rare birds and one entire wall of tropical fish. An electronically controlled waterfall rising 20 feet into the air cascaded down on one side of the room into an indoor swimming pool flanked by huge jungle ferns and exotic flora. If you pressed a button, a wall under the falls swung out to reveal an amply stocked bar. There was a sauna and exercise room where Charles maintained his incredible fitness.

Victoria dallied several days in the baronial splendor of Cestari's villa with its mosaics, pools, waterfalls, and marble Grecian statues, secure in the knowledge that her precious white powder would be arriving Stateside in a matter of two weeks. She was euphoric. Cestari took her to his hangouts in Marseille where le milieu congregated — Le Pussy Cat, the Artistic Bar, Chez Toto, and the Bar de la Rotonde, where his network convened at four and held court for hours.

She was learning more about him and his organization. The Corsican underworld controlled the city of Marseille via its own nucleus of 30,000 accomplices who were prepared to carry out services and maintain silence on the part of the *caid*, the criminal elite. This larger body, known as the phenomenon of *La Gâche*, was said to be the best insulated criminal organization in the world. In fact, a form of solidarity existed between all Corsicans everywhere. Under penalty of death, one was loyal to *le milieu*. No Corsican would dream of betraying a compatriot, thus one would never read about Charles in the newspapers, and law enforcement and politicians would bend over backwards to accommodate him. One of his closest cronies was the operational boss of all French police. Cestari himself was immensely respected. He had even served in the French Chamber of Deputies as a representative from Ajaccio.

Nights they returned to his complex for hours of incredible sex. She knew she was his slave, willing to do anything he asked. Up until Charles, cunnilingus and/or clitoral stimulation had been Victoria's chief methods of sexual satisfaction, vaginal orgasms being rare. Perhaps the problem was that her vagina was so large that the average penis was just too small to do the job, but Charles' bide was truly elephantine, in addition to which he was an insatiable satyr. Thus, she was now having regular vaginal orgasms; Charles was easily the highlight of her entire sexual existence, and she could never get enough, never.

Dolce far niente, as the saying went, no sweeter than as a guest on his 90 foot yacht, cruising the Mediterranean, lolling, lazing, basking in the sun, fucking and sucking their lives away. Drinking *pastis*, Charles waxed philosophical. He told her he saw himself as a *mort-vivant*, a man walking to his own self-inflicted death. He sighed, "Perhaps you see me as a *salaud*. But we are living in a sea of sharks."

She was drawn to the inbuilt icy-still menace of this man, to his magnificent physique and nervous energy and the ever present surface tension. Ah, that relentless, frigid amorality, the alluring coldness that gave him the aura of Satan encased in a block of ice — irresistible!

"Friendship," he said, "is the pivotal point of life."

Victoria dragged on her cigarette, exhaling the fumes in gulps.

"More than anything in this world I prize friendship," he continued. "*On peut toujours baiser, mais l'amitié c'est vraiment quelque chose*. I do not believe in love or in transient passion, only in friendship and the given word, and in a sense of honor. I am Corsican. Honor above all is important to me."

They lay naked together, their bodies' reflections glittering on the yacht's mirrored ceiling. He stared at her with eyes like black diamonds until she could bear his gaze no longer. His dark body enveloped her as he murmured stimulations and stroked her with feathery light fingers, bringing her again and again to newer, greater arousal. Savage, sensual tremors shook her as his body continued its crescendo of thrilling bursts and low sounds escaped his lips.

"*Tu me fascines*," he said, squeezing her hand. "*Tu m'intéresses beaucoup. Tu es ravissante, ma chère*. I want to know all about you." His words sounded great in French, devastatingly romantic and exhilarating. That throaty velvet voice -- *merde*! And being on the yacht, being rocked by the sea, made it all the more so. Charles was her major vice. She wanted to penetrate that wall and reach the soul underneath.

"Life must be lived dangerously in order not to be banal," he said. "You and I, *ma Victoire*, we have chosen to gamble with life." Victoria had never met a man more detached yet more seductive. It excited him to have her on top. He loved her long legs wrapped around his neck.

However, the sex wasn't always 100% the way she wanted it. Slowly, Cestari began showing another facet, a kinky aspect she found humiliating yet was powerless to resist. For instance, he again wanted her to lick his bung hole (she'd gone along with the request in Beirut, but enough was enough). He also wanted sodomy, another turnoff. It was a constant power struggle between them, and Vic swore she was going to get the better of him if it was the last thing she did.

At the back of her mind, she was gathering pieces of a puzzle, that the mystery that was Charles and the strange way he affected her meant something beyond what she could now understand. She was curious about his life and wanted to know everything about him. When he was in the shower she snooped through his drawers and closets. A woman in love couldn't be too careful or calculating. This guy was not to be trusted. Her greater power would derive from having something on him.

She found his keys, including one to his desk drawer, and using techniques Harry taught her, made impressions. She microfilmed documents and photos that looked interesting, got the combination of the lock to his safe.

From her knowledge of locksmithing, she knew one of his keys, a special "government clearance" type, was uncopyable. A Cuban CIA spook ex-lover had once given her such a key and she'd tried copying it, but neither she nor any professional locksmith in town could duplicate it. Knowing Cestari had two copies, she took one.

In his desk she found a series of pornographic photographs of him with a woman who looked familiar — yet Vic couldn't place her. There was Charles, his huge penis in full erection — it was almost obscene for a man to be that well endowed — and this woman, a brunette with a very dark, hairy cunt, her teeth clenched in erotic ecstasy, both staring transfixed at their respective genitalia. Vic took one of the originals and rephotographed all the others in the collection.

They were watching the news on TV that night, sharing a split of Blanc de Blanc, when it hit her who the woman was — none other than Madame Pompier, wife of the President of France! Very interesting. Whereas the woman in the photos had a jet black bush, Madame Georgette Pompier had been known in public for years now as a blonde. The pictures must have been taken at least a quarter of a century ago, but it was unmistakably Madame P — same snotty, vicious face, pouty, cruel slash of a red mouth, the horny aristocrat, game for anything, ruled by her cunt and flaunting it. The pictures were a goldmine, and she knew where the negatives were in case they were ever needed.

Pointedly, Victoria alluded to Madame Pompier. "The French President's wife is hot looking, isn't she? What are they saying about her on the news?"

"Nothing. They are talking about him only."

"Oh. The wife seems more astute than he. She must be very clever. Do you think she's attractive?"

"For a woman of a certain age, she is still goodlooking."

"Do you find her sexy? Would you like to fuck her?"

He laughed, uncomfortable, and shifted his weight. "Frankly, I don't think that much about fucking the President's wife," he said. "I doubt there would be an opportunity, given the restrictions protocol imposes."

"Well, would you have liked to when you were younger, before she became first lady?"

"That might have been different," he admitted.

"Have you ever met her?"

"Yes, in fact, I have. But why are you asking these questions, why — "

"Have you ever fucked her?"

"What gives you such an idea?" he asked, with exaggerated affront.

"Intuition. I just think you have."

He snickered, "So now you are psychic."

"Aha! So you have fucked her then?"

"I didn't say that. What do you think I am, a human fucking machine?"

"Yes, that's exactly what I do think. I think you'd screw anything that walked and plenty that can't."

"Come on," he rose with impatience, "let's take a drink together in town."

She'd made him uncomfortable with her manipulation of the Georgette Pompier affair, and right after that, it was as though he wanted to teach her a lesson. That night he humiliated her sexually by making her lick his bung hole again, knowing full well she hated it; then once again, he forced sodomy on her, the ultimate perverted insult. And after that came bondage — like it was his payoff, like she owed it to him.

He donned a mask. He looked satanic, a devil with a long skinny rat's tail, in a red and black costume, red and black spangles on his cock. In a not so subtle gesture, he even put Boito's *Mefistofele* on the stereo. He said she couldn't have his cock unless she begged for it. She begged. Begged and begged to no avail. He kept refusing to give his cock to her, tormenting her until she was crazy. It was his idea of a joke and she was mortified.

But she still had the second certified check, and she was using it as a wedge. Finally, he agreed to take her to one of his heroin manufacturing labs, because he knew that was the only way he was going to pry loose the second check. She basked in the satisfaction that she could force him to comply.

"It's a dangerous process," he warned. "You can burn your lungs out."

"That's ok, we can use gas masks. I'm sure your chemist does."

They drove about 45 minutes into the winding hills. The odor of vinegar was overpowering as they approached a secluded spot behind high stone walls. Charles said, "You realize I've never shown this to any woman before."

"Not even to your wife?" Vic asked with feigned innocence.

"Certainly not," he replied, indignant, as if his wife were the last person he'd bring here.

"Tell me about your wife. You never talk about her."

He didn't want to go into that subject. All she could glean was that the wife lived in Paris, saw friends for lunch, shopped and liked to frequent art galleries. His only child, a daughter, sold Haitian art in Paris. He was obviously more attached to the daughter than to the wife, who seemed like a non-person.

Cestari shut off the ignition and looked around, on guard. Unlike most labs, this one was not mobile, but a permanent structure. She followed him around a winding path to an outbuilding in back.

Refining heroin was, as Cestari had said, a highly perilous procedure. Used in the wrong proportions, the chemicals could be deadly, improper heating could cause an explosion, the process took days, and apart from the smell that aroused suspicion, you could ruin potential profits in the millions by mixing to cheaper grade # 3 or # 2 when you intended to make the more lucrative # 4 heroin. The difficulties involved in refining were one reason the American market was so dependent on foreigners.

"Using one part acetic acid to one part heroin produces the high quality # 4, whereas for # 3 you are using 6 parts acetic acid. If you goof on the manufacture then you must give up trying to produce # 4 and go to # 3, which will mean an inferior product and far less money," Cestari explained.

100 tons of opium was needed to make 10 tons of # 3 heroin, the smoking stuff, called purple heroin, whereas six times this amount was necessary to make an equal amount of the coveted # 4.

Vic watched the *poudre blanche* being manufactured, watched Cestari's stocky, efficient chemist, Andre Comine, surrounded by microscopes, bunsen burners, beakers and chloroform, mixing sodium carbonate and acetone, tartaric acid and acetic anhydride.

Pouring in water in a series of carefully controlled steps, he heated the mixture to 1000 degrees centigrade, boiled and filtered it. The process was repeated several times, after which the resulting solution was dehydrated via evaporation. The resulting powder obtained would contain 95% heroin, which would then be raised even higher by a continuing process with alcohol, ether and hydrochloric acid. It was in these final steps that Comine outdid himself, achieving what other chemists could not.

The transformation process was long, requiring 17 steps and over one day to do it. Morphine base was treated with acetone, heated to 212 degrees, acetone pumped off, the base treated with carbon black to whiten it, neutralized with caloric acid, baked in sludge, dried, sifted. The process had to be repeated several times until the desired purity was attained.

Afterwards, she finally broke down and gave Cestari the money. He took it casually, an almost disdainful look on his face.

When he found the key missing from his trousers, Vic made light of it. "Probably fell out of your pants, maybe last night when you took your cock out. Anyway, why do you need that one? You have others, don't you?"

"Yes, you're right. It will probably turn up."

The next evening, they were enjoying a leisurely supper together at the Artistic Bar, when four ski-masked gunmen armed with MAT 49 submachine guns barged in. Vic looked up from her bouillabaisse and screamed. She only escaped by running for cover into a pipe barrel. Charles got lucky too, but three of his bodyguards were killed.

Cestari was so shaken that after that he forgot all about the key.

CHAPTER 43

"I'm going to teach you how to suck a man's balls," Sam said, turning to Laura in bed.

He'd told her, that first time in the greenhouse, that sexually he was traditional except in one respect, and that he would reveal the details later. Now was the time. He gazed at her naked body as he rose from the bed. "I have just one special sexual request," he said. "If you do this, I'm your slave for life."

"Anything you want — name it, it's yours," Laura said, watching him head for the bathroom.

"You do a great job sucking cock — let's see how you do with something slightly different," his voice rose above the sound of the water faucet. He returned with a saucer filled with warm water and got back into bed. Placing the saucer under his testicles, he spread out his legs.

He told her how to coordinate the sucking with the right amount of liquid, and the rhythm of sucking with the rhythm of his balls floating in water. The art was subtle and sensual, bringing eroticism of an astounding level if executed to perfection.

"Now you know something few women know," he said afterward. "You picked it up right away." He was more than satisfied — so much so, in fact, that he opened a drawer by the bedside to give her a surprise gift, a diamond bracelet. "You're everything a man could want," he said, moving closer, touching her breasts. "Do you know how it excites me when you're sucking my balls that way, and I think about you servicing me – "

"Servicing — like a whore?"

"Exactly, just like a whore. And you don't fit the image — that's what makes it so exciting." He squeezed her hand.

"If I'm not your image of a whore, what am I your image of?"

"A nice Sicilian girl," he chuckled.

"Which you don't go for."

"Till now. Now I'm addicted for life."

Their romance was blossoming in smoky piano bars, flashy nightclubs and posh eating spots across the country, with quiet lunches and dinners in private suites in Reno, Tahoe, Miami, Vegas, L.A., Palm Springs. When they were apart he always sent flowers.

"You need somebody like me," he said.

"So you keep telling me. Soon I may start believing it." But she believed it already.

He phoned every day and they'd talk for hours without running out of things to say. Thankfully, there were no up and down emotions. The relationship offered her a safe, secure feeling, not the kind of happiness that being with Frank would bring, but something comfortable that gave her a sense of being anchored.

Sam turned her onto a whole new sexual dimension she'd never known before. Like with the saucer — she loved to suck his balls that way, to please him and give him pleasure. He said she was *viziosa*. She told him he had a madonna/whore split in his psyche.

"Where do you get that from?" he wanted to know.

"It's true. And so typical of Italian males."

"Who says?"

"Everyone who knows anything about Italian men," Laura replied. "The Italian male finds it easier to function with a woman he considers a 'whore,' because of the split in his psyche. It stems from the Italian male's relationship with his mother, who's a madonna. Italian men think they should honor and protect madonnas, so it's very easy for them to end up marrying the wrong woman — a madonna. The Italian male can never fully accept the sexuality of his wife, his sister or his mother, he can never accept that all women are both madonna and whore — "

"You've got it all figured out, haven't you? Now I know why they say Sicilian girls are *furba* as hell."

"Maybe it's just as well you'll never divorce your wife," Laura said. "If you married me, the pattern could repeat itself. I'd stop being the whore and become the madonna, you'd be bored and find yourself another whore. Then our sex life would be ruined."

"Impossible!"

"It's true. This is one reason an Italian man should never, never make the mistake of marrying his mistress — it can't work. They'll both be miserable for the rest of their lives."

Obviously Sam's wife hadn't mastered the art of sucking his balls in a saucer of water the way she had. Frank should see her in her glory, sucking and fucking the most powerful man in Chicago. Eat your heart out, Frank. Little do you dream what you're missing.

Sam might not be young like Frank, he might be old enough to be her father, but his stature was unquestionable and his power an aphrodisiac. He treated her like a princess and showering her nonstop with expensive gifts. Besides, she was comfortable with him. People who considered Sam dangerous and sinister didn't know his other side. He was thoughtful and attentive and he made her laugh. She was important in his life, she had the power to turn him on and the power to divert him from his family. She was more exciting to him than any woman he'd ever known.

She had fallen in love with a man who was strong and in command, a man with the quiet instincts of a barracuda and the studied impulses of a cobra. She had fallen in love and didn't know quite why, why he was so fascinating to her, if it was Sam as a person or his position, where the dividing line was, why she needed him and needed to prove something to herself, why she was so consumed. He brought her something — a tremendous rush, a charge she could find nowhere else. She was addicted.

He had walked miles for her and removed obstacles. Then why was she ambivalent? Yes indeed, she relished being Sam's whore, performing the role to perfection as no one else could, yet even so, she felt the pangs of longing for something Sam could never give her, only Frank. Often in bed with Sam, her thoughts were of Frank.

Yet at the same time, as strong as her feelings were for Frank, she still resented his marrying someone else, even if the marriage was nothing but outward show. She resented his family life and pose of domesticity, fantasized the facade crumbling and Frank turning to her. Sometimes in her mind she'd tell him off. But when all was said and done, she still refused to accept anything as final — some day Frank would come around. Never mind he'd started a family. Give it time.

For now, she was relishing Sam, enjoying being in love with him — even if something was missing.

CHAPTER 44

Everything was moving along at a clip. Vic's heroin was selling like hotcakes, her other enterprises were booming, and plans were progressing for Sapphire Bay, for which luckily, she'd gotten herself reinstated. Furthermore, her old balling buddy Robert Francis Casey, newly elected Governor of New York, was set to be inaugurated, while the latest major event in the life of another erstwhile balling buddy, Anthony Zino, was an assassination attempt in the lobby of the San Carlos Hotel that hit all the papers.

"Next thing you know, he's going to be blaming it on me," Victoria commented to Harry.

"He's got a bunch of grievances against you, that's for sure," Harry agreed.

Zino was pissed by the LFM's going over his head to the Teamsters through Laura's connection to Sam, thus cutting him out. He also nursed the beef over Jack's gambling debts, blaming it for weakening his power in the mob, which indeed could have brought on the assassination attempt. And of course, he still had a personal axe to grind with Victoria over the heart attack, Pega Palo, and gonorrhea.

Harry said, "You've had nothing but *tsouris* from this guy — he's screwed you in every sense of the word."

"Damn right. Shit, I like to lie down when I get fucked."

"You can say that again. It's virtually certain he was behind Georgia's murder, probably in tandem with Casey and Mike Giordano. Besides, he knows too much about LFM operations. Listen, the feds are dying to get something on Zino. If they could nail him on tax evasion or anything, they'd be pleased to put this public enemy behind bars."

"Are you suggesting I become an informant, Counselor?"

"Makes sense, baby. Build good will, improve your profile with Uncle. You'll have an easier time sleeping."

"You may have a point, Harry. I'll take it under serious consideration."

Meantime, Vic sent Governor Casey an anonymous greeting on the eve of his inauguration: "Warning — what happened to your pal Tony Z. in Manhattan could happen to you in Albany."

"Don't you remember my voice?" The sound was strange, disembodied, as if coming from inside a tunnel.

Tania froze. "Who is this? Who's calling? What do you want?"

"You don't remember ..." The voice trailed off. Click.

Someone was playing games again. The phone would ring and no one would be on the other end, or it would be a wrong number. Sometimes the calls came in from the overseas operator, other times there was nothing but dial tone. The odd thing was that these calls were on Jack's private line, and very few people had that number. She hadn't bothered to disconnect Jack's phone in all this time. Who would still be calling Jack? Why was it a dead ring? What was going on, Tania wondered?

A conclave of La Femmina bosses convened in London for the joyous occasion of Deborah Cook's big wedding at St. Paul's, Knightsbridge. Deb was stunning in flame pleated tulle at a champagne reception at Claridge's following the ceremony. The groom, Calouste Derounian, was a rich Armenian born in the Caucusus, a naturalized British subject, owner of international banks in the mideast, France and the U.K., who represented a four-nation oil interest, and whose wealth was estimated in excess of sixty billion dollars.

Calouste's car was a tourist attraction in London, a metallic blue Daimler upholstered in lizard skin, boasting a bonnet modeled on the Parthenon and a Steinway installed in the back seat so Calouste, a dedicated musician, could practice his Chopin. Once a year he booked the Albert Hall and invited music loving friends applaud him in concert. Twice a year the car was flown to his villa in the south of France.

Deb had recently spearheaded a masterful coup with the complex transfer of Offshore Fiduciary Fund money representing underworld proceeds from loan sharking, casino skims, prostitution, tax evasion, numbers and narcotics. This operation bagged the La Femmina organization $200 million worth of assets for a mere $50,000 cash outlay, accomplished mainly through multi-level tiers of paper corporations masterminded by Carole Curtis. The result: the LFM syndicate now controlled the premier vehicle for laundering in the Caribbean, and owned a coveted list of names of investments and investors, including organized crime figures as well as government officials, dictators and other tax evaders world wide. Deborah, Calouste and the Daimler left on a honeymoon in his elegantly appointed private jet.

Tania saw Corrado briefly in London this trip; though she longed to be with him for greater periods of time, schedules did not permit. But every experience shared with him, however fleeting, was magical. He was not only her lover, he was a friend and advisor who taught her about banking, credit, business. And they talked endlessly, about art, history, philosophy, literature, travel, food, fashion, films, everything.

Whenever a realization flashed through her mind that other women existed in his life, she would hastily push the thought away. All right, this man was tied to a loveless marriage and to a one-dimensional mistress (admittedly gorgeous, but more shadow than substance); so what? The mistress couldn't provide what she could, and the marriage had no value. These relationships were meaningless, superficial and unworthy of a man of his distinction. Let's face it, he had nothing going with Valentina but outward convention, and Ingeborg was a bimbo. Tania, and Tania alone could provide what Corrado truly needed.

She hoped he realized that. Otherwise, she was going to have to find a way to make him understand.

CHAPTER 45

Upon finding her initial heroin orders from Cestari were still too large, Vic cut them down, in fact, even delayed one whole month's supply entirely. She had also come to recognize belatedly that the price Cestari was giving her wasn't as good as she'd originally bragged about. When all was said and done, she was still making out like a bandit on the heroin; however, her underlying feeling was one of resentment that Cestari should have done better by her.

Then, other aggravations impinged. Vic had been expecting a fat lump sum from a deal with Anthony Zino. She told Harry, "That jai-a-lai fronton in Connecticut. You know I set that up. I made the introductions. It's my deal."

"I dunno why you never got it in writing from Zino."

"Zino's a standup guy," Vic insisted. "He won't cheat me." But then she heard the fronton deal had gone through, and Zino wasn't returning her calls. When she finally got ahold of him, he told her the money wasn't released yet. She checked it out, found everything he said was bullshit.

Finally, she admitted, "The cocksucker fucked me out of my cut. First he screwed us by insisting Jack's share of the gambling concessions be turned over to the mob. We had to forfeit 50% plus vig, and he's fucked us over down the line ever since."

Vic thought better of becoming enmeshed in a legal skirmish with the likes of Zino. There had to be other ways of dealing with the guy. But how?

While the bug Harry planted at his hotel netted no information on Zino's sexual activities, which presumably had been conducted off premises, it did provide something better, and it was dynamite — Zino had not been born in the U.S. as his passport claimed, but in Sicily. At the age of four, he'd entered the country illegally, smuggled in in a coffin.

Harry said, "We got the SOB this time, hon. We can have this guy deported any time you want."

"Not a bad idea, Harry. It's definitely an option that's getting more and more attractive."

LFM operations occupied Laura's agenda on a stepped up basis, as shylocking, numbers and narcotics continued raking in the dollars, while her legitimate enterprises were multiplying as well. She'd concluded deals for a tobacco vending machine company and a truck parts sales agency, as well as a trading company selling auto equipment and used machinery. A situation was in the works for a scrap iron business in Queens, and she was signing a contract on a company that operated 700 washing machines in apartment buildings in the Bronx. She finished setting up a cellulose insulation and manufacturing plant in Staten Island; she was negotiating purchase of bowling alleys in the Westchester-

Connecticut area, and she had recreational projects going in four states. She was also a partner in a transfer company and a brokerage house.

In the works was a syndicate-owned bank in the Turks and Caicos Islands, where no reserves were necessary to make loans, and by now she had secret offshore accounts in the Bahamas, Liechtenstein, Luxembourg, Sark, Austria, Andorra, Campione, Monaco, Gibraltar and Switzerland.

An LFM partnership Laura headed was interested in an operation in Las Vegas that had been put up at a cost of several million but remained idle because it lacked a casino. A pal of Sam's with a record for fixing baseball games couldn't get a license and needed a front. He would be their silent partner. Another pal of Sam's, head of the culinary workers, the most powerful union in the state, guaranteed them a license would be granted. But he was found shot to death by rivals.

Sam paved the way for the LFM group to go in by clearing out the competition that was behind the murder. Next, Sam worked out terms with the Teamsters to allow truckers to come in from out of state. Ivy Schlatter, Boss of Cleveland, took leave of her Shaker Heights garrison for the Nevada desert to run the LFM owned Ali Baba hotel-casino complex. That was their first Vegas property. Another was soon to follow.

The Chicago mob's reach encompassed satellite cities of Milwaukee, Cleveland, Detroit, Kansas City, St. Louis, Los Angeles, and to a certain extent, Las Vegas, which was supposedly open territory but Chicago-dominated. Now, after years of lucrative skimming, the Cleveland group in Vegas was in serious trouble and was looking to unload its Nevada holdings. Its leader was under federal indictment for tax evasion and facing a host of other federal criminal prosecutions. With the Chicago family's seal of approval, a consortium of LFM's negotiated terms to purchase Cleveland's holdings.

They purchased 300,000 shares, representing 25% of the outstanding stock of the company, which owned three casinos, for a total price of 30.5 million, at $35 a share, well below the trading price for the previous month. The agreement was signed pending the gaming commission's approval for the license, which would be granted, it was anticipated, in three months. The seller then took off on a vacation.

The LFM's went to work with lawyers and accountants. Lily, Carole and Deborah headed a team that boosted the stock, using boiler room tactics alongside high class promotional methods. They sold a third of the shares, then plowed back money into the market, acquired more shares, inflated those, and created a false appearance of active trading. After the stock was driven way up, the company was unloaded to a merger partner, and the price plummeted to $10, at which point the seller reclaimed the company and sold the casino to St. Louis and Detroit mob interests, under the auspices of a notorious mob attorney/degenerate gambler.

Sam's clout helped their status as women of respect, but even without Sam's help Laura had been having spectacular success in every direction.

Hopefully Frank was taking notice.

CHAPTER 46

Media buzz had it that Senator Nick Condon was a viable presidential candidate and a rising star, although it was still conceded that no one could successfully challenge the popular incumbent, Herbert Tree. Thus, most seasoned politicos were playing coy, hanging back from declaring candidacy. Nick was one of the few who'd stuck his neck out and identified himself as available for the office.

As Nick's reputation and visibility increased, it became a greater challenge to be alone with him. Secrecy heightened; excitement intensified. To deflect attention, he and Jasmine always used beards, political aides and trusted cronies.

The couple was meeting clandestinely all over the country, an opportunity for Vic. Thanks to the bugs Harry planted, they were getting some great stuff. Knowing in advance from phone taps where the two were headed, Harry would simply plant surveillance devices in the hotels in which they were scheduled to rendezvous. And sometimes they caught the duo together in public as well.

For instance, Jasmine slipped off to meet Nick in Baja California, Mexico, where they spent a weekend together, watching kinky floor shows, drinking Margaritas and Carta Blancas, listening to mariachi music, shopping, then driving to Rosarito Beach and riding horses on the beach.

They walked out of a sex show, bored. "Other people need kicks because they don't have what we have — what we have is something most people will never experience," Nick told Jasmine. "What a mistake our destinies didn't coincide out front — what a team we'd make. You have the right kind of ambition for me."

Later, back at the hotel, he said, "What's wrong with me that I want you more than anything? When I'm not with you, I think of you all the time." After they made love, he said, "I think you're the most sexual woman I've ever been with, not just because you're so horny, but it's your focus, your amazing concentration, the way you really get into it and stay with it full force and never lose the charge — the way you go for it."

"Eureka!" Vic, watching the videos, exclaimed to Harry. "Can you just imagine if this guy gets the nomination?"

"Better yet, let him make President," Harry said. "We'll own the whole country, hon."

Nick was a man of contrasts, in some ways a babe in the woods, in others a man of the world, a combination of guilelessness and sophistication, erudition and naiveté. He and Jasmine seemed like two consummate narcissists feeding each other's vanity. On another tape, Nick was saying, "It doesn't wear thin."

"What?"

"You. Whenever I'm with you I want to watch you. You fascinate me."

Jasmime stood at a terrace threshold, her eyes steady, arms raised slowly, sweeping her hair upwards in a seductive pose.

"What do you want, Jasmine?" Nick asked. "What are your greatest dreams and fantasies?"

"My biggest ambition is to give you head on Air Force One when you become President of the United States." Jasmine stretched, cat-like, arching her body, and slowly, sinuously, approached. Sliding up to him, she opened his robe and bent toward him. Then she moved her tiger mane hair away so he could see what she was doing to his cock. When she came up for air, the camera caught Nick's eyes, fogged with passion, staring at her taut body. Now her breasts brushed against his chest and her tuft teased his erection. He kissed her throat, her ear, her shoulder, the protrusion of her nipples.

Victoria watched as Nick trembled visibly and as moments later, Jasmine slid her leg over him, drew her mouth closer, and then straddled him. They were always ready for each other. Their tongues probed, melding, and then he turned her over, rose high over her and plunged down. There were passionate outcries when their bodies connected; then he lifted her hips and his cock slowly thrust inside her until they both climaxed.

Roused after a restful after-love slumber, Nick stood by the window, gazing at the sea. He said, "I'm so unbelievably happy. It's too much." The lights below reflected on the water at dusk. Behind the buildings in the distance the sky was deep red from the sun. "I think you are so aware of your power it's frightening. And in sex — you are utterly shameless."

Then he dropped what for him was a bombshell. "There's something I've been needing to tell you. A scandalous secret very few people know about me. Darling, I was adopted."

"What's so shockingly scandalous about that?" Jasmine asked. "Adoption is routine. Were you illegitimate? Is that what bothers you?"

"That's part of it." Turning, he went back to her. "Why is it I can't tell anyone else the things I can tell you?" he asked. "I can confess all my innermost thoughts — "

"I still don't see why you should feel ashamed about being adopted," Jasmine persisted, "or even illegitimate. So what? Adoption happens in the best of families and illegitimacy is fast becoming perfectly acceptable these days. Do you know anything about your real parents?"

"That's just it. My mother ... didn't have the most sterling of reputations," Nick said, with obvious difficulty. "My mother was a drunken prostitute, if you want to know the truth."

Jasmine touched the stubble of his five o'clock shadow and rested her chin on his shoulder. "Was any of this your fault? Did you have any say in the matter?"

"It's just that in politics, things can backfire. If it ever came out, if she ever surfaced, well — "

"Listen, you can always put a favorable spin on these things," Jasmine said. "Isn't that what handlers and spin doctors are for? I wouldn't lose any sleep if I were you."

"I probably worry too much about my image." He paused, then said, with difficulty, "I haven't told you everything, Jasmine. There's more."

"Ok, Nick, out with it."

He looked stricken. "My mother was black."

"Really? One would never guess, looking at you."

"True -- I turned out white," he said, almost apologetically.

"So you're actually mulatto, then. You don't even look that."

"I know. But suppose this emerged in the campaign?"

"It would be a plus. Tons of people who look white these days are claiming they're African-American, under the `one drop' rule ... it gives them an identity and an advantage they wouldn't have as Caucasians. So you'd automatically have a jump in popularity."

"It's just that I've never related to the black part of me. I was raised in a white environment. To suddenly start being black would be strange, foreign to me." He walked a few steps away and looked at himself in the mirror.

"What are you doing?"

"Looking at who I am."

"And what do you see?"

"I see the face of a man in the fast lane, a man who's made decisions and compromises he has to live with, a man whose life is not really his own, and a man whose greatest pleasure is you. We are unique, you know."

"I'm glad you know that, my love."

Vic and Harry had some powerful stuff — skeletons in Nick's closet, Nick committing adultery, Nick admitting he knew Jasmine was mafia; they even had him snorting coke at her invitation. And now this -- Nick Condon was a closet *schwartze*! Spectacular evidence. In time, it would come in handy.

CHAPTER 47

Tania was in the process of expanding her LFM interests to her native Texas. She was concluding construction loans for industrial and commercial projects out of McAllen, and had wrapped up franchises for outdoor recreational facilities paying ten year residuals totaling a million a month in season. Corrado, who adored Texas, came to see the 1000 acre ranch she'd just purchased in northeast Uvalde County, semi-hill country with wildlife abounding.

He bought a horn that honked "Deep in the Heart of Texas," and a blue and white enamel "Texas and Southwestern Cattleraisers Association" sign to hang on the walls of his European headquarters, together with a Lone Star State flag. At Justin Boot in Fort Worth, he purchased short top boots studded with silver nails, a silver concho belt, and a sharp looking blazer edged with leather arrowheads.

There he was, the quintessential Sicilian, walkin' tall in new lizard boots, even talking Texan — hoof it, hang up yer saddle and stay a spell, y'all, fixin', mosey on up — it was a kick to see him play at being Texan, dudin' up at Tony Ramas and Manny Gammage, sporting Stetsons with hand made creases, ordering custom made chaps, belts and buckles Texas-style, paisley handkerchiefs and Mexican shirts.

At an outing to Texas' Golden Triangle, he learned to sing local ditties like "Talk That Trash, Dig That Mash," and ordered crates of Pearl's beer to be shipped to Europe.

Meanwhile, his dreams of making the family-owned Sicilian bank a viable world entity were in place. He gave Tania a grand tour of the company's newly built offices in Milan, where windows in his luxuriously appointed office looked out on the Piazza della Scala, dominated by Magni's monument to Leonardo da Vinci.

Life with Corrado was an adventure in romantic fullness. When he listened he responded with his entire being. When they held hands, watching a sunset together, strolling arm in arm, she had never felt closer or more in tune with anyone. Theirs was a fantastic rapport. Magical. He was everything she could want in a male counterpart.

Corrado knew something about everything — fashion, art, furniture, jewelry, decor — his taste was impeccable. He brought her to the Lancaster in Paris, where they breakfasted together on *oeufs brouillés en croissants*. There were fresh flowers in every room, and when they opened the shutters, the chimneypots of Paris burst into view. Corrado came up behind her on the balcony and ground his cock into her from behind.

In the South of France, he took her to the nudist colony at the Île du Levant, where they played out fantasies together, sun beating down on their naked bodies. Every rock was private and the only sound was the pounding surf below drowning out their cries of passion. In Sicily, she'd had the feeling of being watched. On the Côte d'Azur, she felt free, liberated.

They spent an evening at Divonne at the Rothschild casino, drove through the seven mile tunnel of Mont Blanc. At the Vallée Blanche Glacier they took a cable car up the jagged perpendicular face of the Aiguille du Midi and stood in the midst of howling winds.

"You and I are the last romantic couple," Corrado said. "With you I exist for this moment and forever. This is all there is. We are all there is. We're the world's last romantic couple."

Whether they met on the Piazza Navona or at Maxim's or the Dorchester or the Peninsula in Hong Kong ... it all blended into one picture, something monumental, pure, total. He aroused powerful emotions in her -- hope, elation. The most minor social pleasures created exalted moments. It was a beautiful courtship — lingering in vine-covered cafés of Fregene, moonlight walks on the Campidoglio, champagne suppers, parties at world class resorts. She treasured every thought of him, recreated every embrace.

Even when they were apart she felt anchored in him, reliving the past and fantasizing the future. Her dreams were like chords binding them together, an admixture of megalomania and idealism. She had the feeling the relationship was for a great purpose, one that perhaps only later she would understand.

She lived for the ecstasies, moist desire and throbbing strength of their joined energy.

In London, over dinner at Wheeler's in Old Compton Road, he told her, "Each time we're together it's as if we've never been apart — as if we don't need the continuity that others require, or that we are better for it."

Tania agreed with the first half of the statement, but not the latter. Rather, she longed for a fuller commitment. He made the pronouncement, "One should never marry one's mistress — it never works." If he was referring to Ingeborg, fine, but every now and then she saw he was still thinking of herself as his mistress, even though she'd made it abundantly clear she was not. What an insult! A mistress was an appendage, dependent on a man — totally untrue in her case. Why was he saying this to her?

Other men popped in and out of her life, but she was obsessed with Corrado, the one man who eluded her. To assume greater importance in his life had become near-mania.

Sipping Chardonnay together in one of Balls' newly-opened salons, Tania and Fiona discussed the Corrado dilemma.

"He resists planning a future. It's so aggravating. I can't understand the attachment to this airhead Ingeborg. What can he see in her?"

"Ingeborg is merely a possession, something to flaunt."

"But doesn't he see what an opportunist and user she is?"

"He doesn't care. Rich men need a mistress as an ego trip, society expects it — it's a status symbol, period."

"But it's also a framework. I could never be any man's possession, and yet I have no framework."

"Face it, Tania, you are unlike any woman this man has ever known. You are quite an unusual person."

"That's what makes it tough. I mean, not to brag, Fiona, but when you compare my accomplishments alongside those of the average male, it's not easy to find a man who can parallel me, let alone one I could truly admire and respect, let alone adore. Corrado fills the bill. This man is so fascinating! Like so many Italians, he has real dimension, a secret mystery — he's lighthearted, yet possessed — he has an absolutely wonderful facade, an incredible persona and a very deep shadow. He continually surpasses himself.

"You know, Fiona, part of what is great about being mafiosa is the element of control — being in the driver's seat in a way I could never be otherwise. I love this feeling of control so much I want it to pervade every aspect of my life. And yet here is Corrado — the one thing I can't control at all, and I can't live without him. I want him completely. There is no other man in the world for me! Tell me, Fiona, why can't I have what I want?"

Another time when Tania was losing sleep over Corrado, in the wee small hours, she phoned Fiona in London, when Fiona's day had already started. Fiona listened to Tania's problem, then said, "What you have to understand, Tania, is that Ingeborg is a whole other archetype altogether. But you needn't worry, luv. When Valentina dies, this bloody Ingeborg won't stand a chance."

"What makes you think so, Fiona?"

"Because given any say in the matter, Italian men never want to marry their mistress; the concept of mistress is superficially important to them, but deep down inside they never feel the mistress is worthy of the kind of respect he accords his wife, his sister, his mother. There's only one way the mistress can get an Italian man to commit to a legal union — blackmail, guilt."

"Are you sure?"

"I'm telling you, when Valentina dies, you'll have it made, Tania, because it will be you who'll assume the legitimate role in his life. Mind you, he may still have his playthings, but you'll be the one with the respectability — you'll be his wife."

"Fiona, you really think so?"

"Trust me. Men like Corrado need a wife, and they are particular about whom they choose; they want a woman who enhances them, a woman with background, intelligence and culture. Ingeborg can't qualify. She may be drop dead gorgeous, I'll grant her that, but everybody knows what she is. She's common! A woman like this is fine to parade around for ego enhancement and outward show, but not to introduce as an esteemed marital partner. A man like Corrado would never risk a person like that."

"You've made me feel a lot better, Fiona," Tania said, and hung up, sure that Fiona spoke the truth. All she had to do was play a waiting game. Valentina couldn't possibly last. It was just a question of time, and her dream would be reality.

CHAPTER 48

"If you ask me, honey, you gotta lead a quiet life for a while," Harry said, and he was right.

Vic was still worried about Zino. No telling what the guy might pull; furthermore, her own profile with the feds was getting to be a problem. She'd been under government surveillance — less due to her own activities than to those of subordinates. In particular, her capo Dolores del Vayo attracted attention when she was sentenced to 15 years in federal prison on a counterfeiting charge, passing bogus bills at Gucci's doing her Christmas shopping. The sentence was eventually reversed by the US Court of Appeals, Doll's defense cost plenty, but the biggest problem about it was having thrown unwanted heat Victoria's way and forcing her to operate with greater precautions.

"If the feds get wind of your involvement with drugs it won't be a healthy situation, especially after your trouble with Dolores. Once these law enforcement jokers get on your tail they never give up," Harry cautioned. "The time may have come to earn your brownie points and tell what you know about Zino."

He had a point; the Zino situation, though potentially injurious, if handled right, might give her a protective wedge and keep the feds from her door. So Vic took Harry's advice, went to the government, told Zino's dark secret, and waited for him to be deported.

Harry said, "The prosecutor's out to get Zino. He doesn't have a prayer."

"Serves the motherfucker right," Vic said.

Let the douche bag spend his energy worming out of this one.

CHAPTER 49

Thanks to Sam Scardelli, some of the biggest LFM projects had been arranged; acknowledging it, Sam joked frequently about being Laura's consigliere. While Laura thrived on his protection and help, eventually, as time wore on, Sam started showing a side he'd kept under wraps in the beginning. He was wildly jealous and possessive. The honeymoon was over.

How had she failed to recognize the warning signs? He was so demanding, always wanting an accounting: where was she going, whom was she seeing, what business did they have together? He phoned several times a day, the long conversations robbed her of valuable time, and when she couldn't be reached he pried into her personal space. She bristled with resentment that he should always be checking up on her and felt entitled to know her every move. When she told him she needed more freedom, he sulked, and she was fearful that underneath he was hiding dangerous emotions. She couldn't stand being controlled, feeling trapped. She resented his access to her business affairs, knowing too much about her, his assumptions of entitlement.

Keeping Sam happy required almost a form of self-deceit. Sometimes she would look at his sallow, shrewd-as-a-ferret face, brow seamed, tight lips turned down at the corners, and suddenly feel frightened at his unguarded, ferocious expression. Moments like these she could believe rumors that he killed sixty-four people.

The status she had once basked in with the backing of the powerful Chicago Enforcer no longer thrilled her as it once had. The appeal of her role as madonna/whore had worn thin and was no longer a factor. She'd played out that angle; she'd been fascinated with her own power and its effect on him, but now she was ready to go beyond it. She wanted to move into a deeper area, an area of heightened passion and pleasure, but that part of Sam was emotionally inaccessible. Where was this relationship going? It had lost much of its original flavor, and now guilt was eating away at her. Sam was still mad about her, but now danger was ever present. She must be careful.

Perversely, she sometimes thought about him dying and wished he would. Death often seemed the only way out. She kept thinking of Frank, wanting to be with him still. When she heard he was having marital difficulties, her thoughts focused on the possibility that a relationship might open up with him at last. She'd been nothing if not patient.

Sam and she still spent time traveling together. In L.A., staying at the Hotel Bel Air, they ordered dinner sent in. They drank champagne, got a little tipsy and threw the glasses against the wall by the fireplace.

Later when they made love, she noticed something odd that had started to happen. Lately there was a withdrawal to him, almost a shrinking, as if he were retreating emotionally from her, as if he had drawn protection around himself, shutting her out. She was aware now how much he kept his eyes open during sex, as if he were watching her even in the most intimate moments, judging her, mistrusting her. Sometimes it even felt as if he had moved totally into himself and were feeding on her, as a succubus. In a surreptitious way, insidiously, he was milking her, squeezing her dry.

Sam's face had drained of color.

"What's wrong? Are you ok?" she asked.

He opened a small gold case, removed a pellet and inserted it under his tongue.

"Nothing nitro-glycerine can't fix."

Heart pills, twice a day. His age was showing, and that bothered her too. She was young and he wasn't, she was restless, she wanted to live, and she had this feeling of being saddled, obligated.

When they got off the plane in Chicago US Treasury men were waiting to present Sam with a subpoena to appear before a federal grand jury the next morning. The government was seeking indictments in areas ranging from income tax violations, violations in interstate travel in aid of racketeering (RICO statutes), infiltration of legitimate business, vote fraud and narcotics trafficking.

"It's a lot of crap," Sam said. "They got nothing."

Sam was right. The government had nothing on him. "I know the tactic they're trying to pull," he said. "They want to use me as bait to get to other people."

It didn't work. He invoked the 5th, so the government reversed its strategy. They granted Sam immunity; this way he could no longer claim his constitutional privilege against incrimination. When Sam still refused to talk, he was cited with contempt. Chief US District Judge Harley Randall remanded the witness to the custody of the US Marshal, there to remain until he obeyed the order of the court — which meant that for the remaining term of the grand jury Sam would have to stay in jail — an additional eighteen months.

His legal team was granted a three day postponement to prepare arguments on a motion. The grand jury reconvened and the judge adjudged him in direct and continuing contempt. Sam's defense motion of a stay of execution of the order pending an appeal was denied; he was booked into the cooler. An emergency petition filed in the US Court of Appeals asking for a hearing was rejected without comment first by the Appeals Court, then by the US Supreme Court. Finally the US Marshal imposed a ban on all publicity.

Laura got the out she'd been looking for, a wish come true, but with complications. She was pregnant. Strange, because she'd been careful, and yet something had interfered. She wanted the child, and in order to give the baby legitimacy, considered the possibility of an in-name only marriage.

Jasmine stepped in, appealing to her powerful friend, international financier Maurice Hirsch. The three had lunch together in Manhattan at The Four Seasons.

"You need a negotiator," Maurice said. "You can't arrange this yourself. I will make inquiries. We'll find you a proper husband, don't worry."

The candidate Maurice came up with was Daryl Matthews, a gay U.S. Attorney.

"Matthews is interested," Maurice said. "He could be useful in many ways. Shall we meet together?"

At first Laura was leery about meeting let alone marrying a fed, but when she learned that as a closet homosexual, Daryl Matthews was never comfortable in the Justice Department and would be glad to be out the revolving door, she agreed to meet him. To her surprise, they struck up an immediate rapport; she felt like they were old friends. He could use a front himself, he admitted, the marriage would give him respectability and a leg up. Soon arrangements were made for "Mr. Laura Lo Bianco," "father" of Laura's child, to come to work for the La Femmina organization as head of their security operation.

Sam was distressed about her pregnancy and the solution she had worked out, but there was nothing he could do about it. Before long, additional charges were brought against him, so that he would be out of commission even longer than the grand jury term, perhaps a few years. Laura was relieved he was out of the way. She had the best of all possible worlds now — success, freedom and impending motherhood.

Later, she found her diaphragm had tiny pin-sized holes poked in it — Sam's handiwork; he had sensed her restlessness, and despite his conventionality, had wanted to bind her to him at all costs.

Excited about her fast-approaching motherhood, Laura was secretly glad he had.

CHAPTER 50

When a federal grand jury indicted Zino on one count of failing to register and be fingerprinted as an alien, and on five counts of failing to notify the Immigration and Naturalization Service of his address for the past five years, Vic hoped the whole thing would soon be over and Zino would be out of her life. But just two weeks later, Harry said, "You won't believe this, but it could be your scheme with the feds is backfiring. You sitting down?"

Vic waited for the bomb to drop. "Yeah?"

"Word from the inner sanctum of Justice is they're getting ready to grant Mr. Z. immunity."

"Shit." They'd been so certain he'd be deported. But sure enough, within only days, Zino was loose on the streets again, with some kind of a deal having been struck. Having Zino roaming around was a threat to her well being. Suppose he discovered she was the one who'd set him up? He'd already screwed her, he could screw beyond where he'd already screwed, even go so far as to whack her. She wouldn't put it past him. Now that he had immunity, she feared for her life.

"The son of a bitch knows too much about us, Harry. He belongs ground up in a car shredder."

"Way to go, hon."

Ultimately Vic found a better way to handle the Zino situation.

After mulling over a major career move, she decided to expand operations to Chicago, switch domiciles at least for the time being, thus move out of harm's way. When Chicago's LFM boss, Paula Derringer, was murdered, the territory was wide open. After Laura got first crack and turned it down, Vic asked for and was granted permission to transfer by the LFM National Commission. She would be the Windy City's Acting LFM boss until such time as a fulltime skipper was appointed. So she set up shop in the Second City and began conquering the town.

From jail, Sam cleared the way for her to open her own handbook joint near the Loop, from which she was soon making good money. Her next move was invading the vending machine business and establishing a record distributorship which she built up to net a million and a half a year, according to her declared IRS statements. What didn't appear on her taxes was the amount she made from counterfeit labels.

In addition, she had a new insurance company that inside of a year was writing about 30 per cent of the policies on all the dives and clip joints along Chicago's Skid Row. Besides this she was managing two Golden Gloves fighters and running several Rush Street joints of her own. The clientele didn't realize the dice games in back were rigged. There were magnets under the table tops, with holes drilled to connect intricate wiring to a basement power source. Additional electronic gear was installed that allowed the croupier to control the roll of the dice, which were loaded with powdered magnesium. There was also a remote unit that could be activated whenever the croupier's body moved in a certain way.

The crap shooter didn't have a prayer in that place. The dice always came up seven when necessary at the right time. The electronic force was so great the dice could actually jump right off the table, and Vic's engineers had devised a special way of dimming the lights so it looked like a split second power failure to accommodate. She was also using a device that signaled via electronic means from a balcony, radioing opponents' hands.

Expanding connections, she added Captain Lloyd Sullivan to her stable of intimates. It was a known fact that at least 50 of Chicago's police captains were worth in excess of five million dollars. All the cops in Chicago were kinky, they had so many rackets going it was unbelievable. And Lloyd was no exception.

Captain Sullivan's sphere of influence was impressive. He was a labor organizer for the syndicate in a score of unions, kept an eye on gambling, handbook and poker parlors and was a wheelhorse in the Democratic party.

He visited the criminal courts building daily, ambling in and out of courtrooms and chambers, conferring with runners who worked for the judges and bondsmen, spending a large part of his time in the felony branch where tens of thousands of felonies were reduced to misdemeanors on a steady basis.

Like herself, Sullivan had a large interest in vending machines, juke boxes, slot machines, pinball and various vices, and in his spare time speculated on the grain market. Lloyd Sullivan was one of the hardest working, most efficient police officers in the business. His best friend was Chief Judge of the Criminal Court.

Victoria found a penthouse with a terrace overlooking Lake Michigan that suited her to a tee. She was humming around the house these days, "My kinda town, Chicago is, my kinda town ..."

Vic's restructuring of the heroin deal never sat well with Charles Cestari, which may have had something to do with his change in attitude toward her. But then, Cestari had been decidedly strange for some time. Always, just when she thought she had him figured out, there would be a complete shift. He'd kept her on a roller coaster, coming on strong again and again, then suddenly tuning her out again without warning.

She was perturbed about their affair losing steam and his turning aloof and distant, but perhaps she understood the psychology of his warped psyche. The guy had a self-destructive streak and couldn't stand things being too good. When he saw how fabulous she was and found himself so involved, he had to destroy things by shitting all over her and their relationship, by degrading it and her. The guy was so incredible at first, but she had come to see how he could switch his feelings on and off. Of course, it was sick.

For some time Cestari was on her brain. Why should she constantly fantasize being with him every time she had sex with Harry or Lloyd or somebody else — especially since Cestari acted so contemptuous? Why was she filled with images

— sitting quietly on his cock, scarcely breathing, sensuality building until, like two animals, their mutual passion burst out. Maybe because no man had ever brought her to those peaks before — maybe that was the nature of his power over her.

The bastard only thought he could fuck and forget — just give her time, she'd get back at him.

CHAPTER 51

At last, after much time and planning, Sapphire Bay, the syndicate's crown jewel, including a hotel and two casinos, theatre in the round, three restaurants and spa, yacht and beach club on an island with miles of sandy beaches, was ready for business. The La Femmina partners chartered four jets to shuttle guests to the grand opening. It was a media event splashed across the world press, with tons of tropical fruit, gourmet food, and a few hundred cases of Mouton Lafitte Rothschild on tap for 1200 of the globe's elite being comped for the weekend. Guests were given half a day of free gambling, free girls and free studs on demand. There were floor shows with name performers.

The hotel, built on ten and a half acres, fronted on a big bay, was built around a savannah of royal palms, mango and banana trees. Graceful flamingos glided on a lakelet in front; there were tropical flowers everywhere; purple bougainvillea and white jasmine permeated the soft air, and drums in the distance pounded from the tangled rain forest and stark volcano peaks in the hills. There was a rumor that somebody spotted Jack Riley, to whom the LFM owed this whole setup — but naturally, that couldn't possibly be; Jack was long gone from the firmament.

A great deal had happened in the past couple of years. Laura's baby daughter, Diana, was already one year old, Laura was divorced from Daryl, who had served his purpose in her life but remained a friend and LFM associate, and Sam was still in jail.

They said it would never happen. He married another woman, but nevertheless, Laura had always known Frank was the man for her. When she looked up to see his nut brown figure in white bathing trunks, her heart began to melt and she had a flash of insight that everything would be changing now.

Frank Gantry's lean body radiated a bronze-like glow. That face -- the full lips, fiery dark blue eyes, as blue as the island's Sapphire Bay, the shock of hair falling across his forehead -- he could have stepped out of a Michelangelo fresco. She was hoping he'd accept her invitation to the opening, but hadn't dared believe he really would.

It was carnival time. Festive masqueraders dressed in elaborate costumes caroused through the town. Throughout the day, the tempo increased, until dark, when a crowd converged on the savannah. A funeral pyre for King Carnival was lit, dancers shouted and screamed until the flames leapt high and the King was hurled to his finish. The revelry went on in the streets, building to a climax. Safe inside the hotel suite, Laura and Frank consummated their love, so long in coming. All she wanted was to melt into him, be his forever.

The time was right; they were ready for each other now. It was finished with Wendy, finished with Sam — even if Sam didn't know it.

CHAPTER 52

Lorelei-like, Ayla Kalkavan perched on the bar stool swinging her legs, combing shining coffee-colored locks that swirled around her oval face. Trouble was brewing with LFM drug operations, Ayla revealed in her melodious contralto. Two Munich-bound TIR trucks containing jam (*confiture*, narcotics) were intercepted in Europe on a pre-cleared run, and one of Ayla's Turkey-based henchwomen had been killed. Sandra Martinez added that La Femmina drug shipments had also been intercepted in South America. Were the two incidents related or was this mere coincidence?

A propos of local streets, Harlem's Kami Raines reported, "Demand for product is growing, but so is competition. The market's double what it was four years ago, but another organization is trying to make inroads on our territory."

"Who are they?" Tania asked.

"We hear it's the Corsicans — that they're not content to merely have the production end, they're out to muscle in on North American distribution," Kami replied.

"They could undercut us to get our customers," Lyse Allegret of Montreal said. "The Corsicans have huge stocks — 200 tons of morphine in Marseille alone, and plenty in the middle east too. They have the processors, the growers, the labs, they have an edge."

Jasmine said, "The situation certainly bears watching. We'll monitor closely."

Obviously, Cestari was masterminding. Vic was angry at him now not only for playing with her feelings but for making moves on LFM territory. She would do everything in her power to contain the problem. Attempting to find out more background information about Cestari's life, she tried phoning his wife and daughter, even made an appointment with the daughter in Paris, claiming to be interested in buying the Haitian art she specialized in. Then, running into Cestari on a business trip back to the Big Apple, she confronted him and demanded to know what the hell was going on.

"Why are avoiding me?" she persisted.

He accused her of phoning his wife and turned livid. "Don't you have any sense of decorum? You are so American," he sneered, like it was a dirty word. How dare he refer to her in such a snide, pejorative manner, insult not only her but her country? Had this sleezebag frog never heard of political correctness?

"Yeah, I'm an American, goddamnit, and proud of it," she shot back, her voice rising.

This was taking place in the lobby of the Pierre Hotel and people were staring. Cestari gave her a basilisk glance, shook his head and stalked away. She realized she'd committed a cardinal sin, creating a scene in public. But it was his fault.

He'd screwed her in too many ways: first, shortchanging her on the heroin, sending her diluted product — which he denied but which her people confirmed — and she believed her people before she believed him; then avoiding her, making himself scarce with no explanation; and now even trying to move in on LFM turf.

Later, back home, dropping into a floral-scented bath, Victoria opted for a relaxing pick-me-up from the disappointing day. Drying herself in front of the full length mirror, she stretched her arms upward and admired her shapely breasts and the rest of her nude body. Tanning had given her a coppery bronze glow. Her body looked great.

Theatrical bulbs on the vanity mirror cast a flattering pink glow over her face. It was hard to figure why a woman as brilliant and attractive as she was had to fight so hard for every inch. Just why was it she had to struggle for supremacy in every area of life — money, men, sex, business? As she doused herself with cologne, she was still thinking about Cestari. He was a consummate prick. How had she ever been fascinated with him?

The thing she most wanted at this point was to show him up. Not that she'd object to fucking him again, because now she'd be under no illusion, she'd put it in proper perspective. But when all was said and done, Cestari was beneath contempt and she was going to get the upper hand come hell or high water.

She took copies of the porno pictures of him and Madame Pompier, mailed one to Maurice Hirsch at his office off the Champs-Elysées in Paris, and another to President Georges Pompier of France at the Palais d'Élysée. That would fix Charles Cestari's wagon, but good.

Revenge would yet be hers.

CHAPTER 53

Having recently thrown his hat in the presidential ring early in the game, Nick Condon was out stumping. He was reaching the American people in supermarkets, shopping centers and hotel ballrooms, town meetings, school auditoriums, churches, and TV studios, being photographed with hard hats, students, babies, soccer moms. He was visiting farms and chemical plants and auto factories, offering one and two sentence sound bites to questions that the audience clapped for with standing ovations. He journeyed to Appalachia, to urban ghettos, he visited migrant workers. His genius was to link everything in a cohesive vision of the future.

Nick had a high profile as a member of the Senate Judicial and Banking Committees, and his senatorial experience had given him a good perspective of the political landscape. As momentum slowly gathered, the press was saying he was closer to the mood of the people than any of his rivals. He had the pulse, he had the knack. His advertising campaign was working like a charm.

"Come to California, be with me. I need you," Nick said over the phone, and Jasmine hopped on the next plane to meet him at a hideaway up the coast near San Simeon.

"I didn't think you were coming," he said, embracing her.

"You should know me better," she murmured in his ear.

Following preliminary foreplay, they sank down on a king-sized mattress strewn with muted Victorian-shaded cushions. They made love, captured for posterity on the video cameras Harry had set up. Then, side by side, they talked about something that seemed to be more of a problem to Nick now than before.

In the beginning, Nick had made light of Jasmine's mafia activities. Perhaps he hadn't really believed what she told him. Gradually, though, he seemed to take it in stride. Frequently he would joke about it, while other times he seemed more concerned and asked questions, trying to pin her down. Jasmine was usually evasive. Now he wanted to probe deeper.

"Come on, Jasmine — the truth, the whole truth, and nothing but — "

"You've had the whole truth, Nick. I told you from the start that I have my own mafia."

"And drugs?"

"What about drugs?"

"Just how deeply involved are you?"

"Didn't I make it clear ages ago that my townhouse was paid for by cocaine? You've enjoyed snorting my coke on occasion yourself. What else can I tell you?"

"I guess what I'm trying to determine is — er, are you, that is, are you a — " he struggled to get the words out, sounding laughably ingenuous, "are you a dope dealer?"

"Is the pope Catholic?"

"Jesus!"

"Why are you shocked? Listen, Nick, what I do is a whole lot more honest than most politicians, who should all be locked up they're so crooked. So what's the big megillah?"

"I can't believe it. Here I am, a man elected to public office, hopefully on his way to the White House, in bed with — " he shook his head in disbelief — "an unconvicted drug dealer."

"So I'm a sociopath — and you're a square. But I love you madly all the same."

It turned out his advisors had heard rumors about her activities and were telling him he shouldn't be seeing her anymore, that he should cast her out of his life.

"Spare me," Jasmine said. "This is character assassination."

"I didn't mean it the way it sounded, darling. You know how I feel about you."

"You can be such an asshole sometimes, Nick. Are you saying these spin-doctor jerks can change the way you feel about me?"

"Nothing changes how I feel. What I'm saying — "

"You're a man who's always taken tremendous risks. The public doesn't know, your family doesn't know or doesn't care, only gossip seems to be upsetting you. All of a sudden."

"As you know, honey, I'm in a sensitive position."

"And who are they to judge? They have a double standard. Lawyers, judges, Wall Street, corporations, bankers, film and sports stars — everybody's into so-called `crime.' Look how the great fortunes were made. Go back and examine the impeccable families of today — Rockefeller, for instance — the end justifies the means. Look what old man Kennedy did. Crime enabled Kennedy and Rockefeller to purchase respectability for their dynasties, and listen, it's worth the risk. Crime is the only fair way in an unfair world.

"What is the mafia but an invention of the politicians and the press? It's a gimmick that provides law enforcement an excuse to look like heroes, to make it seem like they're doing a job, when actually it's a part of a conspiracy to let the people at the top operate with impunity.

"What about all the billions in bogus collateral floating around the Fortune 500 companies? That's establishment. The taxpayer covers it. It's how our system works. The rules are made by the system which sets things up to their advantage, our disadvantage.

"How much do you know about the history of the mafia in the United States, Nick? The serious founding and funding of organized crime in our country began in 1870 as a Disraeli brainstorm. This mafia began in New Orleans as an official arm of the establishment. How naive and gullible can a brilliant Harvard graduate, Rhodes scholar, Yale Law Review, future President of the United States be?"

Nick smiled ruefully but said nothing as Jasmine continued, "Look at you, son of an alcoholic prostitute; the rich family that you were fortunate enough to be adopted into saw to it you had every advantage, and to cinch it you marry a well-connected woman from a socially prominent family for an added leg up in life. No matter if you have nothing in common with this woman — she's a great wife for you — and the press says you have it all.

"But to me you're a typical politician who's never worked in the real world, and consequently knows nothing about real life, nothing about business, free enterprise, or struggle. You're all for government handouts to ease your guilty conscience, handouts that will keep people slaves barely getting by, while the mafioso establishment — you — use mafia tactics to further your own interests and keep the rest of the peons in chains. Then you use the so-called mafia as an excuse to show off your law and order. This country is set up for two systems, establishment or welfare. Suppose you don't fit in with either, what then? You've no choice but to be an outlaw, which is what we are.

"Drugs fill a need. And look at the double standard. People don't condemn their favorite stars, athletes or even politicians for using drugs as a crutch or an escape or a release. That's cool. Drugs are politics, baby."

Nick Condon was heedless, Vic decided as she watched the tape, the man thought he was invulnerable, that he could get away with anything. Lucky they had all this on tape.

Condon was given to mercurial changes of mood. Now, as his cock rose once again, he was ready to put a quick end to this discussion. "We have an unusual relationship," he told Jasmine. "Let's keep exploring it, baby, let's go to the bottom with it."

He directed Jasmine's head to his crotch. As her tongue found his erection, he groaned deeply and said, "I'll never give you up, never."

CHAPTER 54

A faint blue haze of Gauloise cigarette smoke, like a halo in the lamplight, lingered over Maurice Hirsch as he stood stroking his lantern jaw with large, strong fingers. He was dressed in a pale green open necked silk shirt, Brioni mustard colored slacks and soft leather Gucci loafers. His rough-hewn body was pale mahogany from prolonged tropical exposure. Despite his age, Hirsch was still the master of a world in which he moved with the vitality of a man half his years. Both his face and every area of his body were tucked by skillful surgery, not quite masking his advanced age and worked-over appearance.

His meticulously groomed, well barbered face twisted into a taut grimace that passed for a smile. He knew he could trust Jasmine, count on her. The two of them went back a long time, as far back as when she was a young teenager. He even claimed some credit for her development into the fantastic woman she had become. But that was another story.

Now he told her, "I need a favor. The President of France has appealed to me. Compromising pictures of his wife, taken with the Corsican, exist." He reached into his pocket and pulled out a photo of a much younger Charles Cestari and Madame Georgette Pompier locked in sexual embrace.

Jasmine studied the photo without comment as Maurice continued, "Someone sent this to President Pompier as well. An anonymous note says there are more where this came from. Pompier wants the entire set. I've spoken to Cestari, who denies all knowledge, although he cannot deny the subjects in the photos are himself and Madame, taken some thirty or more years ago. You can imagine the embarrassment this would cause if it became a scandal. Can you help?"

"Me? What could I do?"

"Your associate Victoria Winters has an inside track with Cestari — they had quite a liaison, *l'amour fou* — they were seen all over Corsica and the South of France together. Perhaps she can find something out, locate the full set."

"I'll ask. But with Victoria, it's quid pro quo. Nothing for nothing."

Maurice smiled. "What can I do for her?"

Jasmine thought a moment. "Cheaper supply? Arrange a discount, perhaps?"

"I will attempt to negotiate something more favorable than present terms," he promised.

Maurice was still financing Cestari; Jasmine hadn't yet convinced him to sever the tie in favor of the LFM court. Unfortunately, Maurice was a creature of habit, not easily prone to change patterns. He and Cestari had been doing business together for years and Maurice was reluctant to upset the applecart. Still, Jasmine kept trying to chip away.

Now Maurice asked, "How do you read the upcoming U.S. presidential elections, my dear?"

Initially, nobody had believed anyone running against incumbent Herbert Tree would stand a chance; however, just as Jasmine's consigliere Sandra Martinez predicted, inside of just a few months, the formerly popular President's rating with the American public plummeted, and at this point, it was too late for most would-be opponents to jump into the fray, too late to raise campaign funds. Nick, on the other hand, had a head start, so he was now one of the frontrunners. It was good he'd listened to her advice.

"Nick Condon stands a good chance," Jasmine said. "His one serious rival for his party's nomination is Robert Francis Casey, Governor of New York."

"Very interesting," Maurice mused, deep in thought.

"Whoever gets the nomination could win the presidency against Tree. Tree is slipping fast."

"Tell Condon I want to make a campaign contribution," Maurice said. "And will you arrange a meeting between us?"

The very next week, Nick and Maurice held a secret, informal get-together in St. Martin. Soon thereafter, Maurice negotiated a better price on LFM heroin supply with Cestari, and Vic, printing copies of copies, produced an entire set of photos to Maurice's satisfaction.

Robert Francis Casey had a lot of solid northeast support and posed a serious challenge to Nick Condon. As the nominating convention neared, it looked like Casey and Nick were in a dead heat. Casey's rise in politics having been facilitated by blackmail, his camp now threatened to release embarrassing material showing Nick in erotic dalliance with various women, including Jasmine.

However, the tactic failed. Vic and Harry, having patiently bugged Casey over the long haul, now produced evidence so explosive it forced Casey to abandon his plan, in exchange for their withholding the damaging material on him. His strategy sabotaged, Casey could only compete on a may-the-best-man-win basis, and thus he lost the nomination to Nick.

Nick just might end up in the Oval Office yet.

CHAPTER 55

Tania's business interests were prospering, but her love life remained the attachment to one romantic ideal. Why wouldn't Corrado budge, why did he stay stuck with Valentina? She was sure he was using her as a shield, protection from commitment. And every time she heard he'd been seen with Ingeborg, she had a fit. Fiona kept telling her not to worry.

"Ingeborg is just an opportunistic bimbo, whereas you, Tania, are a woman of distinction," Fiona said.

"Yet Corrado seems to respect her more," Tania lamented.

"Absolutely not true. Ingeborg is a flashy, shallow international whore with no substance, strictly out for what she can get — there's no contest between the two of you."

Fiona's assessments made Tania feel better, but still — what else could the future hold other than this formlessness, meeting in corners of the globe, joined in erotic unions snatched between deals and appointments and meetings and plans? Corrado had her heart and soul but she did not have enough of him. She resented his other ties. Why did he need them? She wanted more than this.

She wanted to have his child. He asked her to wait. "I am far too conventional a man for this lifestyle," he explained.

"But I love you and I want to have your child," she said.

"And so you shall," he promised. "We will have babies and babies, as many as you want. Please be patient. I know it's difficult — but Valentina is slipping fast — it can't be much longer."

So Tania, respecting his wishes, agreed reluctantly, and turned her attention to more business. This part of her life was a spectacular success. Her clandestine enterprises were well-concealed behind tiers of offshore corporations, holding companies and trusts; she had scores of legit enterprises as well; everything was rolling her way, and LFM had enabled it all, made her rich beyond imagination. Actually, in terms of financial security, she didn't really need the LFM any more, but she treasured her membership. It was like a game to her now, and she was constantly upping the ante.

More and more she was drawn back to Texas, and over time, to philanthropic and cultural activities that never would have been possible without the LFM. She had fully explored the limits of power in her business life, she controlled that segment to perfection, but it wasn't enough — because she did not have power over her own feelings, over herself.

On one of Fiona's visits to Texas, Tania said, "I sometimes think, as we go along, that maybe Corrado doesn't really need love — companionship and sex, yes: love no. He can buy all the sex he wants, which he does with Ingeborg — it's strange, because we - he and I -- are so great together sexually, so why should he need anyone else?

"He appreciates the passion and energy in our relationship, but he doesn't realize its source — a whole level of feeling. My sense of this man is he's very diversified sexually, that he shows me one part of himself, but he goes elsewhere for things he doesn't get from me — kinkiness, for instance."

She longed for a conventional lifestyle with a male counterpart who fit her high powered lifestyle. Corrado was too traditional and guilt-ridden for divorce, and the marriage also served as a buffer. This way he could have his cake and eat it.

The situation was becoming intolerable. She had waited and waited. He kept saying his wife didn't have much longer to live, but after all this time, she wasn't dead yet. How much more patient could she be?

Even in togetherness, Tania saw the foreshadowing of a dream in decline, and the knowledge that this was not to be.

CHAPTER 56

The drama mounted — bands, crowds, banners, airports, planes taking off and landing, a much ballyhooed bus trip throughout the country. The papers contained endless photos of Nick munching on hot dogs, pizza, knishes, souvlaki. Nick spoke about the future, about reorganizing the country; the country needed a change. The same old bull shit, except Nick did it better. He was the media's golden boy; he could do no wrong.

Tania reminded Thomas Kelly, Jack's uncle, he owed them, and Kelly threw the labor movement behind Nick. With union weight supporting him, Nick's chances for the presidency were enhanced.

Maurice told Jasmine, "Tell Nick I want to make another `campaign contribution' — three million dollars in his personal account, under the table, in Switzerland or wherever he wants." Jasmine planned another meeting between the three of them at Maurice's favorite Gotham haunt, The Four Seasons. True to his word, Hirsch pledged support to Nick and contributed three million privately. In return, Nick declared he was in favor of improving relations with France, and could be counted on to do everything to cooperate with President Pompier.

Things were looking good for Nick. He had style, charisma, and smart advisers; with the opposing party divided, the incumbent losing ground, and the country ready for a change, he was fast being viewed as the proverbial knight on a white charger. Entertainers and big Hollywood stars were rallying around him. He was glamorous, he had California mystique and magic, voters trusted him, he knew how to make the most of issues, and he had an uncanny sense of the public mood.

Slick Nick, his enemies called him, Nick the snake oil salesman. The guy could sell anything and charm his way out of any situation, he was a past master of doublespeak; that ready smile got him out of any corner anybody tried to back him into. He didn't answer directly, he bullshitted and played everything down the middle, and it was working for him.

Would Nick be the first illegitimate President of the United States? The first black Commander in Chief? Jasmine advised him to bring the issues of both his blackness and bastardy into the open; as an adoptee, he was sure to gain sympathy and voter identification, ditto being African-American. But Nick's spin doctors, busy with other strategy, hadn't gotten around to it yet. Then suddenly, it was all over the news — Nick Condon was pretending to be other than what he really was, hiding his true identity, when in reality his real mother was a black boozed-up drug addict/hooker whom he was ashamed to acknowledge.

Although initially it looked like a scandal, ultimately Herbert Tree not only hoisted himself on his own petard but enhanced Nick when the tactic backfired. Nick's national speech on searching for his birth mother, how he felt about his illegitimacy and her abandonment of him, newly found identification with his black roots, his gratitude toward the family who adopted him, won high marks all around. The public respected Nick for his honesty and rallied behind him; who could forget the sincerity of his speech, confessing to the whole nation? He was an even greater hero than before, and Tree a worse skunk.

It was going to be an unusual first couple, Jasmine thought: Nick might be a womanizer and sometimes recreational coke user, but you certainly couldn't deny his brilliance and dedication; the wife, Heather, was tight-looking, a lawyer by profession, a woman who prided herself on her efficiency. It was impossible to imagine Nick having sex with her.

When Jasmine saw Nick again, he asked, eyes glazed over with passion, "How does it feel to sit on my cock again?"

And she answered, "Like heaven. Like I'm home."

Vic's hidden cameras recorded it all.

In debates Nick was nothing short of brilliant. He knew how to put the opposition on the defensive, always appearing better informed and more at ease than his opponent. President Tree, on the other hand, was surprisingly tense, swallowing nervously after every sentence. Nick's genius was being able to throw off Tree's timing and rattle him during attacks, making Tree look like a jackass and sound like a kvetch.

"You were fantastic, Nick," Jasmine said, throwing her arms around him and kissing him.

Nick smiled. "As Napoleon said, never interfere with the enemy when he's in the process of destroying himself."

But Nick wasn't going to be a shoo-in. He needed Illinois to win, which was where Victoria came in, playing Sam Giancana to Nick's John F. Kennedy by rigging the Illinois votes and delivering the state. She was in a good position to do just that: first of all, when Sam Scardelli went to jail, not fully trusting his cronies, he appointed her as watchdog; so Vic was, in effect, in addition to her LFM duties, the Acting LCN Enforcer in Chicago (unheard of for a woman — and law enforcement never suspected).

The first Tuesday in November, Nick won the office of Chief Executive of the United States, albeit narrowly. A new era was beginning.

CHAPTER 57

Why had Tania been thinking so much about Jack these days? He was history, a bad chapter of her life, her biggest mistake, yet lately he kept popping into her mind. She did owe him a lot, as much trouble as he'd been — Sapphire Bay never would have happened but for his paper that started it all in motion so long ago.

Strangely, she kept hearing reports about people having seen Jack. Aside from the rumor of his having been observed in the distance at the casino opening, it was reported Jack was sighted playing backgammon somewhere else in the Caribbean. Then after returning from a trip to South America, Jasmine told Tania, "You're not going to believe this, but Jack — or someone who looks just like him — is alive and well in Brazil."

"It has to be his double," Tania said. Yet she couldn't help wondering, as her mysterious phone calls continued on Jack's line.

Jack, were he alive, would be interested in LFM gambling operations. Reports from Nevada indicated enterprises in Las Vegas, Reno, and Tahoe were doing great — the slot machines in Vegas alone were taking in over a million a month, the skim ran around $12 million a year, and even the gift shop was a gold mine. Concurrently one of boss Ivy Schlatter's top lieutenants, Marcia Knowles, was being courted for the office of state senator. On the other coast, meetings had been set with lobbyists and assemblymen, influential well-placed New Jersey lawyers had been signed up, options on boardwalk property firmed in the syndicate's big push into Atlantic City.

The one puzzling thing was Sapphire Bay. Revenues were off: a hoped-for turnaround hadn't materialized. No one could understand it, and all agreed it was a matter of concern.

Pink stucco walls stood out against a gleaming sea where Sardinian waters were the clearest blue in the Mediterranean. The village of Porto Rotondo was but a short drive from the nearby Costa Smeralda of the Aga Kahn. Lavender bloomed above the rim of the Mediterranean, juniper bushes and blueberries were everywhere and the aroma of sage was overpowering.

A five acre project developed by Venetians, Porto Rotondo resembled a provincial village with a Venetian flavor — it even had a canal, with boats docked outside the doors of many of the homes. There were only two hotels in town, the Sporting Club and Villaggio San Marco, where Laura and Frank were staying with Laura's daughter and her nanny.

It was a beautiful place to be. They swam at the secluded beaches and coves, took coffee at the local bar in the great meeting place at Porto Rotondo's piazza. They ate wild boar roasted on a spit, served with *risotto alla milanese*, and Sardinian wines, of which the island had over 100. Every night there were parties and dinners, the most famous of which was the annual White Party, to which guests wore white pants and see-through white shirts, singular spots of color being expensive jewels and antique chain belts.

Laura's relationship with Frank was all she had ever dreamed of and more. Frank was sorry they hadn't been together years ago. "But let's not waste time in regrets," he said. "Let's be happy we're together now."

The relationship was idyllic in every way but one — the specter of Sam. Laura could now understand her affair with him for the father fixation it was; it was arrested development, in a way. She was over Sam, but feared him all the more. He would not easily relinquish his claim on her; no matter that he'd been out of the picture in jail, he still felt entitled. She wanted him to know there was no future for them, but she was afraid to make it any clearer than she already had tried to do. She worried, to what lengths would Sam go in seeking revenge?

"We're safe here together," Frank reassured, and joked, "We have the Venetian mafia to protect us."

But Sam would be out of jail soon. What would happen then? She was madly in love with Frank. But Sam and she had a child together, he had that hold on her. The stay at Porto Rotondo would be coming to a close. A meeting of LFM investors in Sapphire Bay had been called to discuss their slackening gambling revenues. Sam would soon catch up with her, she would have to face him.

To make matters worse, his wife had died of cancer and he even fancied their marrying now. Surprisingly, losing his wife came as an emotional blow; even though they had seldom been together, he was attached to his role. Now that he was free, he was anxious to cement another security blanket. The last time Sam called from jail, he talked about adopting Diana, adopting his own child. "No one has to know the real story," he said. He wanted this for appearance sake. He was so conventional, so old-fashioned.

"Let's talk about it when you get out," Laura said, uneasy, sensing his suspicion over the phone, wondering how much he knew about her relationship with Frank. She had done her best to prepare him, telling him there was someone else in her life; he seemed to hear but not hear. Not to worry, Frank said, but that was easier said than done, particularly when strange things were happening. For instance, on one occasion they were told the hotel room next door was vacant, yet all night long a light shone through the crack, as though the room were occupied. She was sure someone must be surveiling them. Why did Sam always make her feel threatened?

Maybe Frank was right — it was foolish to allow her life be ruled by fear. Laura tried to push Sam out of mind and enjoy the tranquility of Sardinia. But then, her short peace was interrupted by shocking news from home.

Laura's lieutenant Kamzen Raines ran Harlem. Kami had six underbosses under her, each with a crew of workers. Her captains oversaw the mills where mill hands bagged heroin, cutting it, adding manite or quinine, measuring it into bags with colorful trademark tapes for clientele along the seaboard.

Kami had sought material advancement, life on her own terms, and she got it. Her legit interests included a parking garage, a gypsy cab company, a wholesale record distributorship, a meat company, bars and clothing stores, and real estate all over the east coast. Together with her boyfriend Billy Powells, Kami had built a beautiful place on Staten Island, where their home boasted an indoor swimming pool, gold fixtures, and marble floors imported from Italy. Three of Kami's kids attended the exclusive Staten Island Academy. How many women could boast as good a life? She dreamed it, she demanded it, she achieved it. She had outdone her role model, Madame Stephanie St. Clair.

Additionally, all her capos had made it big; several were millionaires many times over. One, Le Donna Fesnay, was a successful music business promoter and producer, a cover operation she'd built up from narcotics profits. Another, Francine Cooney, owned a concert promo agency in Jersey City and her own record label, with subsidiaries including a chain of record stores in the south.

Kami and her boyfriend were among the 600 elite blacks from the New York, Philly and South Jersey areas who gathered three blocks from the Atlantic City boardwalk to hear one of Kami's recording stars perform. Kami sat at a ringside table, surrounded by several bodyguards; Billy, who was clad in a white mink cape; two grown children, son Le Beau and daughter d'Amber; and her stepson Charlemagne. The audience was glittery in diamonds and furs.

All of a sudden, Kami looked up to see Billy Powells slump and one of her bodyguards crash into the cream of turtle soup. Kami dove for cover. Tables overturned, customers screamed in panic as a volley of bullets flew into the smoked mirrors, sending glass shattering for yards. Billy was shot in the face, Kami's bodyguard was dead, her stepson Charlemagne was killed, daughter d'Amber wounded and six other people seriously injured.

No one had noticed the vigilantes enter, dressed in similar flashy attire as the rest of the crowd, weapons concealed under flowing capes and wide brimmed hats. Because of the noise level and silencers, the shots were inaudible.

It didn't take long to find out who was behind the carnage: Corsicans, in cahoots with Canadian organized crime and renegade New York LCN factions that were rumored to include Anthony Zino, recently released from incarceration. Led by Charles Cestari, the group was striking at the roots of the LFM distribution network, as part of the scheme for challenging the LFM on its own turf.

An emergency LFM meeting was called in Manhattan, with crime figures from across the nation attending.

"Many of Cestari's people are illegal aliens and/or Canadians from the crime infrastructure in Montreal," Lyse Allegret explained to the assembled. "As you know, it's a snap to get across the Canadian border — Americans and Canadians are interchangeable. So Cestari has been moving his people from Canada onto the streets of New York, looking to consolidate his power in our backyard."

"We control and supply the major black, Cuban and Dominican networks," Laura said, "but these lousy Corsicans are trying to crowd us out. We'll have to launch aggressive countermeasures."

Victoria came up with a plan to neutralize Cestari's power: Maurice Hirsch, not satisfied with just a set of Cestari/Madame Pompier sex photos, wanted the negatives destroyed, in fact, was even willing to pay a million dollars for the job. The figure was nothing to sneer at, but they could do even better. With Vic's scheme, they could oust the Corsicans from the heroin scene. "We begin by severing the Cestari-Hirsch connection," Vic said, "by weakening it at its source."

Vic had keys to all Cestari's places — Marseille, Corsica, Paris, Beirut; she had a set of his car keys, she had the combination to his safes, keys to his desk and file cabinets. She knew where everything was. She could get into his drawers, locate the negatives — that was not a problem. But above and beyond that, she had something else in mind. She'd been to Cestari's lab in the South of France, made careful note of the location, and could find it again. Her idea was to spoil a big heroin batch, in order to turn Maurice Hirsch against Cestari.

Aided by Kami, who after the Atlantic City massacre had sworn revenge, Victoria's plan swung into effect. Kami and her people went into the lab, surreptitiously ruined the batch — worth a fortune to Maurice — then bypassing security measures according to Vic's instructions, picked off the negatives exactly where Vic said they were at Cestari's villa. Vic made sure she was highly visible in Paris when all this was taking place in the South of France so she would never be suspected.

Not long afterwards, Maurice confided to Jasmine that Cestari and he were having serious problems: Cestari's chemist Comine was to convert a very large supply of morphine base into # 4 heroin, as usual, Maurice said. However, a mistake made during acetylation process, possibly incorrect use of chloroform or ether, resulted in the unwanted appearance of byproducts, compelling the chemist to switch to the cheaper, lower grade pinkish-brown # 3, "purple" heroin, which had almost no market value whatsoever in the western world, (used only for smoking — "chasing the dragon" — by Asians). The loss meant tens of millions of dollars of potential profits. Cestari claimed it was sabotage but Hirsch didn't buy the story and was furious. Now Maurice was going after Cestari with a vengeance, and was out to destroy him. Well and good.

"Maurice coming over to our side is a big step," Jasmine said, "but we do face a major hurdle in heroin production — our big challenge is going to be manufacturing # 4 in sufficient purity and quantity."

"Why is that a problem?" Tania wanted to know.

"It's hard to do. Usually the chemist will end up with a slightly brownish product. The Corsicans alone have mastered manufacturing large quantities of white # 4, the kind the American market covets."

"We've resolved other seemingly insurmountable obstacles. Now we'll just have to work solving on this problem."

CHAPTER 58

Through the mysterious stranger's heavy brocade Chinese mandarin robe, Jasmine felt his erection rise as he drew her closer on the dance floor. At an elegant masquerade luncheon in the South of France, red and green parrots fluttered on stems at each individual table, while 200 gallons of eau de cologne had been emptied into the swimming pool.

She knew almost nothing about this romantic stranger in the black mask, except that he spoke English like an American. At the end of the afternoon as the setting sun fell behind the palm trees to cast its rays over the calm sea, they removed their disguises and went swimming together, nude, and made passionate love.

The unknown stranger who brought her to the heights of erotic pleasure was Marc Jabry. He was handsome in an offbeat way, with keen, penetrating eyes and thin lips, the kind that a smile made disappear. The nose could have been sculpted by a master. His hair, streaked with grey, was neatly trimmed in a style that elongated his face. They gazed at one another for a long moment. He had captured her imagination with his combination of strength and restraint.

He was the Chairman of a major pharmaceutical firm, a licensed physician who gave up medicine to pursue his interest in pharmacology and business. He projected a quality of agelessness, as though he might have stepped out of a different century or another time warp. He was a seductive, charming man of the world with a penetrating mind and a fiery articulate personality. He was an amateur painter. His gleaming teeth betrayed a recognizable rapaciousness that gave him dash and danger. Jasmine's intuition told her he could be important in her life. Already, he had cast his spell.

After dressing, he took out a small Carlo Fracchi embossed leather booklet and Mark Cross gold pen and wrote down her name and phone number.

They made plans to meet again in New York. "I'll call you soon," he promised.

Jasmine was ready for another important relationship in her life and was eager to know him better. Things were different now that Nick was President. Since his election, he'd been incredibly busy. Although they still rendezvoused, usually via the secret Washington underground tunnels connected to the White House, and although it was exciting at first, Jasmine craved an out front partner.

When she accepted the invitation to dinner at Jabry's luxurious art-filled triplex, she found herself becoming increasingly intrigued by this cultivated self-made man who by all reports grew up in a roughneck section of Kansas City, later worked as a roustabout in the oil fields of to finance his medical education, gave up medicine to enter business and was able to climb to the top of the international corporate world where he now served in the position of Chairman and CEO of Polo Pharmaceuticals as well as its holding company ACF, located in Philadelphia.

Jabry was multilingual, smooth, polished, the owner of a 100 million dollar art collection. In addition to his Fifth Avenue apartment, he owned an Acapulco villa, a manored house in the horse country of Virginia, and additional homes in the Bahamas, Paris (on the Île de la Cité, near Maurice) and Damascus, Syria.

A chandelier shed warm light on Miro and Riopelle canvases, prominent against beige wall coverings. Comfortable and relaxed, Jasmine and Marc sipped brandies together. At the end of the evening, Jasmine had the sense that a remarkable destiny could be in the cards for them.

One snag: Jabry did have a wife; however, the couple led completely separate existences and were nearly always apart. "There hasn't been anything between us in years," he said; so that was a start.

She didn't know why he affected her as he did; perhaps it was something secretive and private that she responded to, the unknowable in him. She was impressed by the scope of his connections around the world and the part of him that forever remained a mystery. He had a compelling power that made her feel wholly a part of him, as though he could impart his force to her. He walked with a slight yet discernable limp, which somehow made him seem vulnerable and aroused her protective instincts.

She researched his background, compiled a dossier on him and discovered he had an interesting, somewhat murky past. Back in Kansas City, he had having been adopted by a well-connected Syrian mafia family.

His company, AHP, with headquarters in Philadelphia, functioned as a holding company for 94 US and 84 foreign subsidiaries. They operated 29 plants in the US, 3 in Puerto Rico, and 77 foreign manufacturing facilities in 28 countries. The telephone was answered with the firm's phone number instead of its name, in keeping with the company's low profile policy, and their name never appeared on their packages. The company did no p.r. whatsoever, either for itself or its products, which grossed 4 billion the previous year. As CEO of a multi-billion dollar company, Marc had great legitimate cachet, but intuition told Jasmine this man was into the clandestine — hadn't Maurice said enigmatically that Jabry could be "very useful — work on him, my dear"?

"I'm rich beyond belief," Jasmine told Sandra, "I'm in control of every aspect of my life, except that the romantic, emotional side could use some support."

"No doubt about it -- you definitely need a male counterpart to establish a life with," Sandra agreed.

"Marc would be ideal. What a great façade. He's romantic yet tough. I could definitely be content to share my life with this man."

"He's more than you think," Sandra said. "He could be very useful to us as well."

"Strange — Maurice intimated as much. How do you mean, Sandra?" Jasmine could tell when Sandra's psychic powers were plugged in, and she was eager for the input Sandra could offer now.

Sandra said, "I mean, this man could hold the key to the problem of our heroin manufacture. Approach him on that level as well."

"I will. If he can solve that problem, he's a godsend. I want this man, Sandra. He's perfect. The only kink is the wife. "

"Not unsolvable," Sandra said. "It can be handled."

"You have my permission," Jasmine smiled demurely.

CHAPTER 59

Victoria's soldiers were harvesting bumper crops of marijuana on federal lands, and there was a big market for it. All her enterprises were flourishing: her international commodity firm was working on a deal with a refinery in the Bahamas, also closing a situation with a chain of Illinois gas stations, and she had a great scam going with the brother of the ex-Governor of New Jersey to avoid paying taxes at empire state filling pumps. On the dockets was a company making cellophane sheets for meat packaging, a confirming house for import finance, electric and pneumatic operated smoke vents for the Philippines, a trash reclaiming plant to be located in Guam that would produce energy and guarantee nine million a year in profits, and she was also developing 32 acres of raw land 25 miles southwest of Disney World as a tax shelter.

And so on. Wouldn't you think that with all her legitimate enterprises and considering the contribution she was making to the nation's economy, the feds would stop fucking her over? Yet she surprised FBI officials late one night in her office, installing an illegal bug. Her legal team used the fact of breaking and entering to gain immunity from prosecution.

Subsequently, another potential indictment was squelched at Justice Department intervention. But it was often nip and tuck with these situations. For instance, there was the arrest in Florida of one of her top bagwomen, Gloria Dempster, for attempting to smuggle half a million narcodollars out of a La Femmina-owned Florida airport. Customs agents confiscated the money and filed felony charges against Gloria.

Gloria Dempster was a classy, savvy lady who happened to be black. Working closely with Gloria's legal counsel, Vic devised a strategy. First they played the race card, charging discrimination, then they successfully argued that taking money out of the country was not illegal. Gloria was found guilty of not reporting the cash to Customs, but this violation was only a misdemeanor, since it was a first offense. The Hon. Marcus Tannenbaum, *amico nostro*, threw out the charges.

But all these things were tricky, they took time and energy to fight, to say nothing of money. And immunity was not unilateral. Today's untouchable was tomorrow's crook. You never could tell what direction the next betrayal could come from. Being the acting LFM boss of Chicago sounded impressive but it was a thankless assignment, and at this point, she was resenting having to hack the hinterlands. She was feeling neutralized, away from the action. Chicago as a local phenomenon was one thing, powerful to be sure, but its additional power derived from tentacles across the country, especially out west. Chicago was a great place to reach out from, if you knew where and how to reach.

The La Femmina Caribbean casino, in which Vic had points, was the damnedest thing. Nobody could figure why, but for some time now it wasn't making the profits it should. You'd think the security force, all those ex-Justice Department hotshots led by Laura's former husband Daryl Matthews, would be able to come up with an answer, but they were as in the dark as anyone else, supposedly. Maybe if she were closer to the action she'd be able to figure it out herself.

When all was said and done, nothing in the world was quite like Manhattan. She'd about had it with the steady Chicago grind. In the first place, the town was loaded with racket guys, most of whom were into bustouts and scams, who when you came down to it didn't have the brains to do a whole lot else. The really smart Chicago guys had branched out in other directions.

Chicago was the crookedest, most mobbed up town in the United States. It was strictly a low class operation. Out of 1000 gangland type slayings in the Chicagoland in the past 50 years, only 1/100 of a percent had been successfully solved with arrest and conviction. That told you something about Chicago. It told you about their law enforcement and judicial systems, such as they were. Everybody there was on the take and the competition was fierce.

Originally, Sam was supposed to see she got a fair shake, but ever since Laura had given him the horns Vic was getting the short end of the stick. And even if Laura hadn't dumped Sam in favor of Frank, Chicago would still be what it was, with or without Sam Scardelli's contribution.

She'd had her season in hell. Now Vic wanted out of this crummy, corrupt town. Sooner or later everyone wanted to move beyond this garbage dump of crooks and kinky cops, this lousy berg where you always had to clear everything with guys with third grade educations and records as long as the block but no convictions, all of them with at least a dozen to several score brutal murders to their credit.

Florida, Vegas, the Caribbean -- they were all open territory, and most of the Chicago mob with any brains went there or L.A. Here there was just too much federal heat. It was always the same story. Locally, law enforcement was no problem, but the feds were worse here than anywhere else in the nation. She was ready to move on to other challenges.

She had interests in many parts of the country; her options were open. Harry liked the idea of Florida or Hawaii, but Vic had her eye set back in the northeast. She missed the old days in Manhattan as head of one of the Four Families. Rose was minding the store as acting head of the old Victoria Winters regime. Vic was beginning to feel like Joe Bonanno must have, out of the action in Phoenix, and she missed her great old apartment at the Woodward, besides. Maybe it was time to relinquish her role as Acting LFM boss here, and return on a permanent basis to the scene of her early success. Sure, get the hell out of Chicago. It made a lot of sense.

CHAPTER 60

At The Four Seasons, Jasmine and Maurice Hirsch compared notes and exchanged information. By now Hirsch had cornered the European market in black poppies, the non-narcotic alternative to opium for legitimate pharmaceutical consumption. Turkey, Hirsch said, was a producer of both the red and black poppies. Angry over Cestari's double cross, Hirsch now wanted to cut off Cestari's opium supply by curtailing Turkey's red poppy production.

For years, American drug manufacturers had been vainly lobbying at world congresses to curtail opium growing so that they could move in with synthetic patents, forcing other manufacturers to license from them. Only four countries currently produced licit opium. Knocking Turkey out of the box as a red poppy producer would be a major coup from which Maurice stood to gain handsomely, clearing the way for his black poppy industry to take off. The American drug company lobby would be all for it as well. The plan would also enable the LFM's to corner the American heroin market.

Henceforth, future LFM illicit opium supply could come from Asia's Golden Triangle, an advantage being cheaper deliveries. This area had been producing 50 billion dollars worth of heroin a year for the Asian market; the LFM's could step up production and redirect supply. The most important thing now remained to perfect final product, # 4, to satisfy the U.S. customer.

To the French government, Cestari and his network had become a giant headache, Maurice said. A number of years back, the President of France had enlisted underworld figures, Cestari among them, to work with French secret service in counter-terrorist activities. But France's current President wanted to get rid of this underworld influence in order to make the French intelligence services, SAC and SEDCE, responsive to him.

Maurice said confidentially, "Eliminating the Corsican connection must be done in the strictest confidence." Executing plans would require the sub rosa cooperation of both the Presidents of the United States and France. Maurice would take care of Pompier.

It would soon be time for the LFM organization to call in their markers from Nick Condon. But first, Jasmine had to gain more ground with Marc Jabry. Marc had invited her for a Mediterranean cruise on his yacht Persephone and to his home in Damascus. On the Mediterranean, gliding over smooth waters, watching the stars together in the darkness, Jasmine had the feeling of being transformed to another dimension.

Marc's quality of erotic languidness was a contrast to Nick's hard-edged strength. With Marc, it was a slow, burning, smoldering sexual excitement, like being perpetually poised at an abyss. When he kissed her with drawn-out tenderness and exploratory curiosity, it was like the seepage of juice from tropical fruit, some rare nectar, as enigmatic as the man himself. Marc's sensuality was a surprise needing to be evoked slowly, quietly, patiently, as if drawn from him like opium latex. His hand pressed against her. His eyes were compelling, soft. Jasmine had the sense of being understood in a very oblique way; there was serenity and healing in their melding. He lit up a Disque Bleue and she saw its smoke curl in the air. Overhead a flock of birds flew toward the sun. She watched the smoke go into the atmosphere and disappear.

"Never feel guilty about drugs," Marc said — not that Jasmine did. "We're doing the drug addict a favor, offering an opportunity — freedom of choice. Once they get into the habit of saying yes, no becomes harder, but it can always be done — if they want to refuse, they can. The problem is most people have no will.

"In the majority of cases it's not drug addiction which gives rise to the psychological disorder, but individuals already suffering from this who become drug addicts. Even the National Health Institute tells us this. Another way of looking at it — drugs are a test of the degree of temptation and control a person can exercise in their lives. How big a slave are you?

"The abuser, the addict, is retreating to dependency, to the utmost childlike level. It's a withdrawal from life. It is not your fault they put themselves in a state of such irreversible physical dependence. I am not my brother's keeper," he said, lifting his glass. "Excuse me, I am not.

"Drug addiction is a regression to babyhood, avoiding responsibility for life, and a way of coping with emptiness and hopelessness. They make a political football of it, yet how many people worry about the wealthy addict, the movie star, the rock star, the athlete, doctors and other rich junkies? No, the cause for concern is always the part it plays in urban crime. Poverty already exists there, but they make it an issue out of their own guilt.

"Opiates have been used since the dawn of time to allay pain and provide the feeling of wellbeing. The psychological addiction is hard to cure — but so is suffering from physical, emotional and psychosocial pain. Who are we kidding? Life is tragic. Euphoriants, for many people, are the only crutch they can find to get through it all."

Among Marc's hobbies was collecting old manuscripts alluding to the use of the poppy by ancient cultures for spiritual insight. One of his goals was to rediscover these ancient secrets, to unlock beneficial uses of the poppy for modern times.

"Can you imagine how enriching the whole drug culture could be with the right drug and dosage, set and setting? If drugs were left in the realm of magic and ritual where they belong, we would have fulfillment, not emptiness. Drugs should involve theatre, religion, catharsis, understanding; ceremony should be attached to it, not the ritual of needle stabbing the arm, but the kind of ritual that has real correspondence with theatre and enactment."

Damascus, the oldest continually inhabited city in the world, was a bustling metropolis as early as the 7th millennium, and considered ancient in the 9th century, BC. The Eastern Gate, Bab-al-Sharqu, dated to the Roman period and opened onto the famous Roman Road. Six of the seven Damascus gates were medieval, dating from the 12th through 15th centuries. One time the city was ten times the size of Paris and even now was bigger than Rome; old Damascus alone, within the original city walls, was an area of nearly 350 acres. An almost magical atmosphere permeated the city with its red roofs and square stone buildings. It was full of mosques, public baths, caravanserais, and contained hundreds of houses of 18th and 19th century vintage.

In the ancient quarter, Marc pointed out the Temple of Jupiter with its columns from the Roman period, the mosque of the 7th century Ubyad dynasty, and to the right, the Via Recta, Street of the Straight, which led to the famous "covered suq," the Hamadieh Suq.

"Arab houses have always traditionally been large," Marc said. "eighteen, twenty rooms and more, in order to maintain extended families. Sons, when they married, would move in with their parents. Now this custom is less in vogue, and some of the great old houses have fallen into disrepair, as the younger generation has moved into the more modern parts of the city and found new ways. The old houses have become schools, tea houses, inns and especially warehouses."

Time seemed suspended. It was as if behind the courtyards, secret events were transpiring.

Situated in the Christian quarter of Old Damascus, Marc's family home had been constructed over three hundred years ago by a Turkish pasha. It was an elegant twenty-eight room mansion, reached by streets that wound north from the Roman arch, on the Street called Straight, to Swaff Road. Its garden proliferated with damask roses, jasmine, bougainvillea, cypress, palm and citrus trees. The courtyard tiles had been laid over two centuries ago. They strolled through the complex of gardens and reception halls.

Ten generations of Jabrys had lived in this home. It had sixteen halls, nineteen small basement rooms, fourteen fountains, a five room hamman or Turkish bath consisting of Roman baths, cold, hot and steam rooms. There were five inner courtyards and an exterior courtyard for horses.

The doors were one of a kind, paneled in marble with massive cedar window cornices carved a hundred and fifty years ago. Jasmine admired the 18th century damascene hand carved ceilings and painted beams whose designs were formed to integrate with the oriental carpets. Two hundred year old mirrors were set into the beams overhead.

One room contained priceless porcelain and Bohemian glass displayed in a gold brocade Ottoman tent; another salon was decorated with calligraphic inscriptions; there was a display of rare calligraphy, including an egg with the entire Koran inscribed, as well as a grain of wheat exhibited under a magnifying glass, bearing calligraphy.

Marc had unique freedom to run certain enterprises, thanks to the Syrian Ba'ath party. He had offered the party a deal that would provide badly needed jobs for unskilled labor. In exchange for allowing him to maintain control of his family enterprises, the government permitted him to operate his factories and employ Syrian workers, who made tiles, pottery, copper products, insulated wire and other things.

As Jasmine gleaned more about Marc's Damascus operation, she learned that in the basement he warehoused several tons of opium and morphine base. From time to time he would sell off stocks to pharmaceutical companies on the black market. In a remote part of the country, a three hour drive from Damascus, he grew thousands of hectares of opium poppies.

After the cruise ended, they checked into the Georges V in Paris. Room service delivered langouste and Piersporter to their suite, where they discussed clandestine arrangements in which he would divert to the illicit market morphine base for the LFM group. Polo Pharmaceuticals was the perfect front. Vital to their own future was the manufacture in sufficient purity of a large quantity of white # 4 heroin. To this end Marc's chemists would be engaged behind the scenes perfecting the white powder.

Jabry's pharmaceutical knowledge extended to other areas as well. For instance, he confessed to a rare sexual problem regarding his ability to orgasm, that he suffered from perpetual priapism; it took him forever to come, sometimes up to two hours, unless he took a particular medication, a mideastern herb, which normalized his sexual metabolism. Jasmine asked him to stop taking the drug, to sample his eroticism *au naturel*, and reveled in long hours of exotic pleasure.

Not long after Jasmine's return to Manhattan, Sandra phoned to say, "Guess who croaked?"

"Can't imagine."

"I wanted you to be the first to know. You'll be happy to hear it was painless — thanks to an amazing, undetectable Amazonian herb. It won't be long now, Jazz — can I be your maid of honor?"

"Absolutely," Jasmine promised. "I wouldn't dream of having anyone but you, Sandra."

The nuptials were performed in London at St. Clement's Dane in the Strand. 15,000 lilac blossoms festooned their Clermont Club reception, for which an eight piece Cuban orchestra was flown in from Paris. The couple cut their wedding cake with the ancient Sword of Ramillies, carried in battle by John Churchill, the first Duke of Marlborough. The cake itself was a 150 pound replica of Marc's home in Damascus. It was a marriage made in heaven, with a brief honeymoon cruising the Dalmatian coast aboard Marc's yacht, and after that, it was back to business as usual.

CHAPTER 61

Laura, her baby daughter Diana, and Frank Gantry were sharing a large flat in Soho. Laura had never been happier: she was with the man she had always desired and loved, she had a strong sense of her own identity, she was a mother and a successful entrepreneur — she had it all. Still, there was always the specter of Sam Scardelli.

Even if Frank hadn't come into her life, she could not have continued with Sam. One good reason she fell out of love with him was her dislike of being controlled. She was a powerful woman with a strong will, and could not stand someone overseeing her. She was into a far better mode without Sam than she ever could have been with him.

While finishing out his jail sentences, Sam had ample time to brood. He had been betrayed and lost face. He tried to prevail upon Laura's sense of duty as a mother, saying they should be together for their child's sake. She told him there was someone in her life; she told him again. It was as if he didn't hear. Laura was his, she belonged to him, she had humiliated him. Even so, he could forgive her more easily than Frank Gantry. She would come to her senses; the true guilty party was Gantry; the problem of Gantry would have to be taken care of.

Making matters worse, Frank had taken over a Hollywood studio that was building an offshore casino on territory that Sam had a proprietary interest in. Sam had once held an option on the land -- negotiations had dragged, and his jailing had halted things. In the meantime Frank went in, got all the clearances and necessary permits and put the deal together. To add insult to injury, some of the money to finance the deal came from a bank controlled by an old Chicago crony of Sam's.

Laura dreaded Scardelli's release. Finally, just before his sentence was finished, Sam appeared to accept the inevitable. "I know it's been a long time. You had a life to lead," he said, "and you have my blessing." Despite his words, Laura didn't trust him. He could have something up his sleeve. But there were matters to discuss, not the least of which involved their child. Ultimately, they would have to meet and talk.

Shortly before Sam's impending release, Laura and Frank were staying at Frank's condo in the Bahamas. Frank's brother Tom, who looked so incredibly like Frank the two were often mistaken for twins, would be arriving after their departure to use the condo for the following week. Frank was heading for California, while Laura was finally going to Chicago to meet Sam. Neither she nor Frank liked the idea, but they knew that sooner or later Diana, at least, would have to be discussed.

Sam Scardelli had a score to settle. Laura was with Frank Gantry, the same *stronzo* who aced Scardelli out of two business deals, a land development deal and slot machine concession representing millions in potential profits. The *ladrone* would pay. More than anything he'd ever wanted, Sam wanted Frank's balls on a platter, and he had a hit man from Sicily, a zip named Orlando Gentaccia, ready to oblige.

"*Farlo fuori*," Scardelli hissed, waving his Montecruz panatella at the swarthy, mustachioed zip. "Take him out."

That very afternoon, Gentaccia boarded a plane for the Bahamas. Gaining access to the Gantry cottage early that evening, he waited in darkness until his victim opened the door. Then he pounced, hit the guy on the head with a blackjack, tied him up, gagged him, and turned the volume on the radio up.

The thundering buildup of the Beatles' "Hey, Jude" began, as following instructions from Scardelli, Gentaccia revived Gantry with smelling salts, so the *caffone* would be fully aware of his punishment.

"Hey, Jude," Paul McCartney sang, as Gentaccia ripped open Gantry's trousers. When he flashed the stiletto from his jacket, Gentaccia confronted the look of stark terror that came over his victim's face. He would never forget that look.

Then with one swift stroke, Orlando Gentaccia, Sicilian zip, sliced Gantry's balls off, neat and clean. Gantry fainted before it was done. Gentaccia finished the job with a silenced .38, then scooped up Gantry's bloodied testicles, as per Scardelli's instructions, and hung a "Do Not Disturb" sign on the door. Paul McCartney was still singing.

It could be a couple of days before anyone would become suspicious and try to enter the place and find the mutilated, de-balled body.

Making sure no one saw him, the zip got the hell out. He flew to Miami first, Gantry's mushy testicles beside him in a picnic basket, packed in ice, so they'd stay nice and fresh for the next leg of the trip to Chicago.

What he didn't know was he'd got the wrong man's balls.

Laura arrived in Chicago. Sam had to understand it was over; she loved Frank, the man she'd longed for all her life. Sam and she would make visitation arrangements. They had a lot to straighten out.

In the distance, she heard a clock tolling the hour and at that moment she shuddered, not from wind or cold but from an instinctive foreboding. It was like that old wives' tale about somebody walking on your grave, Laura thought. Prescience, an ungodly belly hunch, that was what it was. She rejected the feeling, put it out of mind as she headed to the Ambassador East.

Strange, how vastly different she felt about Scardelli now than in the beginning. As much as she had once thrilled at Sam's extravagant gifts, she now saw them as ploys to bind her to him. Despite having helped her, Sam had tied up her life, made her feel beholden. She was finished with that now.

"Motherhood becomes you," Sam said, his snake-like eyes narrowing at the sight of Laura.

She was wearing a simple pink dress that emphasized her winter-tanned body. Her luxuriant dark hair cascaded down her shoulders, her eyes gleamed with depth and happiness. To Sam, she was more beautiful than ever, as sensual as before, but with a greater maturity and happiness that made her even more irresistible than he remembered.

He looked a lot older, Laura thought, older and worn. He had booked them a private dining room in one of his favorite spots. "I wanted to make this a very special event," he said, "because you're very dear to me."

Laura took a sip of wine. Her eyes clouded over. "Thank you for everything, Sam. Thanks for understanding, and thanks for being my friend." It sounded hollow. But it was over and she had to say something nice.

He said, "Anytime." The stub of a fat cigar clamped between his teeth, he made a chopping motion with his hand, then squinting, asked about Sapphire Bay. How was it going? Laura told him there were problems, no one understood why. Sam nodded and for a moment seemed to contemplate her in a peculiar manner that was almost scary. Then he reached for an antacid pill and took it with ice water. The reptilian eyes were steady. A nerve throbbed silently in his cheek. His eyes held their intense focus. He rubbed his hands; his jaw line hardened and his brow seamed. The conversation continued as though things were normal between them. He said he accepted her decision, that he wished her happiness.

She had outgrown this relationship even before Frank reappeared in her life and they made the commitment. It was dead, although she would always feel an attachment for Sam, but now she wondered how he could have been such a part of her life for so long. She knew she'd loved him, but how different, how much fuller were the feelings she had for Frank.

Sam sipped a shot of Sambucca, contemplating her slowly, as his fingers drummed on the table. He'd had the chef prepare a cooked to order specialty, Sam said. He couldn't wait to have her try it.

In the kitchen, Armando Morini, the chef, took the package from its waxed paper and unwrapped the newly arrived testicles, soft and pulpy, still bloody. He put them under the water to rinse, donned plastic gloves so as not touch the gentle fleshy folds with his own bare skin. He ran the water over them for a full minute till they were thoroughly clean.

Then he poured some Progresso olive oil to heat the griddle. He let the flame get red hot before turning it to low. He placed the balls on the pan to brown lightly on both sides, flipping them after simmering one minute to lock in flavor and juice, to give that delicate crusty quality.

In a separate pan he heated the herbs and spices, mushrooms, garlic, parsley, *fines herbes*, chopped celery, half a carrot finely grated, oregano, a dash of cinnamon and fresh basil. Sauté lightly. *Ah, delizioso*! This is the way to prepare a man's balls.

He let the whole concoction simmer for three minutes in a delicate, specially prepared *salsa di pomodoro*, very light, very fresh -- *purissimo*. After that he placed the balls in the oven to bake at 350 for ten minutes. He brought them out on a silver platter garnished with greens. Laura smacked her lips and picked up a fork. Testes *alla parmigiana, Signora* — sprinkle on a little Romano, salt and pepper to taste. *Delizioso!*

"*Mangia, mangia,*" Sam urged.

And Laura did. "Mmm," she said, looking up from her plate, "what is this? I've never had it before."

"A once in a lifetime specialty — *mangia, mangia!*"

Sam watched Laura with satisfaction, seeing her eat the sautéed testicles, smiling to himself when she remarked she was expecting to talk to Frank soon.

"*Telefono per Lei, Signora,*" the waiter said, beckoning Laura to the phone.

"That must be Frank now," Laura said, rising. She'd left word he could phone her here.

When she returned to the table, she was visibly shaken. "Sam — something terrible has happened," she said. "That was Frank calling — "

"Frank?" Sam turned ashen.

"Frank's brother Tom Gantry was murdered. Oh, Sam, it's so horrible — they cut Tom's balls off."

Sam choked on his cigar and his elbow accidently spilled Sambucca all over his pants.

CHAPTER 62

An urgent LFM meeting had been called to discuss heroin plans. Jasmine said, "The Golden Triangle area grows about 80% of the entire world crop, most of which has been for the Asian smoking market. The Triangle is capable of producing more, so we'll increase production. The major problem has been in the conversion process -- white heroin of sufficient quantity and purity. Now that we have just about conquered that, we're ready to proceed to the next step."

"Which is?"

"Take out the Corsicans."

A hush fell over the room. The idea sounded preposterous.

"How do we do that?" Laura asked.

"With help. The President of France wants to get rid of these guys, he says the Corsicans have to go. We'll have full French cooperation. Now all we need is Nick, to form a super secret White House drug agency, a sort of hit squad."

"You think you can talk him into that?" Tania asked.

"He might be a tough sell," Jasmine admitted, "but I'll certainly give it my best shot."

"Not to worry," Vic spoke up. "When you people all see what I have on this dude, you're going to kiss my ass in Macy's window. We'll get Condon, no problem."

Victoria had something on Nick, all right. Tapes, stills, videos — in flagrante delicto, in every position known to man — the President without his pants, the President in raunchy dialog, the President at his stud best — red hot; the President snorting coke, admitting he knew about the female mafia, that he was head over heels in love with a mafia leader/drug dealer named Jasmine Shields, that he was passing as white, that his mother was a black hooker. The President's balls were on the line, for sure, his reputation, his very life and future at stake.

The Florida sky was streaked with a sunset of yellow golden rose. The skiff pulled up alongside the luxury yacht, the Persephone. Nicholas Condon, President of the United States, boarded the yacht to meet Jasmine.

The FBI warned him she was dangerous. Sure, he'd known about the women's mafia affiliation, but he'd discounted it. Jasmine and her La Femmina mob sisters had created an empire rivaling any on earth. Now the La Femminas were conceiving something far more audacious and daring than any of their previous undertakings. Jasmine had summoned Nick to do something he wouldn't want to do. But he wouldn't have much choice. Despite himself, Nick would be forced to play a major role, and he would deliver because there was no way he could refuse.

First he would say no. Then he would realize he had to say yes. The plan was tailor made, it would make him very rich and a hero to the American people, besides. And no one would ever suspect. Who even dreamed there was such a thing as the La Femmina female mafia organization?

They needed him — but for what? Nick would soon find out.

She was married now, but that shouldn't stop them — it never stopped him, so why should it bother her? Ah, Jasmine — what was her secret, the source of that mysterious power, and how to account for the sway she always held over him? It wasn't her beauty alone but rather something that transcended it. He thought of the hypnotic quality of her touch, the light gestures of her long tapered fingers, the formations of her mouth when it closed around his cock, the promise of her lips, the casual fall of tawny hair around her shoulders and the heavy scent of exotic perfume that always clung to her, the sweep of her arm, and the knowing smile that played across her face.

Jasmine Shields was a claimer, taking what was hers. That was what he was afraid of now, that she had something up her sleeve, this woman he loved, this new breed of international capomafiosa the likes of which the world had never before seen.

She had always fascinated him. There was something otherworldly yet very in control about her. She looked like she could buy and sell the world, which in fact she could. As the charismatic leader of a powerful group of lady mafiose, Jasmine Shields ruled a over several billion dollar empire. Hers was a different power than his — more lethal, more potent. She had a rare gift for bringing out others' lust and greed. Her mere presence could make a man feel daring and wild, take chances, do things he never thought of.

He looked directly into her amber eyes. Ah, that opulent body, sinuous and inviting, tempting with its swelling breasts, thin torso and long silky legs; the delicately challenging, half mocking smile ... she was always simmering beneath the surface with that enigmatic expression, that undercurrent of intensity and volatile sexuality. That was it, wasn't it, the whirlpool of sexuality that was all-consuming, sucking people in, shooting them out before they knew what happened to them. She had an infinite belief in herself and her powers.

Her hair shone softly in the subdued light, her eyes gleamed erotic. Her skin was porcelain perfect. She outlined the plan. He listened, speechless at first, aware he was turning pale. For the President of the United States to be pulled into a scheme like this was unthinkable. Jasmine Shields — who was she, really? He still didn't know after all this time. How could she dream of putting the office of the President at risk?

Of course Nick didn't want to do it. Like many politicians, he liked to court danger, but not this kind. He trotted out all the standard objections — against his principles, too dangerous — excuses were something he needed for his conscience.

"The plan is simple. Choke off the Corsicans' main supplier, Turkey — shatter their worldwide influence, and create a new LFM monopoly with the support and protection of the U.S. government.

"In Cestari's group are many French intelligence people, thugs who often performed dirty tricks. France wants them out. They're trouble. Look at it this way. The problem of narcotics is not going to go away. So as a pragmatist, knowing if one group doesn't have drugs another will, what you do is manipulate it to your own ends by bringing it under your personal control and direction. The super secret White House intelligence agency will support itself — through the cut it receives on narcotics."

"No, no," Nick said, "it's unthinkable."

So at that point, Jasmine ushered him into another cabin, where she had footage ready to show. At first he didn't recognize himself because his face was turned away. But then he knew.

"How does it feel to sit on my cock again?" he heard himself ask.

Jasmine was in shadows and there was a black square over her face. Her voice had been altered, but he recognized her body and remembered his own dialog. "Like I'm in heaven. Oh, honey, honey, yes! Yes!"

She began moving on top of him, swiveling, screwing; he saw his own face contort, his mouth open wide, his eyes close in exquisite pleasure. Of course he remembered — his garconnière in Washington. His reaction now as he watched the scene play out was an admixture of anger, betrayal, and morbid curiosity.

"How could you do this to me, Jasmine?" he asked, still in shock.

"Actually, Nick, I didn't know anything about it, scout's honor. This is the result of one of my associates, and it was done behind my back as well as yours. But what's done is done. Let's be realistic. When you can't eliminate something, the best thing is to manipulate it. Just think, Nick, you'll have an intelligence operation totally under your control -- your own secret White House force answerable only to you. And think at the same time of money in your personal offshore account — you know, the one Maurice started for you. We're willing to be very generous, Nicky."

He could imagine this on national television. Jasmine Shields, the woman he could never get out of his system, was blackmailing him, the President of the United States -- and he was powerless to do anything about it. She was dead serious. He'd been in denial. But now —

And so, the deal was spelled out, terms reached for where and how the continuing royalty he would earn would be banked. They discussed the relative merits of Switzerland, Liechtenstein, Luxembourg, Cayman Islands, Turks and Caicos, Channel Islands — she was open to them all.

Ultimately, of course, Nick couldn't refuse her.

Jasmine smiled. "Welcome to the female mafia, Mr. President," she said, as the footage froze on a closeup of his erect cock.

Turkey agreed for $2 billion of U.S. aid to get out of the opium game. In Paris at the Palais d'Élysée, President Condon met with Georges Pompier, President of France, and Roger Baiser, French Minister of Justice. The frogs enthusiastically endorsed U.S. policy of a massive media-based antidrug campaign backed up by a super secret team of dirty tricksters. Back home, Condon went on American TV to request national support of his new narcotics program.

The US would buy up Turkey's poppy crop in order to suppress it. France and the US would mount a joint assault on heroin, with arrests, extraditions, and convictions of drug traffickers being the major goals. In addition to the 800 million in indemnities to Turkey for the cessation of their opium crop, Condon asked Congress for 150 million to fight organized crime.

"In order to help I would like to request that the federal government be given wider power in law enforcement, via the formation of a federal strike force and also a special rackets squad," Nick announced in a television address to the American people. "I want our citizens to know that I am asking the congress to give me wider powers of law enforcement. Together we can lick this problem that threatens the very fabric of our society."

The battle was being fought on several fronts. At the same time the Corsican problem was being addressed, rival Italian mafia factions were at each other's throats, the drug war on that territory spiraling to furious heights — dynamitings, bombings, and shootings were a daily occurrence. The "new mafia" in Sicily was heading a campaign to expand internationally, and Corrado, once considered untouchable, was now in grave danger, along with his family.

As far as Victoria was concerned, the move from Chicago back to New York was virtually out of the frying pan into the fire. Was anywhere safe? Mafia rivalries were rampant in the northeast, and a mattress war threatened to erupt.

Heavy duty boys involved in the pizza business ran the cheese factories up in New England and Canada, controlling the warehouses in the cities and distributorships in the suburbs. They brought in illegal aliens, started with "juice" — loanshark loans of forty, fifty grand; they got around the interest by overcharging on the mozzarella. Sales were all cash, unrecorded. Pizzerias were great outlets for drugs and gambling.

Now foul play in the pizza business was undermining Vic's enterprises, her pizza parlors were being vandalized, her trucks bombed and burned, acid dropped in her fermenting milk. They were sending her a message — get out of ricotta and mozzarella, they were saying. Arson and sabotage were dire enough in themselves, but worse, they focused law enforcement attention when you least wanted it. Clearly something drastic had to be done.

Who was behind the moves? None other than her old nemesis, Anthony Zino. He was out of jail; word had it he was in cahoots with Corsicans, and he was dangerous to her wellbeing.

Harry advised Vic, "Remember we once agreed that cocksucker belongs ground up in a car shredder? Wanna give the nod before it's too late? The guy should be eased out of this mortal world, honey, before he eases you out."

"Once," Victoria said, plastering mustard on a roast beef on kayser sandwich over at the Stage Deli, "he was a step up the ladder, but that was a long time ago."

"Agreed we don't need this fink Zino any more?"

"Right on. The fuck's gotta go." Vic laid down her sandwich and held up her right index and middle fingers in the ominous mafia death signal.

"We clip him," Harry said, under his breath.

"Listen, Harry, I'm not going to be maudlin about sending Zino to the Happy Hunting Grounds," Vic said. "We all have to go there sooner or later, so what the hell — help give somebody a premature sendoff, and who knows, maybe you're even doing them a favor."

"Right. Who the hell knows?" Harry agreed. "So how do we take care of old Tone?"

"Any suggestions, Counselor?"

Harry took a swill of coke. "A service issue .45 totally disintegrates the head -- particularly when fired from close range," he suggested. "Millie could do it."

Mildred Hruska, ex-lady wrestler, faithful LFM soldier in Vic's borgata, known as "Mildew." Sure, Mildew could do it. There was a story about Mildew, possibly apocryphal, but nevertheless telling of her character. The tale had it that once Mildew made a 240 pound guy sink to his knees and plead for his life, then pull down his own drawers, after which she took a knife and castrated the cocksucker. After ripping out his heart, she poured gasoline over him and lit a match. Mildew was tough. Sure, Mildew could do it.

Mildew handled the assignment with her customary zeal and aplomb. Simultaneously, on major fronts, terror was being struck to Corsicans worldwide, as France and the US stepped up their heroin war. There were arrests, extraditions, and killings by the White House special assassination squad, and Corsican labs were closed down by the French authorities. Meanwhile, undetected, the LFM were running the successful southeast Asian heroin connection.

News reached Vic from Europe that Cestari had been wounded. As he was driving to one of his Marseille haunts two cars suddenly appeared in front of him. The doors of both opened simultaneously, two men got out and began firing. A .9 calibre bullet pierced Cestari's neck, one hit his feet, another his leg, a fourth penetrated his groin, two others hit him in the chest. He took six direct hits in all, and later doctors found a seventh lodged in his head, an old wound. Bleeding profusely, Charles fell to the ground as his attackers fled.

Although the ambush caused a sensation, it received virtually no publicity. In a hospital in the south of France, Charles' condition was described as critical and he was undergoing a series of operations to save his life -- one behind the cranium, another near his right ear. The bullets could not all be removed at once, and there was the risk he could lose his sight. Too bad. Cestari always did have bad eyes. Presumably, his cock was still intact.

Vic heard soon after he would recover sufficiently to wear glasses. She thought about phoning him for old time's sake, just to see how he was faring. He couldn't be in very good shape. After all, his network was being decimated. Aside from the murders and kidnappings, many of his stockpiles had been seized, sabotaged or stolen.

On top of that, an attempt on Charles' brother's life misfired at an open air rally in Ajaccio. After that, two men were blown to bits trying to bomb the Ajaccio villa. And then at the Wig Wam Cafe, owned by his sister, yet another botched attack took place.

Cestari was under the misapprehension that his ace in the hole was that his team alone could produce in sufficient quantity the pure white # 4 product coveted by the American market. Then came the information that the LFM's could equal, if not surpass his methods, and that their refining capability rested with Marc Jabry, who could refine even more safely and quicker, using the most streamline equipment in a highly secure environment, making up to 99 per cent and even higher purity product.

In desperation Cestari had Jabry killed. But Cestari had miscalculated; he had underestimated the LFM's. They could and were proceeding to process their own pure white # 4 independent of Jabry.

At last most of the leading Corsican chemists were either dead or behind bars. Their labs had been raided and dismantled, disabled, their stocks thinned out. Smugglers, wholesalers and dealers were wiped out. Estimations were that thus far over 100 French gangsters had perished in liquidations set up by the special White House assassinations squad.

Charles Cestari, back on his feet again, hiding out in Brazil, was packing his bags when six policemen smashed through the door. He lunged for his pistol but they grabbed him. Cestari, a karate expert, picked up the six officers like they were puffballs. Finally, overcome by sheer numbers and guns, he was subdued and taken prisoner. Handcuffed and chained, Cestari offered money, six figure bribes each, in exchange for his freedom, plus tickets to anywhere in the world for each member of their families. No dice.

Cestari then grabbed a glass, broke it and slit his wrists, hoping for an easy escape from the subsequent hospital he was rushed to. But after being sewn up in the emergency room, he was placed under heavy guard so that there was no chance of that. His next step was swallowing razor blades. That too failed.

It was going to be interesting to see if France extradited him. A lot of people wanted him back and a lot didn't, both camps in power positions. Although international law gave France first crack at Cestari, they made no move to take him and he was extradited to the USA without notification to the French government. France never did try to get him back.

"And so," Vic said to Harry, "another chapter in the fabulous history of the female mafia draws to a close."

CHAPTER 63

It came as a total surprise when Tania read in the newspaper that Valentina Sofino had died. She would have expected Corrado to phone and let her know. Probably, however, the death had heaped so many burdens on him — family, legal matters and so forth — that he hadn't had time. Well, *meno male*, as the Italians said. He was finally free; this was what she'd waited so long for. Tania grew expectant. She bought an elaborate trousseau, spent an entire week having wraps, facials, hair treatments, waxings, anything she could think of to become more beautiful for Corrado and the future they would soon be embarking on together.

Weeks went by. Why didn't Corrado call? She'd sent condolences, flowers, the whole nine yards. She made excuses for him, until finally she broke down, picked up a phone and rang him. He sounded so strange, vague and noncommittal — maybe because he was still in mourning, and up to his eyeballs with business affairs? When would they get together, she asked; he said it's too early yet, I'll call you as soon as I can.

As time wore on and the communication slagged, she began to suspect something was really wrong.

And then came the shocker to end all shockers: Corrado was married! To that slut Ingeborg! Tania was beside herself. They were supposed to be together always, he said he wanted that, he said he would never marry his mistress, marriage to your mistress never works, then he marries his mistress. Of course, he had always called her his *amica*. How was that for hypocritical bull shit?

What had she done wrong, Tania agonized? Maybe she should have abandoned her values, been his mistress after all. But how? Being subservient was something she could never endure. She was an achiever who didn't need a man's support; it would demean her — she thought he understood that. Mistresses were dependents, takers forced to compromise their integrity to cater to the man. All along, she'd believed Corrado respected her independence, talents and accomplishments — and then he ends up with an accoutrement, a mere trophy, an ego trip he swore up and down he would absolutely never marry — because it would never work.

And yet she and Corrado had this amazingly incredible rapport — sexually, like no other, and friendship-wise too. They were beautiful companions intellectually and spiritually. What was wrong with this man that he couldn't appreciate all they had? Why had he opted for this vapid woman?

Because she pulled a pregnancy, that was why in a nutshell. The time honored feminine ploy. Incredible. Tania had wanted his child, but had respected his wishes — I'm a conventional man, a man with a professional reputation, he said, I would not want this. But I want to have your child, she said, I want our baby, and he said, yes, *tesoro*, just be patient, one day we will be together always, and there will be babies and babies..."

If only she hadn't been so considerate! If only she'd been conniving like most women, and put herself first! Ingeborg got what she wanted, which just showed how the game was played. He had betrayed her. Wait, Jasmine's psychic *consigliere* Sandra said, just wait. His life is going downhill. You'll see, and later you won't want him anymore.

Sandra was right. It didn't take long at all for Corrado's house of cards to cave in. Soon, he was enmeshed in financial troubles of gigantic proportion. After his losing a reported two billion for the Vatican, Italy charged and convicted him in absentia of looting 400 million from his Milanese banks, and his US branches were tottering on the verge of fiscal collapse. That was the tip of the iceberg. Supposedly, he had bled his banks with questionable foreign currency deals and the money was in South America now. His creditors included four major international banks.

A panic ensued. He fled to Switzerland, was arrested, extradited, tried in New York on fraud and grand larceny, convicted to 25 years. He would rot in jail, a shadow of his former self. The tragic Greek hero whose foot was dipped in the Styx had dragged the whole house of Atreus down with him.

She hardly recognized him as the same man. The thing she noticed most about him was how he'd aged. Remembering his élan and optimism, she felt pity for him, but he pulled his own noose -- everything could have been different. Sandra was right — she didn't want him now.

She had loved him. Loved his façade, his spirit, his energy. But what was love without a framework? To exist, love needs boundaries somewhere in the real world. They had connected, had made a supreme statement together; together they became a conduit for something entirely other than what they were separately, a third force.

It was a potent joining but now it was over.

Tania had bought the comfortable apartment on Central Park West just before Jack was shot, and still kept it as her Manhattan headquarters. Although she maintained homes in Texas, St. Moritz, Paris, Rome, the South of France and California, there was a special feeling in her heart for the apartment she and Jack had once shared in the big apple. From time to time she thought of Jack, she thought of him every time his phone rang, she thought of him in connection with Sapphire Bay, which continued operating in the red.

When Tania returned from a trip out of the country, she couldn't believe what awaited. She thought she'd seen a ghost, for larger than life, sitting in the living room, there was Jack Riley, returned from the dead. Jack Riley, her husband of long ago, was alive.

Tania turned pale. "Where did you come from?" she demanded, trembling.

"It's a long story," Jack said. "Are you going to offer me a drink and listen to what I have to say?"

But for slightly greying hair, Jack still looked boyish and youthful. Explaining himself, he told her that a "new liquidity crisis" had hit in the form of "problems with debt consolidation," and that when pressure increased to the point that a mob contract was on him from yet another direction and he feared his number was up, he staged his own death. He couldn't come back until things either blew over, his creditors died, or he hit a big score with which to square his obligations. Finally, conditions had been met and here he was.

"Why didn't you let me know?"

"For your own protection I couldn't tell you," he said. "Now all's well, I'm ready to start over again. I wanted to surprise you. You and I have a lot of catching up to do."

He'd been living mostly in South America, he said. He'd had a heart attack and recovered. His health was wonderful. His luck had reversed. He was doing great. "Remember I said one day I'd score a big win — I did it — a four million exacta at Santa Anita — followed by an even bigger win at Churchill Downs! I was on a roll — so I bet the whole wad at Longchamps and walked away winning another longshot. Practically broke the track."

Miraculously, he was now cured for life of his gambling addiction. "After that, I quit cold turkey, believe it or not."

Jack said he knew all about the LFM's faltering Caribbean operation. "I know what went wrong and I know how to rectify it," he declared.

"How do you know?" Tania asked.

"The casino problem hinges on your pigeon list. You know what a pigeon list is -- a dossier of up to the minute financial info on the high rollers who can afford to drop a bundle."

"Yes, I'm familiar with the term."

"You've heard of the notorious Cellini brothers, Dino and Eddie, who went from Steubenville, Ohio bustout joints to London-and-Bahamas-casino riches. When the Cellinis were being deported in a process known in the U.K. as stoplisting, their pigeon list went for a sum of over two million US. Today a list like that would be worth five times the amount," Jack said. "Few people in the gambling business possess this kind of information. You're looking at one who does," he grinned.

Jack said he knew for a fact that the pigeon list used by the La Femmina casino had been falsified, that erroneous information had been substituted in order to deliberately sabotage their operation. How could he be so sure? Even though he'd been in hiding, he'd kept current.

"I know the identity of every high roller in the business. I know credit limits, I know how to collect debts. I have great gut instincts besides. I can turn things around. I guarantee results. All I ask is the chance to try."

He made her an offer she couldn't refuse.

"You give me nothing up front," he said. "Let me try and if you're satisfied, you pay. First I go into the casino in a position, rout out the insiders who betrayed you and helped switch the pigeon list. Then I organize junkets and make the place start paying off. What have you got to lose?"

The la Femminas agreed to give Jack the opportunity he was asking for.

Jack produced his promised miracle, turning the La Femminas' Caribbean casino around. He presented irrefutable evidence that the enemy was Sam Scardelli. Bitter over Laura, Sam had the pigeon list falsified to hurt operations. His plan was to then go in himself, become a hero by rescuing things, expecting to win Laura back by making her indebted to him.

Another victim of the bloody epoch was Sam Scardelli, whose waterlogged corpse was retrieved from a 55-gallon oil drum off Biscayne Bay. His body became so bloated that the gasses seeping from it broke the chains off the drum, and out popped Scardelli's swollen remains, minus legs, which had been chopped off. Around his mouth were seven neat bullet holes made by a sawed off .22 calibre pistol. At the time of his murder, the Chicago mobster was under two subpoenas and round the clock police surveillance, set to testify before a Senate subcommittee.

Speculations on the motive and identity of Scardelli's assassin varied. One theory was he was slain by the mob for becoming too powerful and challenging other dons. He had secretly bought up 50 property sites in Atlantic City, several tied in with Corsican organized crime. He was also waging a behind the scenes battle with union elements that would allow him to profit from ancillary businesses servicing the Jersey casinos. He would have gotten 2-3 cents per every carton of cigarettes sold in the vending machines, and stood to profit on prostitution, loan sharking and skims, to say nothing of the huge increase in land values that would occur from resales. Property Scardelli had paid $20 million for (using fronts) just two years ago was worth, at the time of his death, in excess of $400 million.

Sam had been involved in a vending machine war with the Philly mob and they had it in for him. But then, so did any number of other people. Another theory was that the killing was made to look like a mob hit, that the Gantria-Gantry family did it in retribution for Sam's having taken out Frank's brother Tom Gantry. As with the death of many mob figures, Sam Scardelli's killing would remain unsolved.

He had lived his life violently. To Laura he showed another side, his better side. Then that started to crack. She had no illusions. This had been her life, it always would be, and the struggle was worth it. Perhaps, in years to come, another way would emerge for her daughter Diana.

But then, perhaps not.

CHAPTER 64 - ALL'S WELL THAT ENDS WELL

Like a deus ex machina, Kal Bolton entered Tania's life a week after Jack's disclosures. Tania went on a visit to Texas and there he was. Everything unfolded rapidly. She was swept off her feet into an affair. It was very romantic. He was the sweetest guy, thoughtful, funny, considerate, eager to please. And soon they were married.

Kal had recently emerged from a legal problem. Having taken over a major motion picture company that was posting a fifty million dollar loss and had not declared a dividend in four years, he engineered a payment which netted him personally over a period of eighteen months, fifteen million tax fee dollars. The SEC filed a complaint that was settled with a wrist slap by his signing a consent decree. Bolton was now working on additional expansion, mainly in the casino and entertainment fields, and Tania was intrigued at the potential of joint ventures, mergers and acquisitions.

The Boltons would divide their time between Las Vegas, Florida, Los Angeles, New York, Europe, the Caribbean, and of course, Tania's native Texas, of which she remained the undisputed capomafiosa. Kal wanted children, he wanted to conquer the world with her. And he was a Texan, too, besides. It was a marriage made in heaven. They would have it all. Her cup runneth over.

Harry Sutro was happy as a clam. Having stuck by Victoria through thick and thin, his devotion was finally being rewarded. Believe it or not, Harry and Vic were tying the knot! While the La Femmina syndicate did not officially "make" men, marriage was the next best thing, a form of legitimacy for a man. At long last, Harry was to find the justification for his existence.

Sutro made himself indispensable when while visiting his favorite Miami shooting range he encountered an undercover FBI agent who tipped him off about a joint task force investigation involving US Customs Service, the DEA, and the FDLE (Florida Department of Law Enforcement) together with the Vice Presidential Task Force on South Florida Crime.

This fortuitous bit of intelligence enabled Harry to know that the task force was ready to move in on their operation. Always quick on his feet, Harry marched Vic into the IRS and declared seven million worth of drug profits as "mischievous income" derived from gambling.

Once that was done, the IRS had no recourse, since it was prohibited by law from notifying another investigative agency of suspicions that the income was derived from narcotics. The law said the IRS could only release findings to a grand jury, not to another agency. And now that the feds had nothing on her, there wouldn't be a grand jury.

Vic paid the tax and walked out scot free. The IRS might have gotten the lion's share of the seven mil, but along with the three million of clean money, Vic had no further worries about surveillance from the feds. Thus, in essence, Harry helped her to launder three million in cash through a federal agency of the United States government.

Victoria was so pleased with Harry's brilliant scheme that she agreed to marriage. It was a big step for her, one she had regarded with trepidation in recent years, but now, she was finally willing to see the error of her ways. As much as she'd resisted "commitment," she now acknowledged: the way of the world was to solidify your base by pairing off, and you might just as well do it legally. Belatedly, she now recognized how important the comfort and trust Harry provided were and the fact that it wasn't easy to find somebody willing to go the distance for you the way he did.

They were married in judge's chambers, in a ceremony performed by Judge Marcus Tannenbaum, who had an avuncular interest in the couple. The vows took all of two minutes, but they would always remain indelible in her memory as the most satisfying two minutes of her life.

"I just sent Pompier my congratulations," Nick said over the phone, "on the last of the great heroin raids — France closed out a big one, and the Corsicans are completely finished now, they're history."

"That's wonderful, Nick."

Jasmine used to fantasize Mrs. Nicholas Condon dying. That mental play ended when she married Marc. Then when Marc was killed, her fantasies started up again. Sometimes she'd see herself pointing a silenced revolver at Heather Condon while the first lady was out jogging, or hiring a hit person to do the job. Perhaps poison would be the best method? But how? The idea appealed to her but she never acted on it.

Then the problem was taken care of for her by a disenfranchised nut from the South Bronx who resented the first lady's bleeding heart liberal do-goodism, condemned her as a phony attorney bitch and shot her with an AK-47 at an open air rally in full view of TV cameras. A shocked nation mourned.

Sandra said he'd come around. Jasmine's mind was at ease. There was still a remaining year and a half to Nick's term in the White House, and he'd be a cinch for reelection.

She waited. Finally one day Nick phoned again and said, "I want to see you. The hell with the FBI. You're the only one who understands me, the only one who counts in my life. It's always been you."

"All is forgiven?"

"There's nothing to forgive. I want to be with you."

"When do I get to go on Air Force One?"

She was already planning what she'd do on board — and after that, planning her invasion of the White House itself.

It was Jasmine's greatest fantasy, and it was well within reach.

CHAPTER 65 - KRISTIN

How can I describe what it feels like to become a made woman, an initiated member of the female mafia? My turn came one summer. Mid-July, the city was in the throes of its worst heat wave in years. Earlier in the day, the temperature had soared to over 100, but by seven p.m., a cooling breeze started moving across the East River. I knew, as I approached the bronze amberglass facade of the exclusive Beekman Place building, that several of the La Femmina top guns were in town for a sitdown, and would attend my big night.

I stepped off the elevator into a luxury triplex apartment. What an inspiring setting — lights strung across the river from the 59th Street bridge glowing on the water; the library's dark green walls and tomato red accents, its Chinese art and Tiffany lamps casting soft shadows on thick oriental carpeting. All of this reflected the La Femmina's trademarks — money and power.

I was nervous. So long had I dreamed about this time, I almost couldn't believe it was finally happening.

From a stereo emerged the gritty, streetwise vocal tones of Lotte Lenya singing "Dr. Krippen," Kurt Weill's chilling song about the famous Victorian murderer, lending a macabre touch that contrasted with the sumptuous décor.

The women who greeted me were the *crème de la crème*, ladies who had mounted to the summit of mafia hierarchy, rich and powerful beyond measure. Collectively, they comprised the strongest female force of their generation. Under them were ranks of underbosses, soldiers, and enforcers. It was the first time I'd ever seen them assembled together, but I knew every one by reputation — each was a legend in her own right.

Sipping drinks, they had been chatting while awaiting my arrival. There was an easy yet dynamic amity among them. I would say that they ranged in age from thirty-something on up past seventy-something, as in the case of New Orleans' crime chief Lucille Rand, who is getting along in years by now, but still, like the old male mafia dons, stays active.

Platinum-haired Ivy Schlatter, buxom and bewitching, pensively moved a long, tapered forefinger up and down the stem of her crystal champagne glass. Ivy started out in Cleveland as boss of the outfit's Mayfield Road wing, and later went on to Las Vegas, where from she now rules a solid entertainment and gambling empire.

Tall, no-nonsense Carole Curtis, reclining on a green Barcalounger in the corner, is a partner in a prestigious Washington, D.C. law firm whose legal skills serve her well in her capacity as head of the D.C. branch of the La Femminas. Present also were ace accountant Lily Wyszowsky and moneymover Deborah Cook; Katherine Sanford, syndicate capo of upstate New York; Susan Goldman, whose turf is Los Angeles; Candace Hastings, boss of Philadelphia; Dove Cameron — her garrison includes an area south of the Mason-Dixon line; Ayla

Kalkavan, head of the thriving La Femmina New England enterprises. There was also Montreal's ever-chic Lyse Allegret; diminutive Chinatown powerhouse Eleanor Lee Wong, and the savvy and sexy, black and beautiful Kamzen Raines.

Naturally, the founding mothers were evident: Texas billionaire Tania Lynn Cutler and Brooklyn's own Laura Lo Bianco, along with the stunning Jasmine Shields and notorious Victoria Winters. All had that indefinable air of confidence, prosperity and success.

Golden-haired Kentuckian Karen Taylor smilingly lifted Cristal champagne out of the ice bucket to refill her Waterford goblet and to toast the future. Just a few short months following this occasion, Karen was murdered. Although officially the crime has never been solved, I can tell you that the force behind her death was her lover, a Washington lobbyist involved with kickbacks on Haitian beef.

And then there was the woman I could thank for my good fortune — effervescent, peppery Sandra Martinez, Jasmine Shields' consigliere. The daughter of a Colombian father and Maryland-born mother, Sandra was striking in magenta gauze with matching cerise iridescent lipstick painted on her full-lipped, pouty mouth. Pale brown inscrutable eyes, a cleft chin and spontaneous smile conspire to make Sandra's Latin charm irresistible.

Embracing me, Sandra planted kisses on both my cheeks and said, "I'm so proud of you, Kris. We all are."

Once these women had been just like me; starting out modestly, they'd risen in the ranks. I admired them for what they'd achieved and hoped to emulate them.

Across the water the tramway was mounting to Roosevelt Island and a boat on the river sounded its fog horn. The assembled capos lifted their glasses to drink to the organization and to my future. If I identified with them it was because we'd all been through similar experiences. Attempts at achievement via legitimate means had brought us all against the proverbial brick walls and glass ceilings of a society that could never accept women as real players. Our consequent plight required a radical solution, and we had all embraced our mafia lives wholeheartedly.

Victoria, in her husky, low, smoke-tinged voice said, "Anybody thinks she's obliged to play by the `rules' doesn't belong with us. Do organized business, organized labor and organized society — let alone organized crime — play by the rules?"

"We're women of honor," Dovey said. "Let nobody ever forget it."

"Come, friends," Jasmine signaled, and we all rose.

The library was an intimate, pleasant room whose high ceilinged surfaces were painted dark green and covered with gold leaf arabesques. Together we stood in a circle under shallow coffers that simulated the effect of fine old leather binding. I was led to the center, while the others surrounded me. The room was filled to bursting with a reverent awe. When Jasmine beckoned, I stepped closer.

"Tonight Kristin Cates will become a made woman."

As the time-honored ritual borrowed from the male mob began, I already felt transported to another world. There was something very mystical about blood. Throughout history, men had known this. Now women knew it too, and I would be in on the secret.

"Kris, give me your right hand, the trigger finger," Jasmine said. Everyone was silent as Jasmine took a needle, punctured the skin of my index finger and squeezed till the blood came out. She said, "Kris, this drop of blood is a symbol of your birth into the La Femmina family. We're one unit, till death parts us."

An almost religious quality prevailed. I trembled, feeling an overlay of some extraordinary, recondite power that seemed to be vibrating to the top of the ceiling.

Tania said, "Kris, do you recognize the importance of this mafia, this thing of ours?"

"I do." My voice quavered at first, then I gained command as I declared, "I accept the honor of being a La Femmina mafiosa. I understand I belong to this organization for the rest of my life and I swear I will never waver in my devotion nor shirk my obligation."

"You know your responsibilities as a La Femmina woman, Kris?"

"I do. My first allegiance will always be to this organization."

"You understand that no man must ever learn the secrets of the woman's mafia?"

"I do."

Laura handed me a piece of paper and a match with which to burn it in my cupped hands. This symbolized the way I would burn in hell if I ever betrayed the secret power of the syndicate.

Jasmine said, "Repeat after me: `I swear on the soul of myself and my family, my heirs, blood of my blood, never to betray any member of the La Femmina Mafia syndicate, and that if I do, I will pay with my life.'"

Respectfully, I repeated the words.

"I will obey every command of the organization ..." Unhesitatingly, I continued the dramatic ritual vows. "I accept all challenges, I agree to prove myself to the satisfaction of this organization. I embrace everyone present as a fellow mob sister, a secret friend for all eternity. I pledge myself for the rest of my life..."

"Now you're one of us," Laura said, embracing me. "Congratulations, friend of ours, *amica nostra*..."

As each capo filed up for the ritual kiss, the energy filling the room was so strong it was almost bursting the walls wide open. The high was contagious. Everyone was radiant. Beaming, the women handed me fresias, gladioli and gardenias plucked from vases, saying, "Congratulations, *amica nostra*..."

At long last, I'd been fully accepted as part of this unique group's strong, united front of incredible solidarity. Their goals paralleled mine — power, respect, money. Now that I was truly initiated, mafia was my secret power too. We were united by a solemn code of *omertà*, silence. No longer was mafia the exclusive bastion of the male sex, no; life had brought each LFM member a special, coveted kind of power such as few achieve. As leaders of the world's first family of feminine crime, these women were transformed, as I would be. It was dangerous but thrilling and exalting. From now on everything would be different. Incontrovertibly. Irreversibly.

This was my destiny and there was no turning back. I had, more than ever before, embarked on a one-way street. Following this beginning of a new phase, nothing would ever be the same.

The good news is the FBI made no cases; all the La Femminas I've spoken about are still free, operating as before.

I too am free — I didn't go into the Witness Protection Program, which was also good news, in fact, great news. Although I might be leading a sub rosa existence for a while, that was no hardship in this era of cell phones, VOIP, the internet, email and fax machines. I can tell you that LFM activities today, including my own, have a far greater scope than ever before.

I can also tell you that politics is crooked, big business, labor, lawyers, accountants, banks, wealthy families, Hollywood, the record industry, sports, and the government are all crooked; they all make their own rules. Why shouldn't we?

All of us, you readers included, can lament lost liberties as Big Brother becomes increasingly imperial. For example, the US had no income tax till 1913, and then it was only 1%. Look what's been happening since. Privacy is a thing of the past; justice is what some government flunky decrees it is. Or some judge. Do you want to remain powerless? We didn't. That's why we fought and will continue to fight.

There are more of us La Femminas now than ever before, with younger women coming up in the ranks all the time. We're a new breed, playing with new rules in a new ballpark.

Rest assured — the world will be hearing a lot more from us; and that's not a threat.

It's a promise.

CHAPTER 66 - AFTERWORD BY DAVID CATES

    There you have it, in her own words, the true story of the La Femmina mafia women, as my mother, Kristin Cates, related to the FBI, which she later novelized, but for reasons unknown, withheld from publication. Following events in this book, Kristin went on to play a much larger role as a second generation made woman in the LFM organization, but that's a whole other story, one which I hope she will someday emerge to tell. I promise to keep informed all readers interested in being updated, if and when I have news of my mother. Readers might want to drop me a line with any leads or ideas about Kristin's possible whereabouts, or should you spot her anywhere in the world, I would certainly appreciate your letting me know. You may reach me on Facebook. (One of these days I will probably break down and join Twitter).

    My sincerest thanks for giving your attention to Kristin Cates' opus magnus. Yours in friendship and appreciation,
    David Cates, 2012

###

ABOUT THE AUTHOR

Jeanne Rejaunier graduated from Vassar College, Poughkeepsie, New York, and did postgraduate studies at the Sorbonne, Paris, the Universities of Florence and Pisa, Italy, the Goetheschule, Rome, and at UCLA. While a student at Vassar, she began a career as a professional model, and subsequently became an actress in Manhattan, Hollywood and Europe, appearing on and off Broadway, in films and television, on magazine covers internationally and as the principal in dozens of network television commercials.

Jeanne achieved international success with the publication of her first novel, *The Beauty Trap*, which sold over one million copies and became Simon and Schuster's fourth best seller of the year, the film rights to which were purchased outright by Avco-Embassy. Jeanne has publicized her books in national and international tours on three continents in five languages. Her writing has been extolled in feature stories in Life, Playboy, Mademoiselle, Seventeen, National Geographic, BusinessWeek, Fashion Weekly, Women's Wear, W, McCalls, American Homemaker, Parade, Let's Live, Marie-Claire, Epoca, Tempo, Sogno, Cine-Tipo, the New York Times, the Los Angeles Times, and countless other publications.

In addition to *The Beauty Trap*, Jeanne published two other novels, *The Motion and the Act* and *Affair in Rome*, as well as nonfiction titles *The Video Jungle, Astrology and Your Sex Life, Astrology For Lovers, Japan's Hidden Face, The Complete Idiot's Guide to Food Allergy*, and *The Complete Idiot's Guide to Migraines and Other Headaches*. Soon, Jeanne plans to publish additional ebooks, including those previously brought out by major New York publishers in hard and soft cover, as well as several completely new titles.

Branching out as a filmmaker, Jeanne produced, directed, filmed, and edited the four hour documentary, *The Spirit of '56: Meetings with Remarkable Women*.

#####

THE BEAUTY TRAP, by JEANNE REJAUNIER

"Here is a novel that can't miss, crammed with all the ingredients that make a blockbuster." - **Publishers Weekly**

"A startling closeup of the world's most glamorous business, an intensely human story." - **The New York Times**

"Jeanne Rejaunier has concocted a sexpourri of life among the mannequins that's spiked with all the ingredients of a blockbuster bestseller."- **Playboy**

"New York's most sought after women find themselves having to make desperate decisions that will affect their very lives." - **Wilmington (DE) News Journal.**

"The novel is rich in esoteric commercial lore about modeling...." **Saturday Review**

"Possibly the most honest novel to appear by a female writer in the past decade."- **Literary Times**

"Miss Rejaunier is most interesting when she goes behind the scenes in the modeling world." - **Detroit Free Press**

"A fascinating inside story of the most glamorous girls in the business, absorbing to read." - **California Stylist**

"This is Miss Rejaunier's first novel. We can't wait for her second." – **Tampa Tribune**

"A powerful novel that takes off like 47 howitzers." - **San Fernando Valley (CA) Magazine**

"If a male author had written The Beauty Trap, he'd be hanged by the thumbs." **- UPI**

#####

JEANNE REJAUNIER

Manufactured by Amazon.ca
Bolton, ON